Michigan
On the Trail of a War Bride

Writer
JULIEN FREY

Artist
LUCAS VARELA

FANFARE · PONENT MON

Thank you to Odette for sharing her wonderful story with me.
To Maud for introducing me to her family in Michigan.
To Pauline for her keen eye and insight.
To Ginette Huerta, Linda Rubalcaba, Michele Thomas,
Karin Amphonesinh, and Daniel Tilliet
for their help with my research.
—

Julien

Michigan, Sur la route d'une War Bride
© DARGAUD 2017, by Frey, Varela
www.dargaud.com
All rights reserved

© Fanfare / Ponent Mon 2020 for the UK edition
www.ponentmon.com

Translation: Matt Madden
Lettering: Cromatik Ltd

ISBN: 978-1-912097-38-8
Printed and bound in the Europian Union

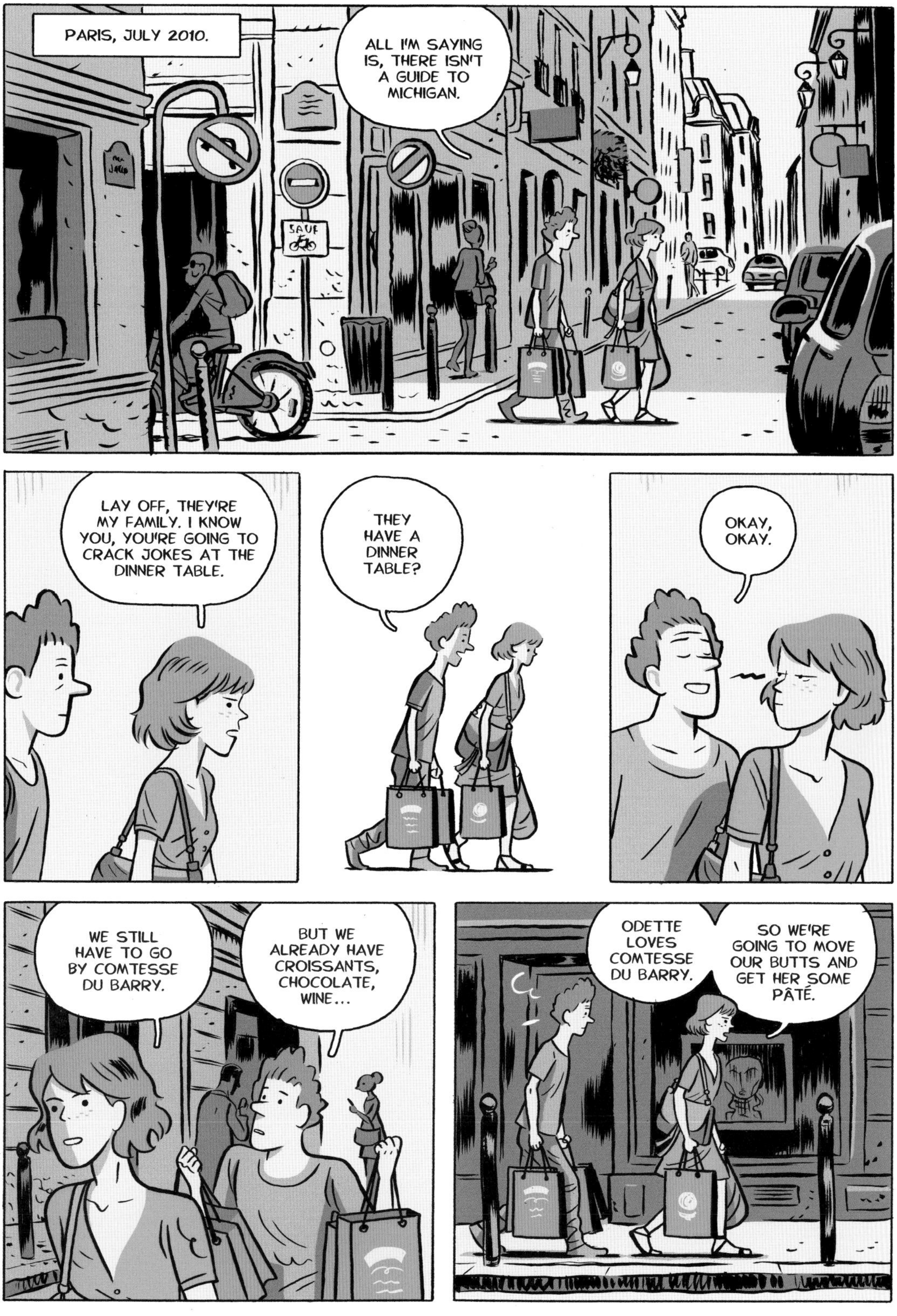
PARIS, JULY 2010.
ALL I'M SAYING IS, THERE ISN'T A GUIDE TO MICHIGAN.
SAUF
LAY OFF, THEY'RE MY FAMILY. I KNOW YOU, YOU'RE GOING TO CRACK JOKES AT THE DINNER TABLE.
THEY HAVE A DINNER TABLE?
OKAY, OKAY.
WE STILL HAVE TO GO BY COMTESSE DU BARRY.
BUT WE ALREADY HAVE CROISSANTS, CHOCOLATE, WINE...
ODETTE LOVES COMTESSE DU BARRY.
SO WE'RE GOING TO MOVE OUR BUTTS AND GET HER SOME PÂTÉ.

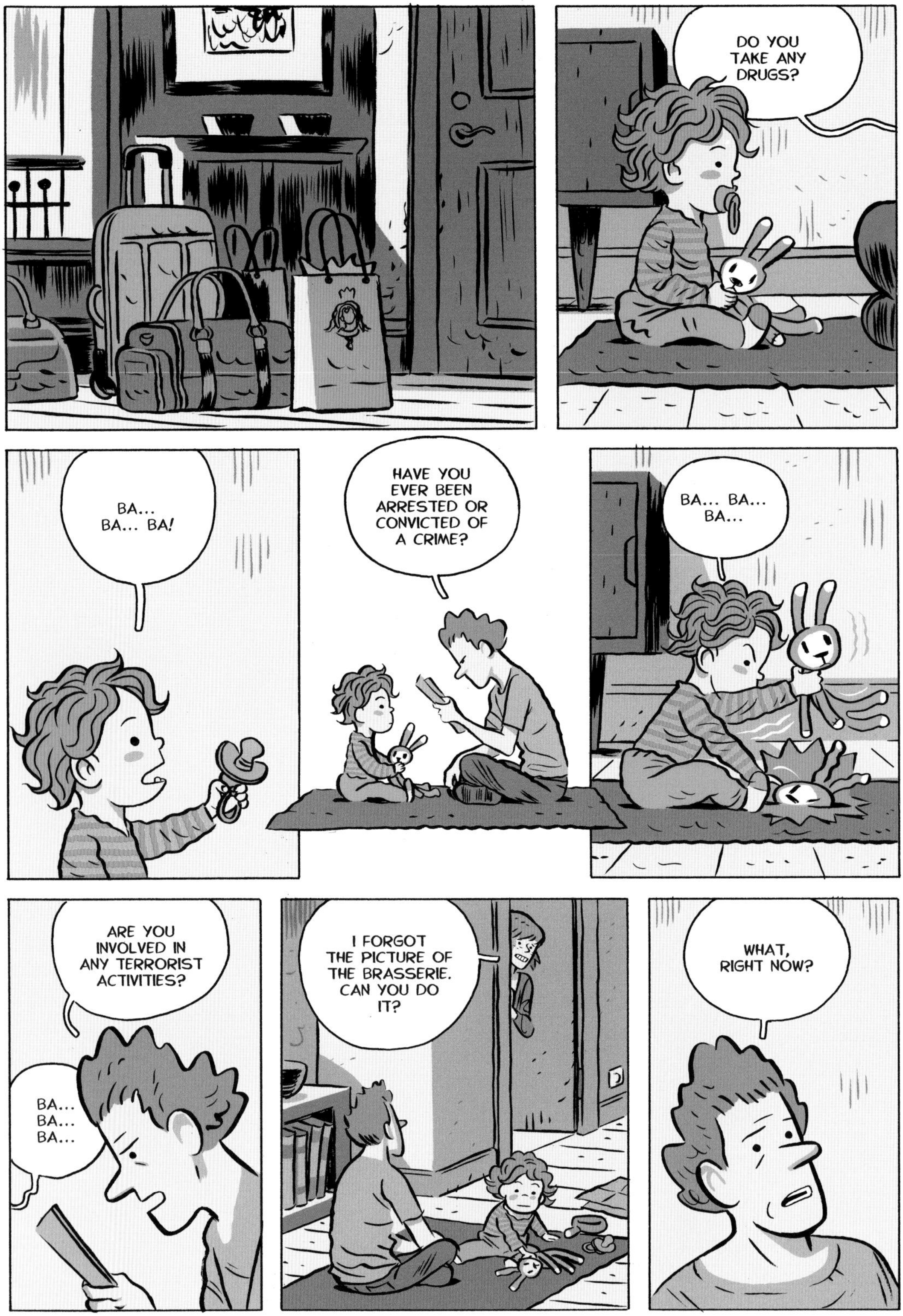
DO YOU TAKE ANY DRUGS?
BA... BA... BA!
HAVE YOU EVER BEEN ARRESTED OR CONVICTED OF A CRIME?
BA... BA... BA...
ARE YOU INVOLVED IN ANY TERRORIST ACTIVITIES?
BA... BA... BA...
I FORGOT THE PICTURE OF THE BRASSERIE. CAN YOU DO IT?
WHAT, RIGHT NOW?

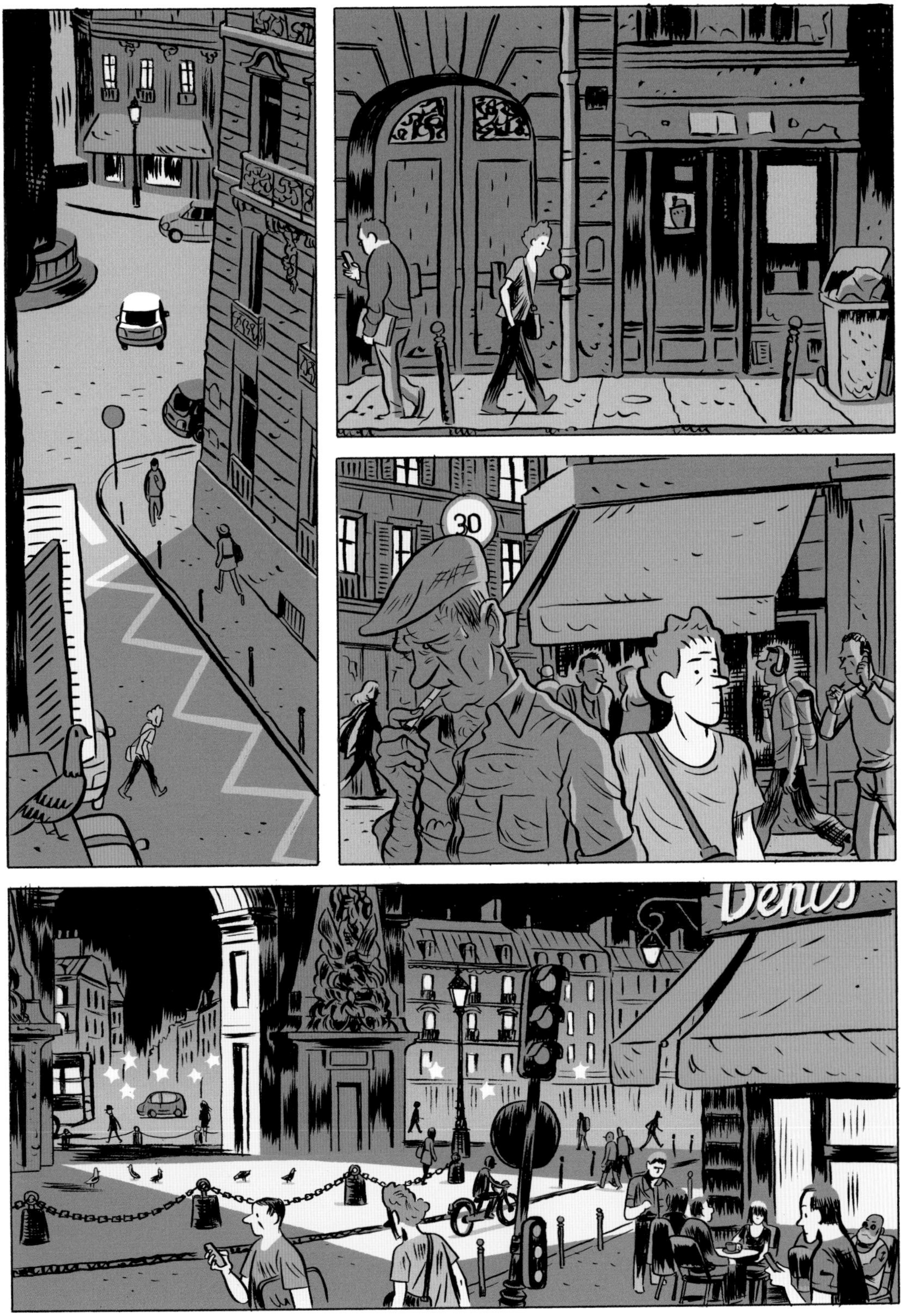
30
Denis

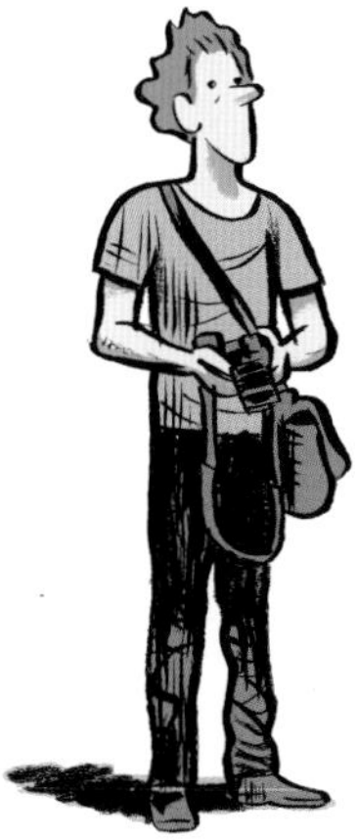

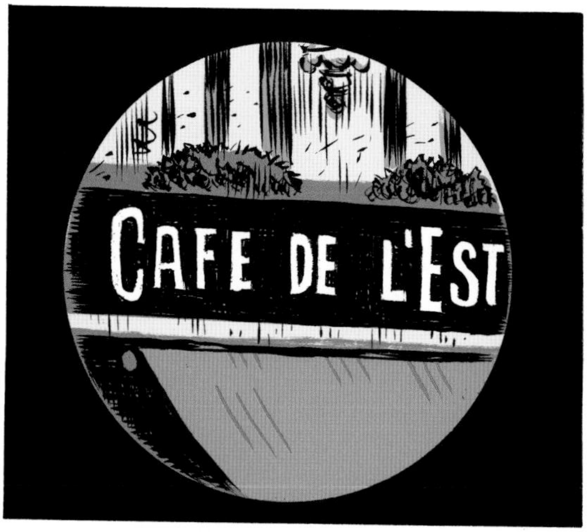
CAFE DE L'EST

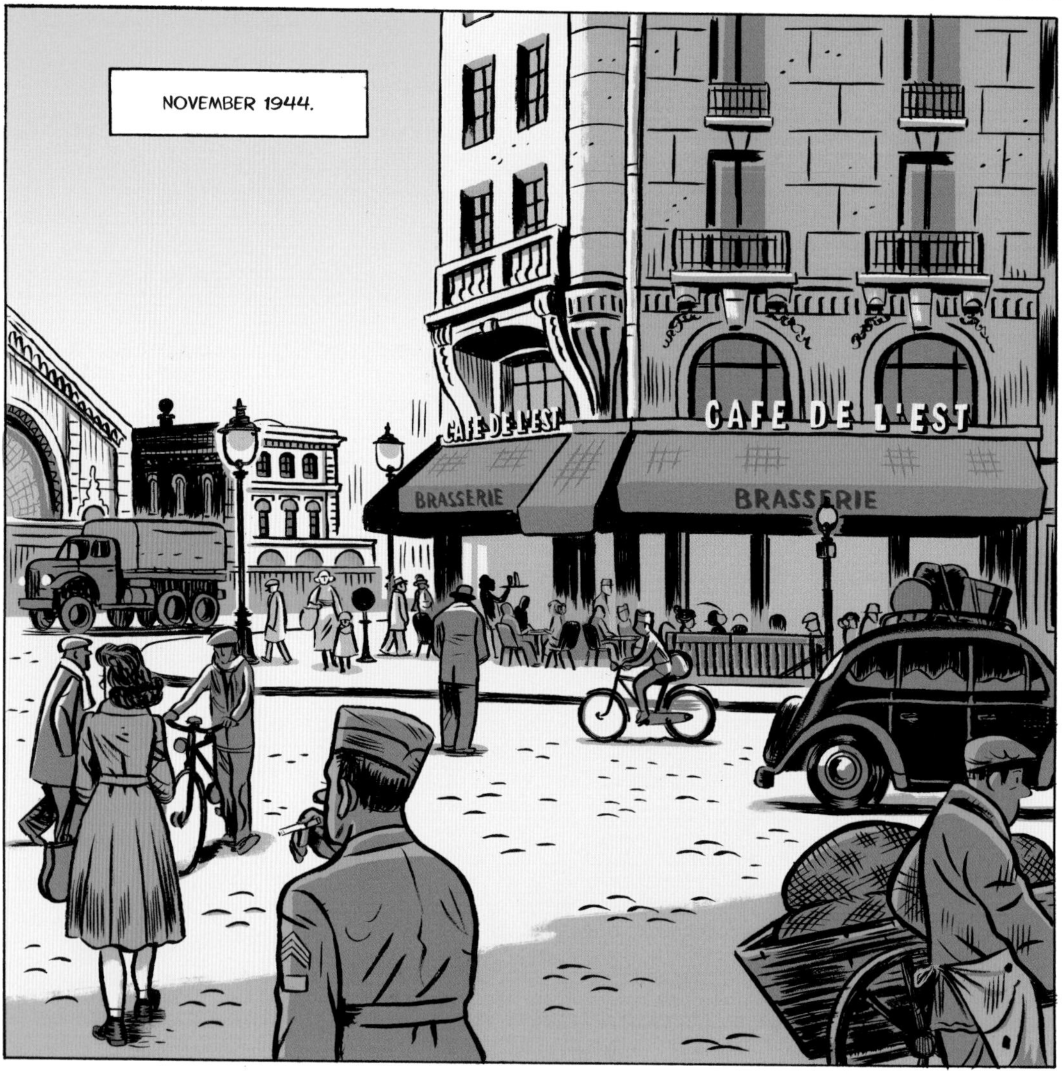
NOVEMBER 1944.
CAFE DE L'EST
CAFE DE L'EST
BRASSERIE
BRASSERIE

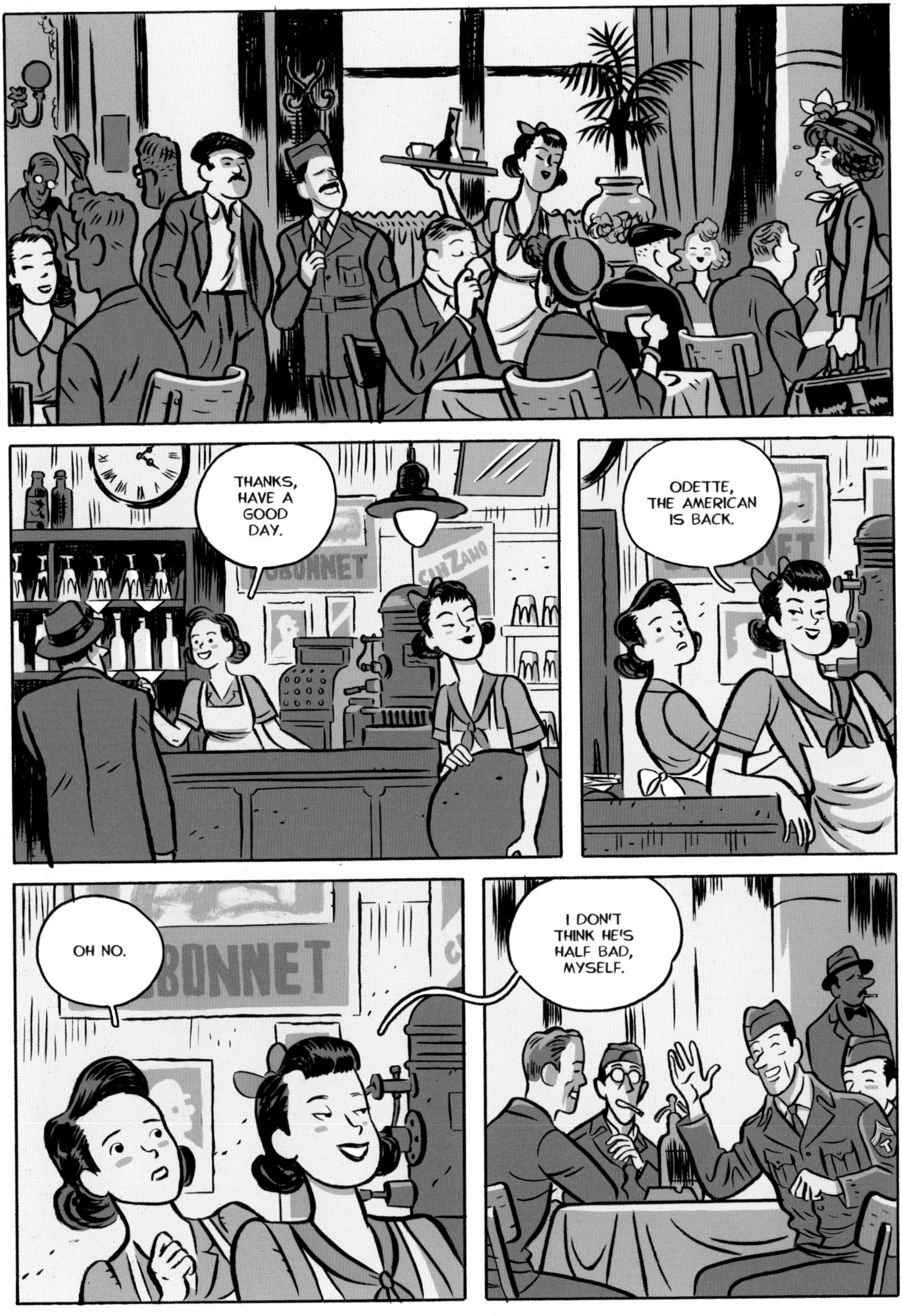
THANKS, HAVE A GOOD DAY.
DUBONNET
CINZANO
ODETTE, THE AMERICAN IS BACK.
OH NO.
DUBONNET
I DON'T THINK HE'S HALF BAD, MYSELF.

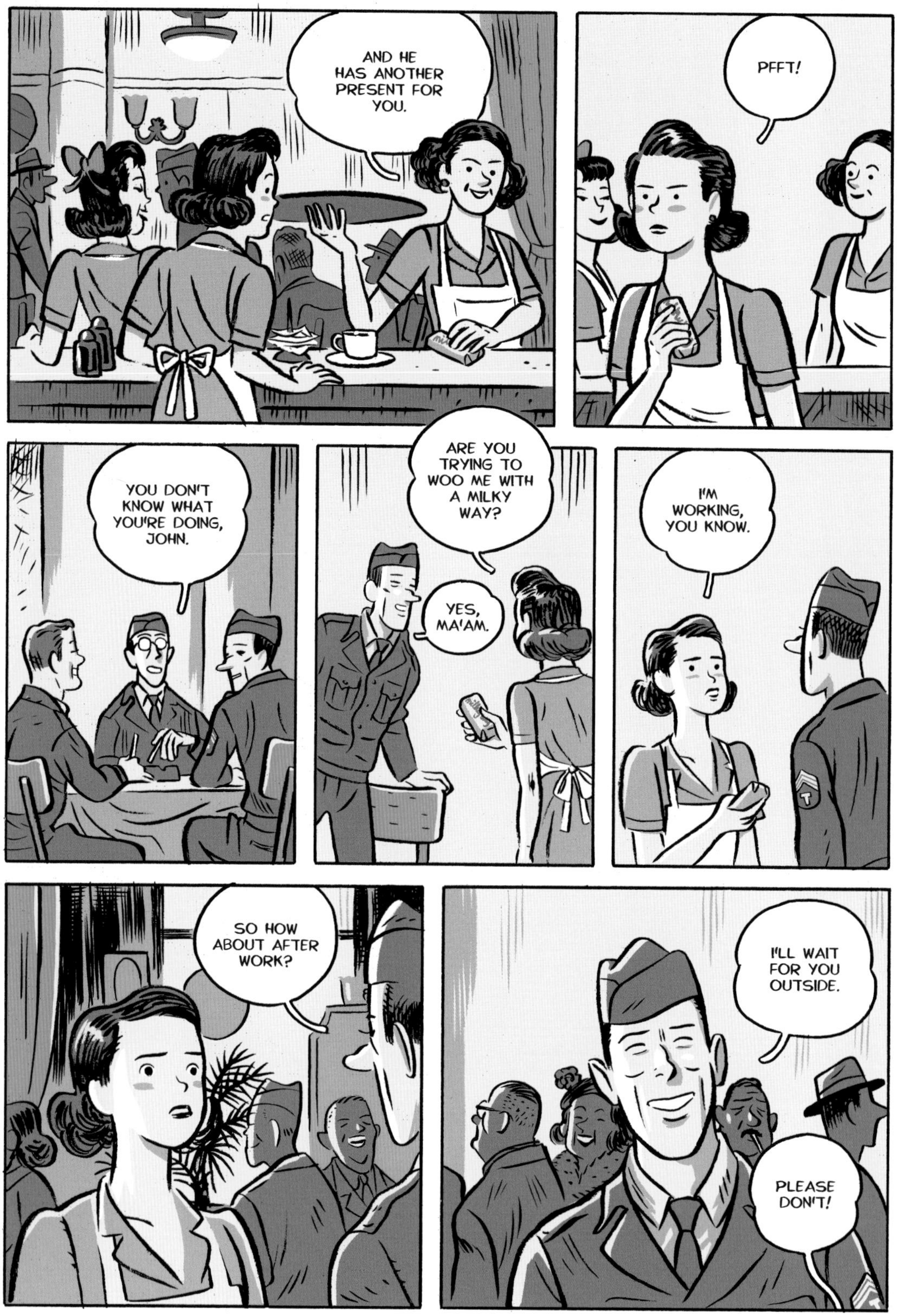
AND HE HAS ANOTHER PRESENT FOR YOU.
PFFT!
YOU DON'T KNOW WHAT YOU'RE DOING, JOHN.
ARE YOU TRYING TO WOO ME WITH A MILKY WAY?
YES, MA'AM.
I'M WORKING, YOU KNOW.
SO HOW ABOUT AFTER WORK?
I'LL WAIT FOR YOU OUTSIDE.
PLEASE DON'T!

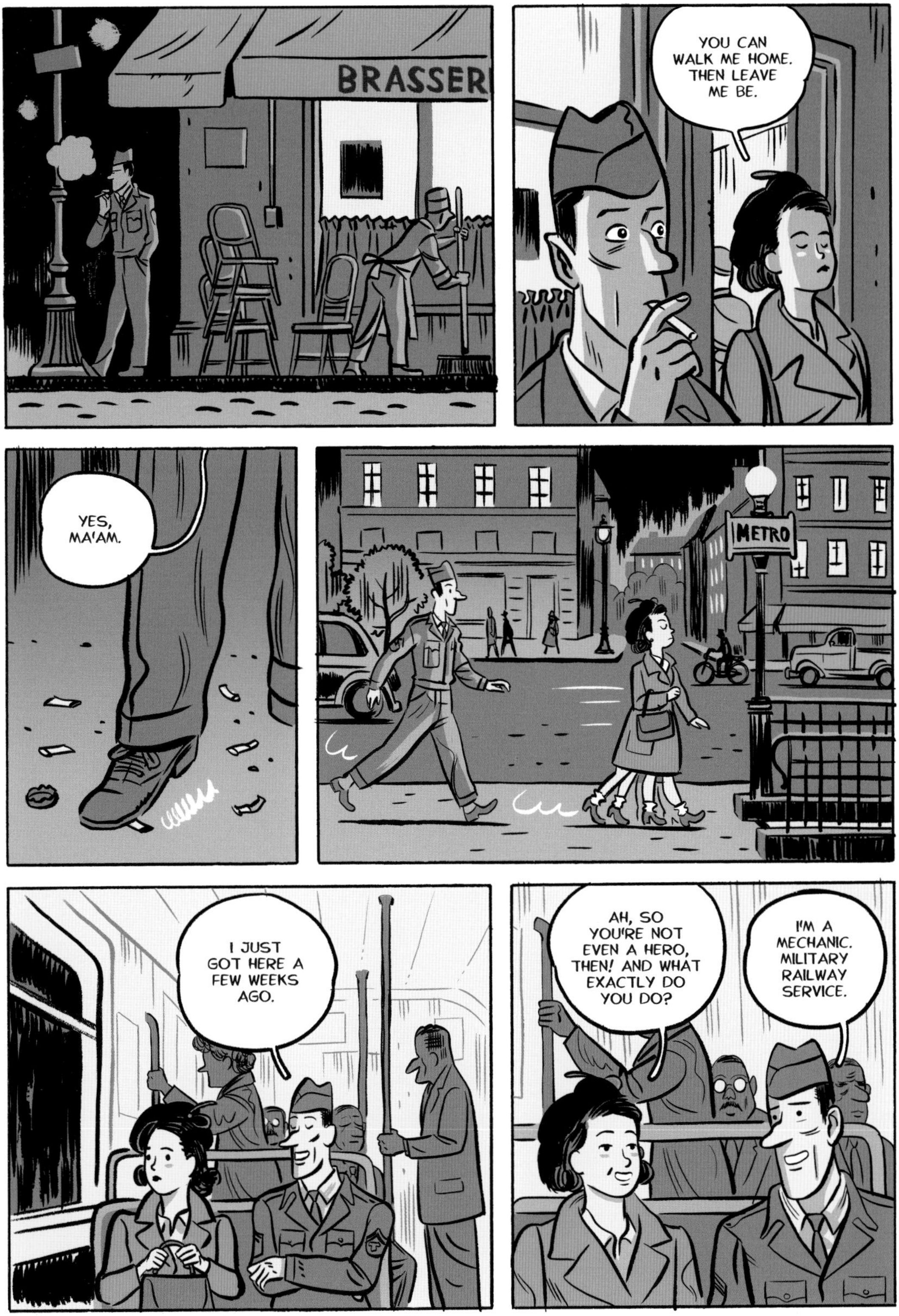
BRASSERI
YOU CAN WALK ME HOME. THEN LEAVE ME BE.
YES, MA'AM.
METRO
I JUST GOT HERE A FEW WEEKS AGO.
AH, SO YOU'RE NOT EVEN A HERO, THEN! AND WHAT EXACTLY DO YOU DO?
I'M A MECHANIC. MILITARY RAILWAY SERVICE.

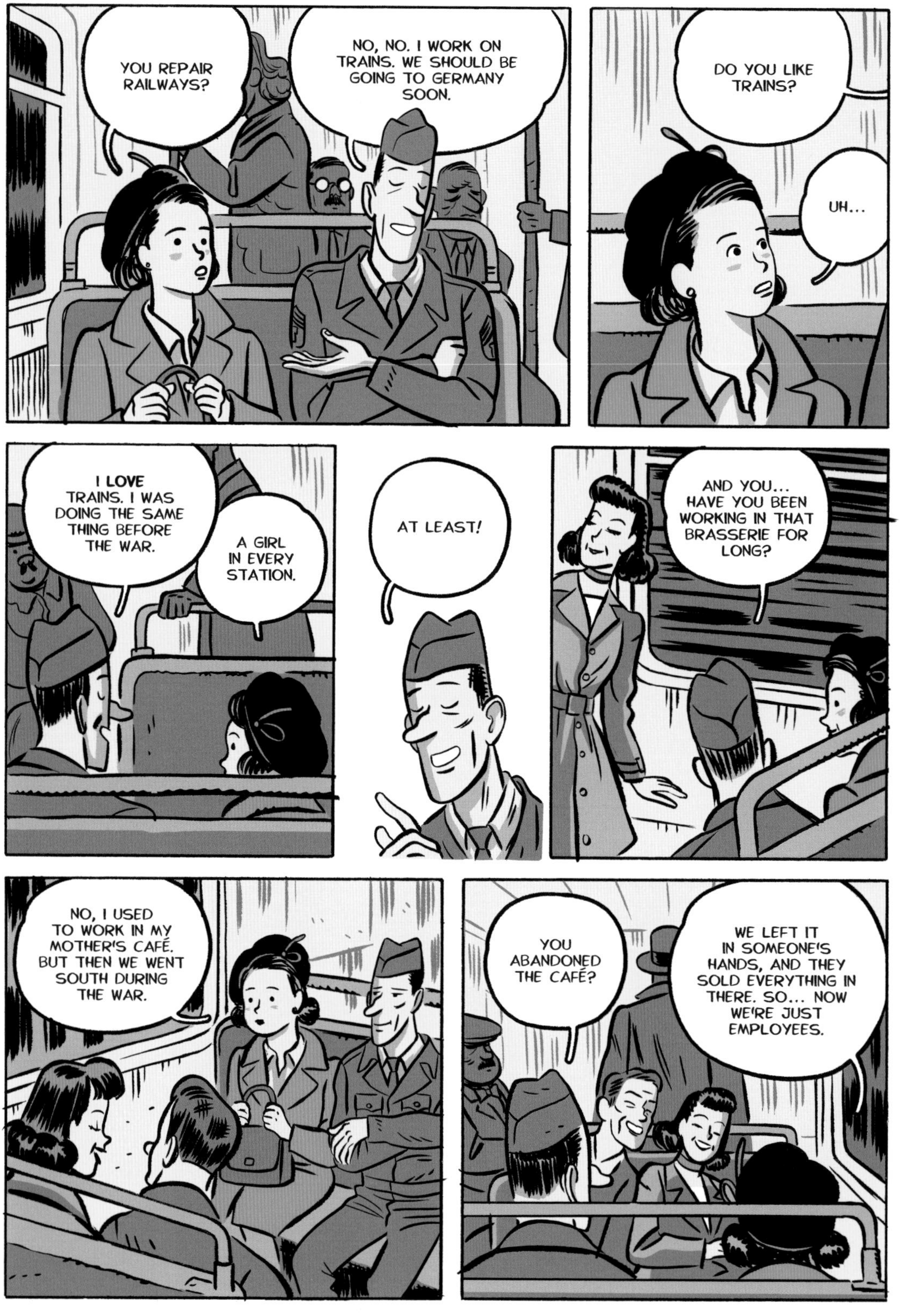
YOU REPAIR RAILWAYS?
NO, NO. I WORK ON TRAINS. WE SHOULD BE GOING TO GERMANY SOON.
DO YOU LIKE TRAINS?
UH...
I **LOVE** TRAINS. I WAS DOING THE SAME THING BEFORE THE WAR.
A GIRL IN EVERY STATION.
AT LEAST!
AND YOU... HAVE YOU BEEN WORKING IN THAT BRASSERIE FOR LONG?
NO, I USED TO WORK IN MY MOTHER'S CAFÉ. BUT THEN WE WENT SOUTH DURING THE WAR.
YOU ABANDONED THE CAFÉ?
WE LEFT IT IN SOMEONE'S HANDS, AND THEY SOLD EVERYTHING IN THERE. SO... NOW WE'RE JUST EMPLOYEES.

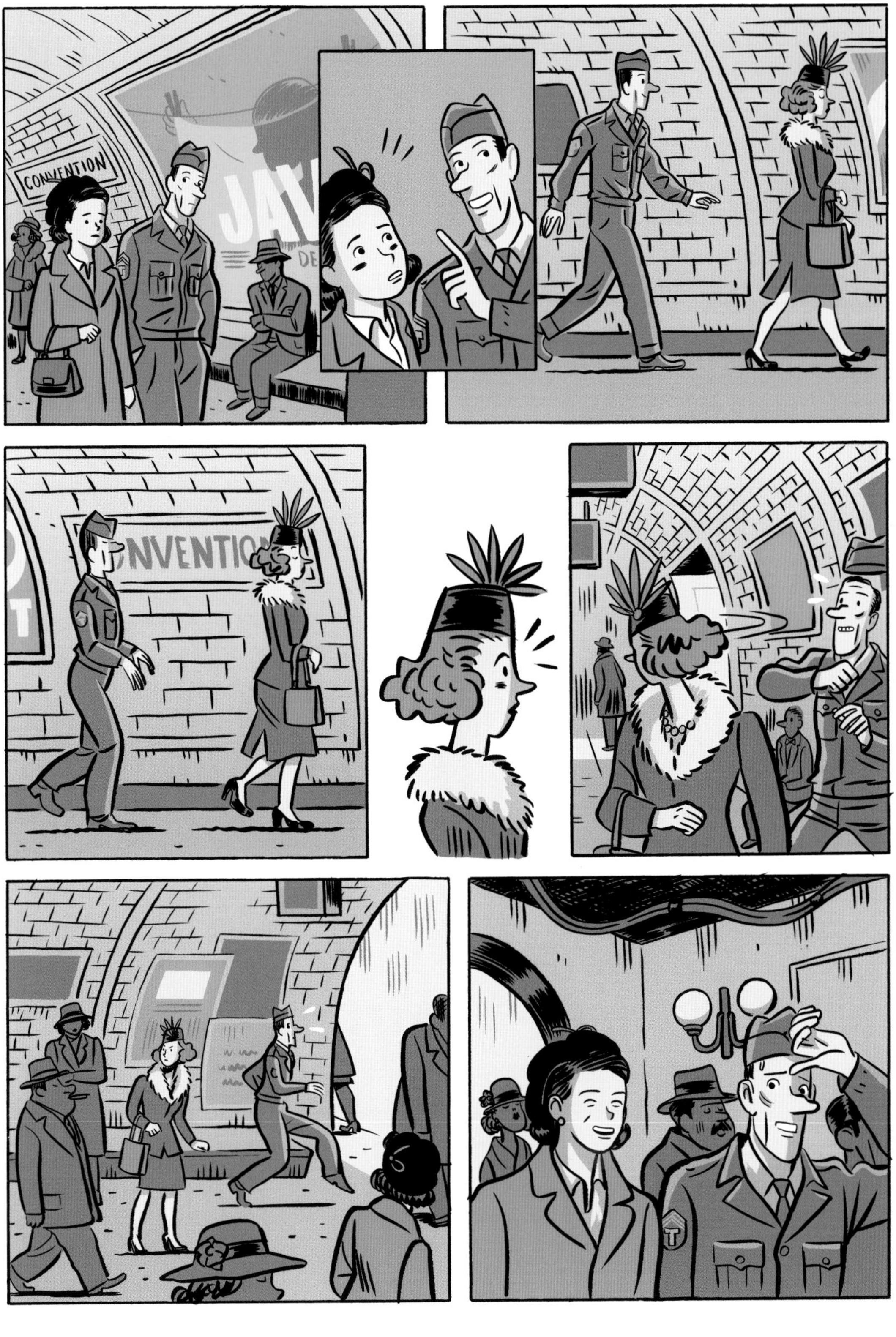
CONVENTION
JAV
DE
CONVENTIO

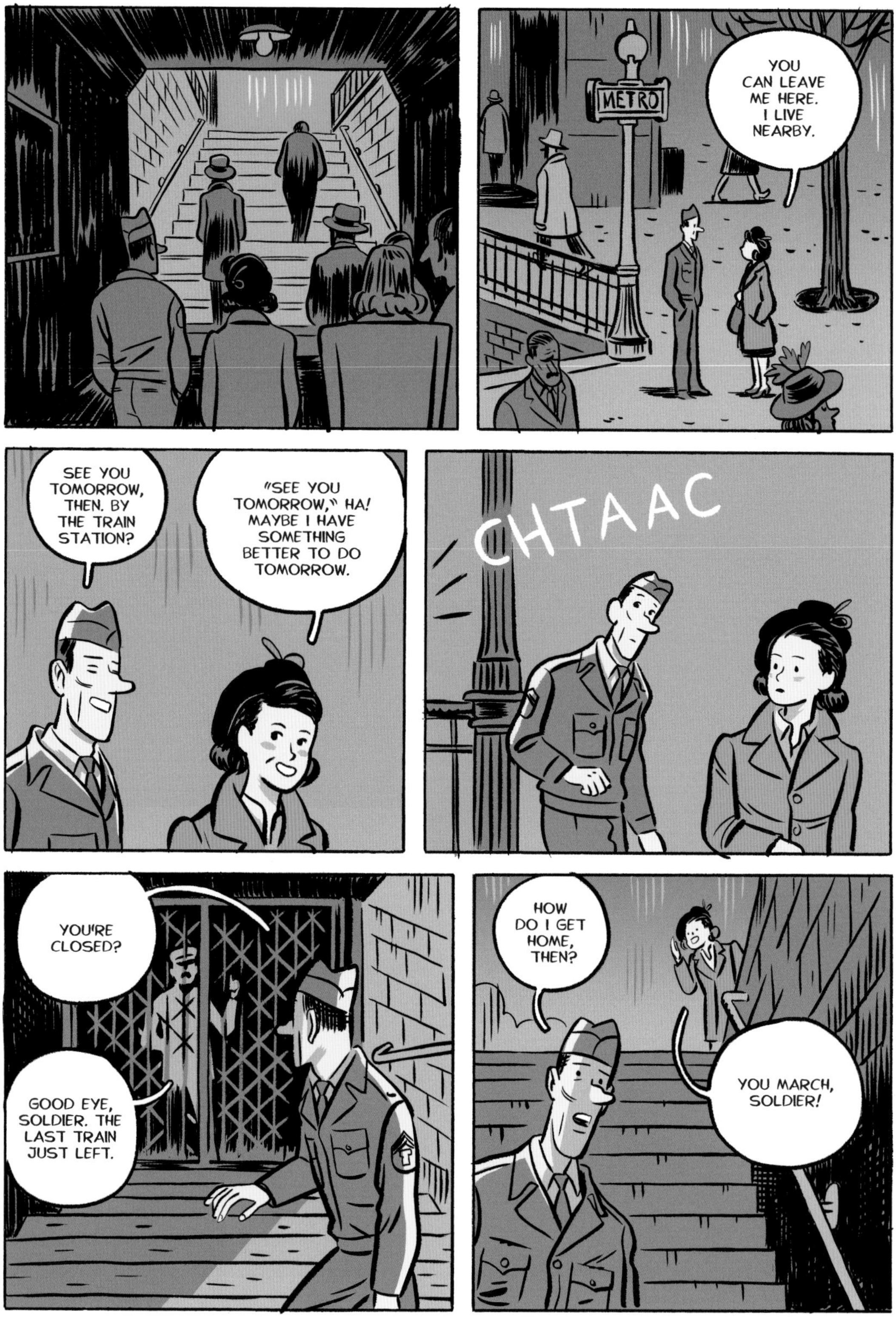
METRO
YOU CAN LEAVE ME HERE. I LIVE NEARBY.
SEE YOU TOMORROW, THEN. BY THE TRAIN STATION?
"SEE YOU TOMORROW," HA! MAYBE I HAVE SOMETHING BETTER TO DO TOMORROW.
CHTAAC
YOU'RE CLOSED?
GOOD EYE, SOLDIER. THE LAST TRAIN JUST LEFT.
HOW DO I GET HOME, THEN?
YOU MARCH, SOLDIER!

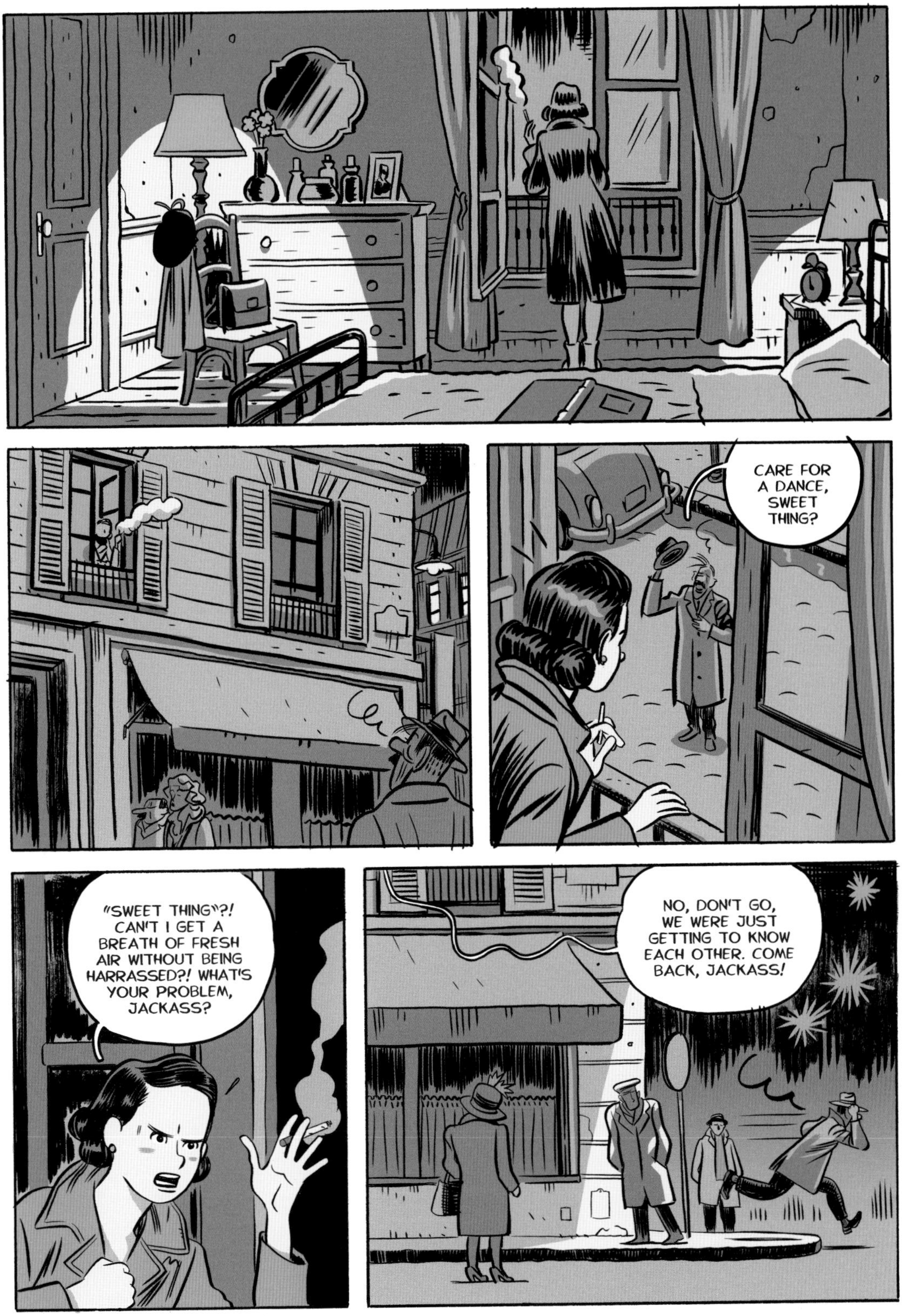
CARE FOR A DANCE, SWEET THING?
"SWEET THING"?! CAN'T I GET A BREATH OF FRESH AIR WITHOUT BEING HARRASSED?! WHAT'S YOUR PROBLEM, JACKASS?
NO, DON'T GO, WE WERE JUST GETTING TO KNOW EACH OTHER. COME BACK, JACKASS!

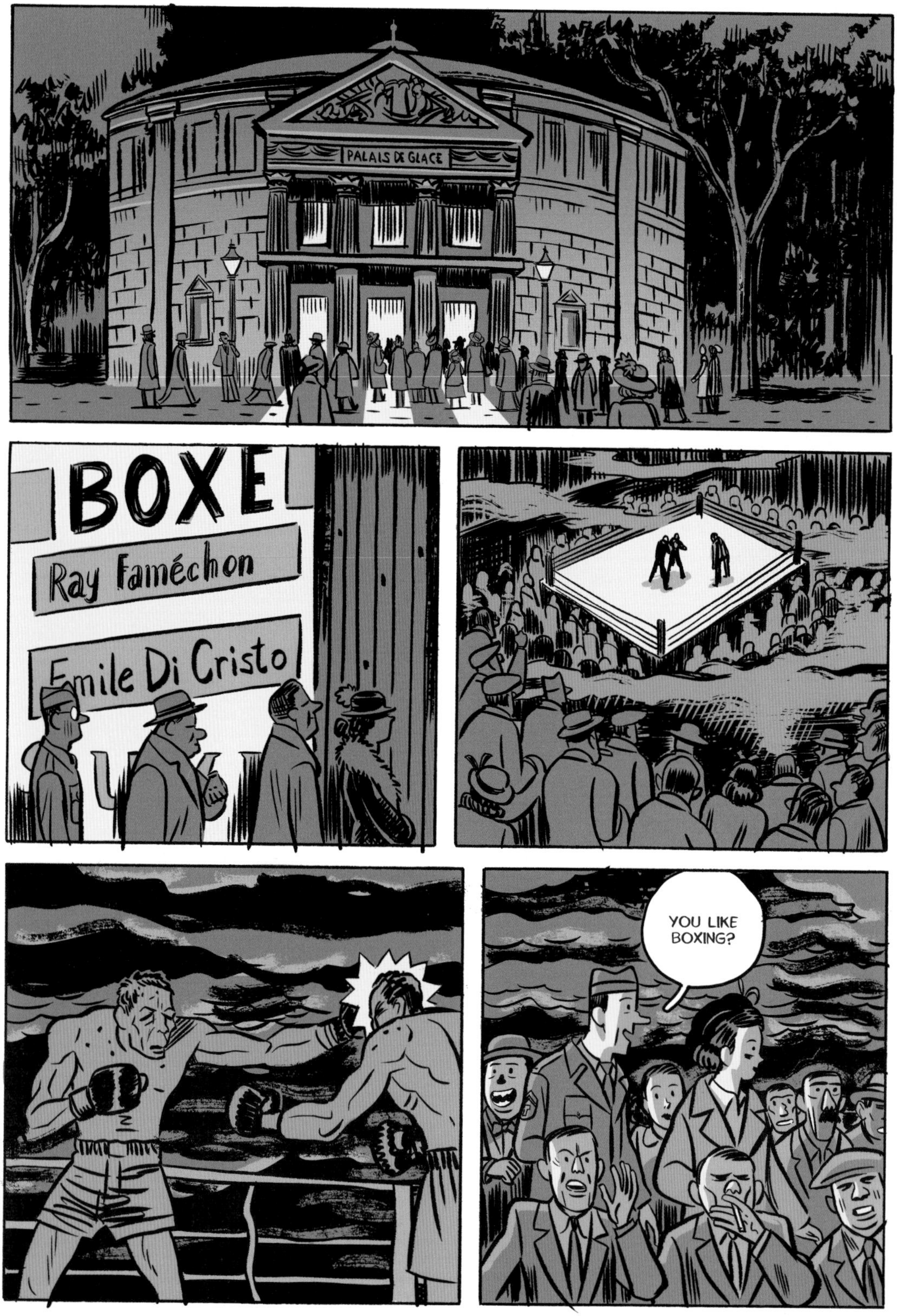
PALAIS DE GLACE
BOXE
Ray Faméchon
Emile Di Cristo
YOU LIKE BOXING?

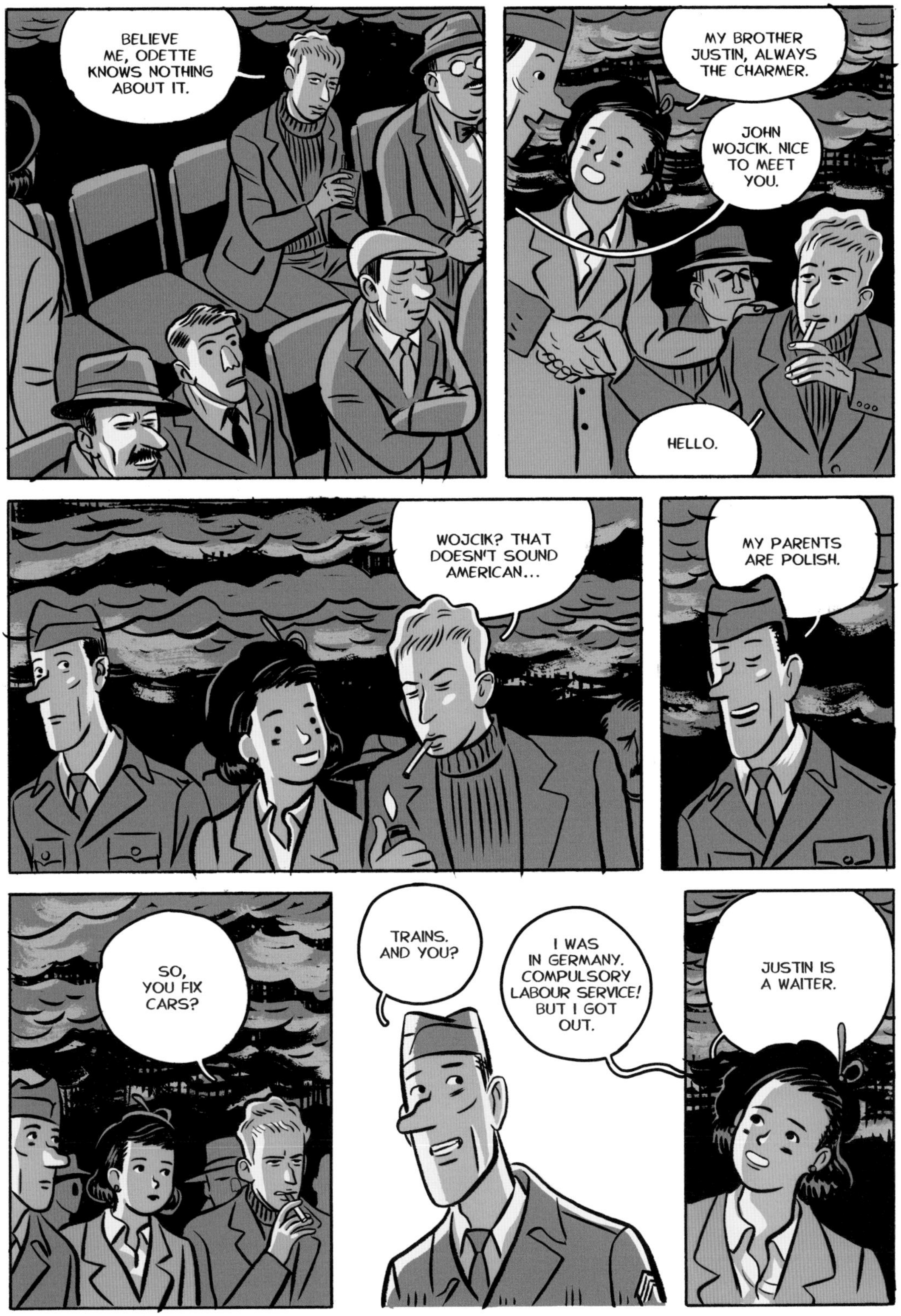
BELIEVE ME, ODETTE KNOWS NOTHING ABOUT IT.
MY BROTHER JUSTIN, ALWAYS THE CHARMER.
JOHN WOJCIK. NICE TO MEET YOU.
HELLO.
WOJCIK? THAT DOESN'T SOUND AMERICAN...
MY PARENTS ARE POLISH.
SO, YOU FIX CARS?
TRAINS. AND YOU?
I WAS IN GERMANY. COMPULSORY LABOUR SERVICE! BUT I GOT OUT.
JUSTIN IS A WAITER.

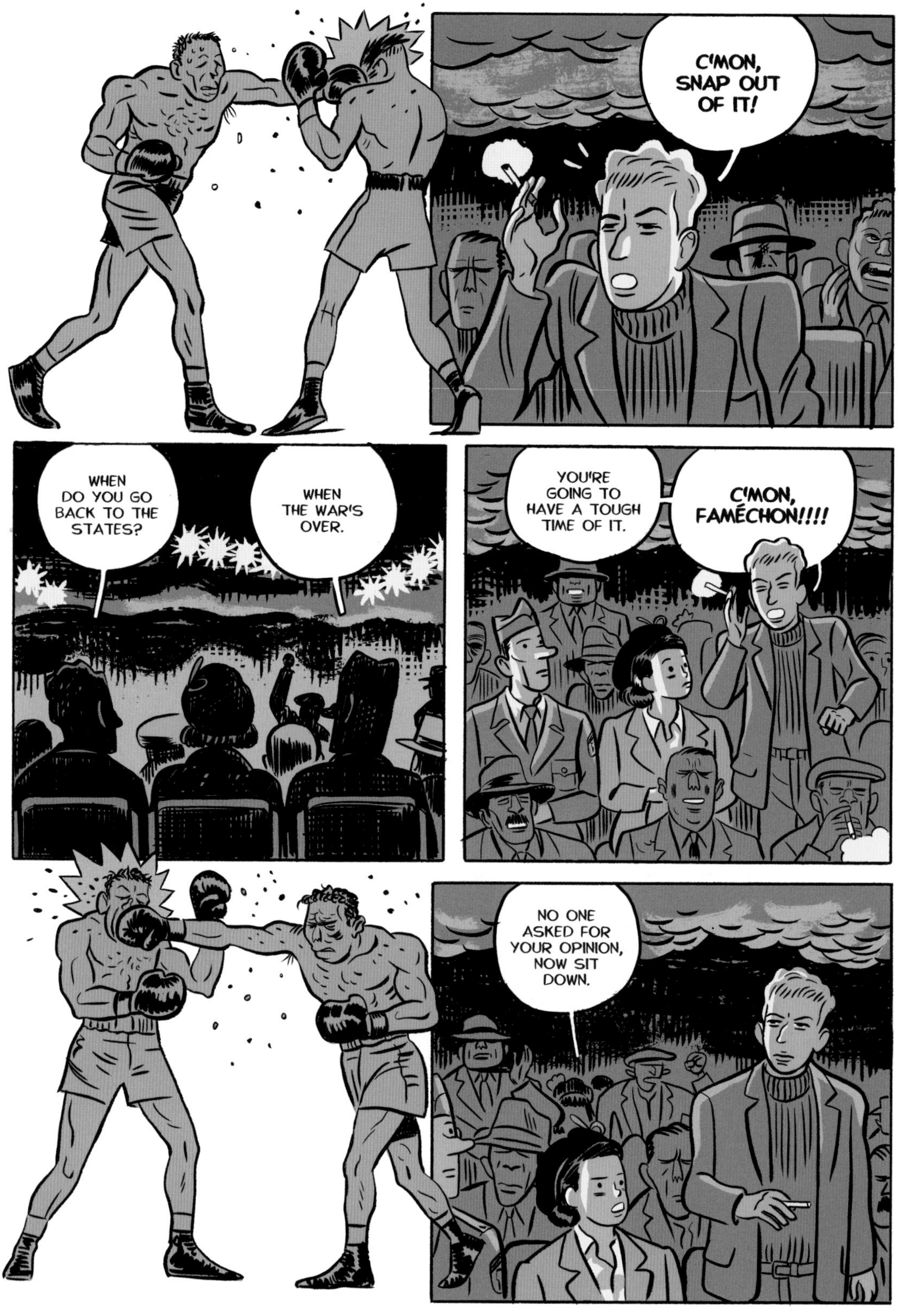
C'MON, SNAP OUT OF IT!
WHEN DO YOU GO BACK TO THE STATES?
WHEN THE WAR'S OVER.
YOU'RE GOING TO HAVE A TOUGH TIME OF IT.
C'MON, FAMÉCHON!!!!
NO ONE ASKED FOR YOUR OPINION, NOW SIT DOWN.

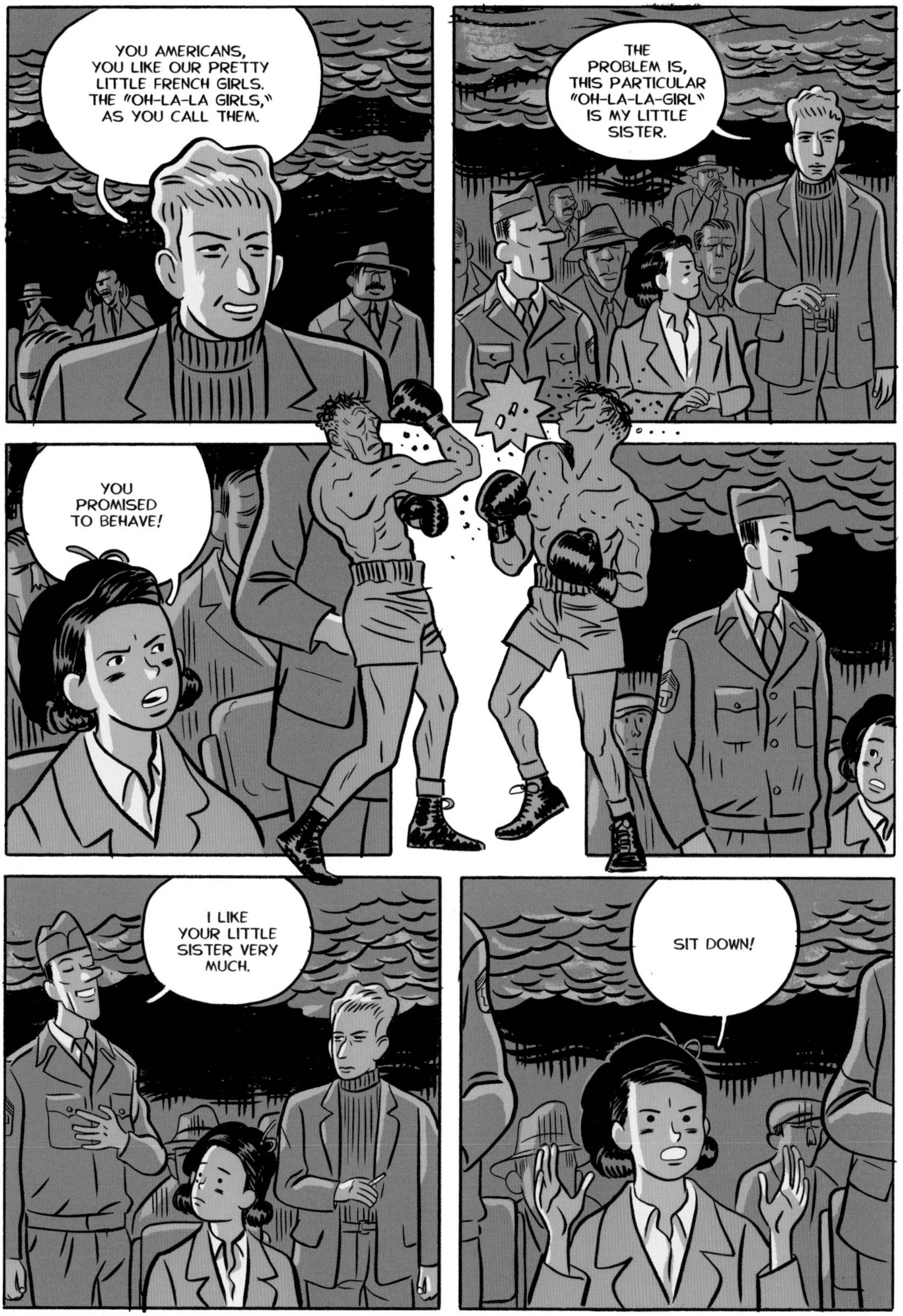
YOU AMERICANS, YOU LIKE OUR PRETTY LITTLE FRENCH GIRLS. THE "OH-LA-LA GIRLS," AS YOU CALL THEM.
THE PROBLEM IS, THIS PARTICULAR "OH-LA-LA-GIRL" IS MY LITTLE SISTER.
YOU PROMISED TO BEHAVE!
I LIKE YOUR LITTLE SISTER VERY MUCH.
SIT DOWN!

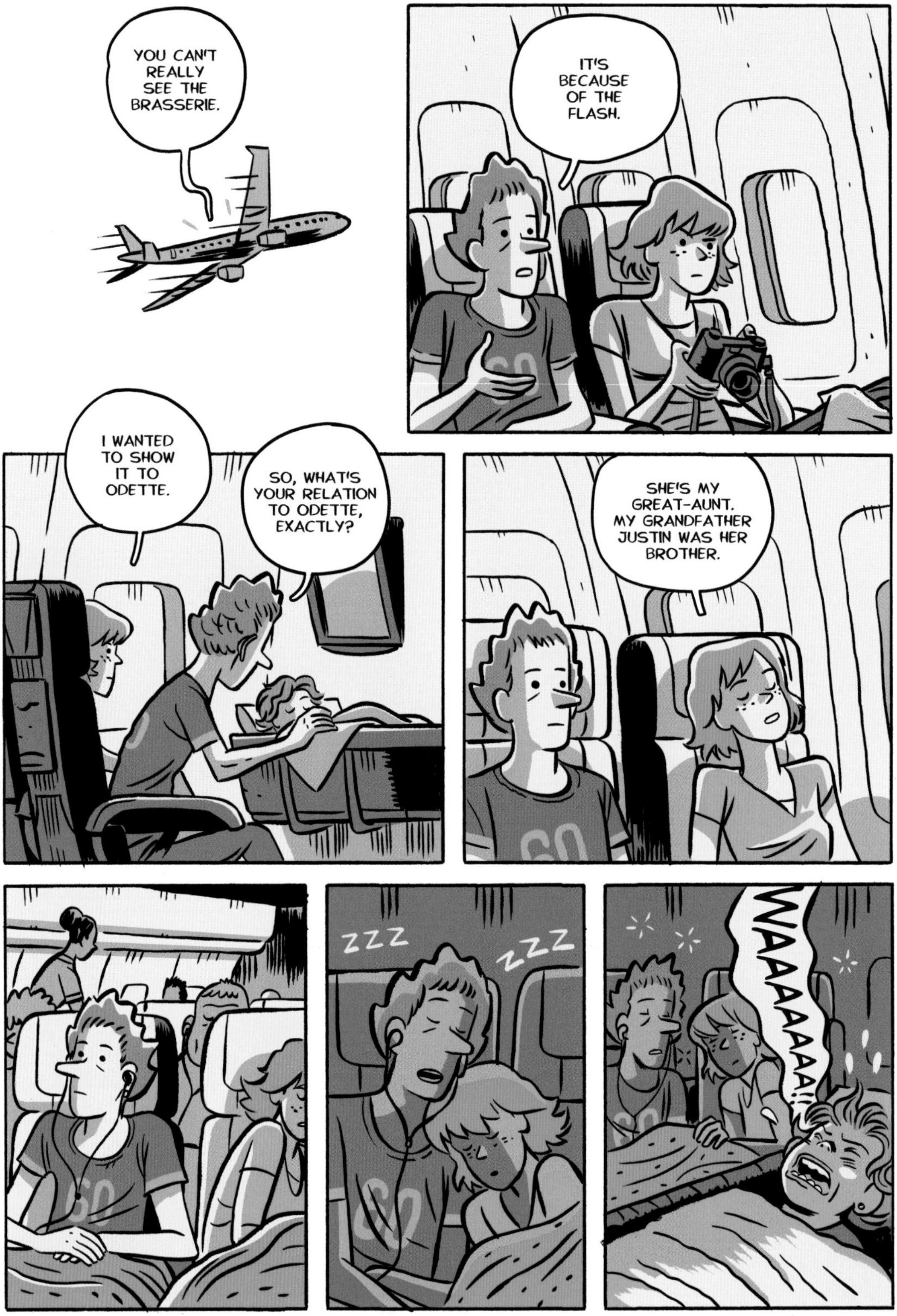
YOU CAN'T REALLY SEE THE BRASSERIE.
IT'S BECAUSE OF THE FLASH.
I WANTED TO SHOW IT TO ODETTE.
SO, WHAT'S YOUR RELATION TO ODETTE, EXACTLY?
SHE'S MY GREAT-AUNT. MY GRANDFATHER JUSTIN WAS HER BROTHER.
ZZZ
ZZZ
WAAAAAAAA!!

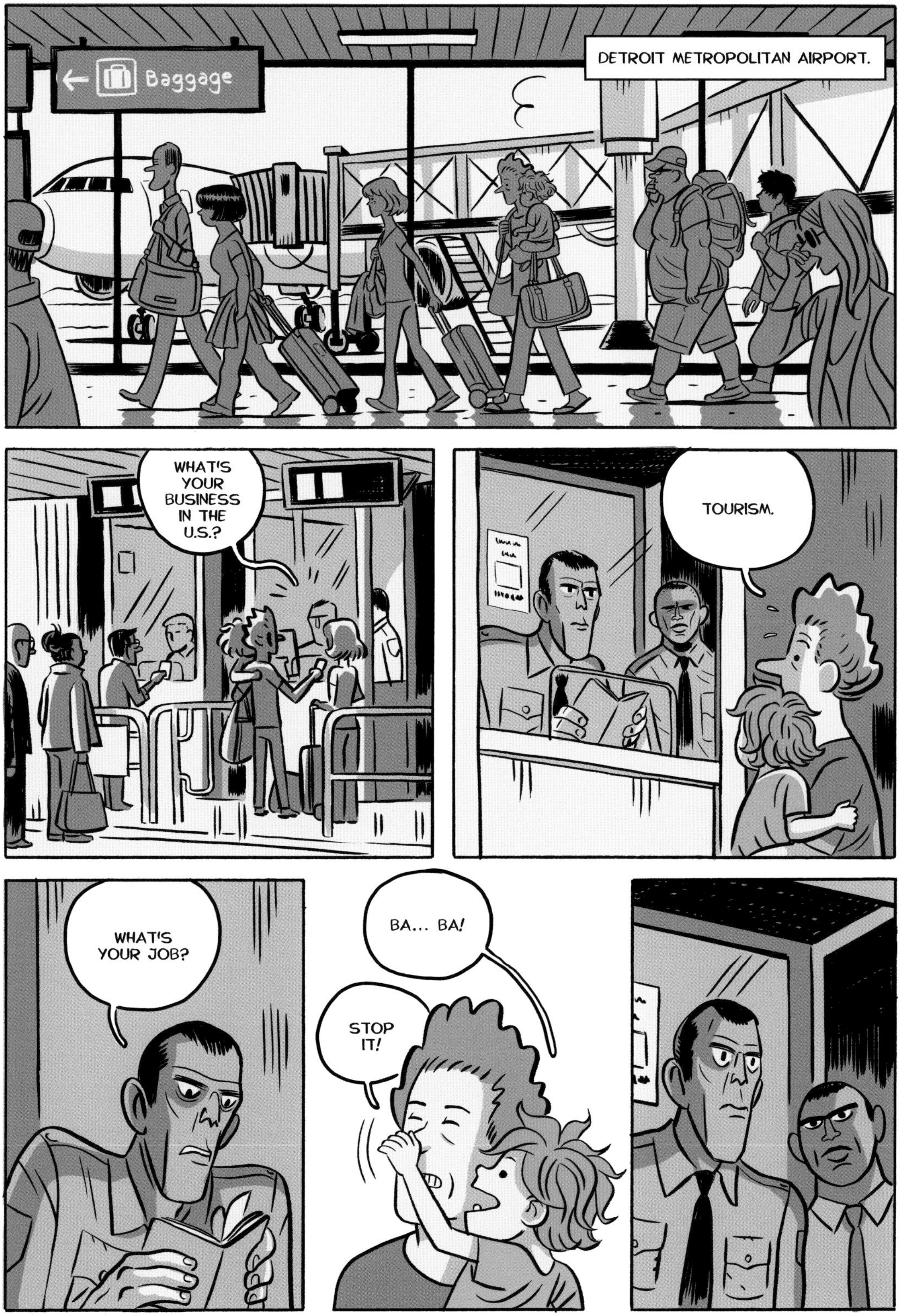
Baggage
DETROIT METROPOLITAN AIRPORT.
WHAT'S YOUR BUSINESS IN THE U.S.?
TOURISM.
WHAT'S YOUR JOB?
BA... BA!
STOP IT!

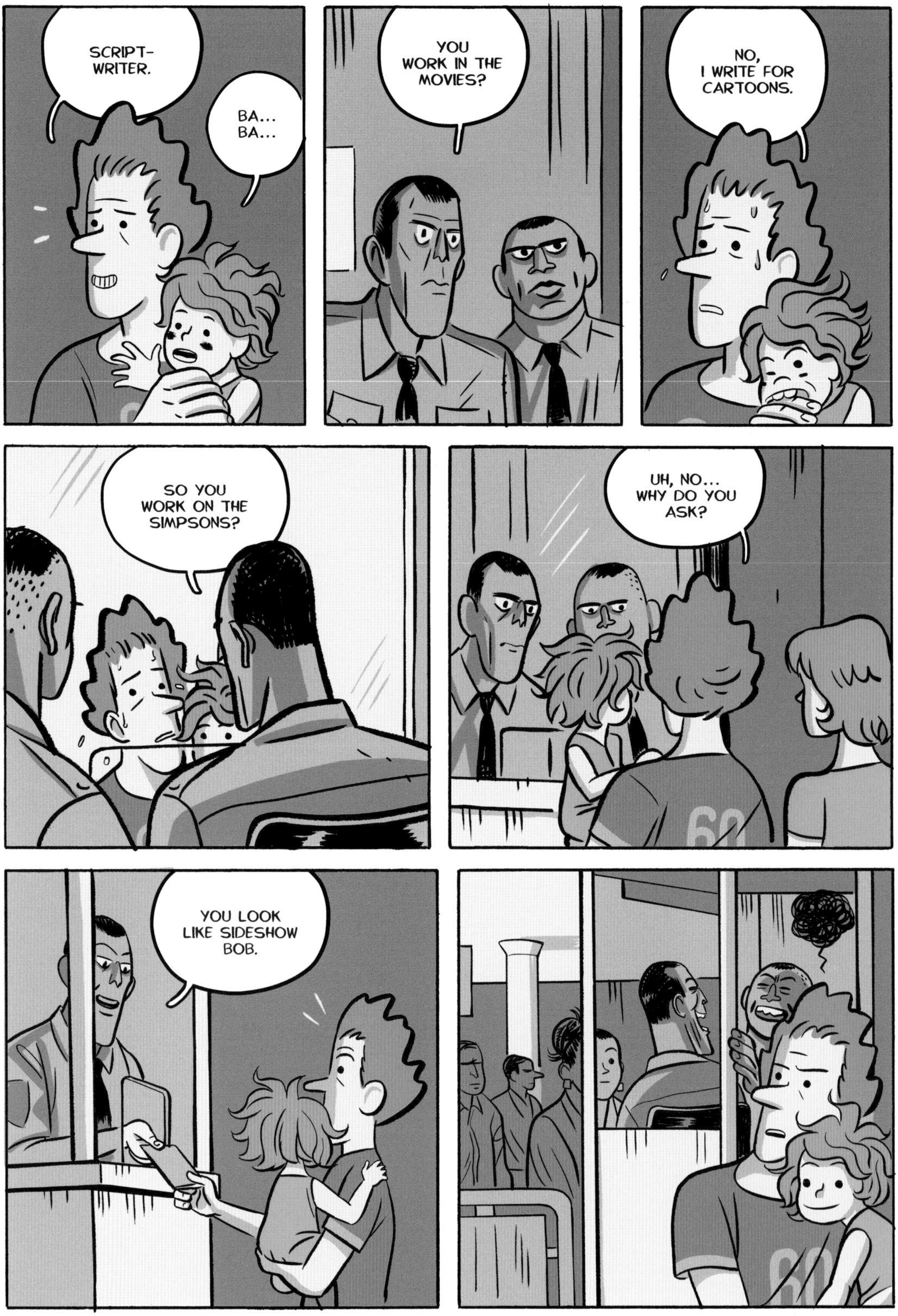
SCRIPT-WRITER.
BA... BA...
YOU WORK IN THE MOVIES?
NO, I WRITE FOR CARTOONS.
SO YOU WORK ON THE SIMPSONS?
UH, NO... WHY DO YOU ASK?
YOU LOOK LIKE SIDESHOW BOB.

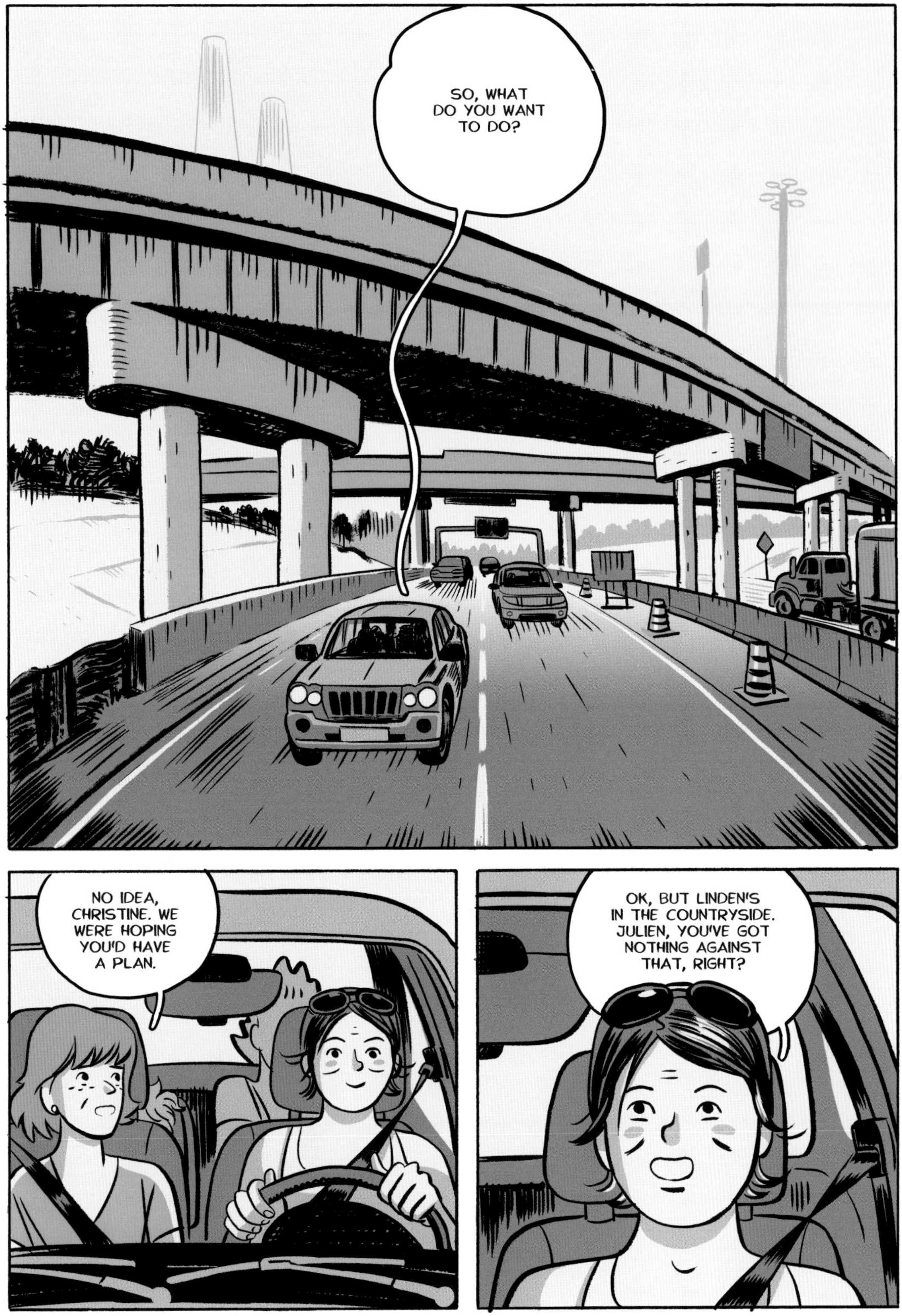
SO, WHAT DO YOU WANT TO DO?
NO IDEA, CHRISTINE. WE WERE HOPING YOU'D HAVE A PLAN.
OK, BUT LINDEN'S IN THE COUNTRYSIDE. JULIEN, YOU'VE GOT NOTHING AGAINST THAT, RIGHT?

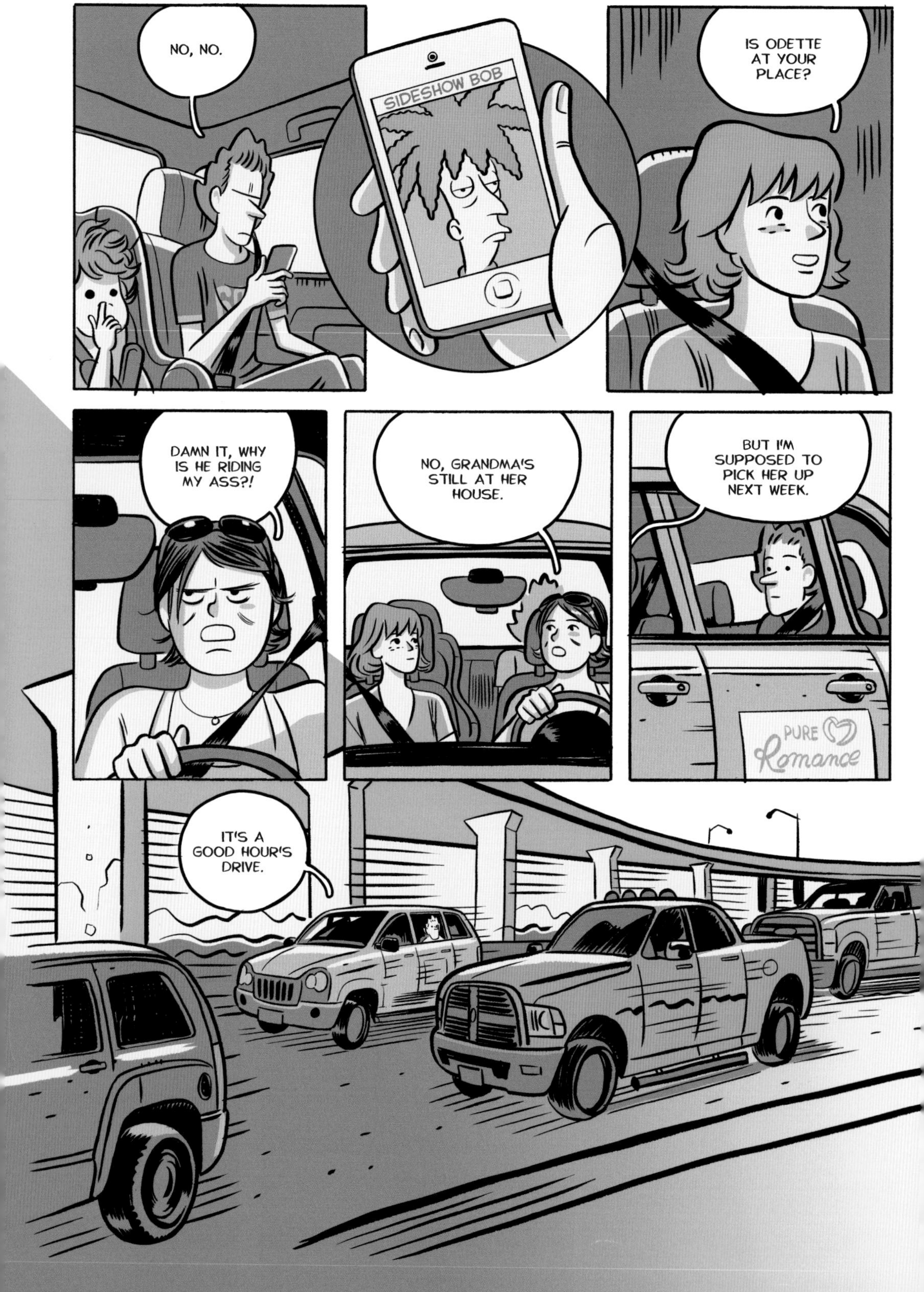
NO, NO.
SIDESHOW BOB
IS ODETTE AT YOUR PLACE?
DAMN IT, WHY IS HE RIDING MY ASS?!
NO, GRANDMA'S STILL AT HER HOUSE.
BUT I'M SUPPOSED TO PICK HER UP NEXT WEEK.
PURE Romance
IT'S A GOOD HOUR'S DRIVE.

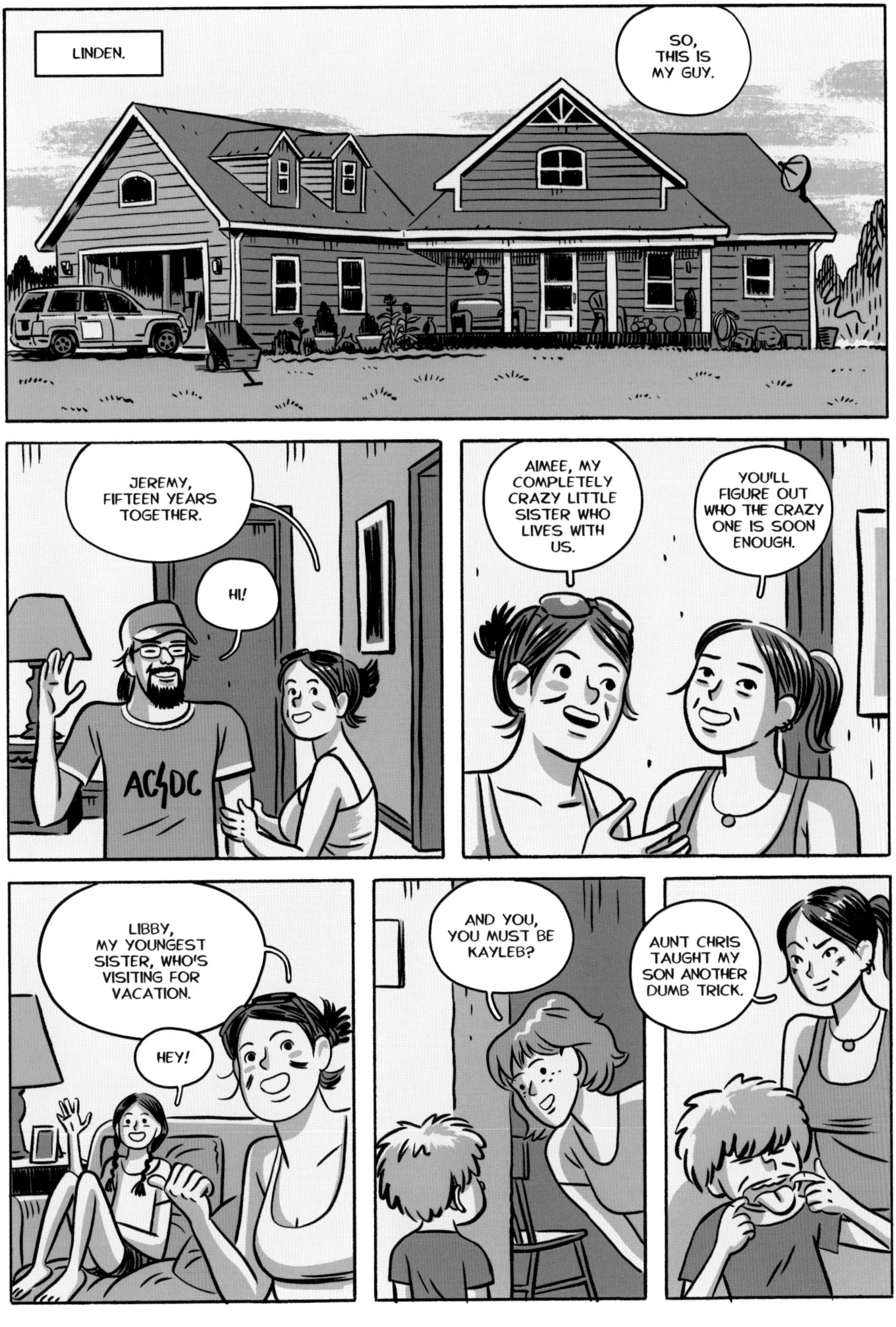
LINDEN.
SO, THIS IS MY GUY.
JEREMY, FIFTEEN YEARS TOGETHER.
HI!
AIMEE, MY COMPLETELY CRAZY LITTLE SISTER WHO LIVES WITH US.
YOU'LL FIGURE OUT WHO THE CRAZY ONE IS SOON ENOUGH.
LIBBY, MY YOUNGEST SISTER, WHO'S VISITING FOR VACATION.
HEY!
AND YOU, YOU MUST BE KAYLEB?
AUNT CHRIS TAUGHT MY SON ANOTHER DUMB TRICK.
AC/DC

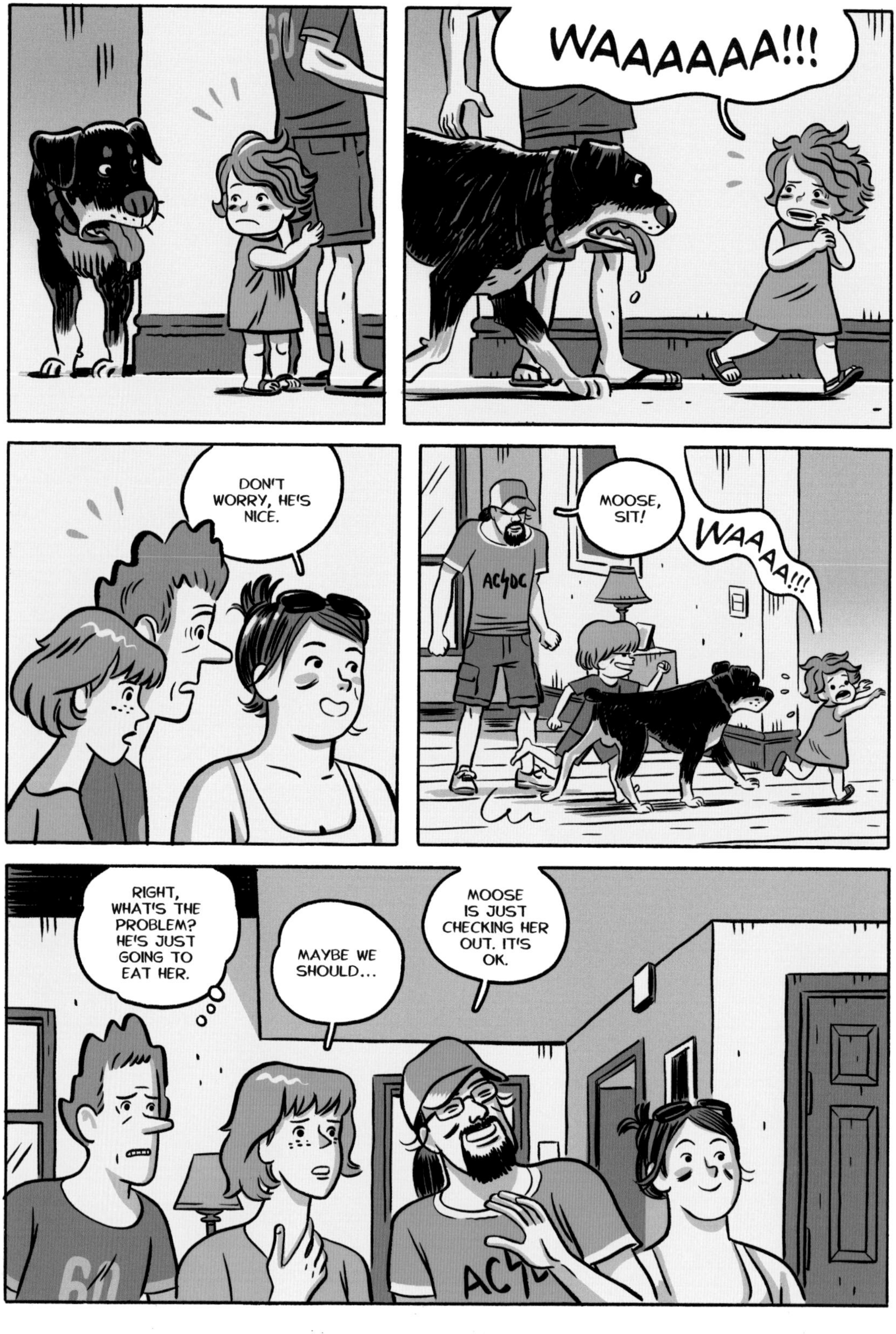
WAAAAAA!!!
DON'T WORRY, HE'S NICE.
MOOSE, SIT!
WAAAAA!!!
RIGHT, WHAT'S THE PROBLEM? HE'S JUST GOING TO EAT HER.
MAYBE WE SHOULD...
MOOSE IS JUST CHECKING HER OUT. IT'S OK.

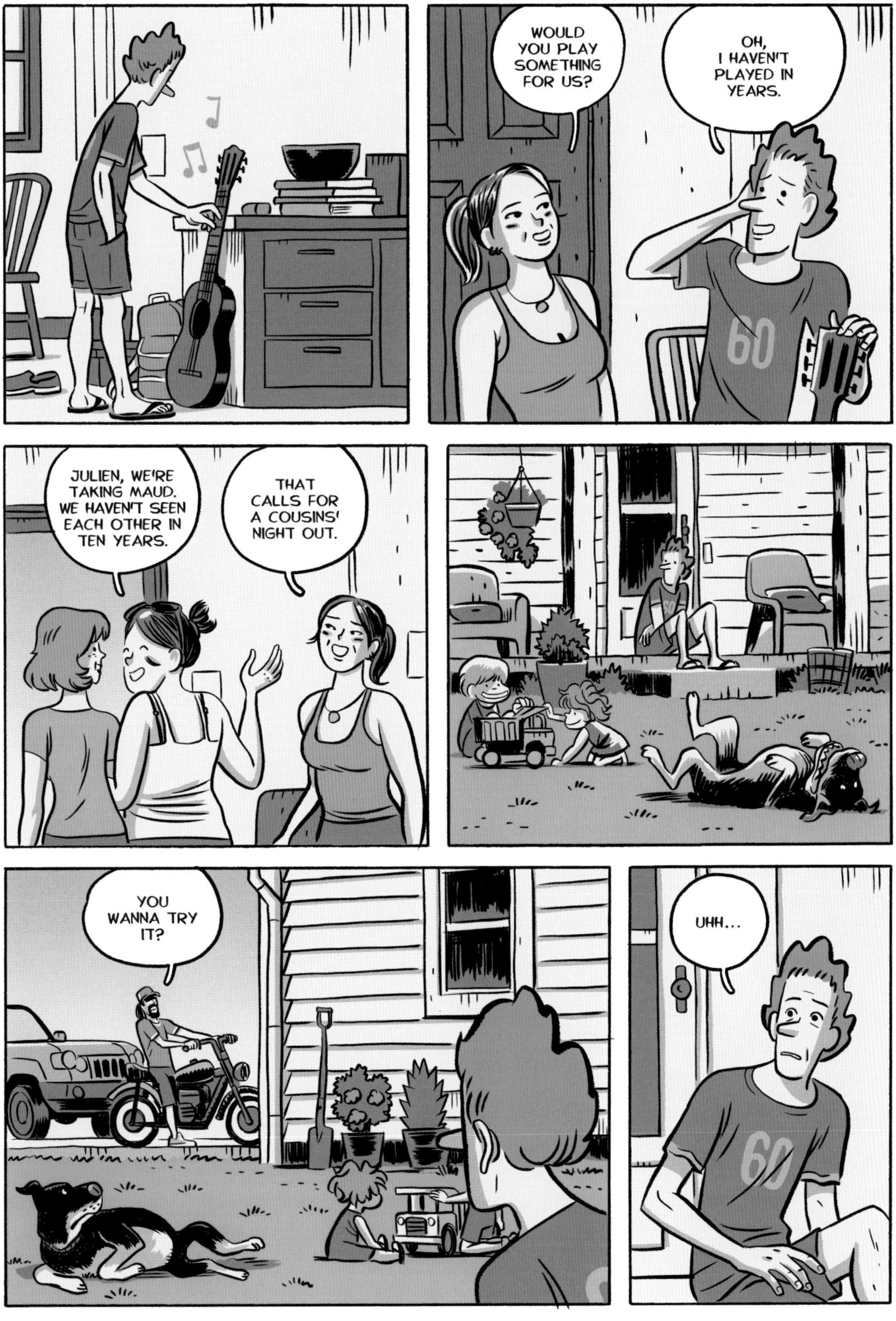
WOULD YOU PLAY SOMETHING FOR US?
OH, I HAVEN'T PLAYED IN YEARS.
JULIEN, WE'RE TAKING MAUD. WE HAVEN'T SEEN EACH OTHER IN TEN YEARS.
THAT CALLS FOR A COUSINS' NIGHT OUT.
YOU WANNA TRY IT?
UHH...

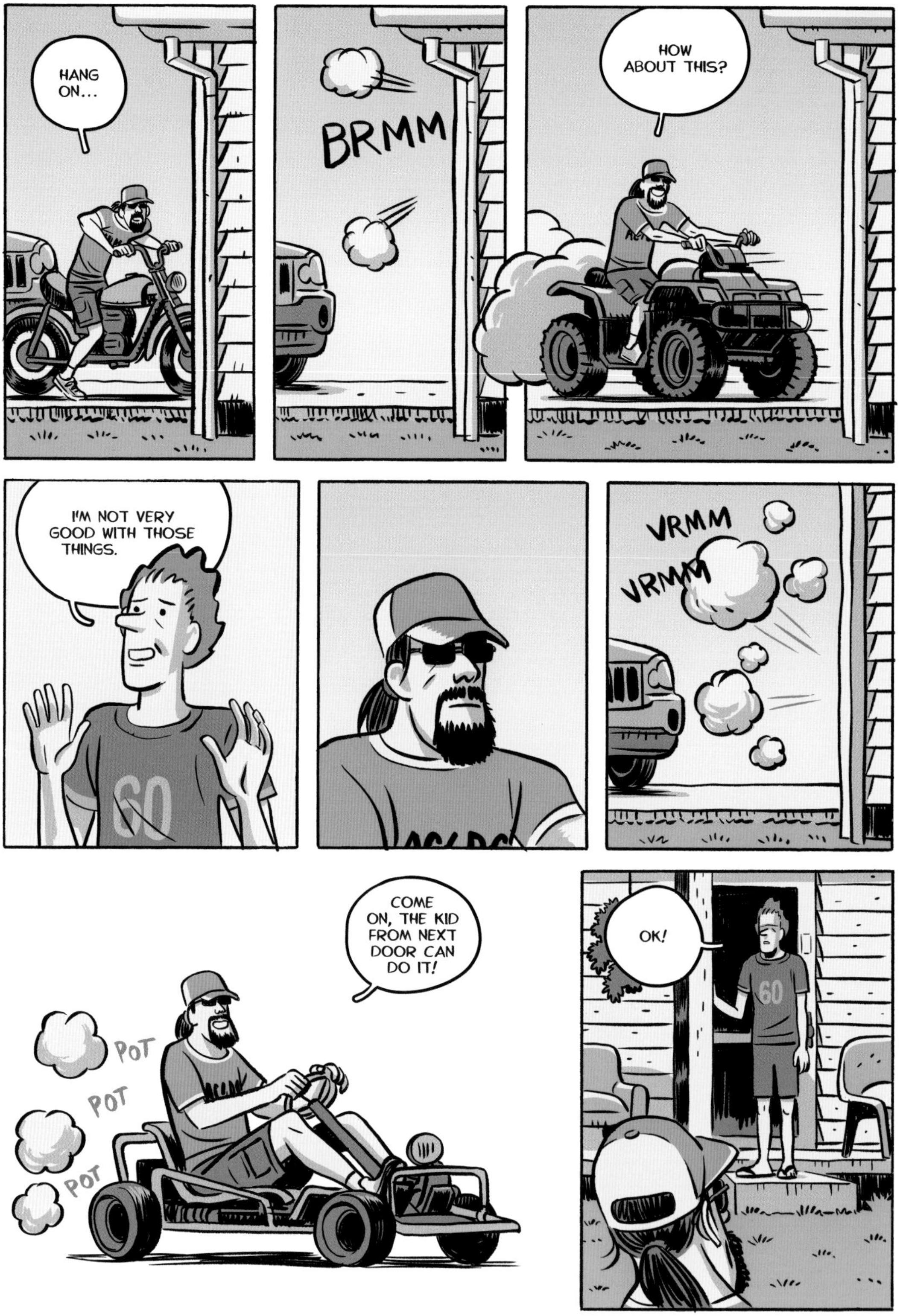
HANG ON...
BRMM
HOW ABOUT THIS?
I'M NOT VERY GOOD WITH THOSE THINGS.
VRMM
VRMM
COME ON, THE KID FROM NEXT DOOR CAN DO IT!
POT
POT
POT
OK!

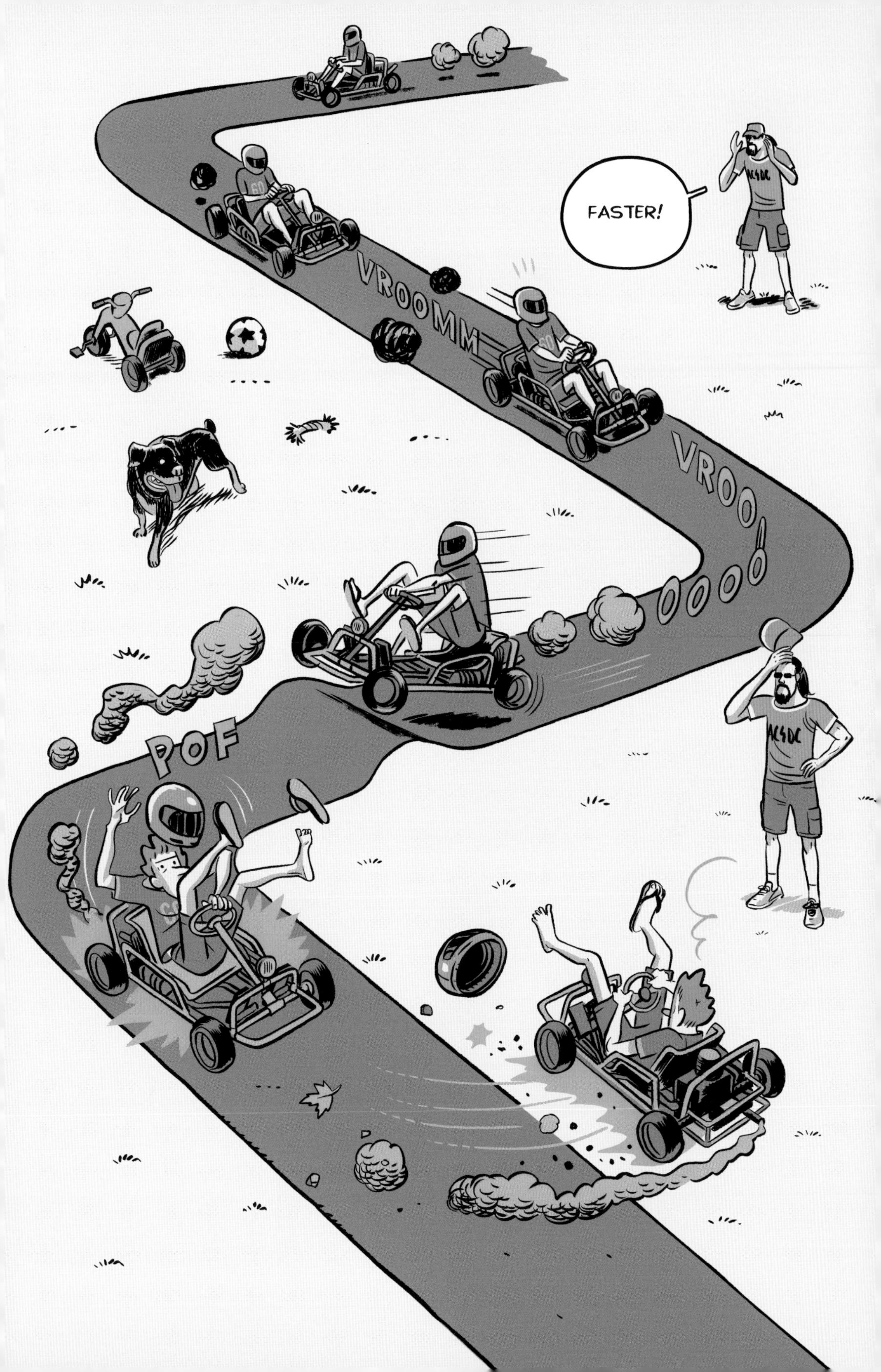
FASTER!
VROOMM
VROOOOOOO
POF

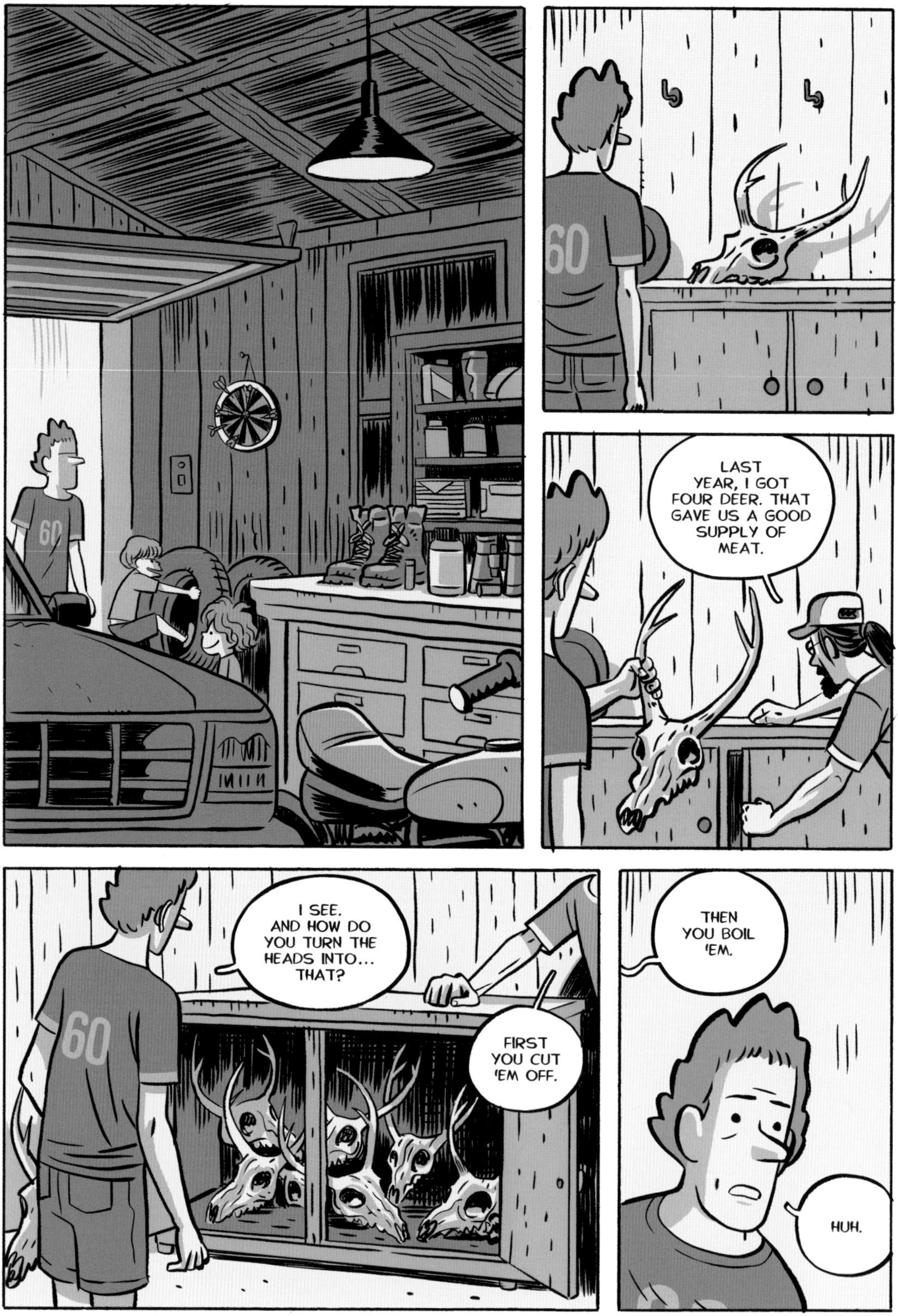
LAST YEAR, I GOT FOUR DEER. THAT GAVE US A GOOD SUPPLY OF MEAT.
I SEE. AND HOW DO YOU TURN THE HEADS INTO... THAT?
FIRST YOU CUT 'EM OFF.
THEN YOU BOIL 'EM.
HUH.

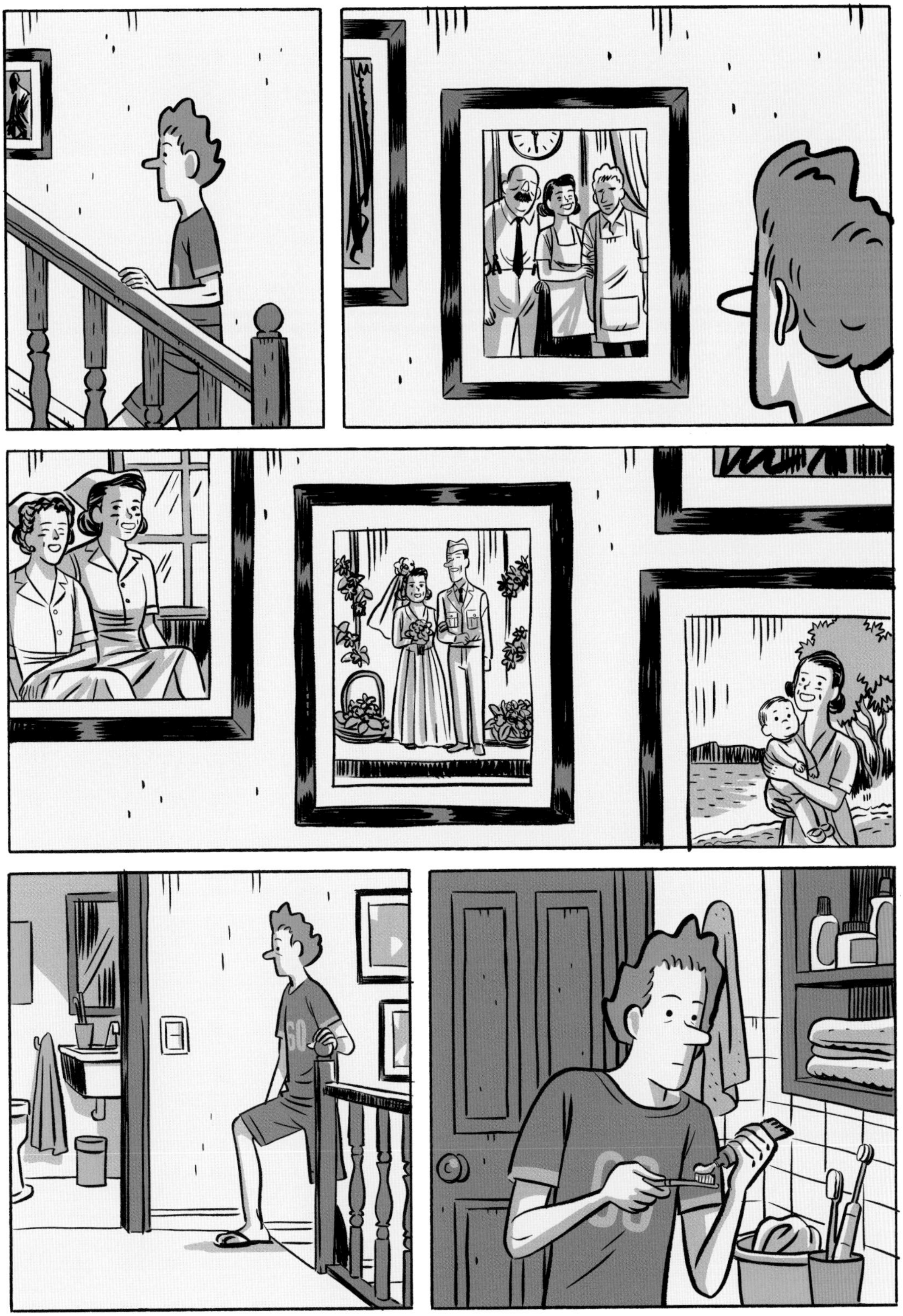

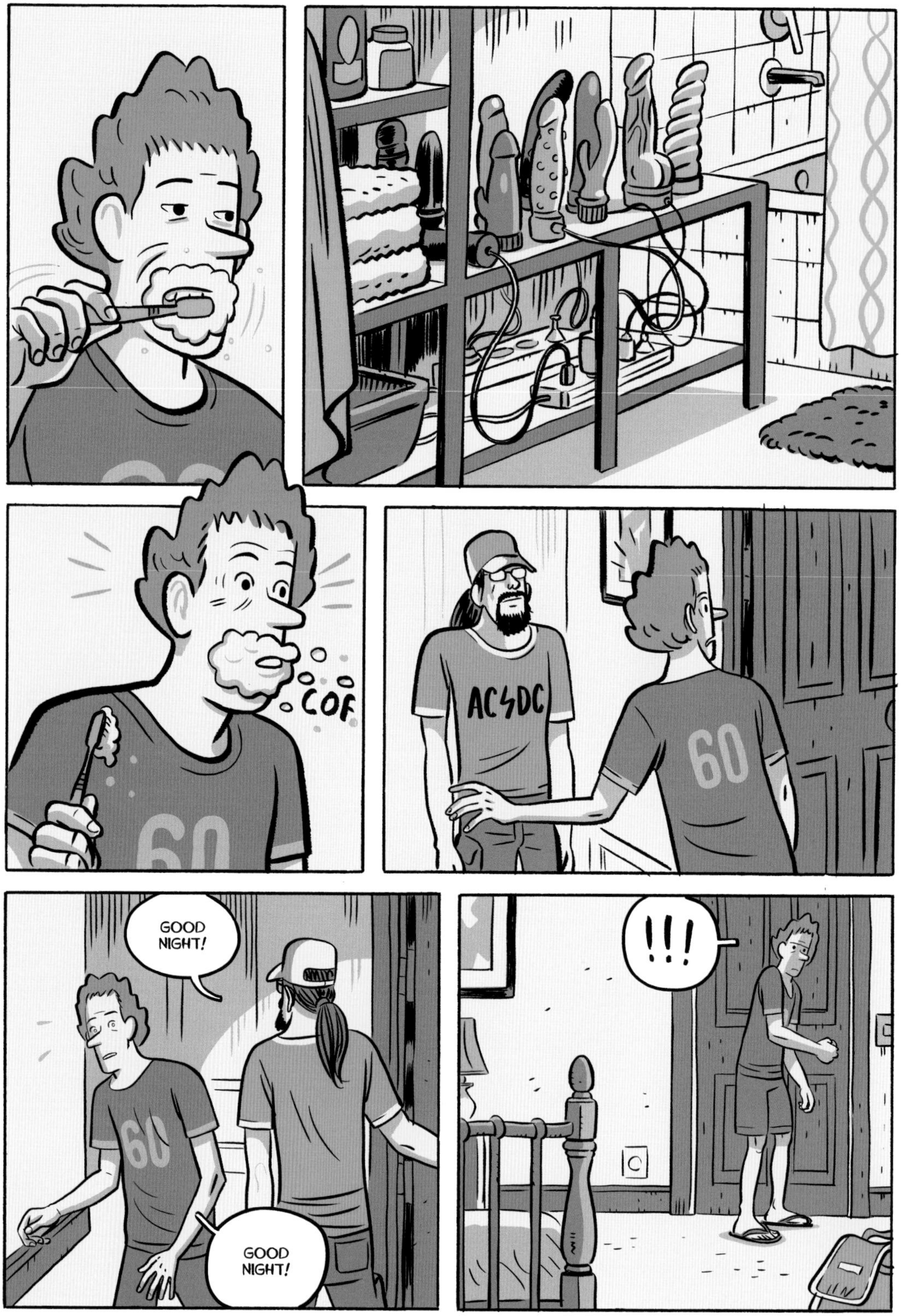
COF
AC/DC
60
GOOD NIGHT!
GOOD NIGHT!
!!!

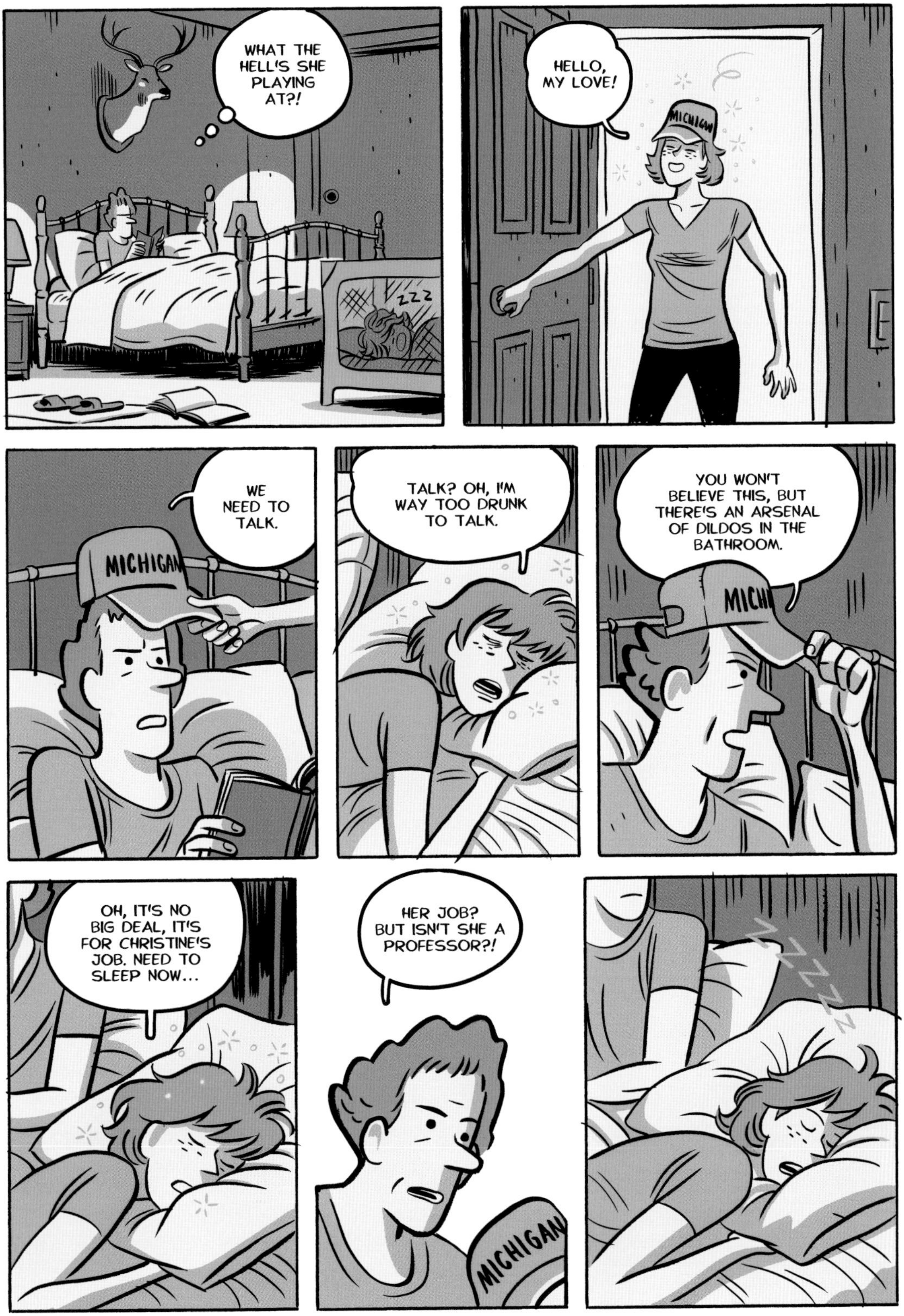
WHAT THE HELL'S SHE PLAYING AT?!
HELLO, MY LOVE!
MICHIGAN
ZZZ
MICHIGAN
WE NEED TO TALK.
TALK? OH, I'M WAY TOO DRUNK TO TALK.
YOU WON'T BELIEVE THIS, BUT THERE'S AN ARSENAL OF DILDOS IN THE BATHROOM.
MICH
OH, IT'S NO BIG DEAL, IT'S FOR CHRISTINE'S JOB. NEED TO SLEEP NOW...
HER JOB? BUT ISN'T SHE A PROFESSOR?!
MICHIGAN
ZZZZZ

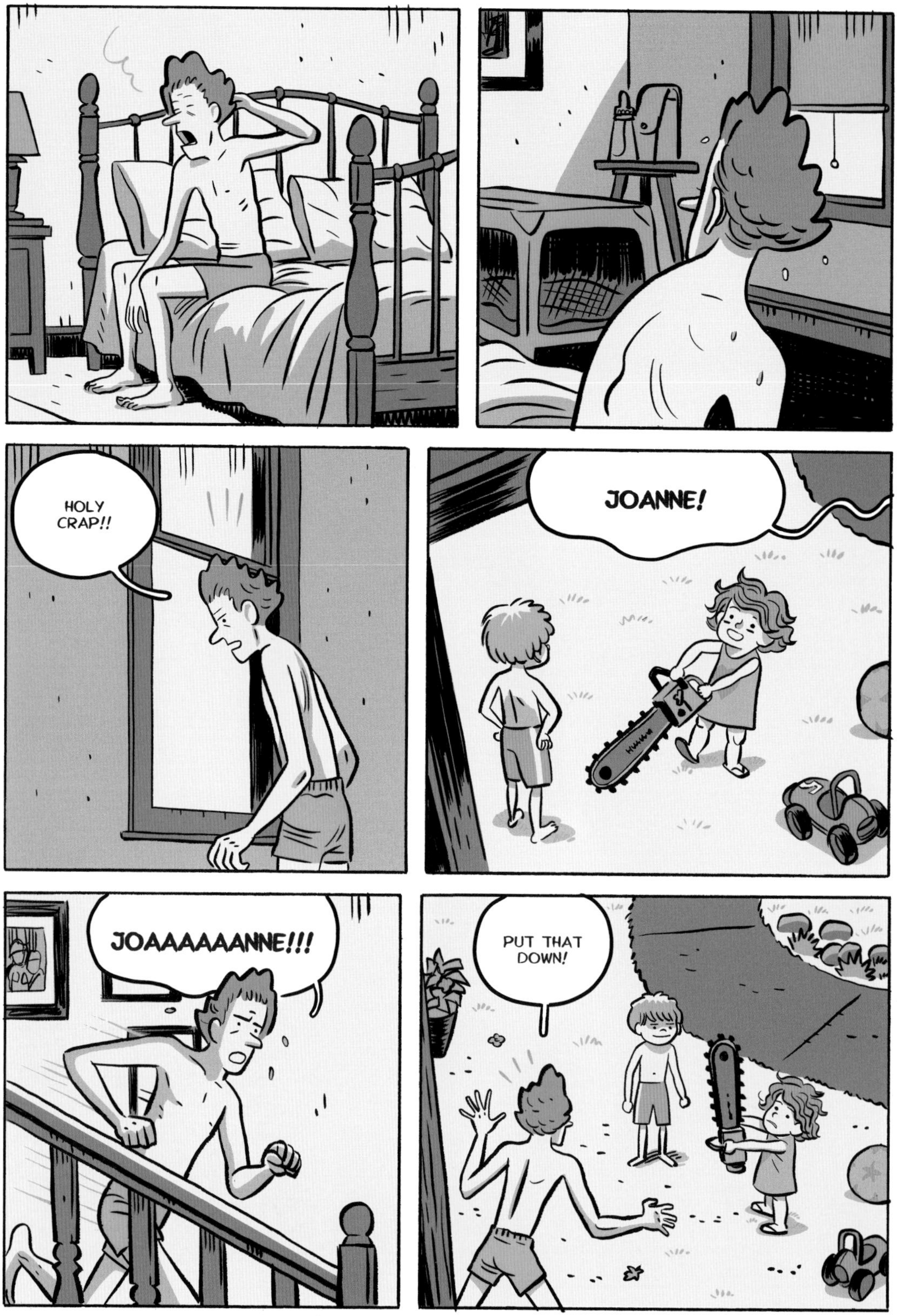
HOLY CRAP!!
JOANNE!
JOAAAAAANNE!!!
PUT THAT DOWN!

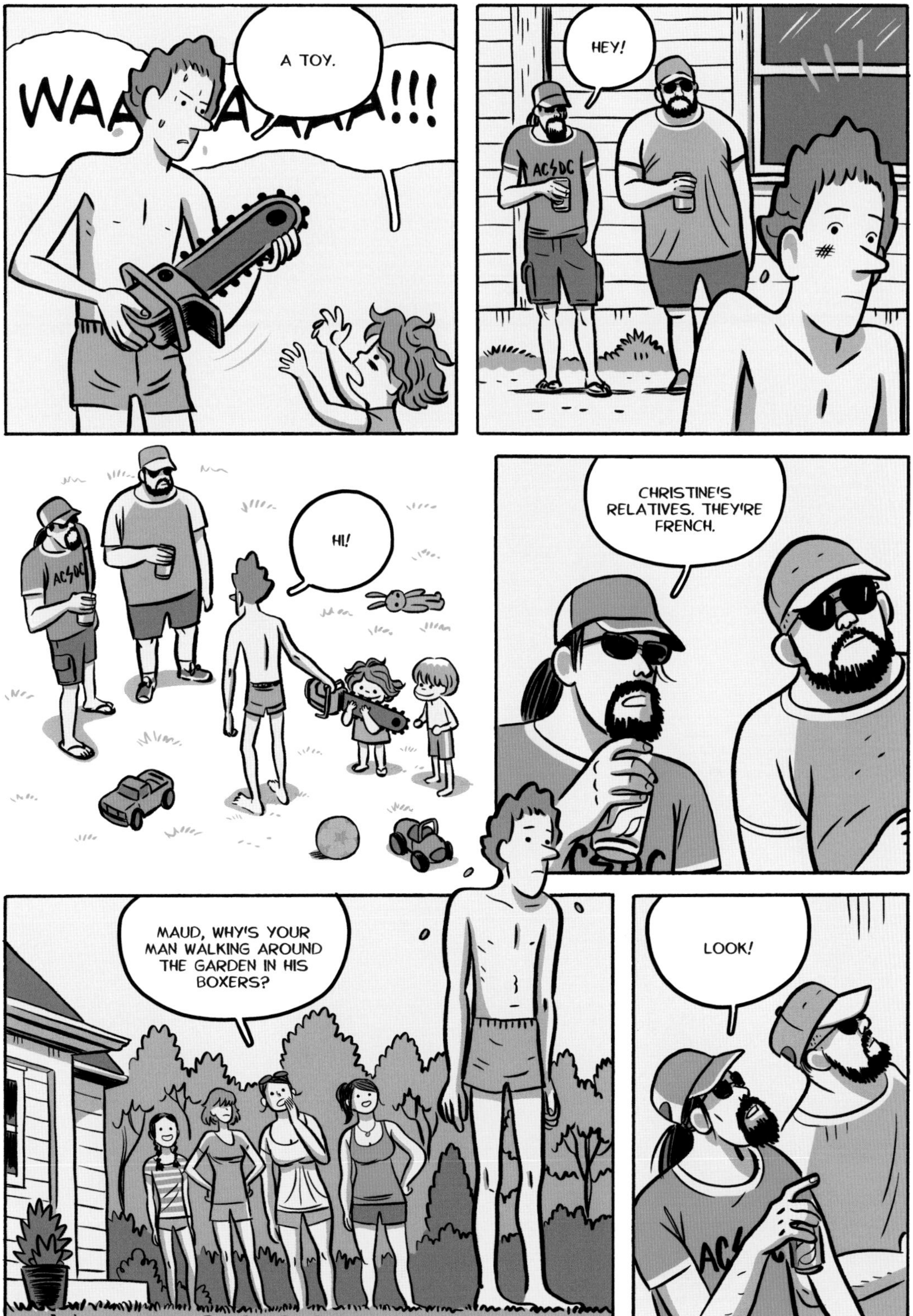
WAAAAAA!!!
A TOY.
HEY!
AC/DC
HI!
CHRISTINE'S RELATIVES. THEY'RE FRENCH.
MAUD, WHY'S YOUR MAN WALKING AROUND THE GARDEN IN HIS BOXERS?
LOOK!

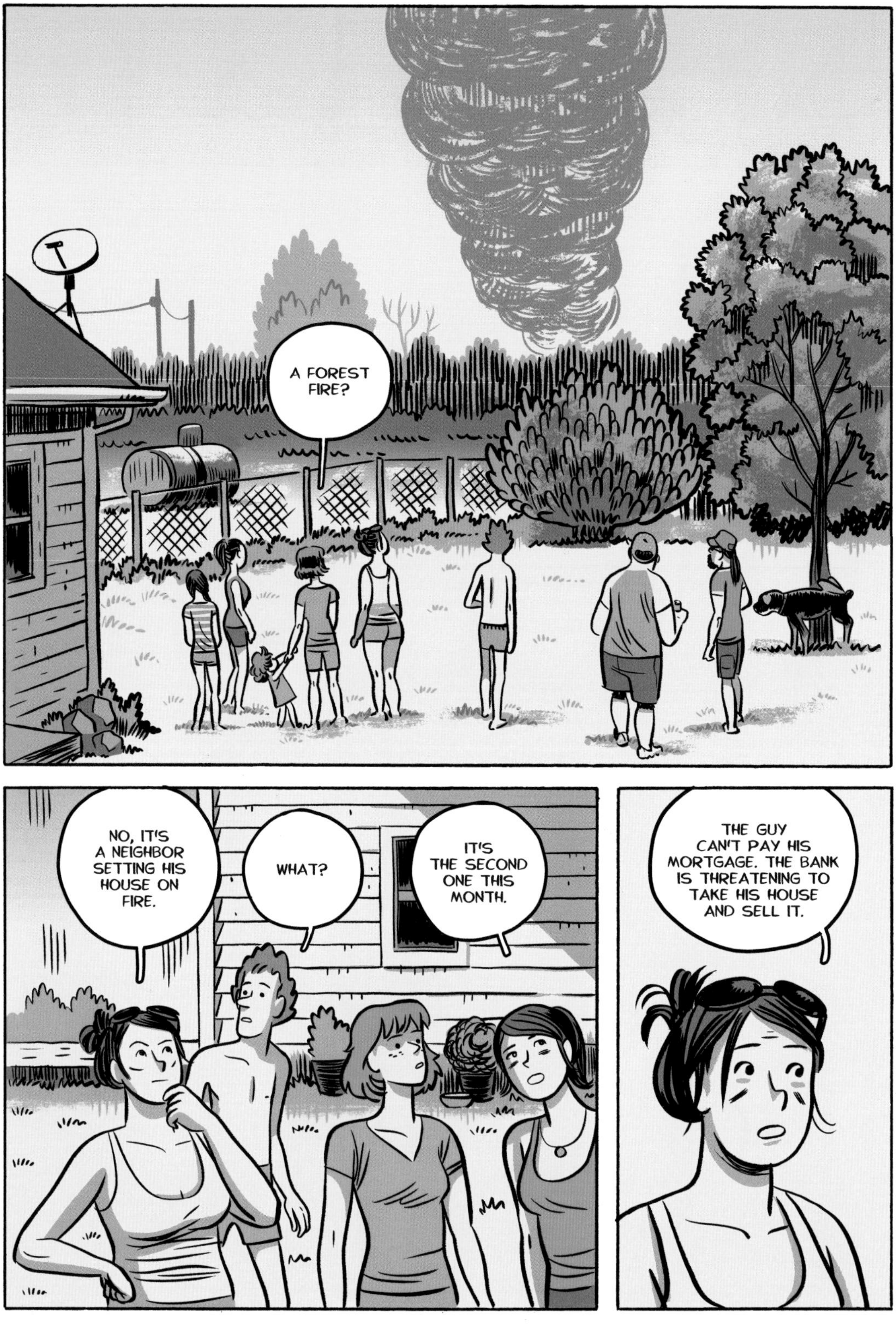
A FOREST FIRE?
NO, IT'S A NEIGHBOR SETTING HIS HOUSE ON FIRE.
WHAT?
IT'S THE SECOND ONE THIS MONTH.
THE GUY CAN'T PAY HIS MORTGAGE. THE BANK IS THREATENING TO TAKE HIS HOUSE AND SELL IT.

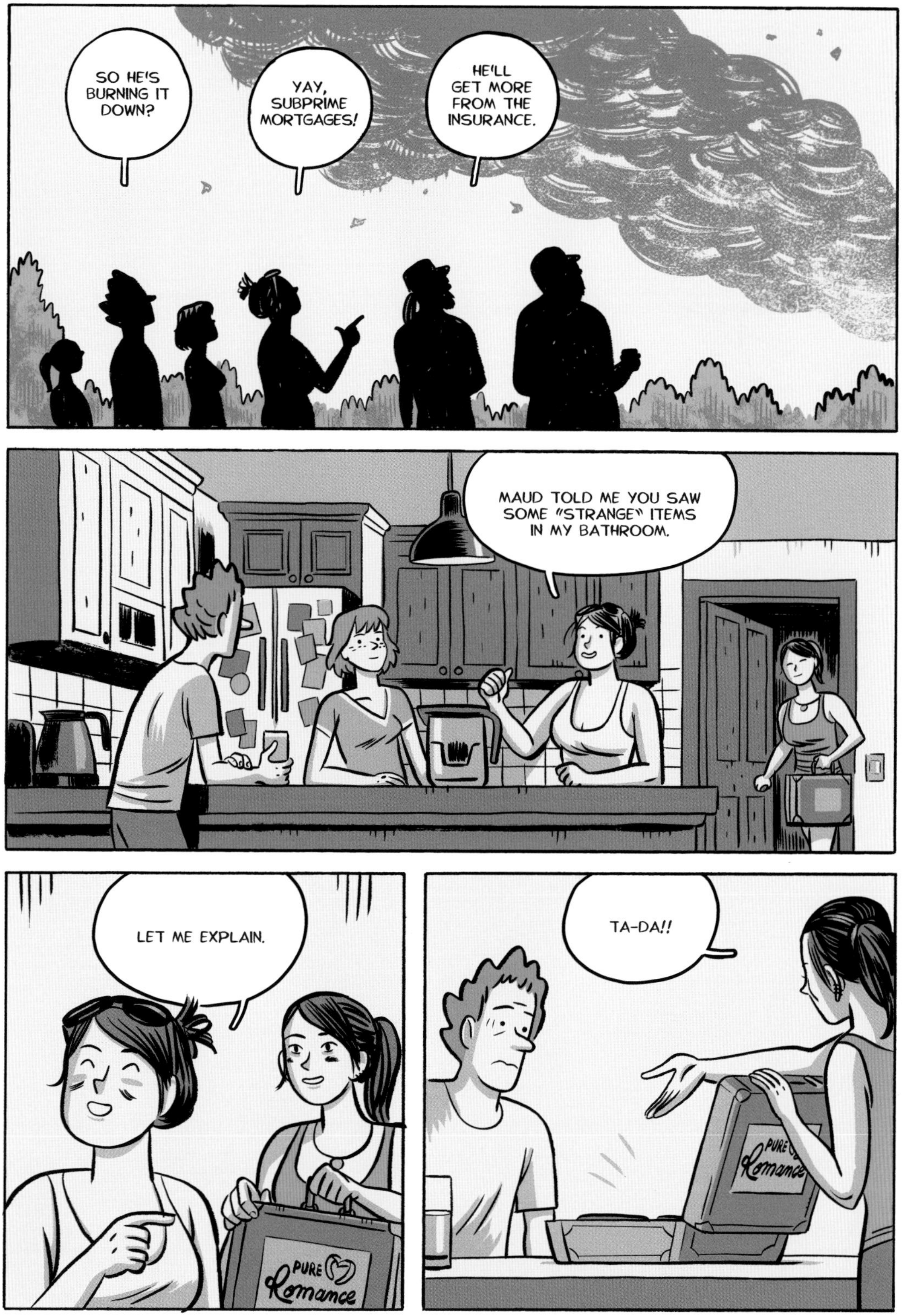
SO HE'S BURNING IT DOWN?
YAY, SUBPRIME MORTGAGES!
HE'LL GET MORE FROM THE INSURANCE.
MAUD TOLD ME YOU SAW SOME "STRANGE" ITEMS IN MY BATHROOM.
LET ME EXPLAIN.
PURE Romance
TA-DA!!
PURE Romance

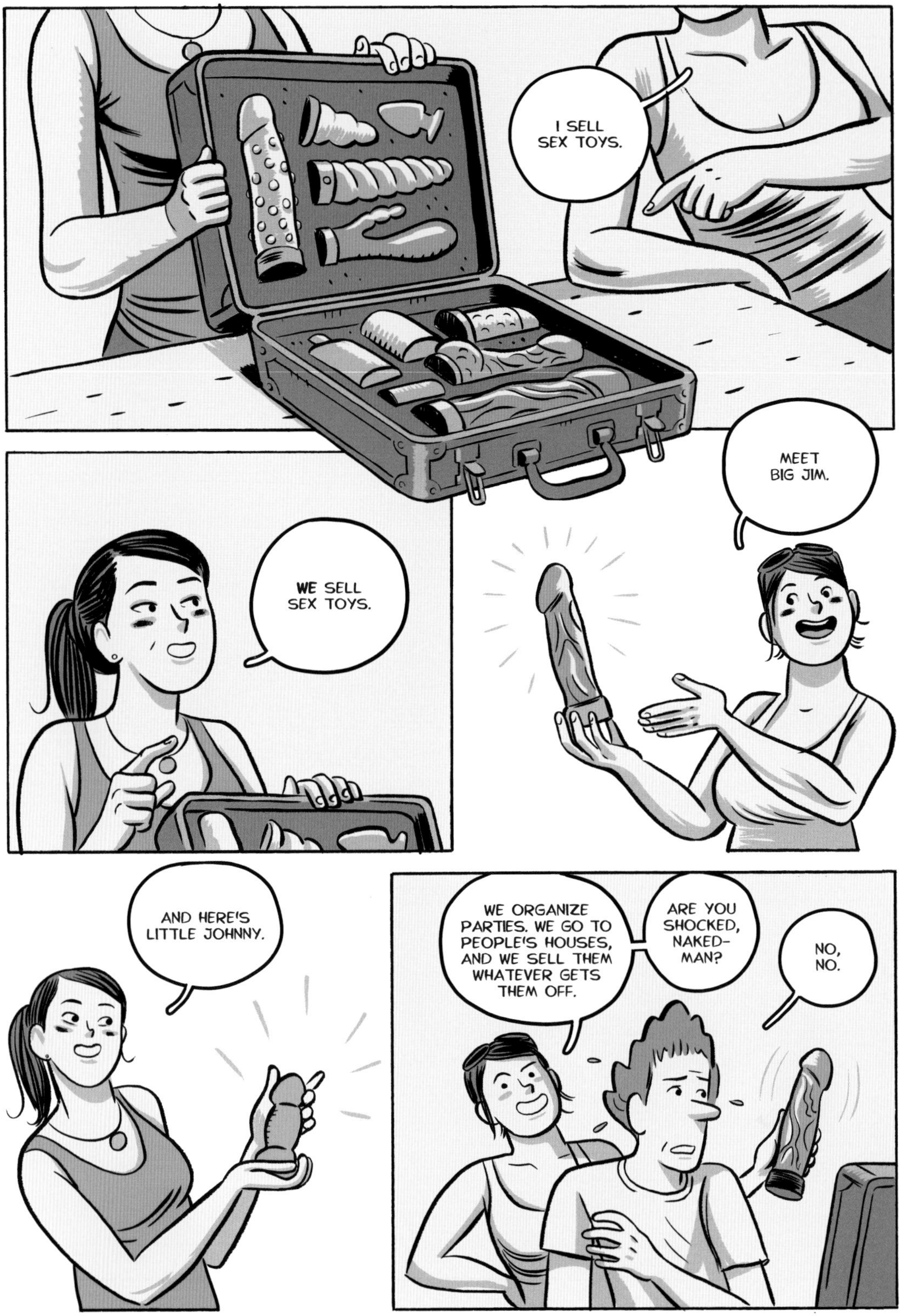
I SELL SEX TOYS.
WE SELL SEX TOYS.
MEET BIG JIM.
AND HERE'S LITTLE JOHNNY.
WE ORGANIZE PARTIES. WE GO TO PEOPLE'S HOUSES, AND WE SELL THEM WHATEVER GETS THEM OFF.
ARE YOU SHOCKED, NAKED-MAN?
NO, NO.

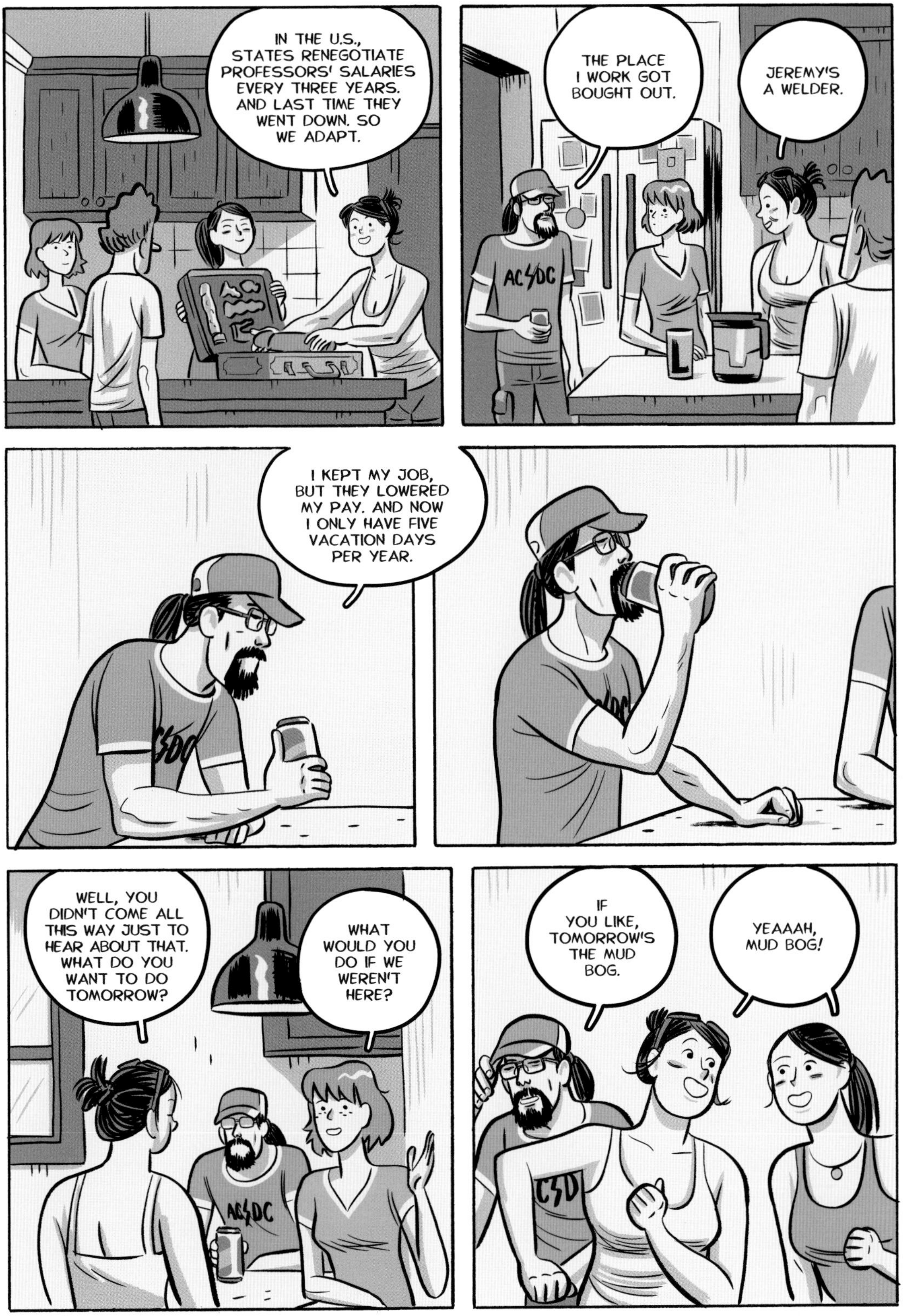
IN THE U.S., STATES RENEGOTIATE PROFESSORS' SALARIES EVERY THREE YEARS. AND LAST TIME THEY WENT DOWN. SO WE ADAPT.
THE PLACE I WORK GOT BOUGHT OUT.
JEREMY'S A WELDER.
AC/DC
I KEPT MY JOB, BUT THEY LOWERED MY PAY. AND NOW I ONLY HAVE FIVE VACATION DAYS PER YEAR.
WELL, YOU DIDN'T COME ALL THIS WAY JUST TO HEAR ABOUT THAT. WHAT DO YOU WANT TO DO TOMORROW?
WHAT WOULD YOU DO IF WE WEREN'T HERE?
AC/DC
IF YOU LIKE, TOMORROW'S THE MUD BOG.
YEAAAH, MUD BOG!

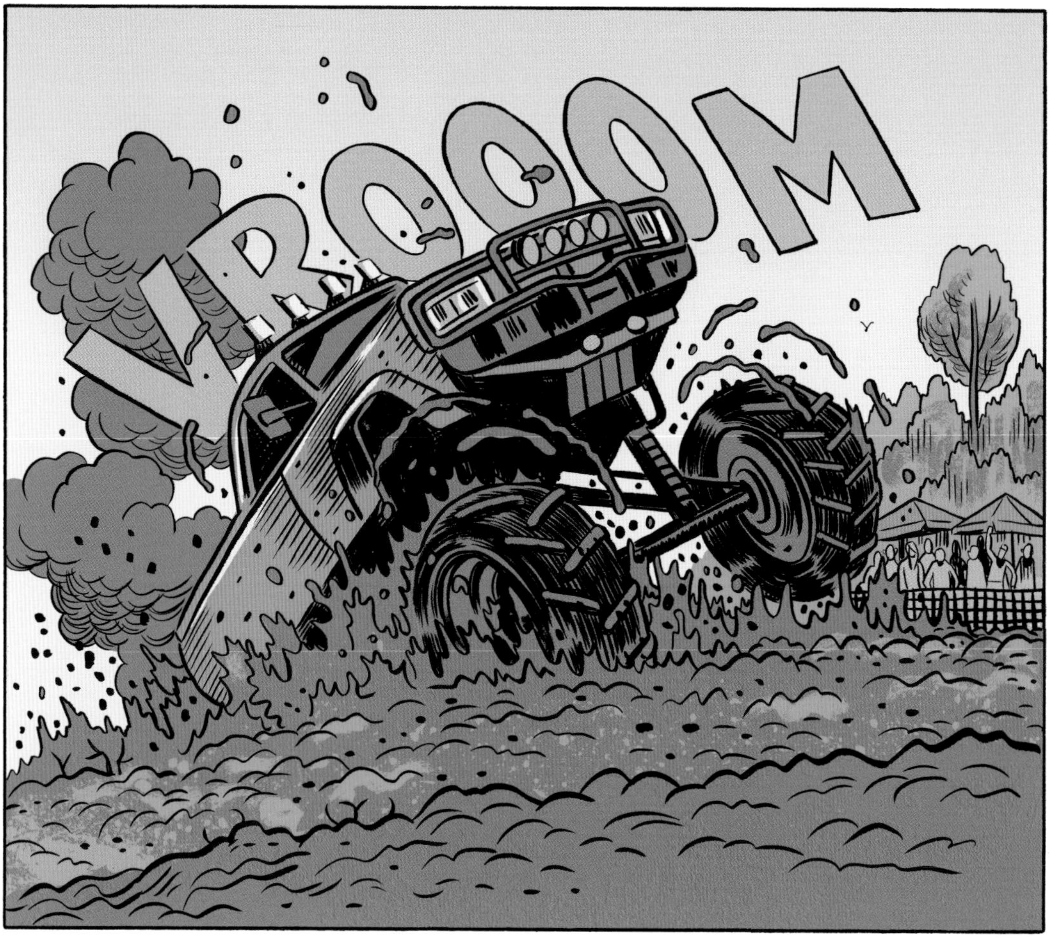
VROOOM

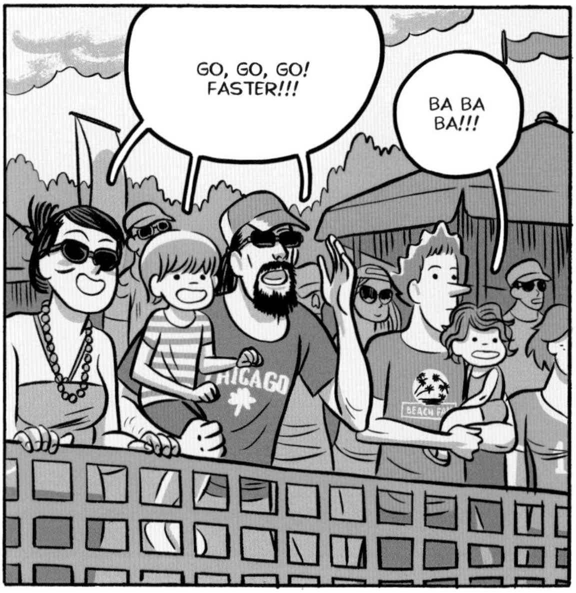
GO, GO, GO! FASTER!!!
BA BA BA!!!
CHICAGO
BEACH

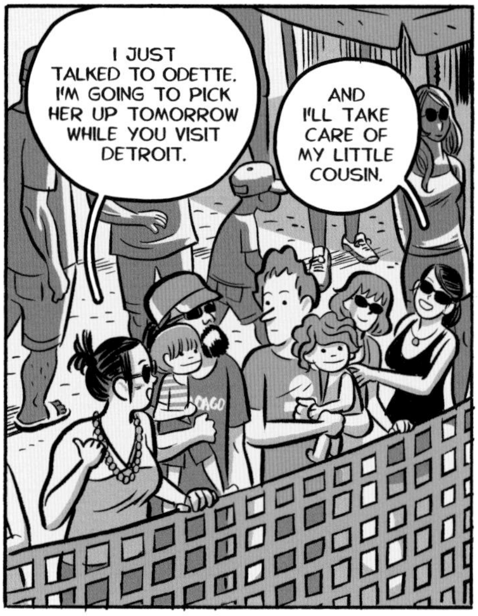
I JUST TALKED TO ODETTE. I'M GOING TO PICK HER UP TOMORROW WHILE YOU VISIT DETROIT.
AND I'LL TAKE CARE OF MY LITTLE COUSIN.

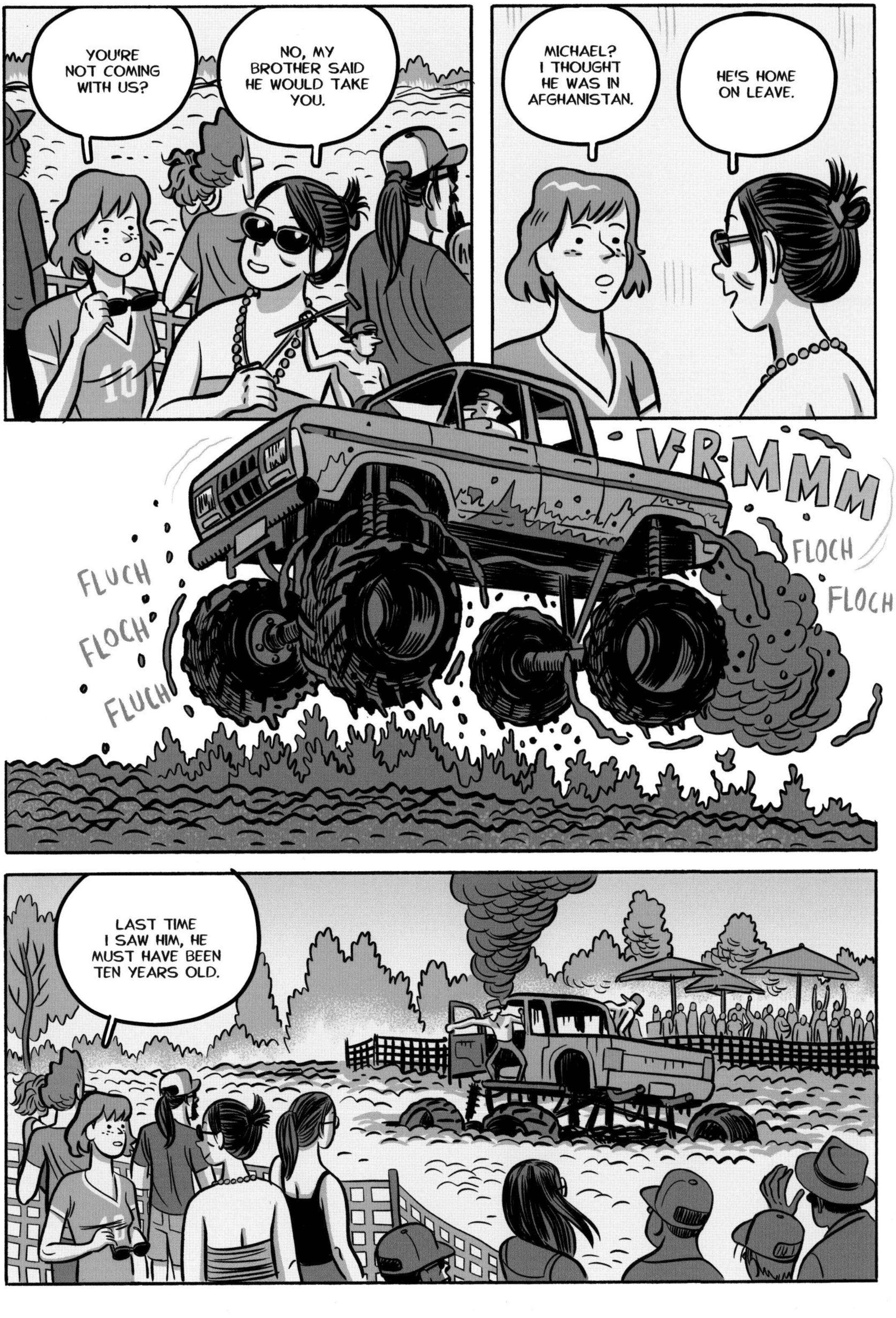
YOU'RE NOT COMING WITH US?
NO, MY BROTHER SAID HE WOULD TAKE YOU.
MICHAEL? I THOUGHT HE WAS IN AFGHANISTAN.
HE'S HOME ON LEAVE.
VRMMM
FLUCH
FLOCH
FLUCH
FLOCH
FLOCH
LAST TIME I SAW HIM, HE MUST HAVE BEEN TEN YEARS OLD.

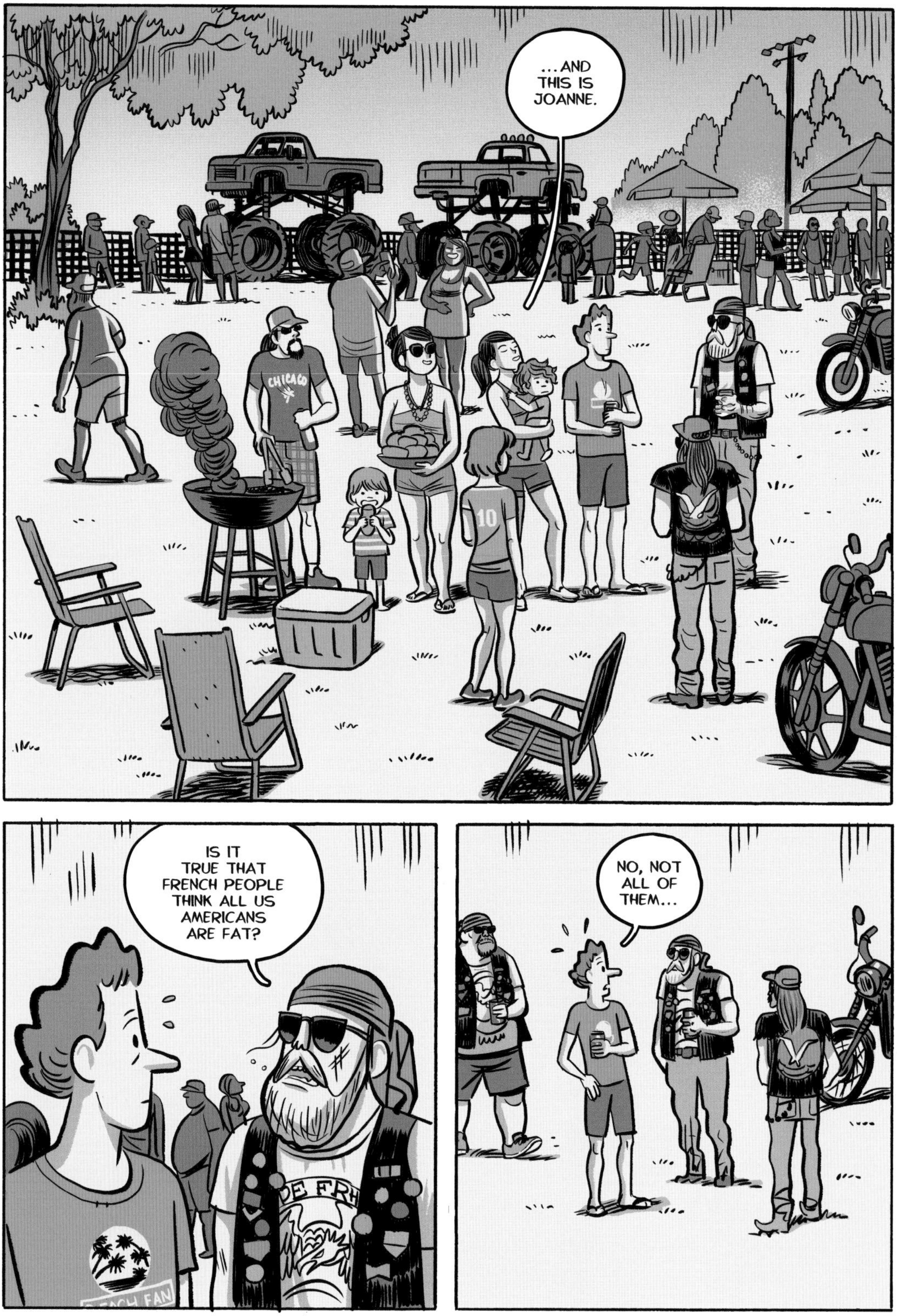
...AND THIS IS JOANNE.
CHICAGO
IS IT TRUE THAT FRENCH PEOPLE THINK ALL US AMERICANS ARE FAT?
NO, NOT ALL OF THEM...

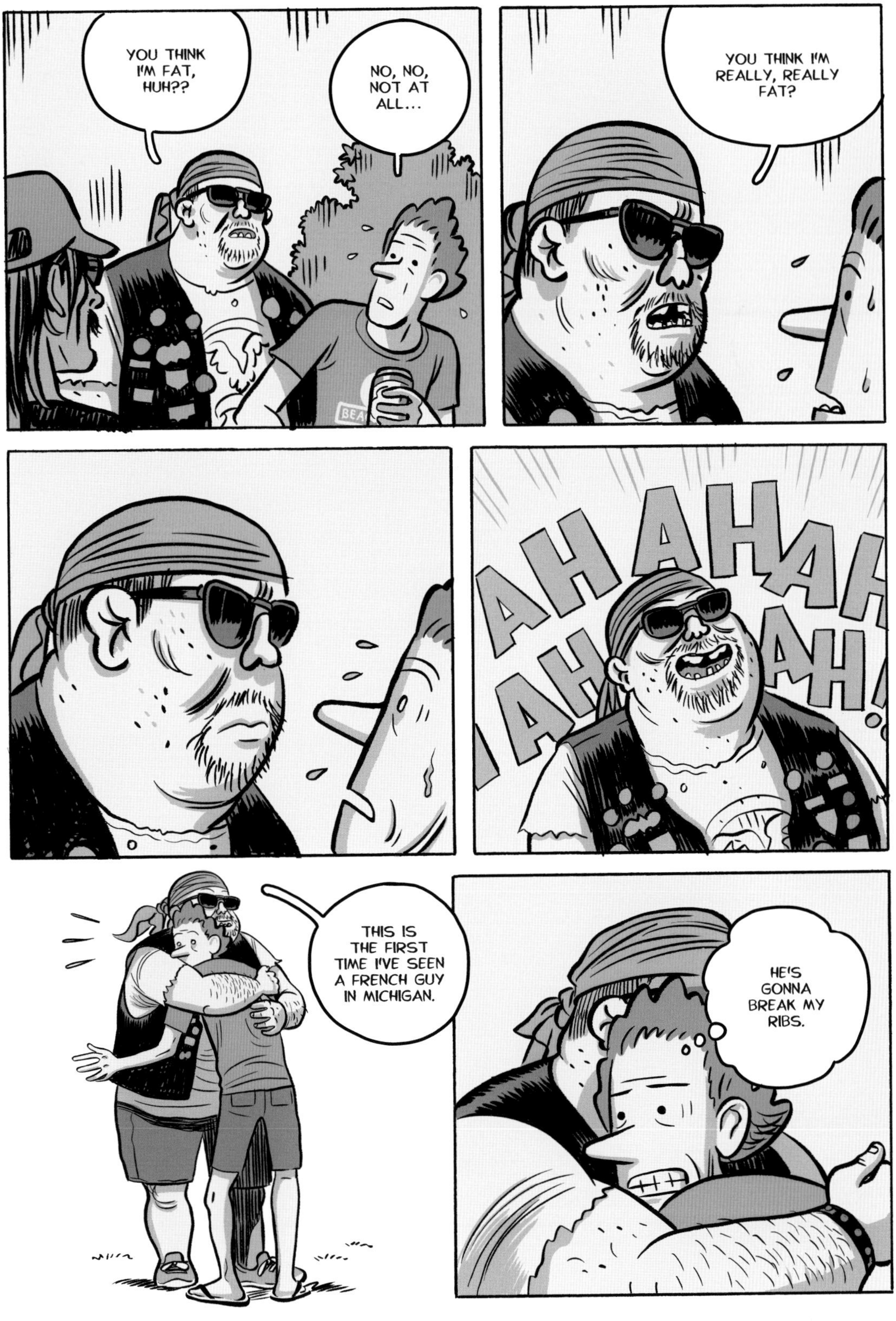
YOU THINK I'M FAT, HUH??
NO, NO, NOT AT ALL...
BEA
YOU THINK I'M REALLY, REALLY FAT?
AH AHAH AHAH!
THIS IS THE FIRST TIME I'VE SEEN A FRENCH GUY IN MICHIGAN.
HE'S GONNA BREAK MY RIBS.

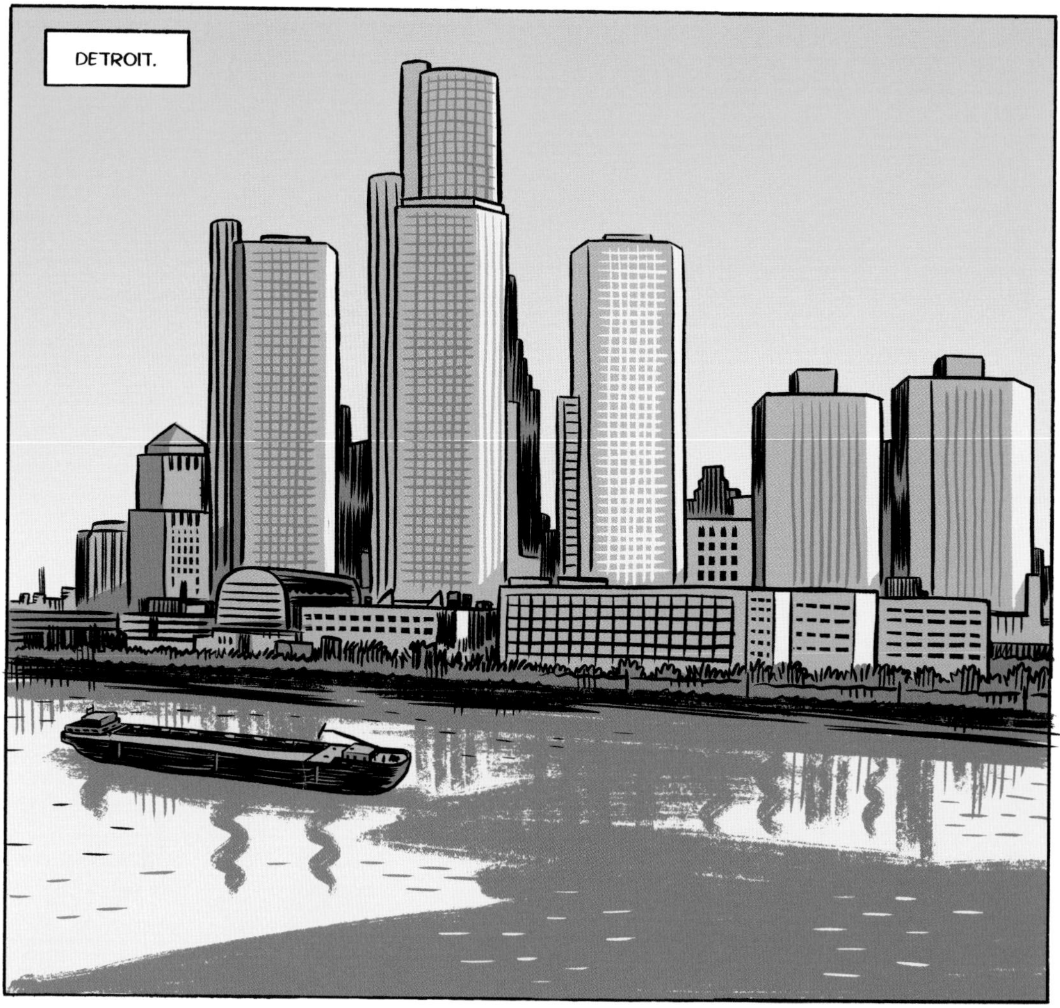
DETROIT.

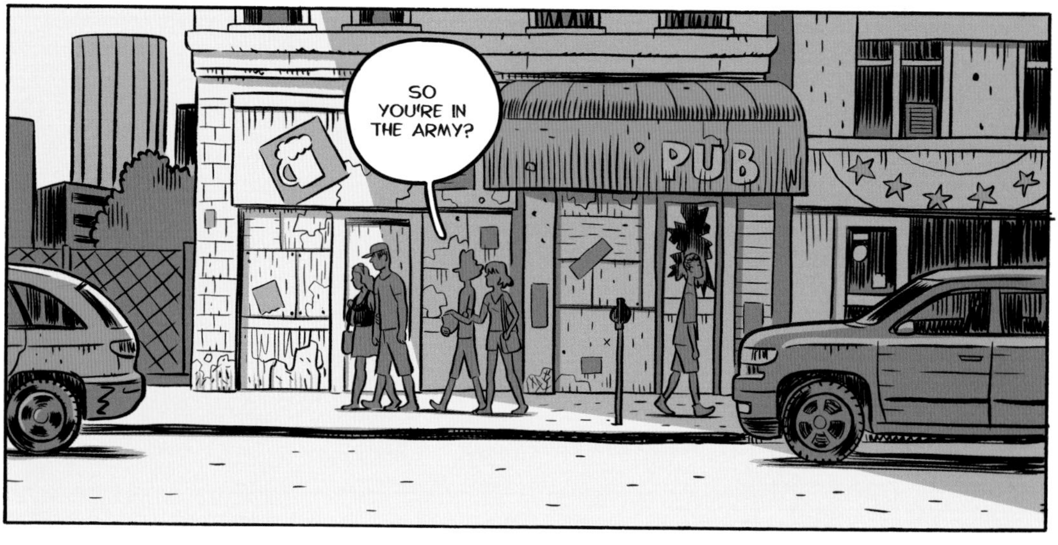
SO YOU'RE IN THE ARMY?
PUB

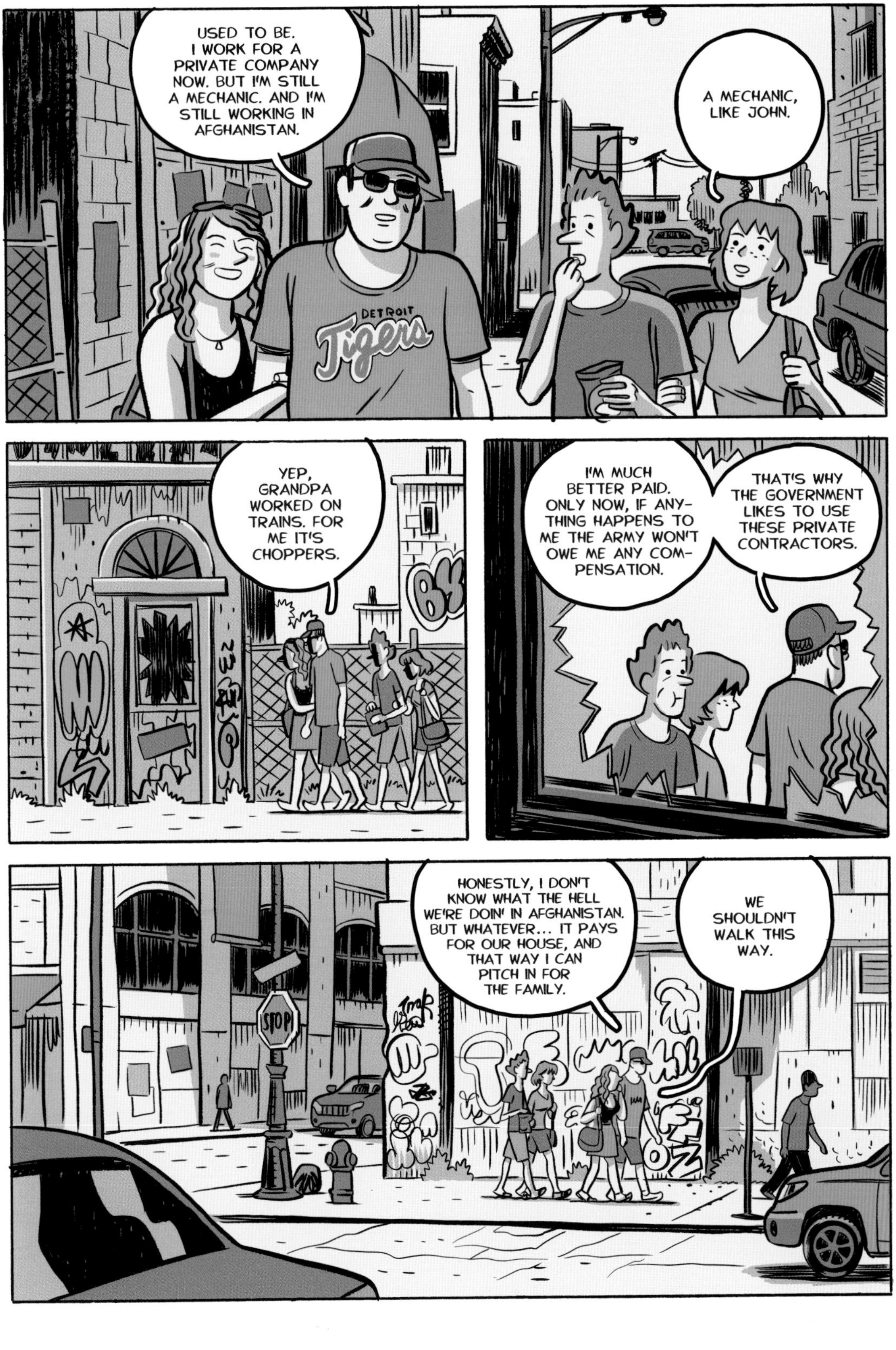
USED TO BE. I WORK FOR A PRIVATE COMPANY NOW. BUT I'M STILL A MECHANIC. AND I'M STILL WORKING IN AFGHANISTAN.
DETROIT Tigers
A MECHANIC, LIKE JOHN.
YEP, GRANDPA WORKED ON TRAINS. FOR ME IT'S CHOPPERS.
I'M MUCH BETTER PAID. ONLY NOW, IF ANYTHING HAPPENS TO ME THE ARMY WON'T OWE ME ANY COMPENSATION.
THAT'S WHY THE GOVERNMENT LIKES TO USE THESE PRIVATE CONTRACTORS.
STOP
HONESTLY, I DON'T KNOW WHAT THE HELL WE'RE DOIN' IN AFGHANISTAN. BUT WHATEVER... IT PAYS FOR OUR HOUSE, AND THAT WAY I CAN PITCH IN FOR THE FAMILY.
WE SHOULDN'T WALK THIS WAY.

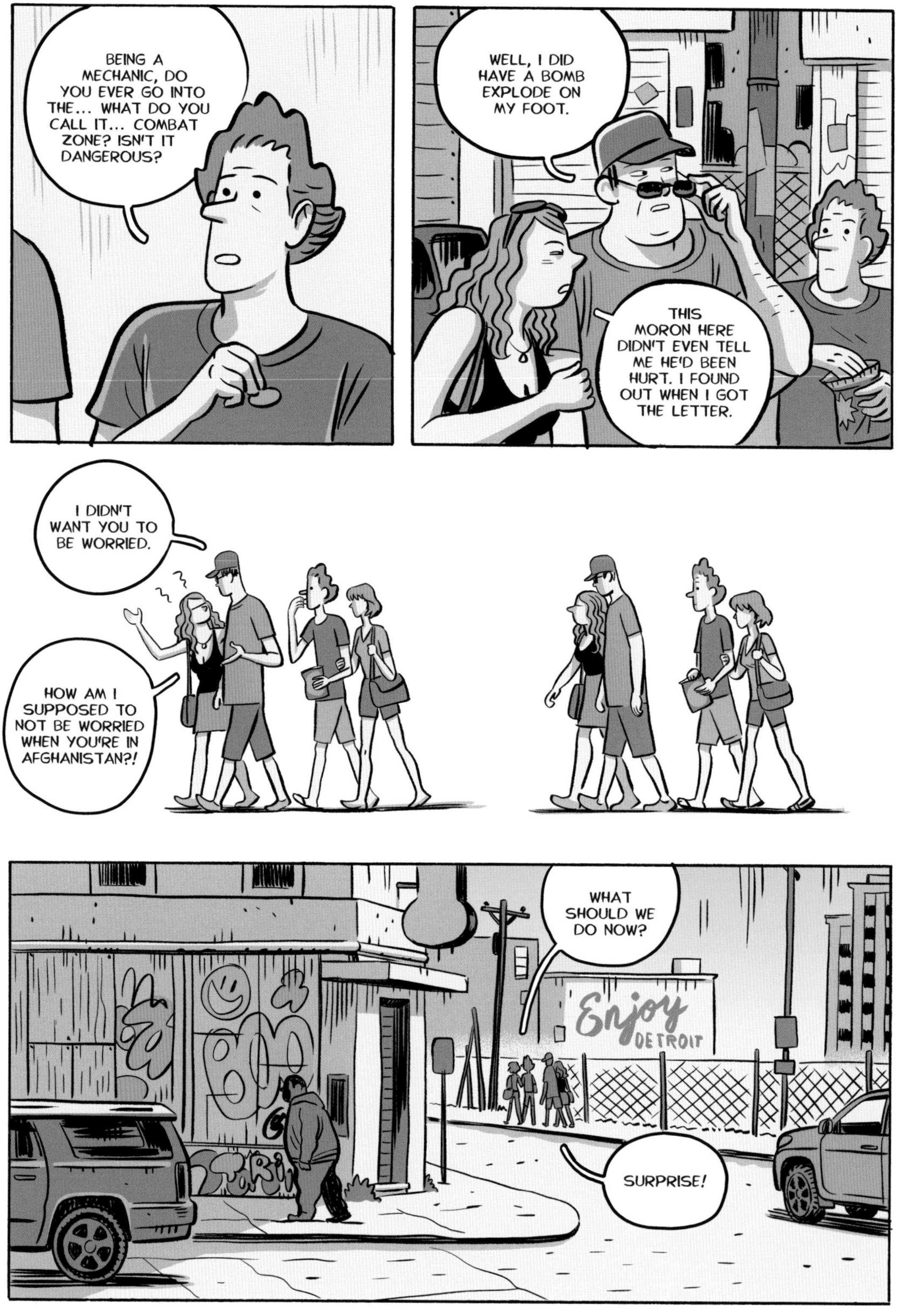
BEING A MECHANIC, DO YOU EVER GO INTO THE... WHAT DO YOU CALL IT... COMBAT ZONE? ISN'T IT DANGEROUS?
WELL, I DID HAVE A BOMB EXPLODE ON MY FOOT.
THIS MORON HERE DIDN'T EVEN TELL ME HE'D BEEN HURT. I FOUND OUT WHEN I GOT THE LETTER.
I DIDN'T WANT YOU TO BE WORRIED.
HOW AM I SUPPOSED TO NOT BE WORRIED WHEN YOU'RE IN AFGHANISTAN?!
WHAT SHOULD WE DO NOW?
Enjoy DETROIT
SURPRISE!

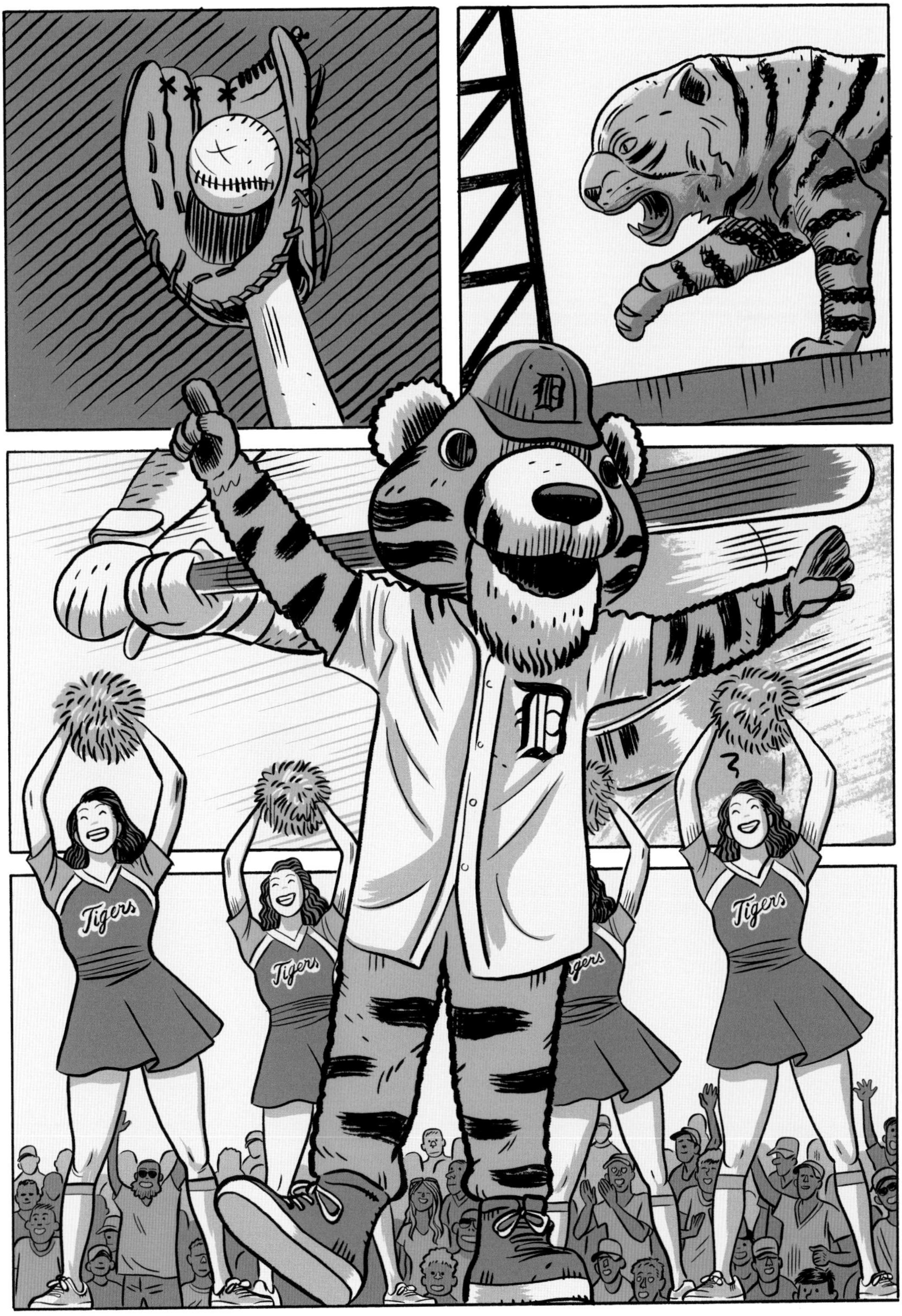
Tigers
Tigers
Tigers

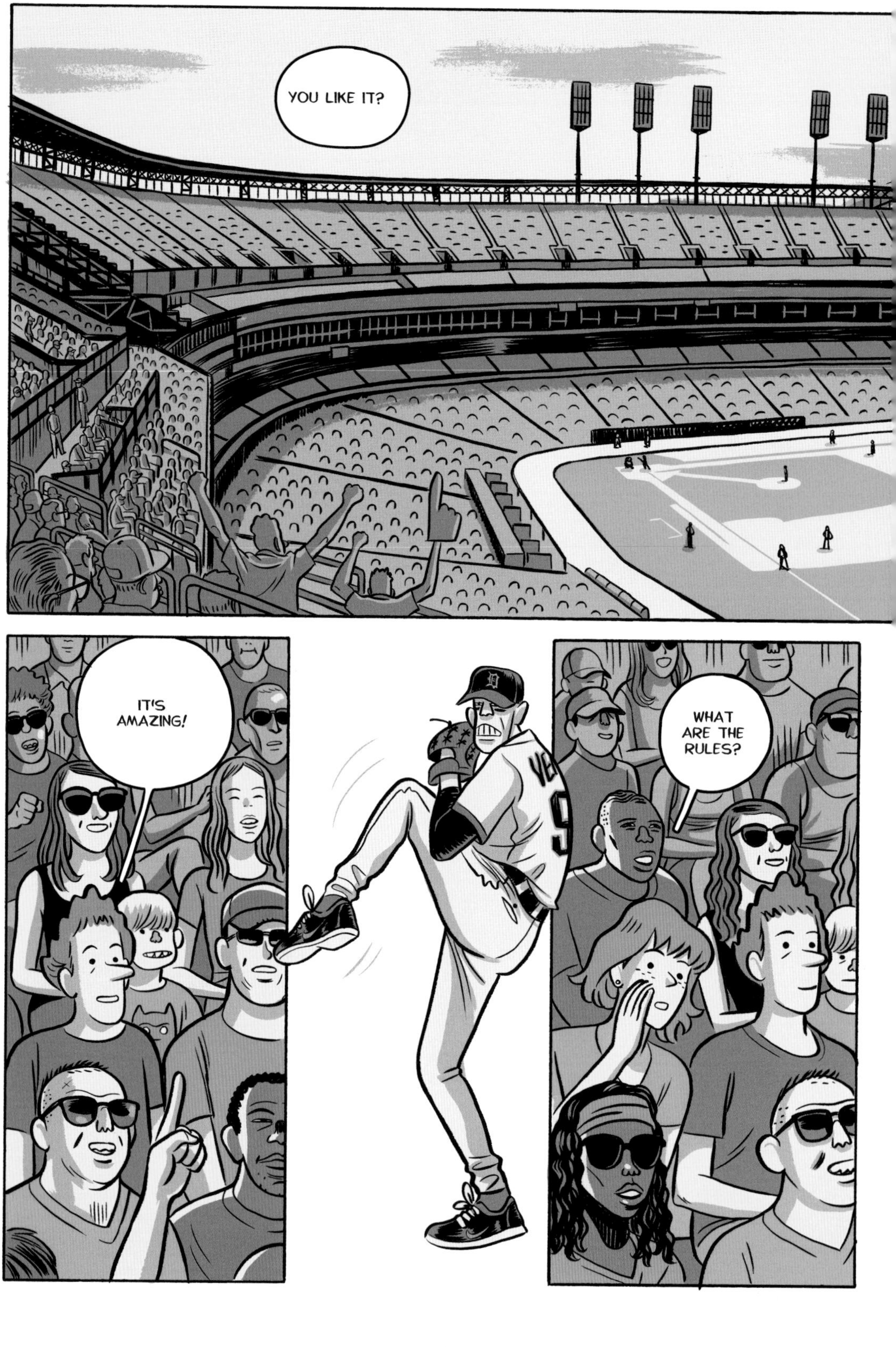
YOU LIKE IT?
IT'S AMAZING!
WHAT ARE THE RULES?

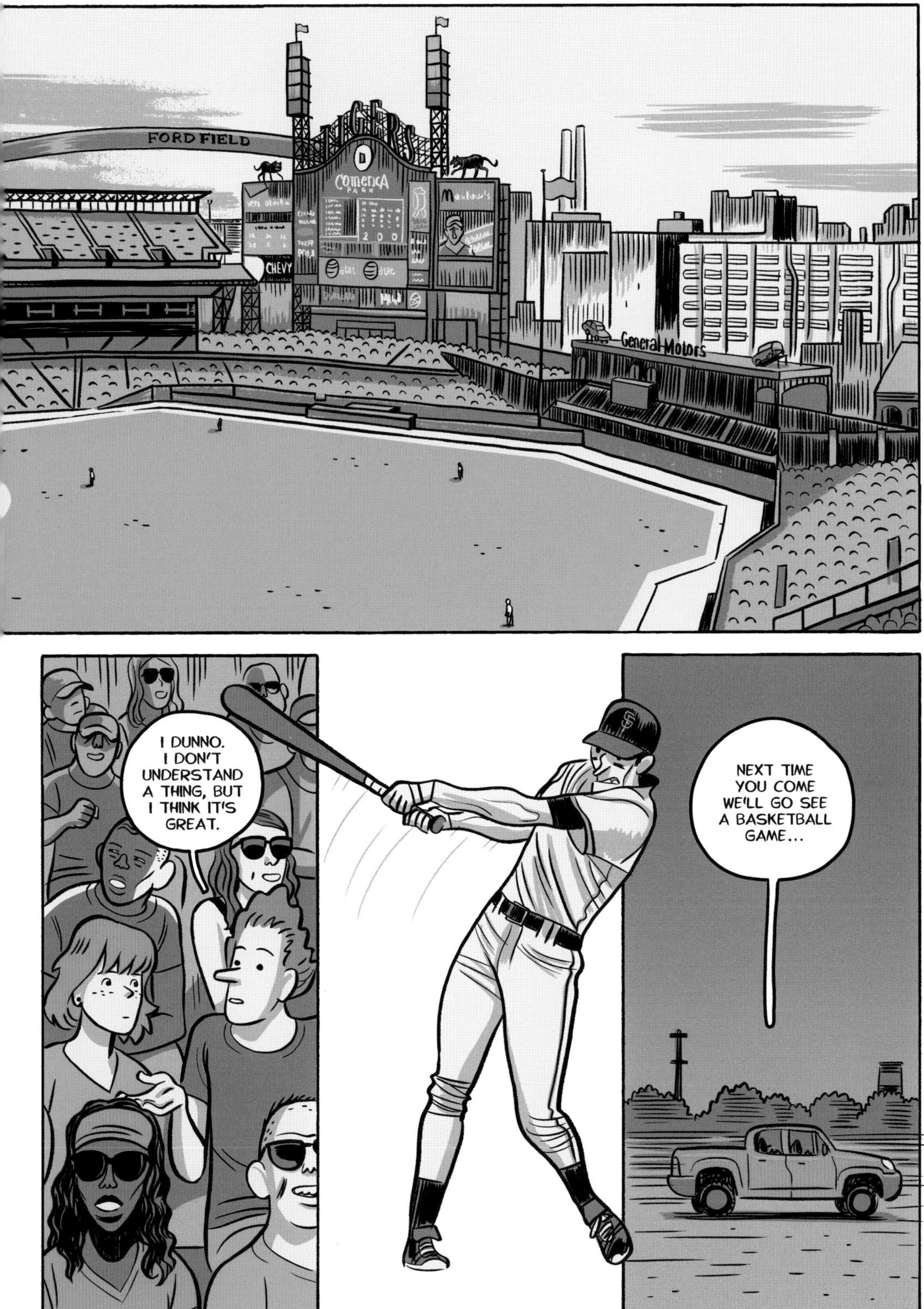
FORD FIELD
Comerica
PARK
CHEVY
General Motors
I DUNNO. I DON'T UNDERSTAND A THING, BUT I THINK IT'S GREAT.
NEXT TIME YOU COME WE'LL GO SEE A BASKETBALL GAME...

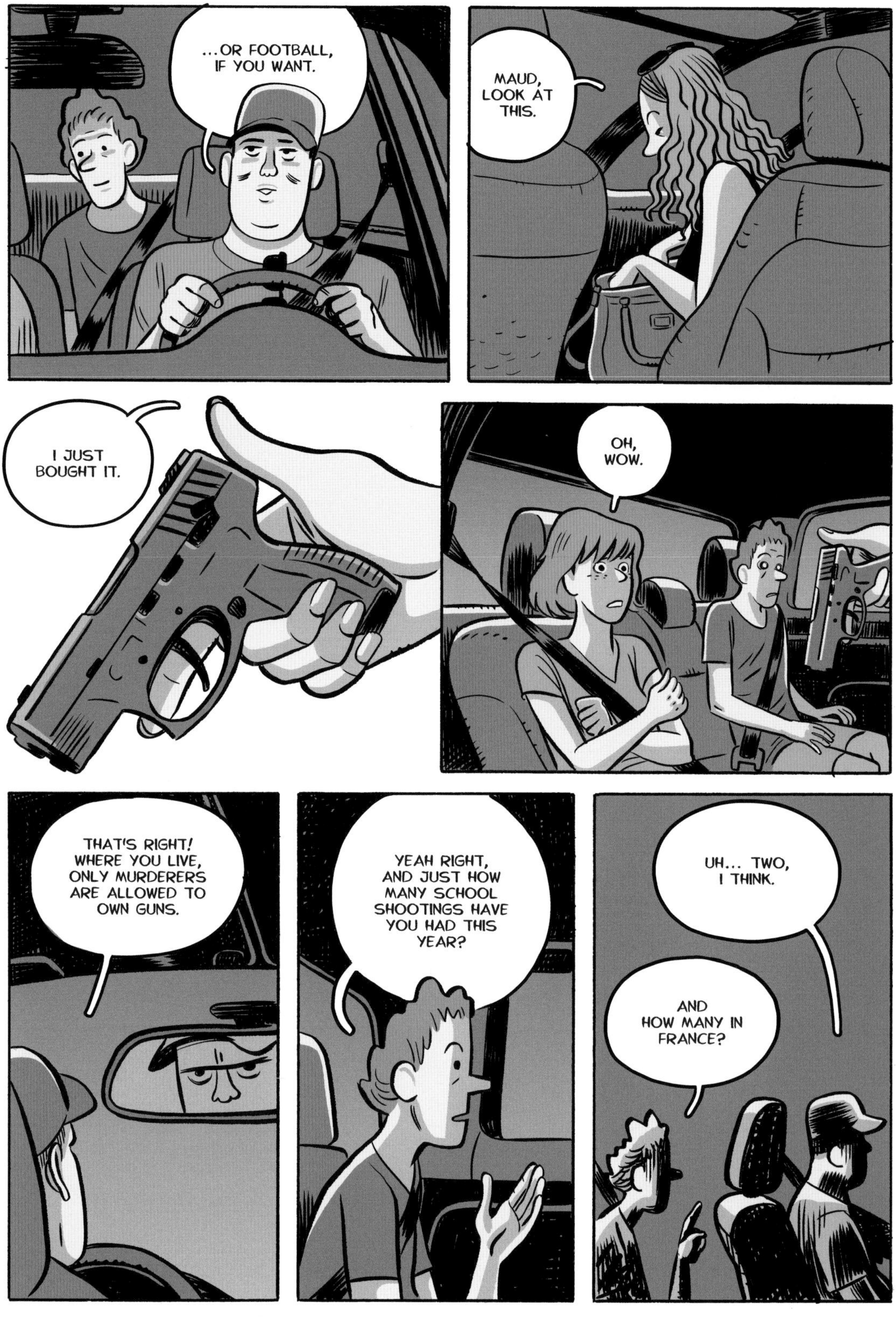
...OR FOOTBALL, IF YOU WANT.
MAUD, LOOK AT THIS.
I JUST BOUGHT IT.
OH, WOW.
THAT'S RIGHT! WHERE YOU LIVE, ONLY MURDERERS ARE ALLOWED TO OWN GUNS.
YEAH RIGHT, AND JUST HOW MANY SCHOOL SHOOTINGS HAVE YOU HAD THIS YEAR?
UH... TWO, I THINK.
AND HOW MANY IN FRANCE?

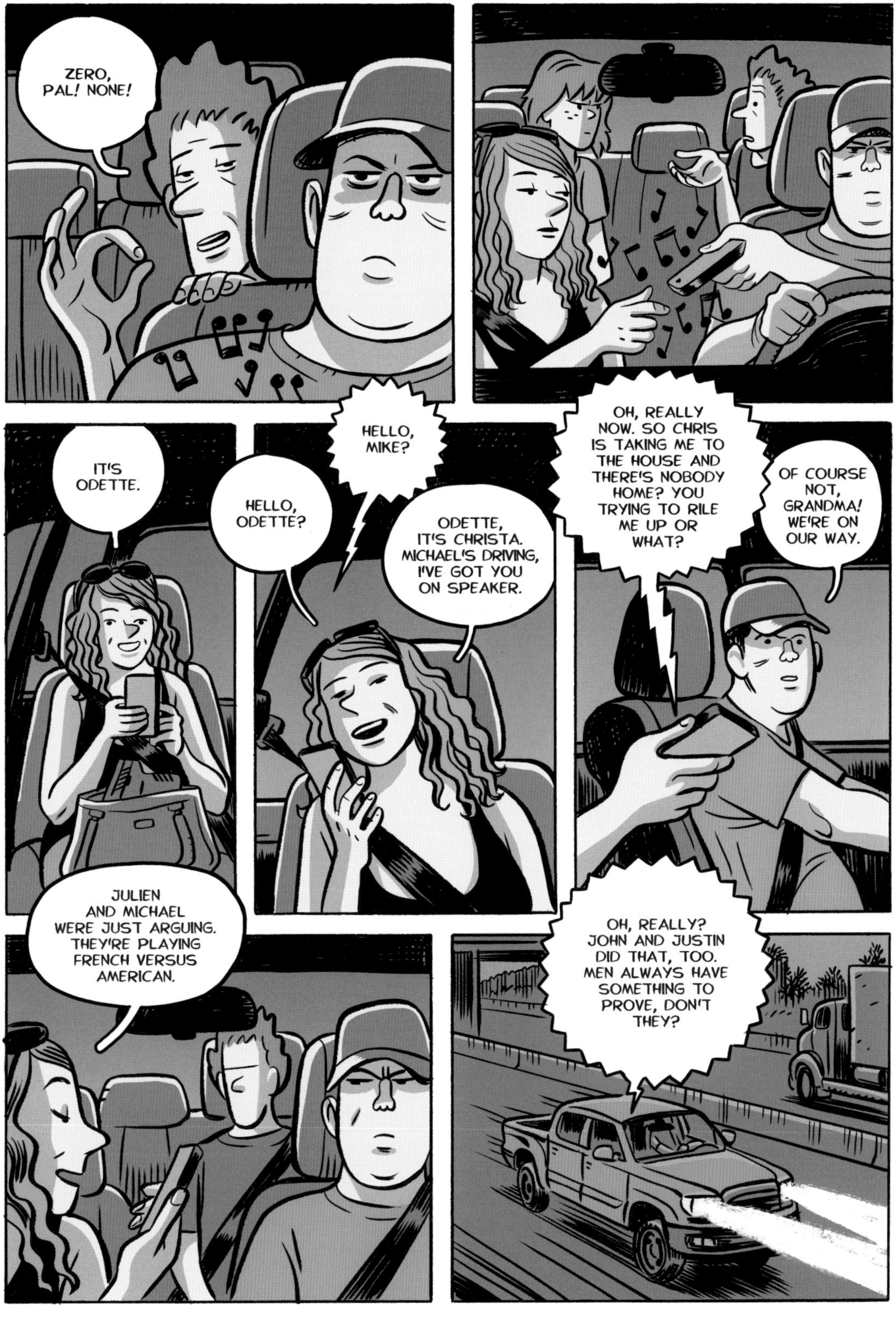
ZERO, PAL! NONE!
IT'S ODETTE.
HELLO, ODETTE?
HELLO, MIKE?
ODETTE, IT'S CHRISTA. MICHAEL'S DRIVING, I'VE GOT YOU ON SPEAKER.
OH, REALLY NOW. SO CHRIS IS TAKING ME TO THE HOUSE AND THERE'S NOBODY HOME? YOU TRYING TO RILE ME UP OR WHAT?
OF COURSE NOT, GRANDMA! WE'RE ON OUR WAY.
JULIEN AND MICHAEL WERE JUST ARGUING. THEY'RE PLAYING FRENCH VERSUS AMERICAN.
OH, REALLY? JOHN AND JUSTIN DID THAT, TOO. MEN ALWAYS HAVE SOMETHING TO PROVE, DON'T THEY?

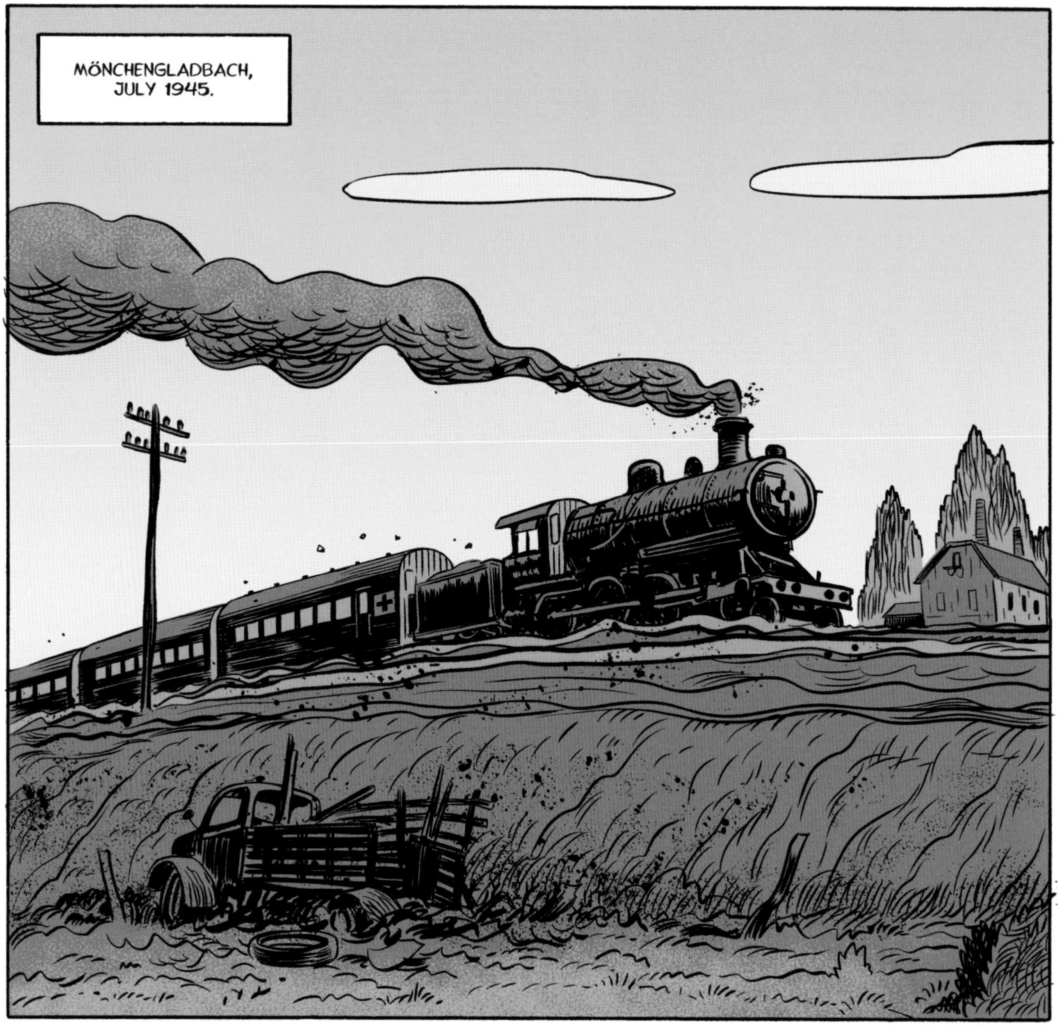
MÖNCHENGLADBACH,
JULY 1945.

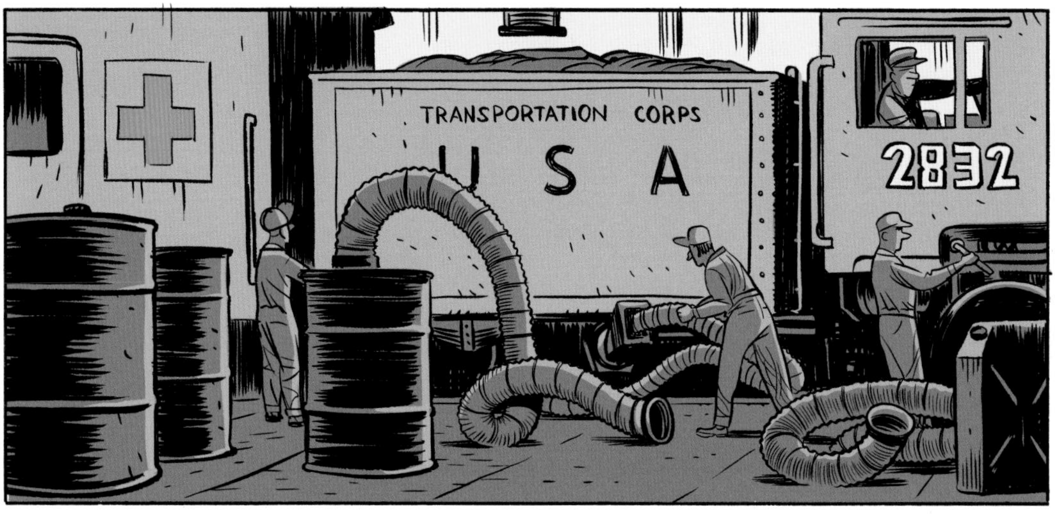
TRANSPORTATION CORPS
U S A
2832

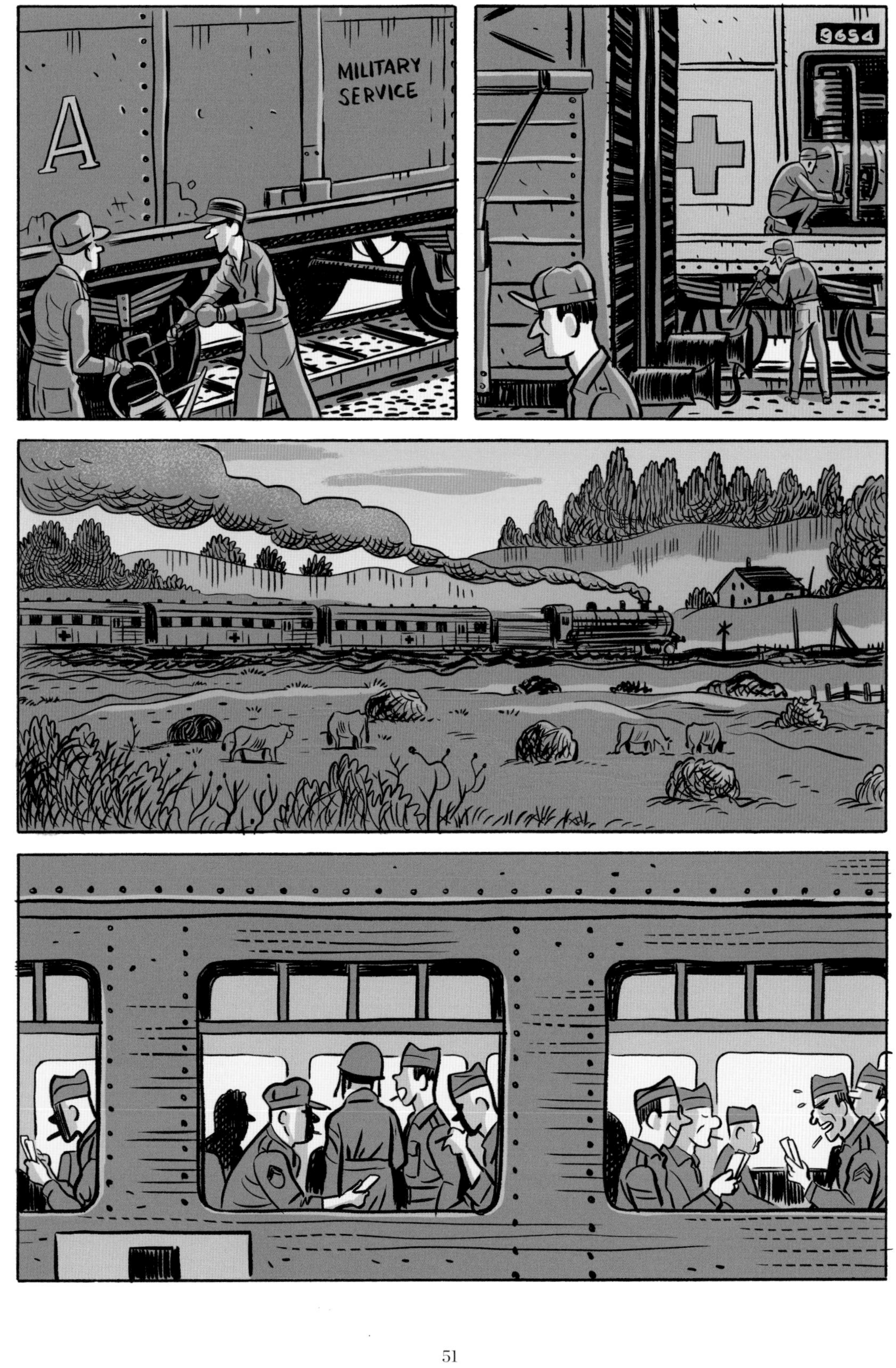
MILITARY SERVICE
9654

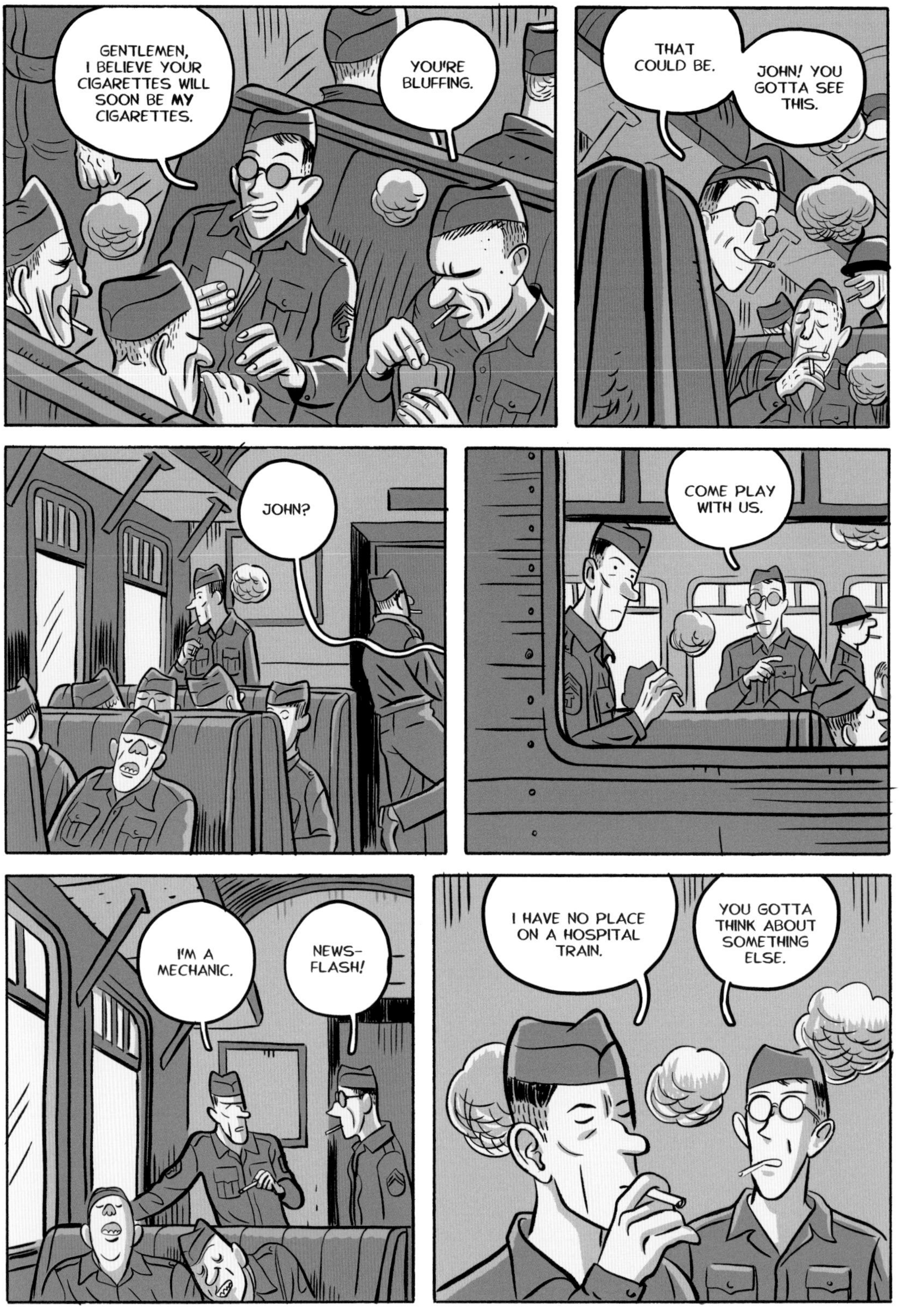
GENTLEMEN, I BELIEVE YOUR CIGARETTES WILL SOON BE MY CIGARETTES.
YOU'RE BLUFFING.
THAT COULD BE.
JOHN! YOU GOTTA SEE THIS.
JOHN?
COME PLAY WITH US.
I'M A MECHANIC.
NEWS-FLASH!
I HAVE NO PLACE ON A HOSPITAL TRAIN.
YOU GOTTA THINK ABOUT SOMETHING ELSE.

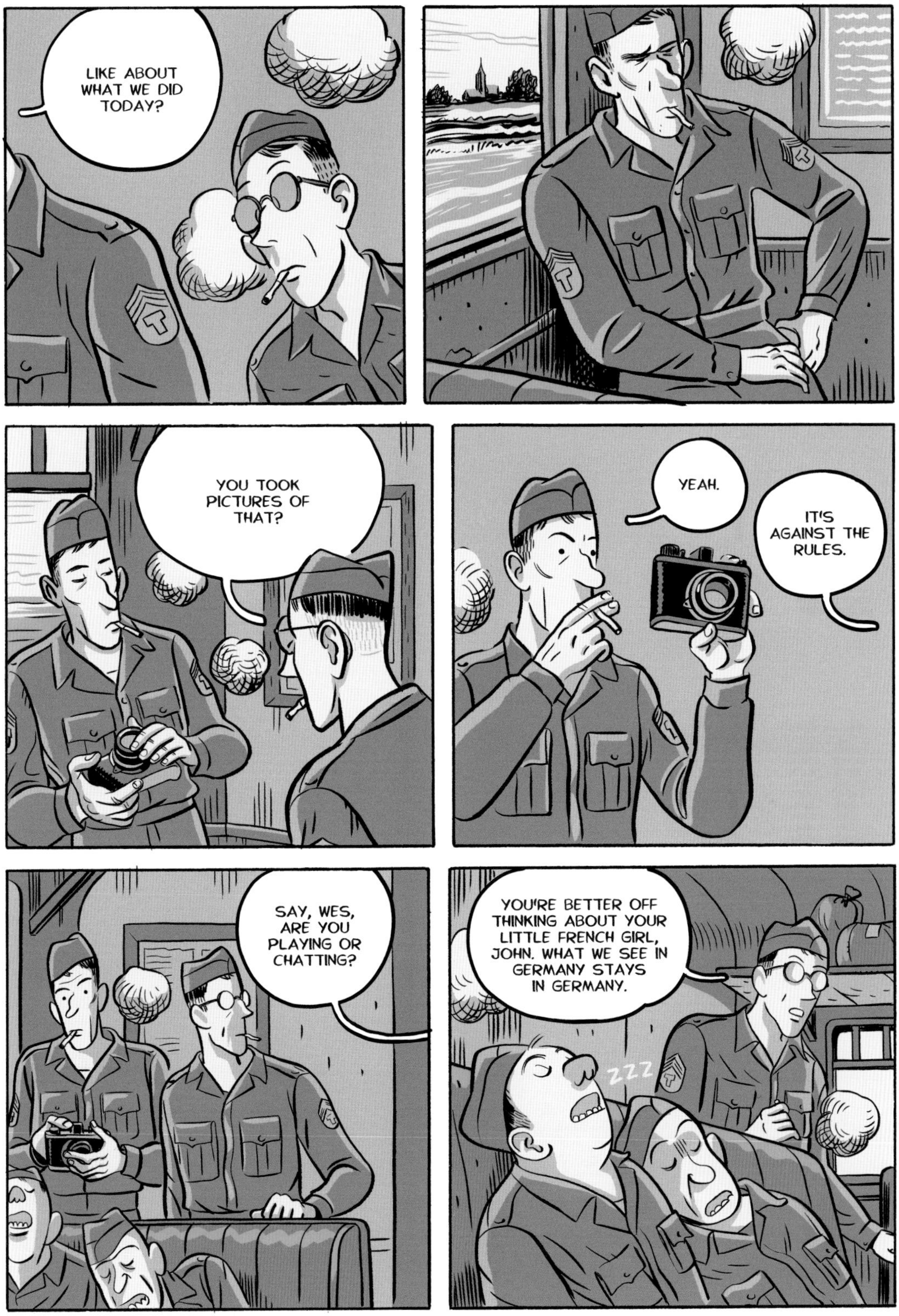
LIKE ABOUT WHAT WE DID TODAY?
YOU TOOK PICTURES OF THAT?
YEAH.
IT'S AGAINST THE RULES.
SAY, WES, ARE YOU PLAYING OR CHATTING?
YOU'RE BETTER OFF THINKING ABOUT YOUR LITTLE FRENCH GIRL, JOHN. WHAT WE SEE IN GERMANY STAYS IN GERMANY.
ZZZ

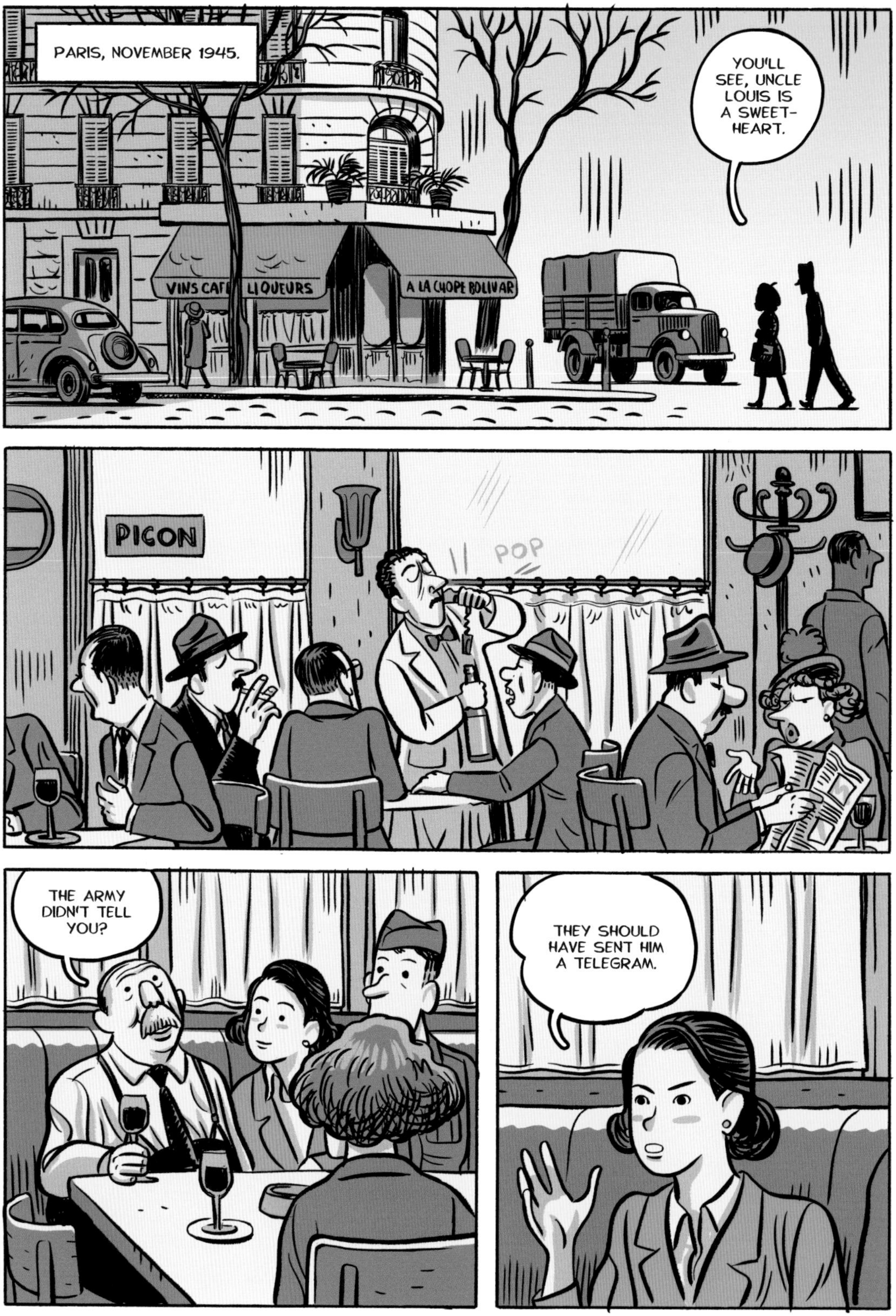
PARIS, NOVEMBER 1945.
YOU'LL SEE, UNCLE LOUIS IS A SWEET-HEART.
VINS CAFE LIQUEURS
A LA CHOPE BOLIVAR
PICON
POP
THE ARMY DIDN'T TELL YOU?
THEY SHOULD HAVE SENT HIM A TELEGRAM.

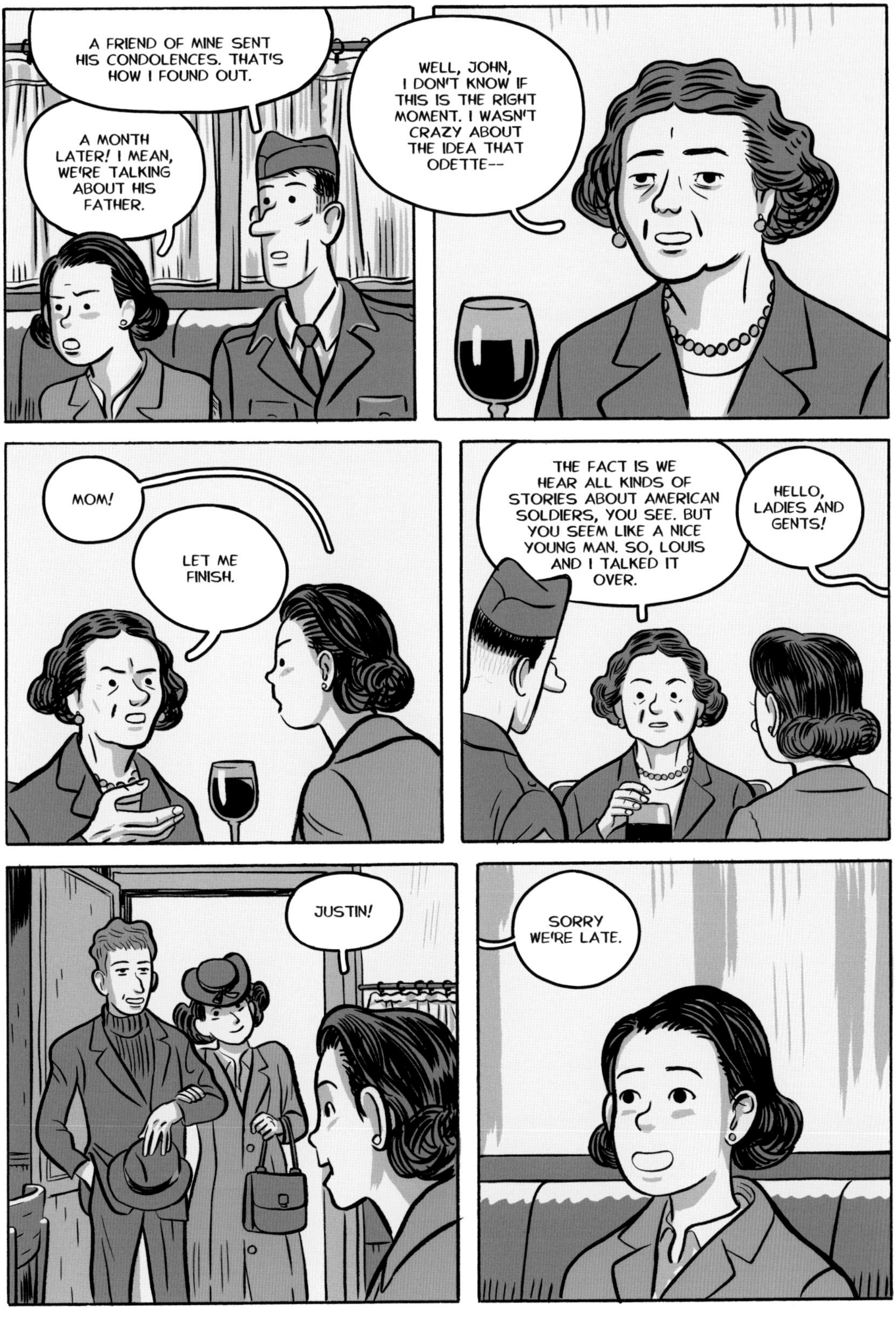
A FRIEND OF MINE SENT HIS CONDOLENCES. THAT'S HOW I FOUND OUT.
A MONTH LATER! I MEAN, WE'RE TALKING ABOUT HIS FATHER.
WELL, JOHN, I DON'T KNOW IF THIS IS THE RIGHT MOMENT. I WASN'T CRAZY ABOUT THE IDEA THAT ODETTE--
MOM!
LET ME FINISH.
THE FACT IS WE HEAR ALL KINDS OF STORIES ABOUT AMERICAN SOLDIERS, YOU SEE. BUT YOU SEEM LIKE A NICE YOUNG MAN. SO, LOUIS AND I TALKED IT OVER.
HELLO, LADIES AND GENTS!
JUSTIN!
SORRY WE'RE LATE.

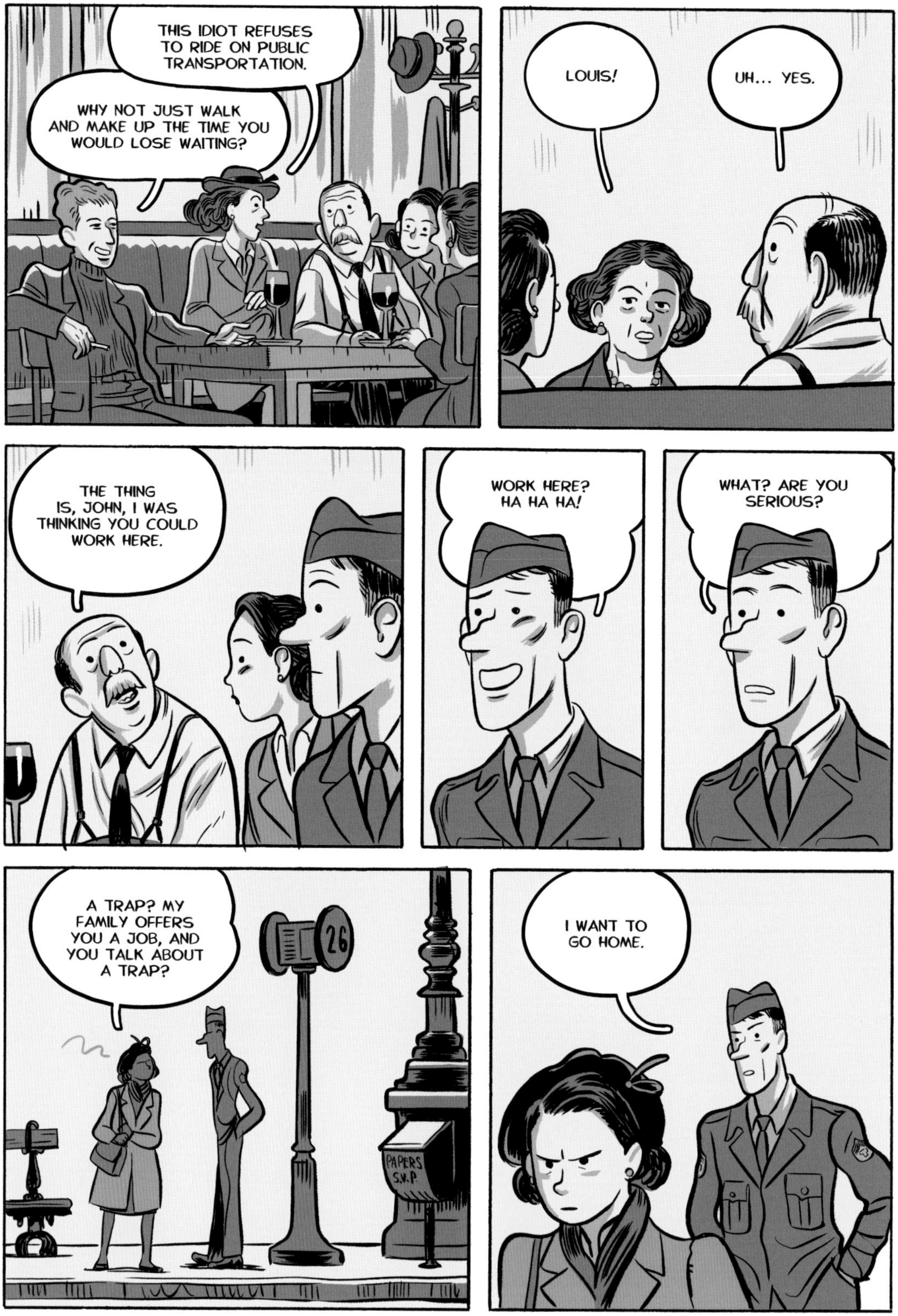
THIS IDIOT REFUSES TO RIDE ON PUBLIC TRANSPORTATION.
WHY NOT JUST WALK AND MAKE UP THE TIME YOU WOULD LOSE WAITING?
LOUIS!
UH... YES.
THE THING IS, JOHN, I WAS THINKING YOU COULD WORK HERE.
WORK HERE? HA HA HA!
WHAT? ARE YOU SERIOUS?
A TRAP? MY FAMILY OFFERS YOU A JOB, AND YOU TALK ABOUT A TRAP?
26
PAPERS S.V.P.
I WANT TO GO HOME.

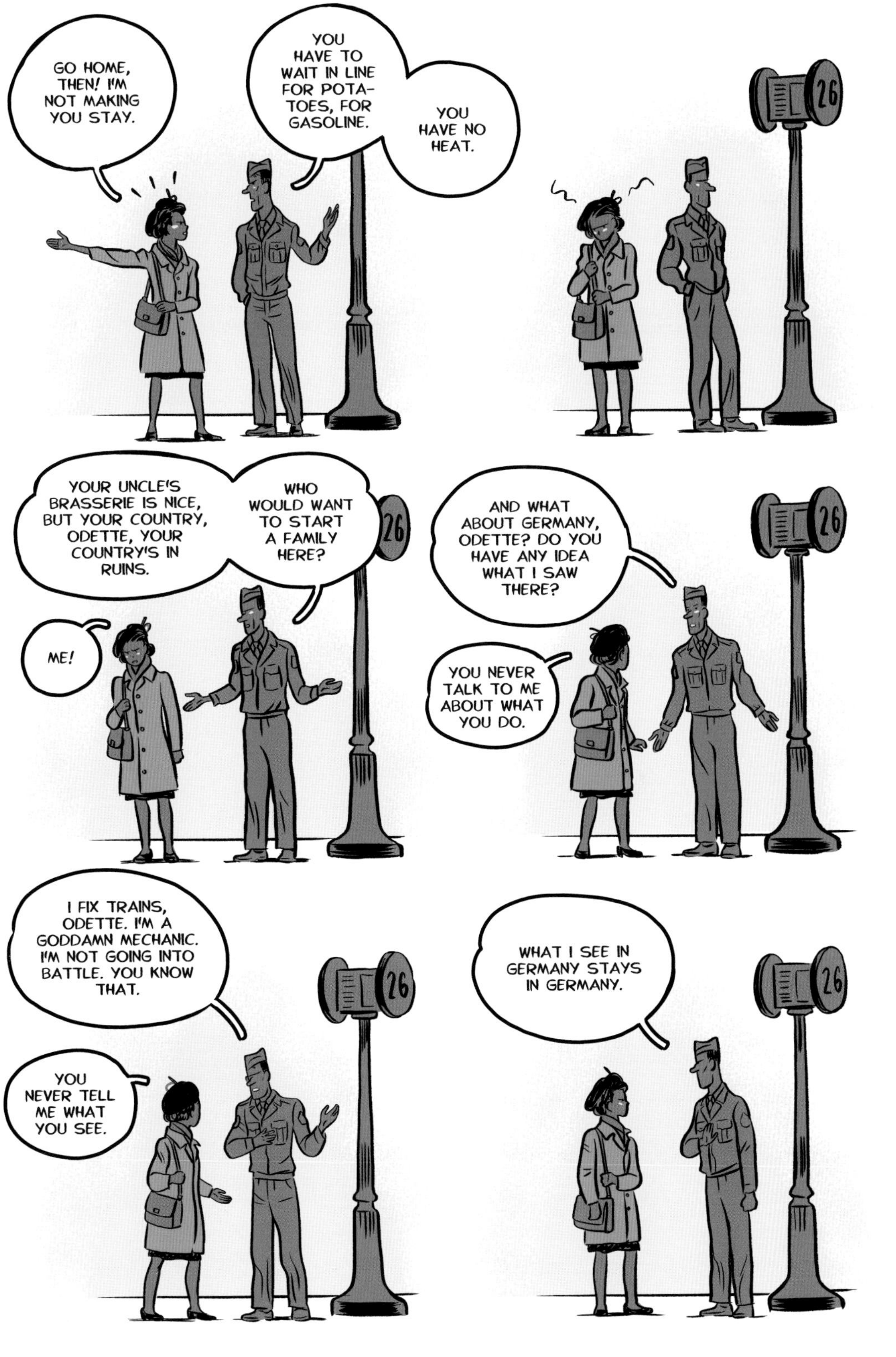
GO HOME, THEN! I'M NOT MAKING YOU STAY.
YOU HAVE TO WAIT IN LINE FOR POTA- TOES, FOR GASOLINE.
YOU HAVE NO HEAT.
YOUR UNCLE'S BRASSERIE IS NICE, BUT YOUR COUNTRY, ODETTE, YOUR COUNTRY'S IN RUINS.
WHO WOULD WANT TO START A FAMILY HERE?
ME!
AND WHAT ABOUT GERMANY, ODETTE? DO YOU HAVE ANY IDEA WHAT I SAW THERE?
YOU NEVER TALK TO ME ABOUT WHAT YOU DO.
I FIX TRAINS, ODETTE. I'M A GODDAMN MECHANIC. I'M NOT GOING INTO BATTLE. YOU KNOW THAT.
YOU NEVER TELL ME WHAT YOU SEE.
WHAT I SEE IN GERMANY STAYS IN GERMANY.

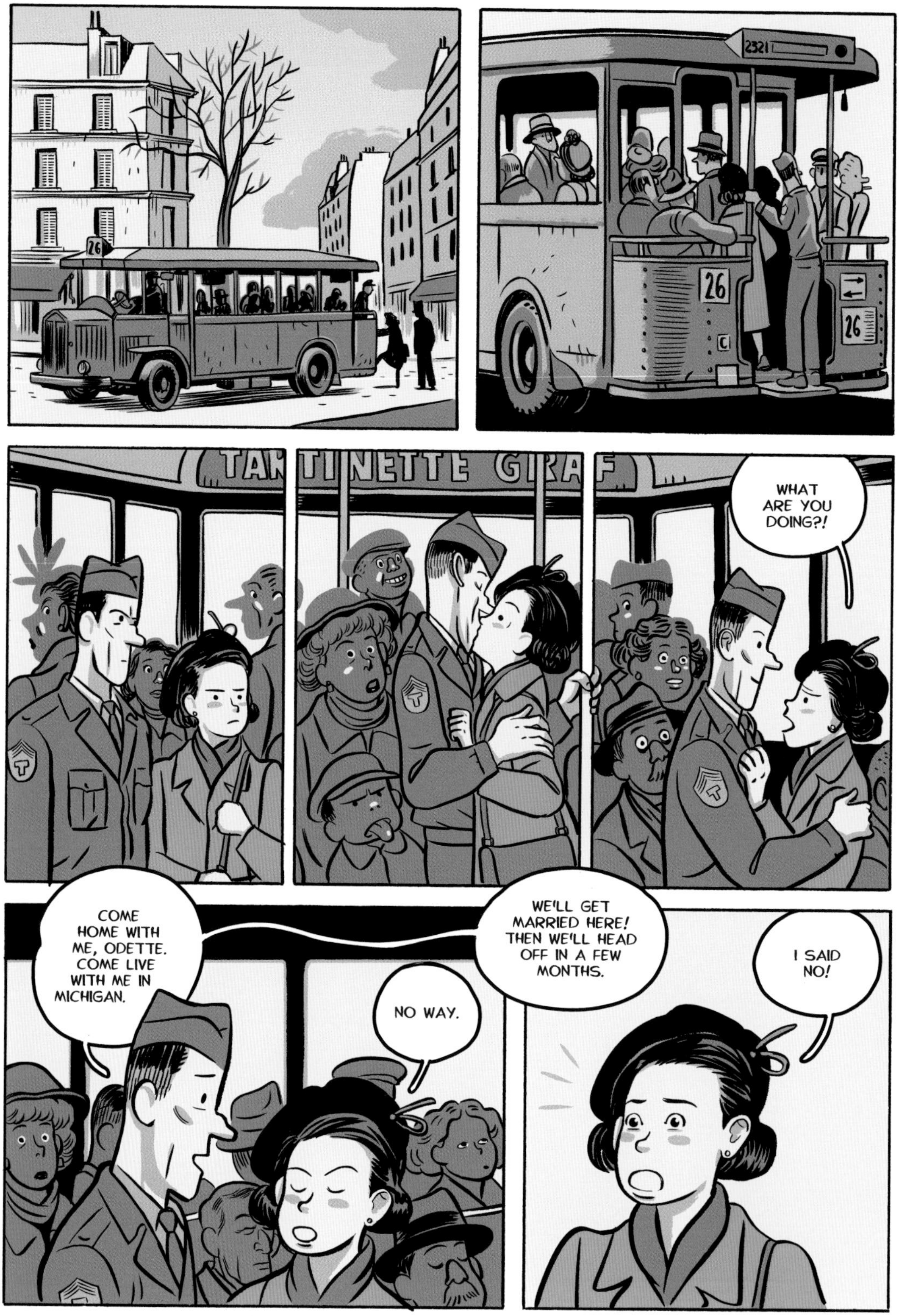
2321
26
26
26
TARTINETTE GIRAF
WHAT ARE YOU DOING?!
COME HOME WITH ME, ODETTE. COME LIVE WITH ME IN MICHIGAN.
NO WAY.
WE'LL GET MARRIED HERE! THEN WE'LL HEAD OFF IN A FEW MONTHS.
I SAID NO!

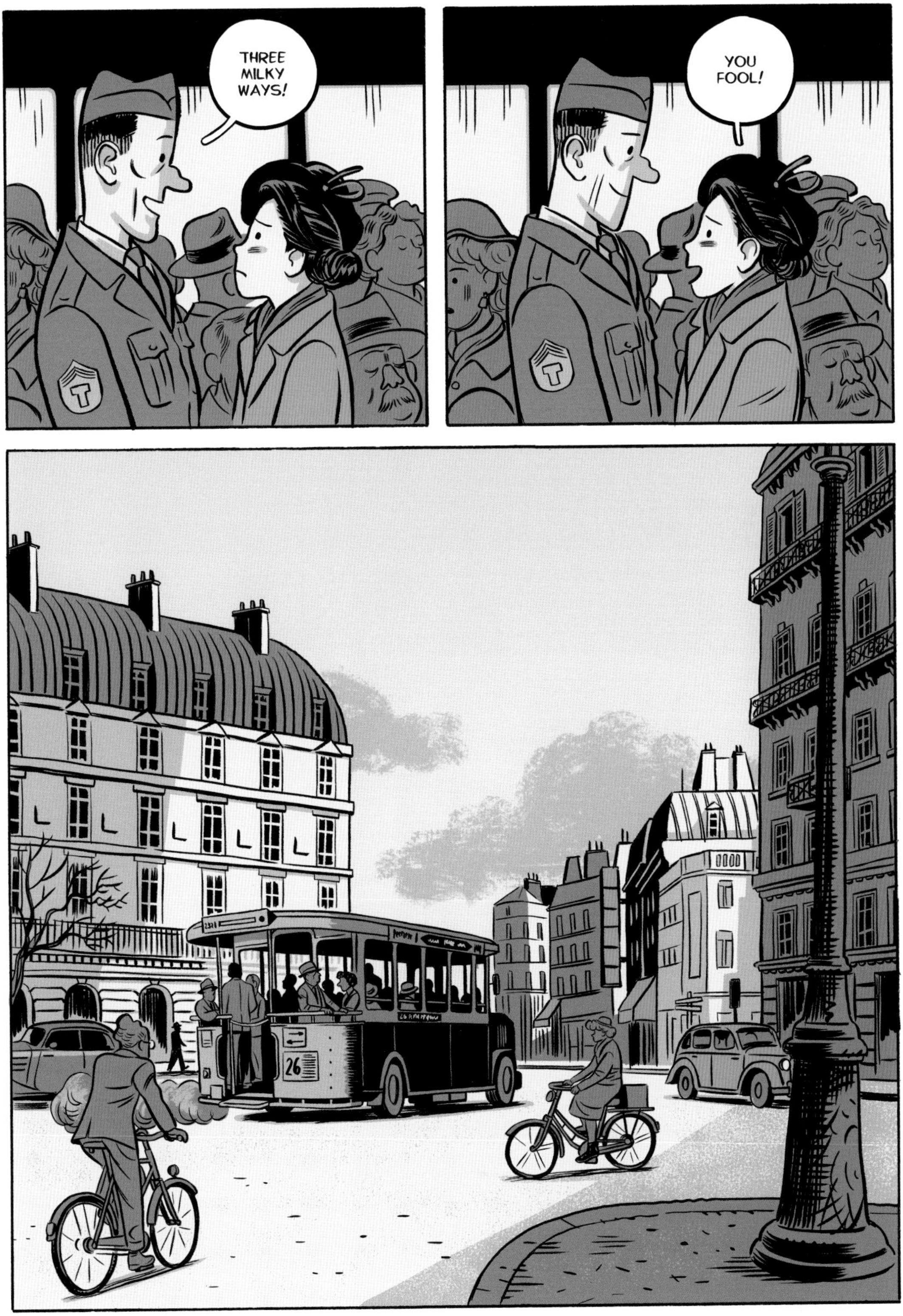
THREE MILKY WAYS!
YOU FOOL!
26

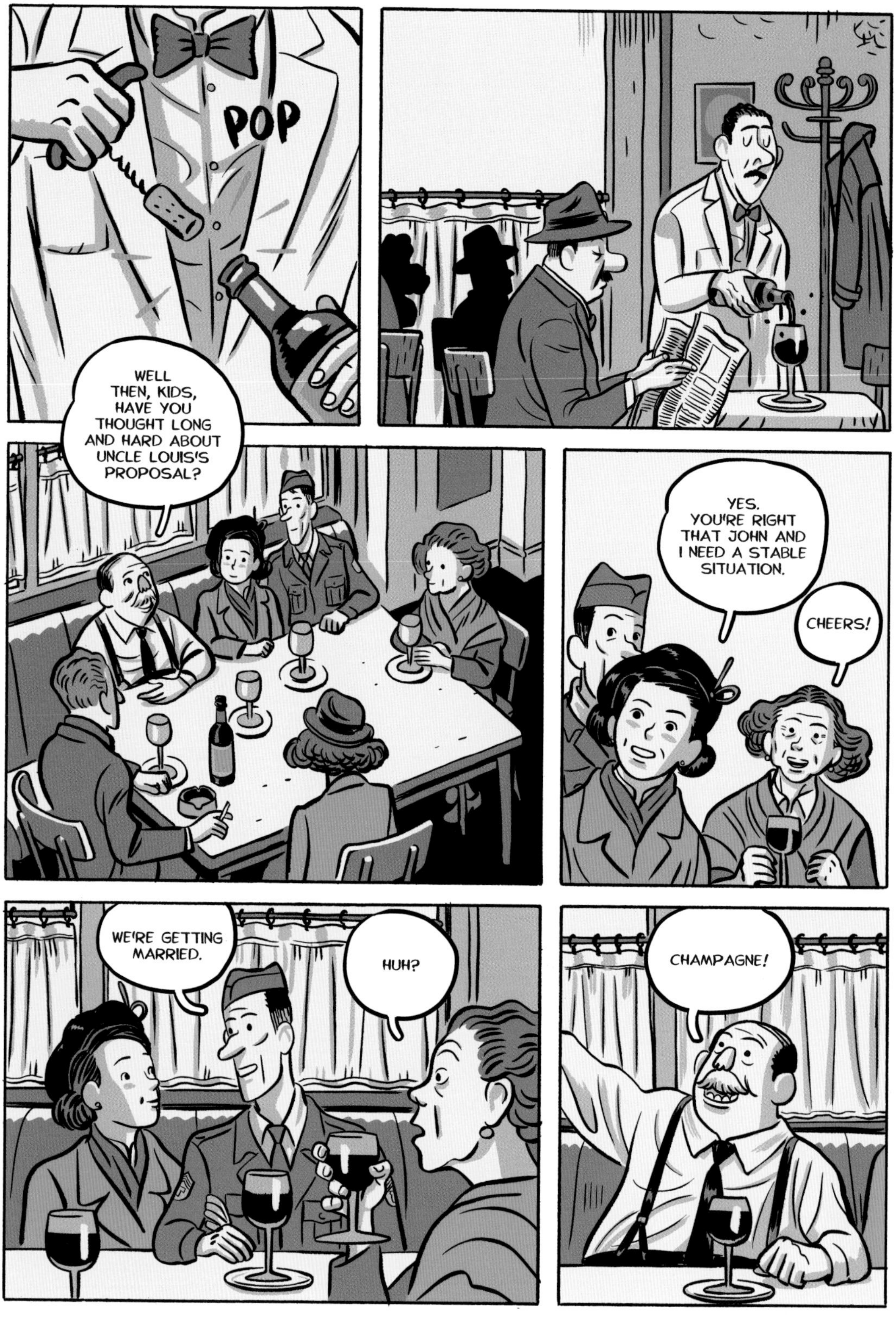
POP
WELL THEN, KIDS, HAVE YOU THOUGHT LONG AND HARD ABOUT UNCLE LOUIS'S PROPOSAL?
YES. YOU'RE RIGHT THAT JOHN AND I NEED A STABLE SITUATION.
CHEERS!
WE'RE GETTING MARRIED.
HUH?
CHAMPAGNE!

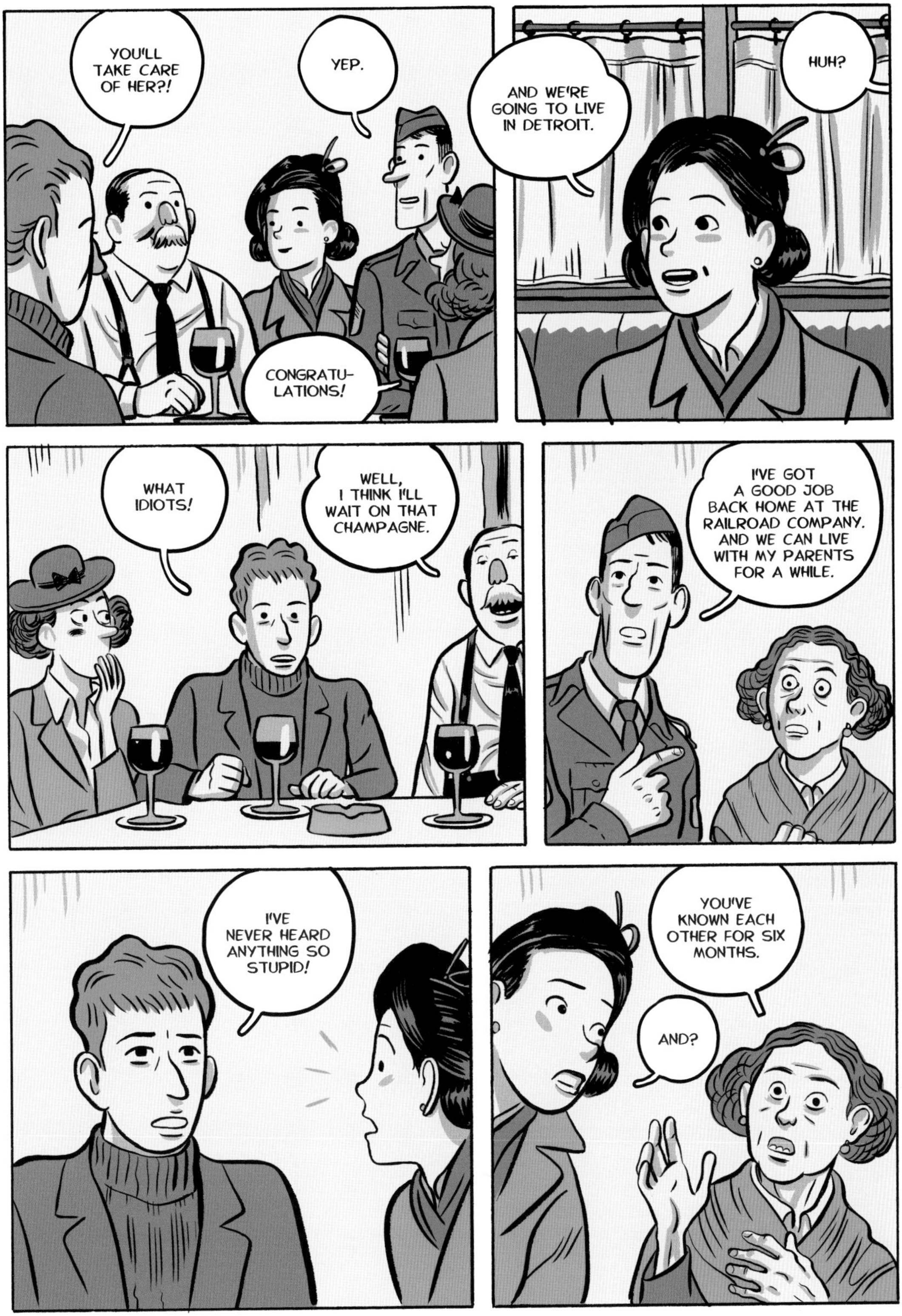
YOU'LL TAKE CARE OF HER?!
YEP.
CONGRATU-LATIONS!
AND WE'RE GOING TO LIVE IN DETROIT.
HUH?
WHAT IDIOTS!
WELL, I THINK I'LL WAIT ON THAT CHAMPAGNE.
I'VE GOT A GOOD JOB BACK HOME AT THE RAILROAD COMPANY. AND WE CAN LIVE WITH MY PARENTS FOR A WHILE.
I'VE NEVER HEARD ANYTHING SO STUPID!
YOU'VE KNOWN EACH OTHER FOR SIX MONTHS.
AND?

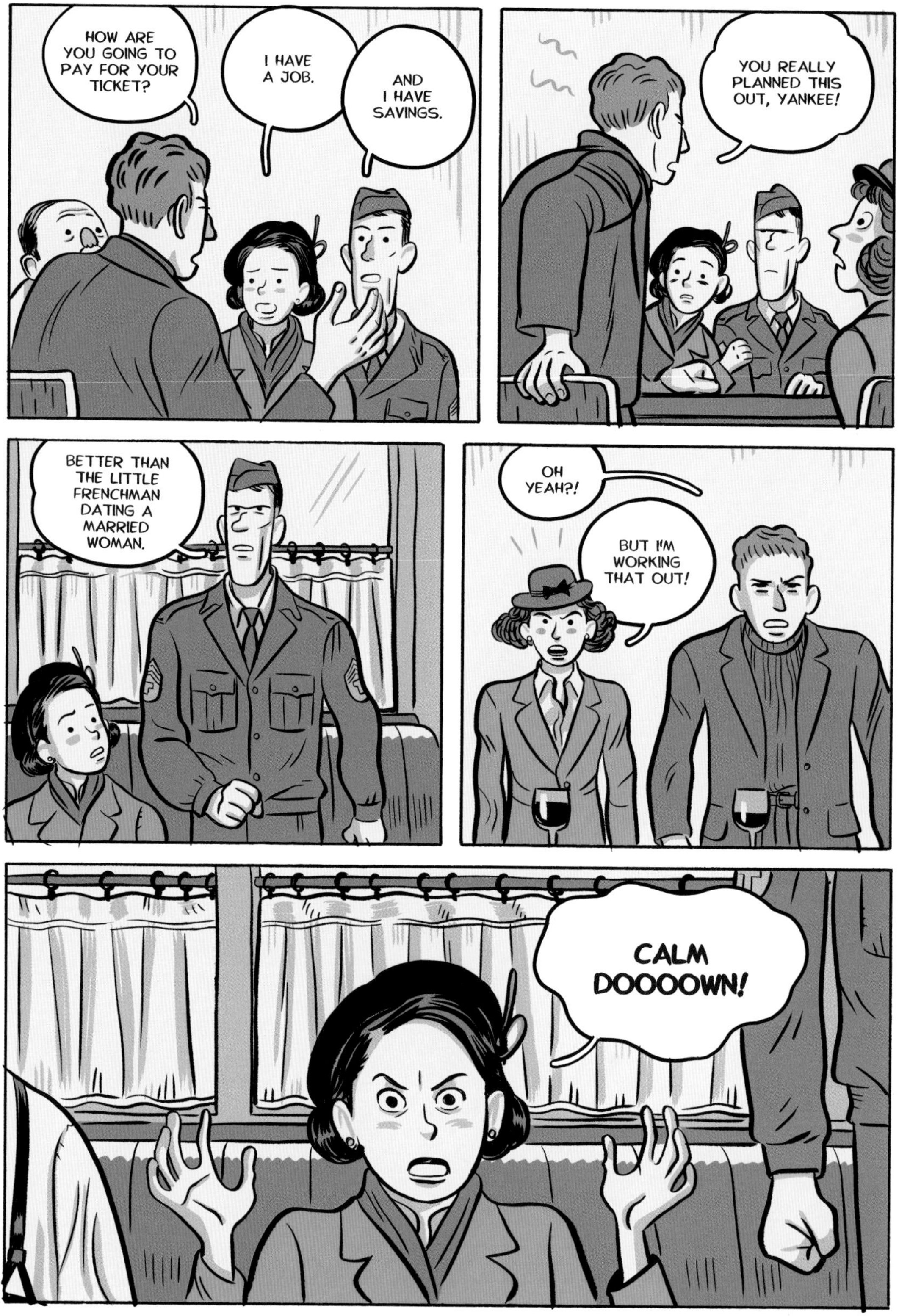
HOW ARE YOU GOING TO PAY FOR YOUR TICKET?
I HAVE A JOB.
AND I HAVE SAVINGS.
YOU REALLY PLANNED THIS OUT, YANKEE!
BETTER THAN THE LITTLE FRENCHMAN DATING A MARRIED WOMAN.
OH YEAH?!
BUT I'M WORKING THAT OUT!
CALM DOOOOWN!

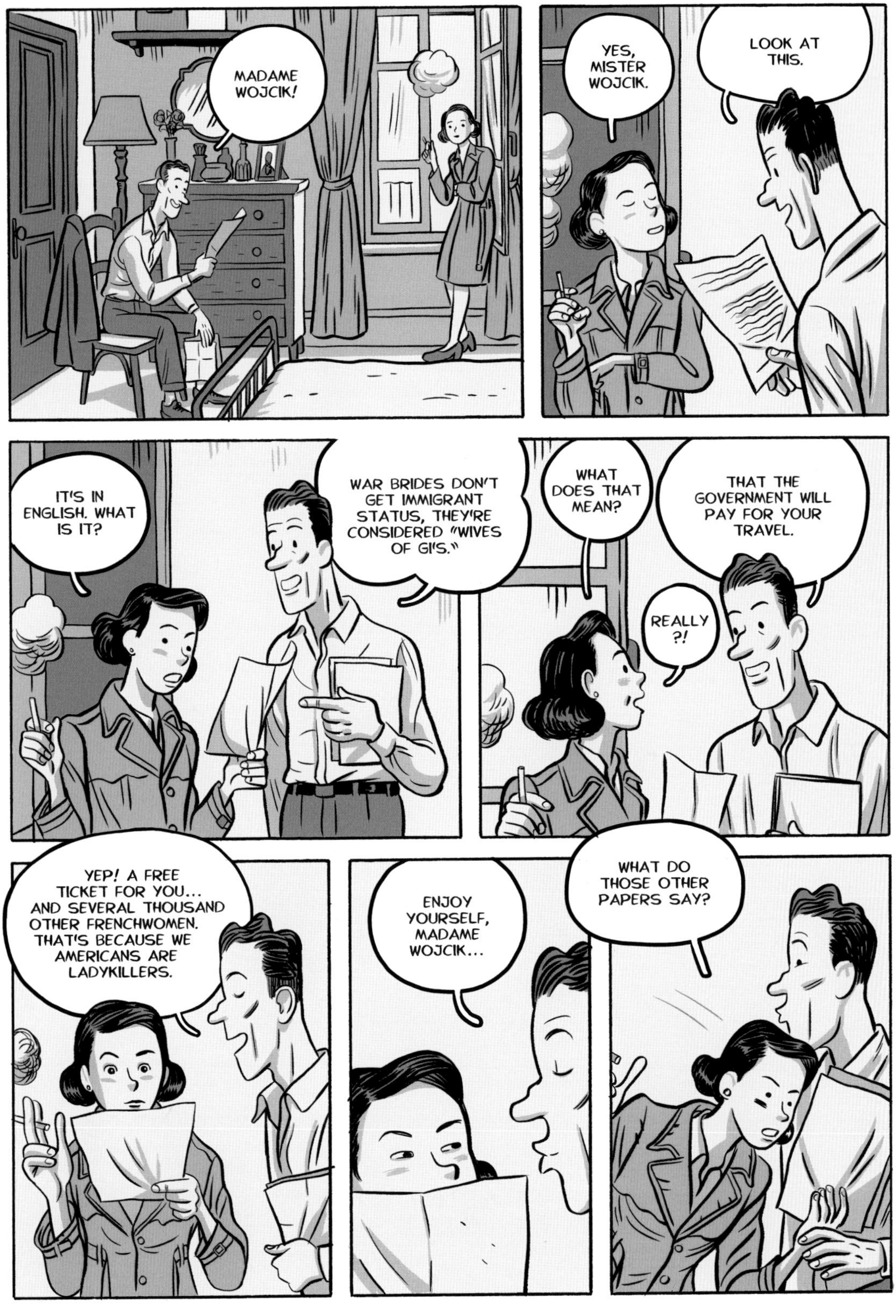
MADAME WOJCIK!
YES, MISTER WOJCIK.
LOOK AT THIS.
IT'S IN ENGLISH. WHAT IS IT?
WAR BRIDES DON'T GET IMMIGRANT STATUS, THEY'RE CONSIDERED "WIVES OF GI'S."
WHAT DOES THAT MEAN?
THAT THE GOVERNMENT WILL PAY FOR YOUR TRAVEL.
REALLY ?!
YEP! A FREE TICKET FOR YOU... AND SEVERAL THOUSAND OTHER FRENCHWOMEN. THAT'S BECAUSE WE AMERICANS ARE LADYKILLERS.
ENJOY YOURSELF, MADAME WOJCIK...
WHAT DO THOSE OTHER PAPERS SAY?

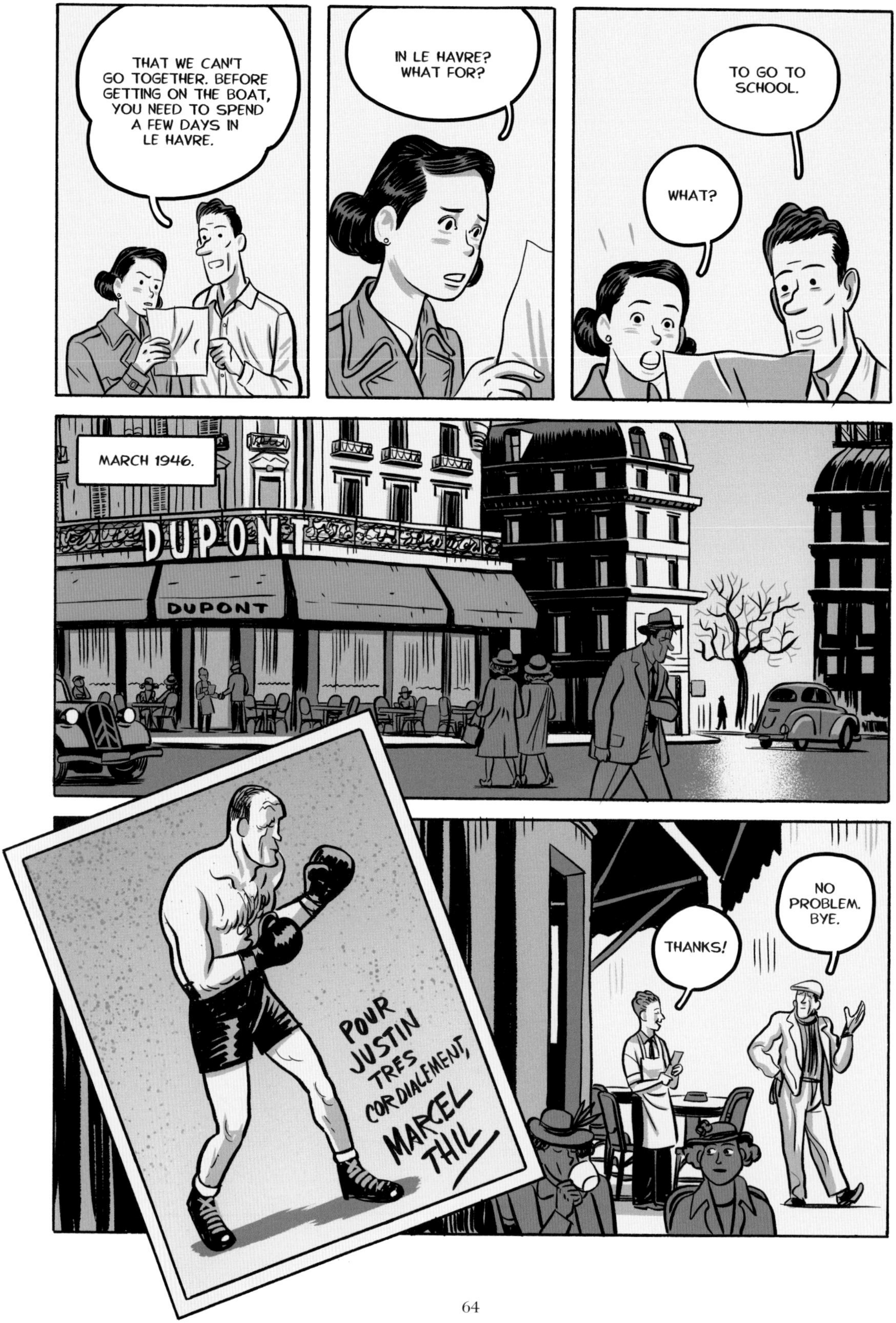
THAT WE CAN'T GO TOGETHER. BEFORE GETTING ON THE BOAT, YOU NEED TO SPEND A FEW DAYS IN LE HAVRE.
IN LE HAVRE? WHAT FOR?
TO GO TO SCHOOL.
WHAT?
MARCH 1946.
DUPONT
DUPONT
POUR JUSTIN TRES CORDIALEMENT, MARCEL THIL
THANKS!
NO PROBLEM. BYE.

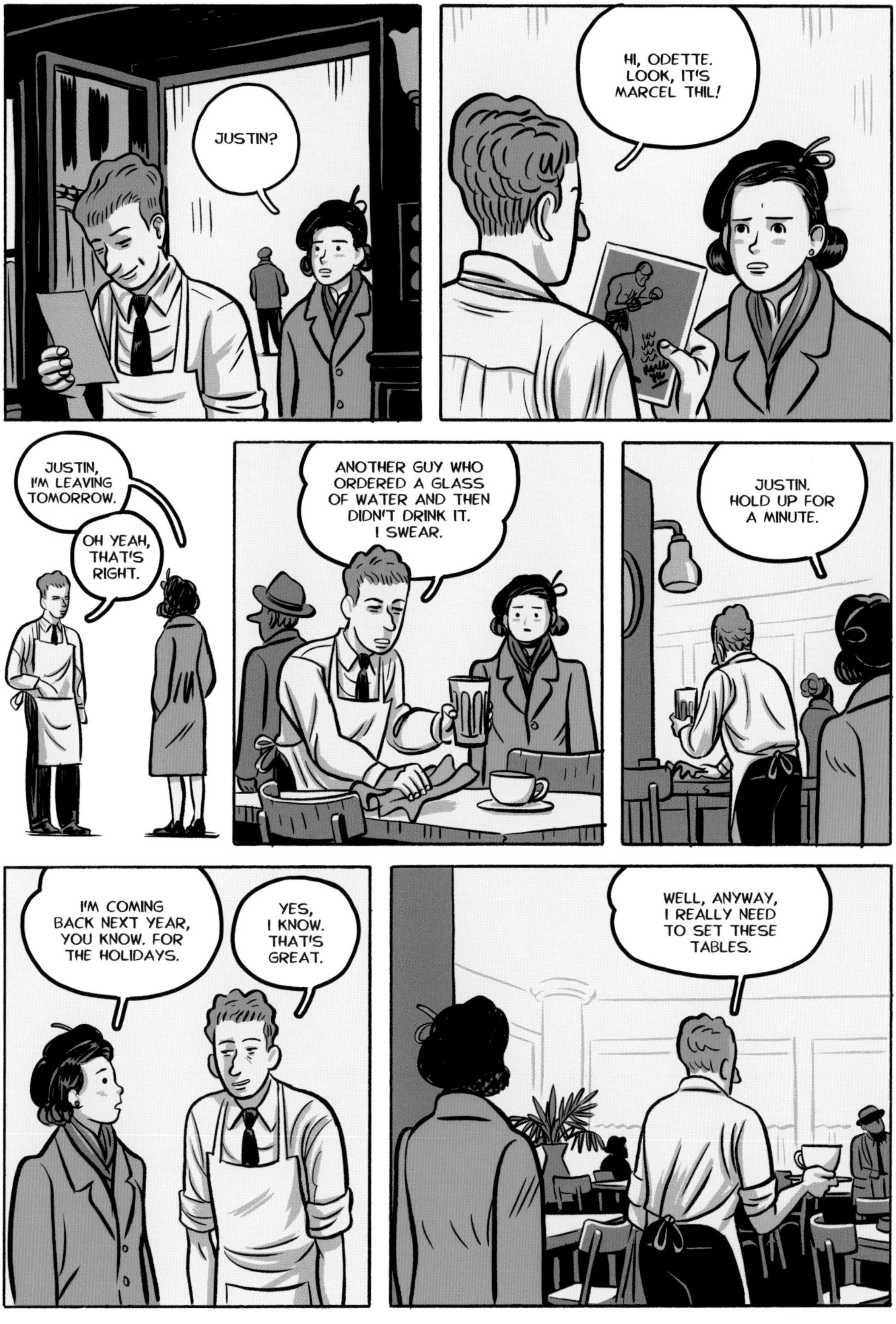
JUSTIN?
HI, ODETTE. LOOK, IT'S MARCEL THIL!
JUSTIN, I'M LEAVING TOMORROW.
OH YEAH, THAT'S RIGHT.
ANOTHER GUY WHO ORDERED A GLASS OF WATER AND THEN DIDN'T DRINK IT. I SWEAR.
JUSTIN. HOLD UP FOR A MINUTE.
I'M COMING BACK NEXT YEAR, YOU KNOW. FOR THE HOLIDAYS.
YES, I KNOW. THAT'S GREAT.
WELL, ANYWAY, I REALLY NEED TO SET THESE TABLES.

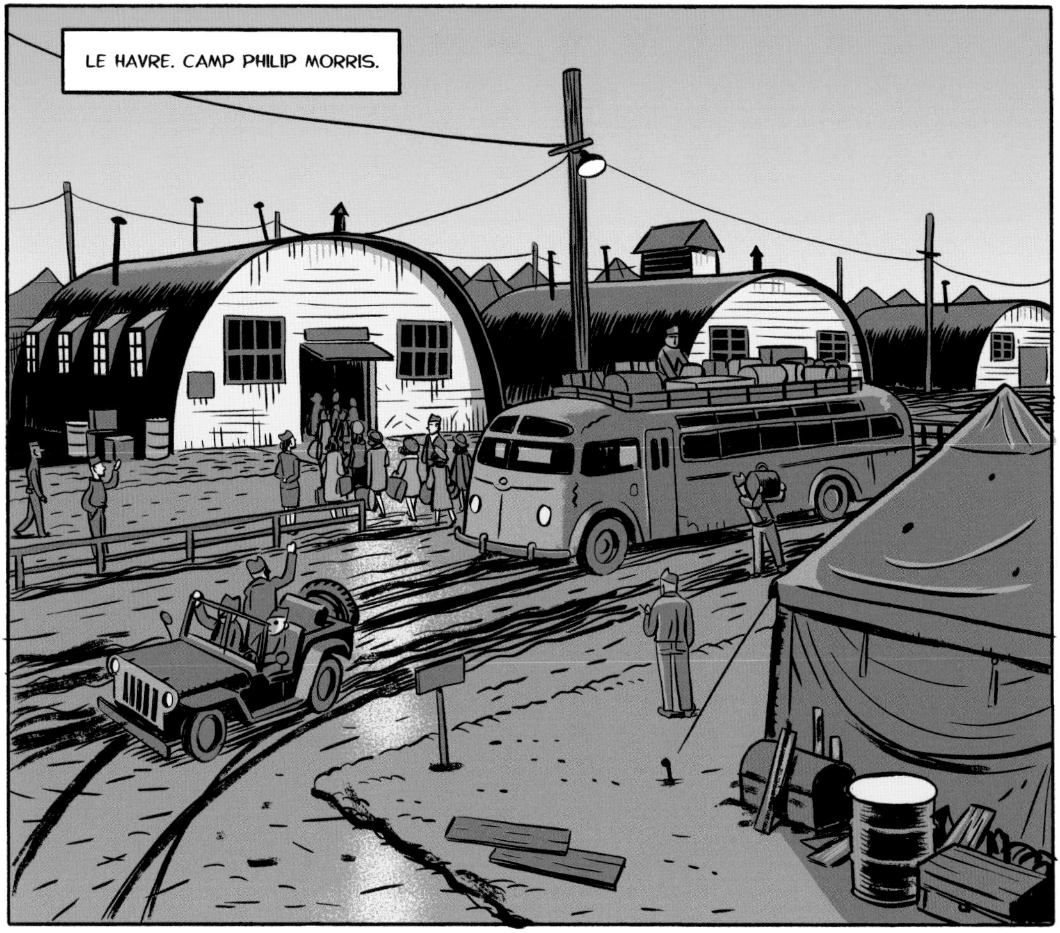
LE HAVRE. CAMP PHILIP MORRIS.

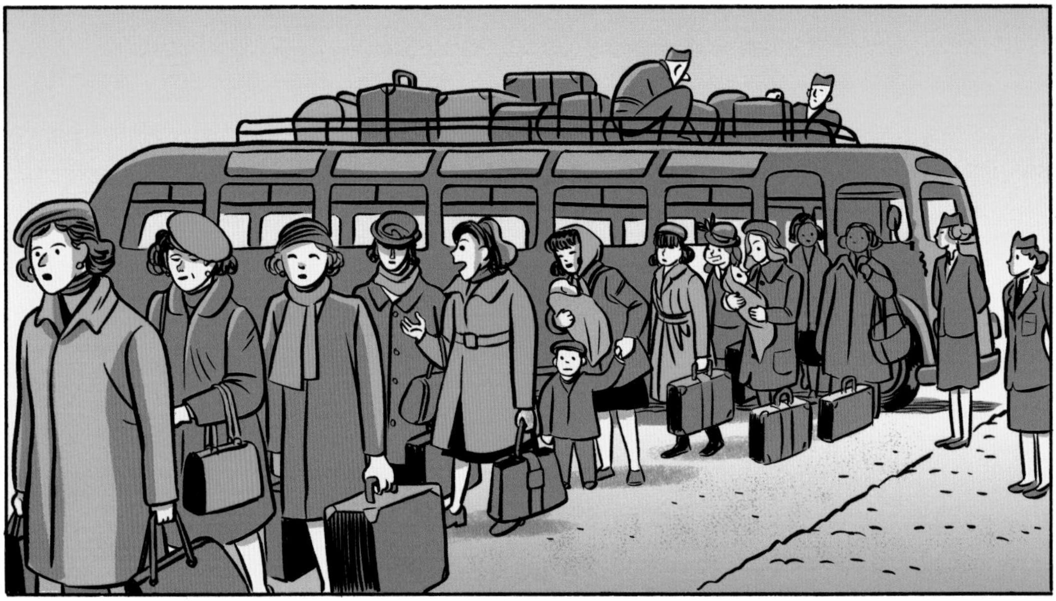

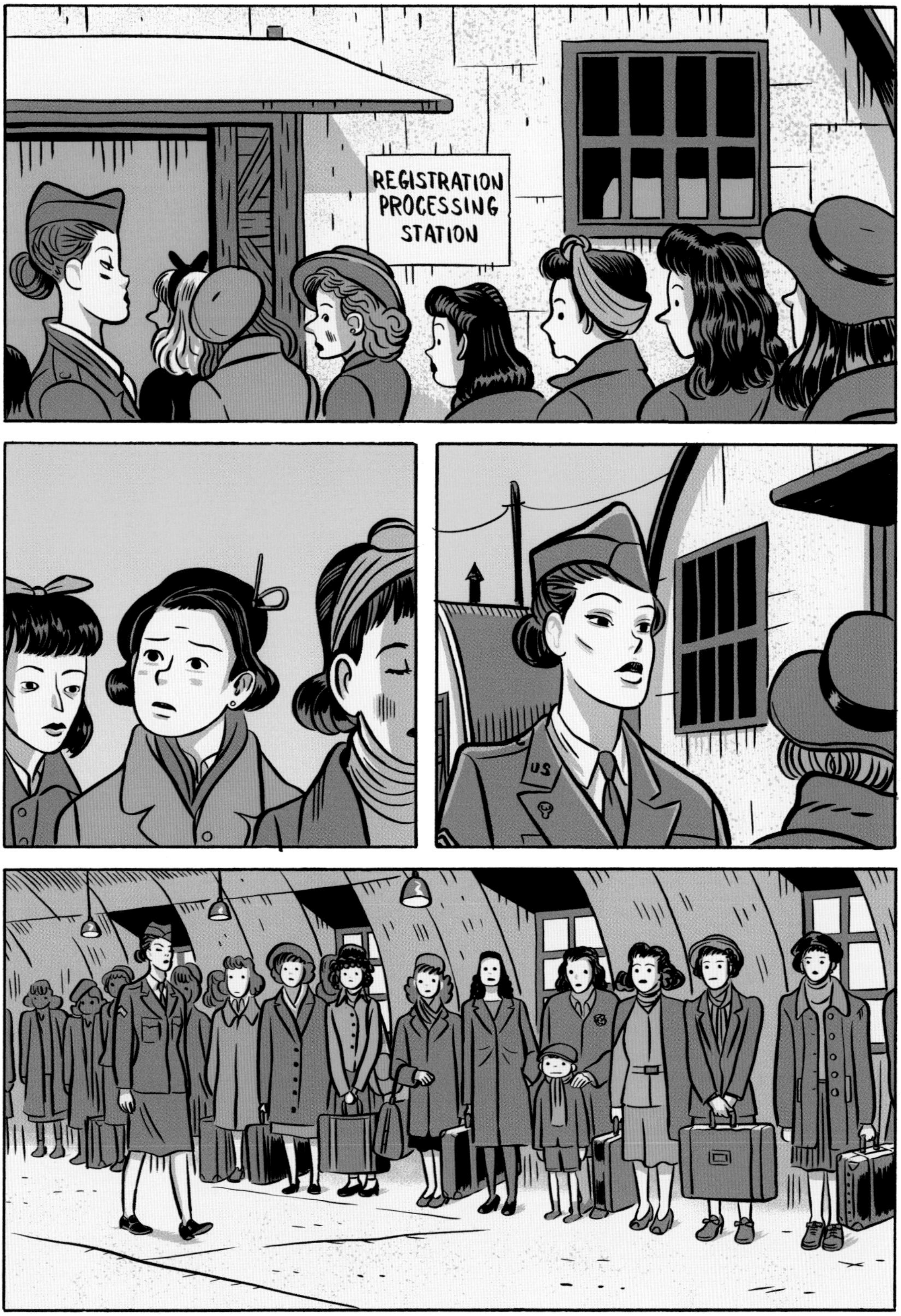
REGISTRATION
PROCESSING
STATION
US

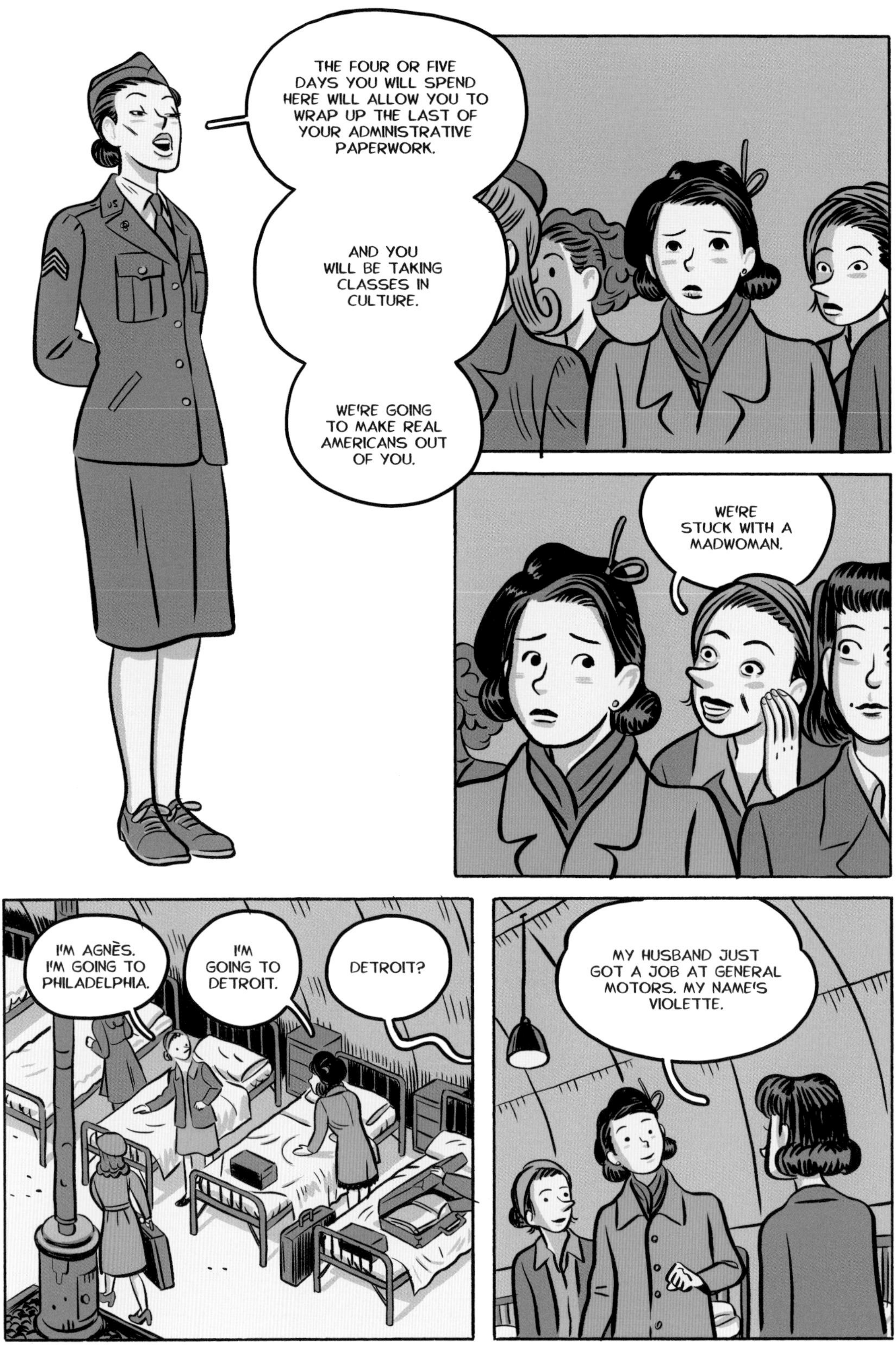
THE FOUR OR FIVE DAYS YOU WILL SPEND HERE WILL ALLOW YOU TO WRAP UP THE LAST OF YOUR ADMINISTRATIVE PAPERWORK.
AND YOU WILL BE TAKING CLASSES IN CULTURE.
WE'RE GOING TO MAKE REAL AMERICANS OUT OF YOU.
WE'RE STUCK WITH A MADWOMAN.
I'M AGNÈS. I'M GOING TO PHILADELPHIA.
I'M GOING TO DETROIT.
DETROIT?
MY HUSBAND JUST GOT A JOB AT GENERAL MOTORS. MY NAME'S VIOLETTE.

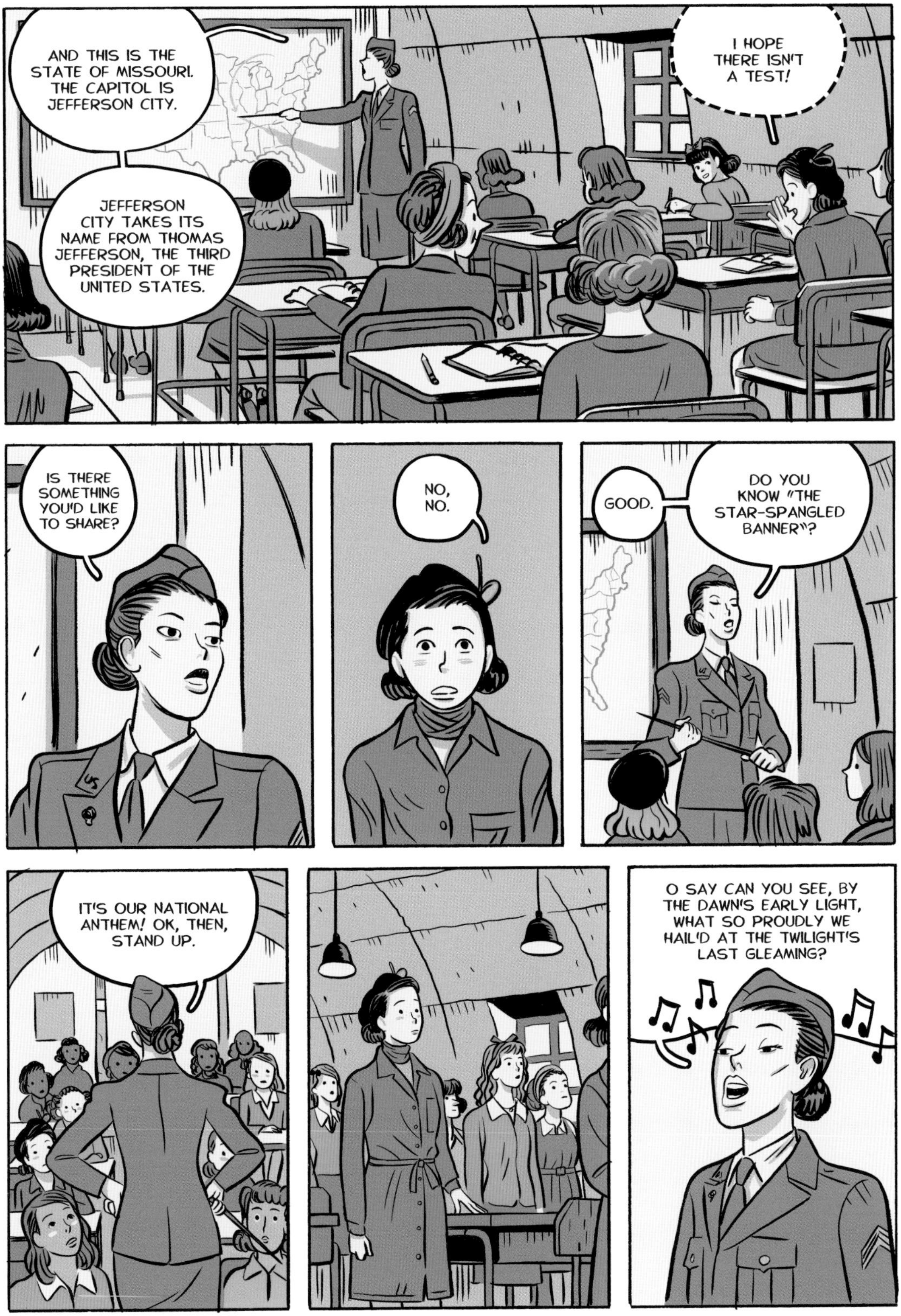
AND THIS IS THE STATE OF MISSOURI. THE CAPITOL IS JEFFERSON CITY.
JEFFERSON CITY TAKES ITS NAME FROM THOMAS JEFFERSON, THE THIRD PRESIDENT OF THE UNITED STATES.
I HOPE THERE ISN'T A TEST!
IS THERE SOMETHING YOU'D LIKE TO SHARE?
NO, NO.
GOOD.
DO YOU KNOW "THE STAR-SPANGLED BANNER"?
IT'S OUR NATIONAL ANTHEM! OK, THEN, STAND UP.
O SAY CAN YOU SEE, BY THE DAWN'S EARLY LIGHT, WHAT SO PROUDLY WE HAIL'D AT THE TWILIGHT'S LAST GLEAMING?

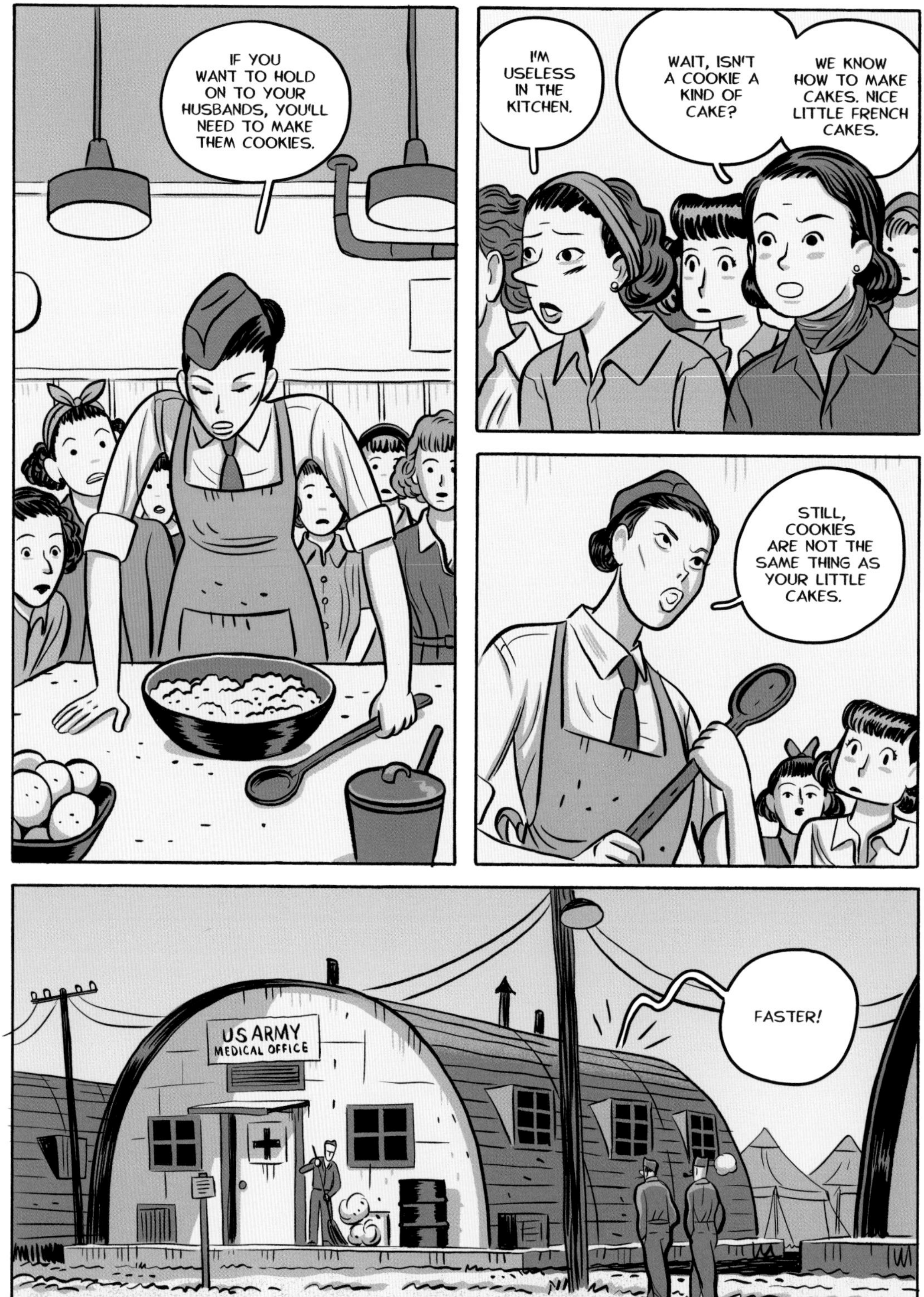
IF YOU WANT TO HOLD ON TO YOUR HUSBANDS, YOU'LL NEED TO MAKE THEM COOKIES.
I'M USELESS IN THE KITCHEN.
WAIT, ISN'T A COOKIE A KIND OF CAKE?
WE KNOW HOW TO MAKE CAKES. NICE LITTLE FRENCH CAKES.
STILL, COOKIES ARE NOT THE SAME THING AS YOUR LITTLE CAKES.
US ARMY
MEDICAL OFFICE
FASTER!

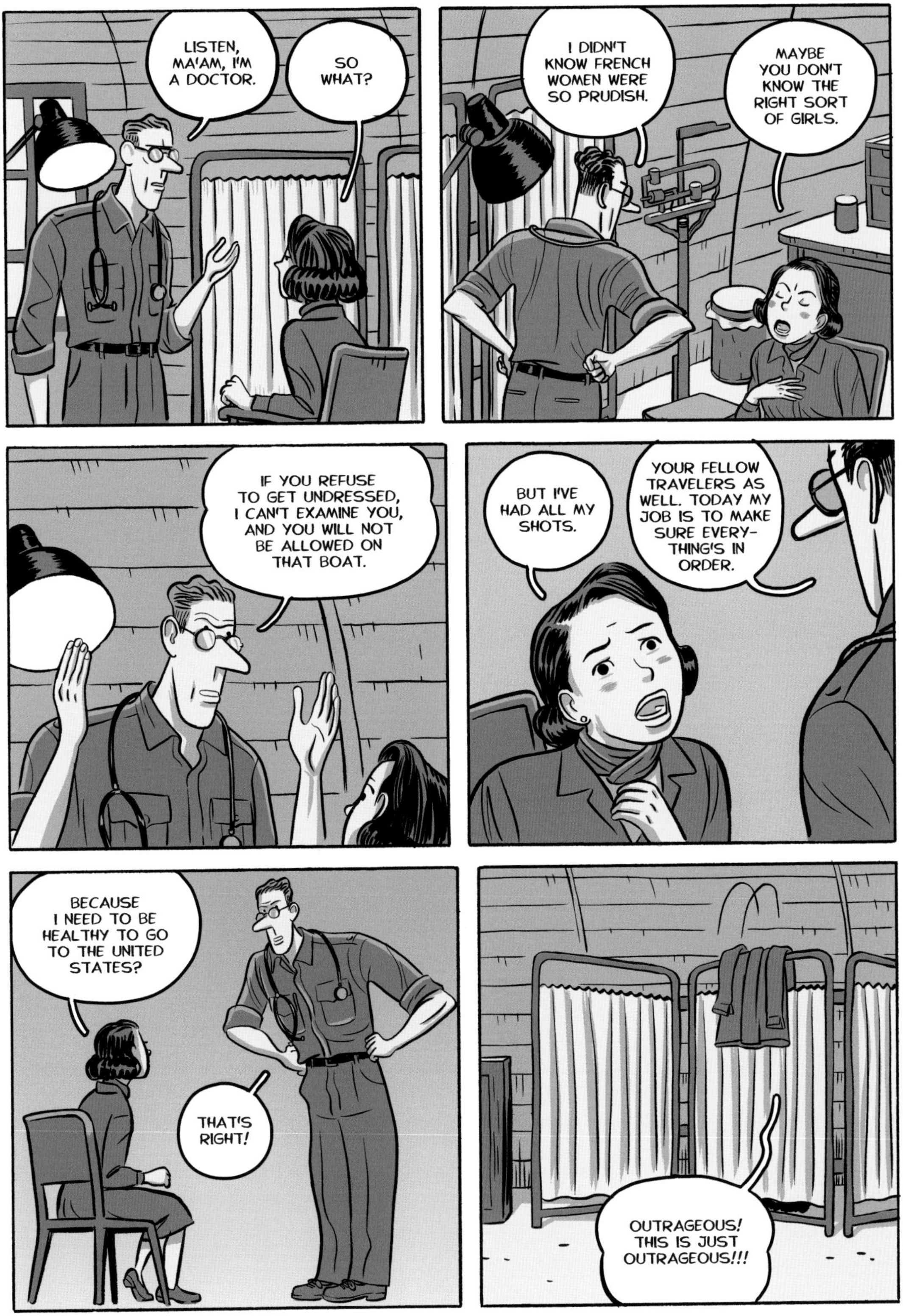
LISTEN, MA'AM, I'M A DOCTOR.
SO WHAT?
I DIDN'T KNOW FRENCH WOMEN WERE SO PRUDISH.
MAYBE YOU DON'T KNOW THE RIGHT SORT OF GIRLS.
IF YOU REFUSE TO GET UNDRESSED, I CAN'T EXAMINE YOU, AND YOU WILL NOT BE ALLOWED ON THAT BOAT.
BUT I'VE HAD ALL MY SHOTS.
YOUR FELLOW TRAVELERS AS WELL. TODAY MY JOB IS TO MAKE SURE EVERY-THING'S IN ORDER.
BECAUSE I NEED TO BE HEALTHY TO GO TO THE UNITED STATES?
THAT'S RIGHT!
OUTRAGEOUS! THIS IS JUST OUTRAGEOUS!!!

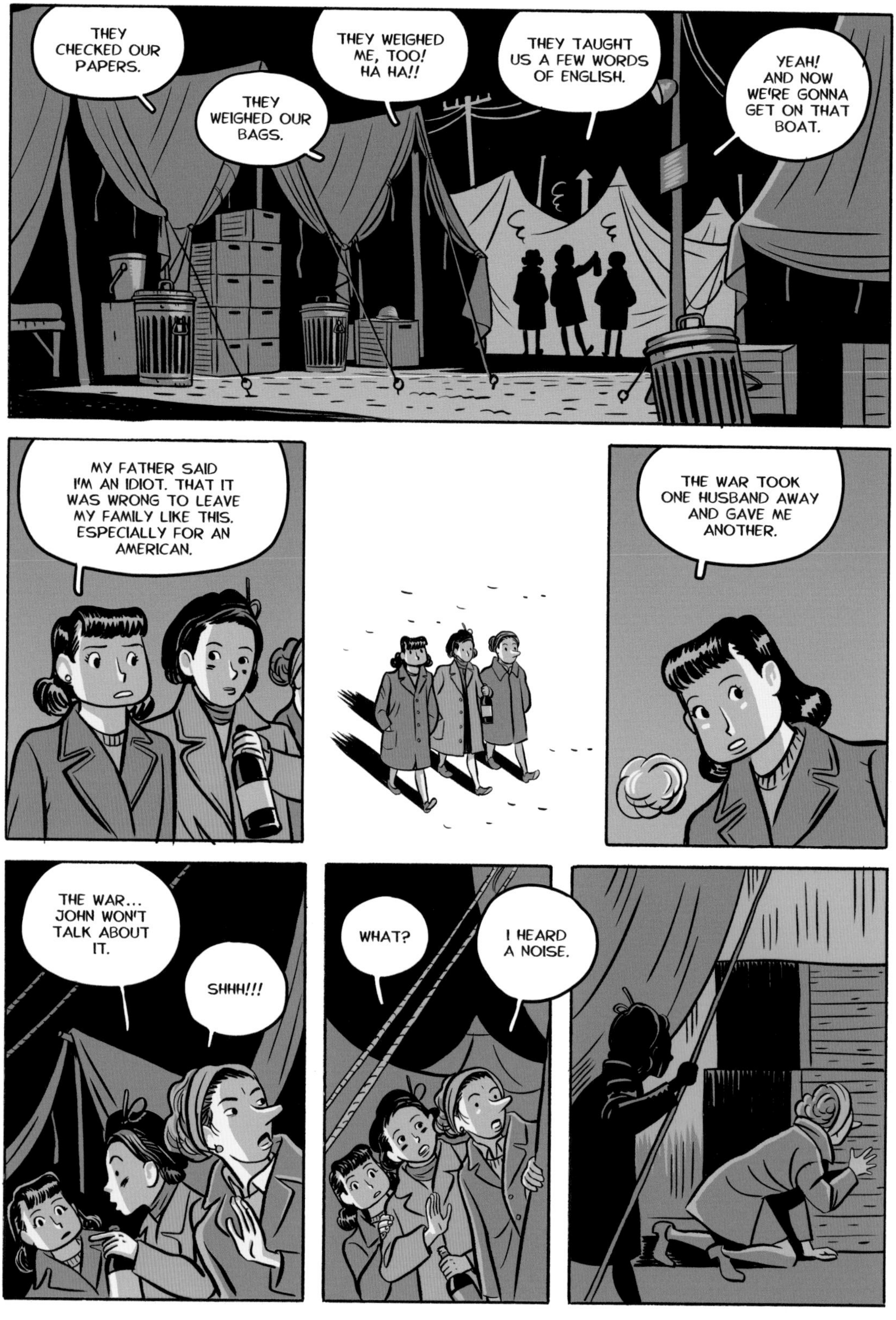
THEY CHECKED OUR PAPERS.
THEY WEIGHED OUR BAGS.
THEY WEIGHED ME, TOO! HA HA!!
THEY TAUGHT US A FEW WORDS OF ENGLISH.
YEAH! AND NOW WE'RE GONNA GET ON THAT BOAT.
MY FATHER SAID I'M AN IDIOT. THAT IT WAS WRONG TO LEAVE MY FAMILY LIKE THIS. ESPECIALLY FOR AN AMERICAN.
THE WAR TOOK ONE HUSBAND AWAY AND GAVE ME ANOTHER.
THE WAR... JOHN WON'T TALK ABOUT IT.
SHHH!!!
WHAT?
I HEARD A NOISE.

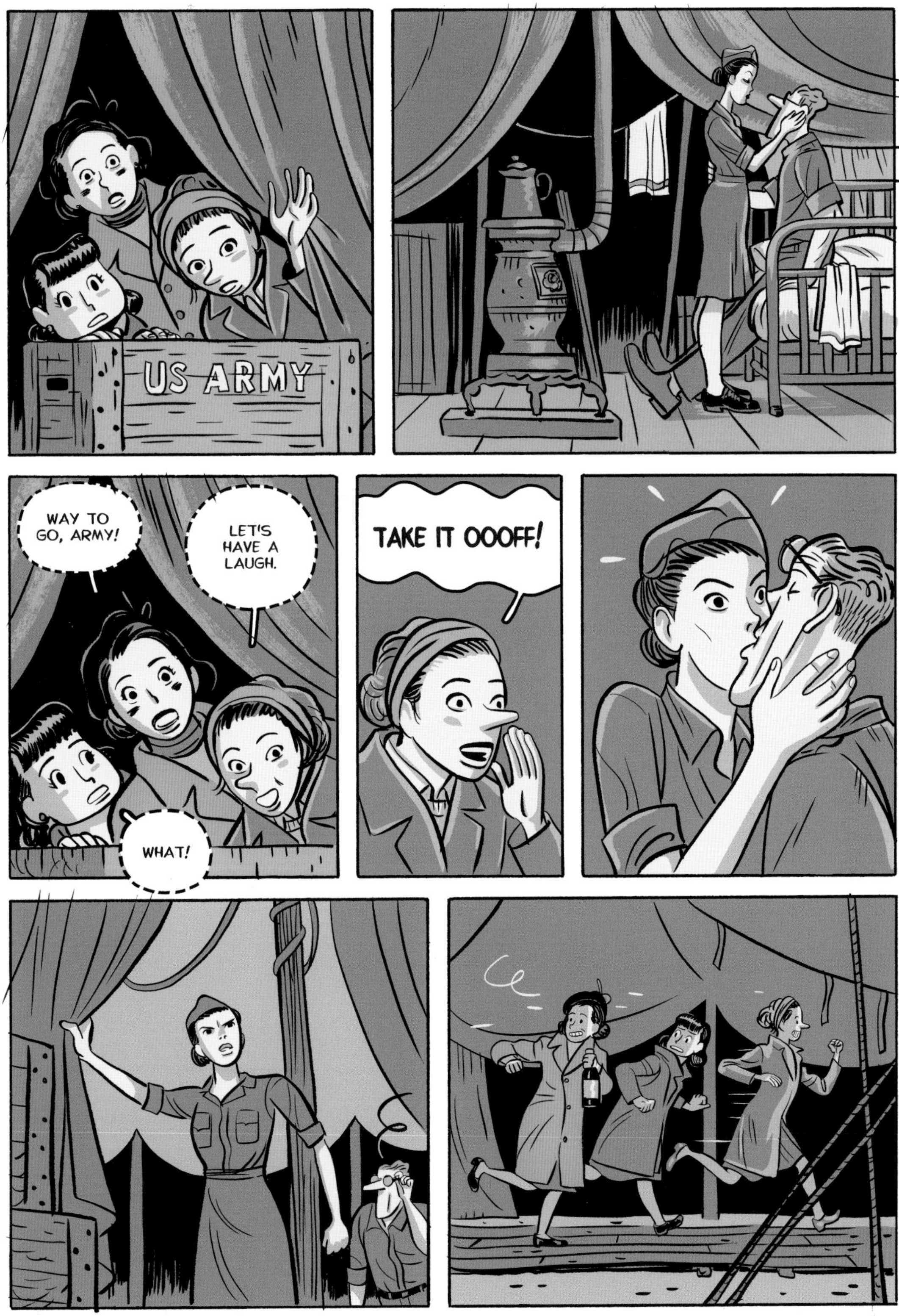
US ARMY
WAY TO GO, ARMY!
LET'S HAVE A LAUGH.
WHAT!
TAKE IT OOOFF!

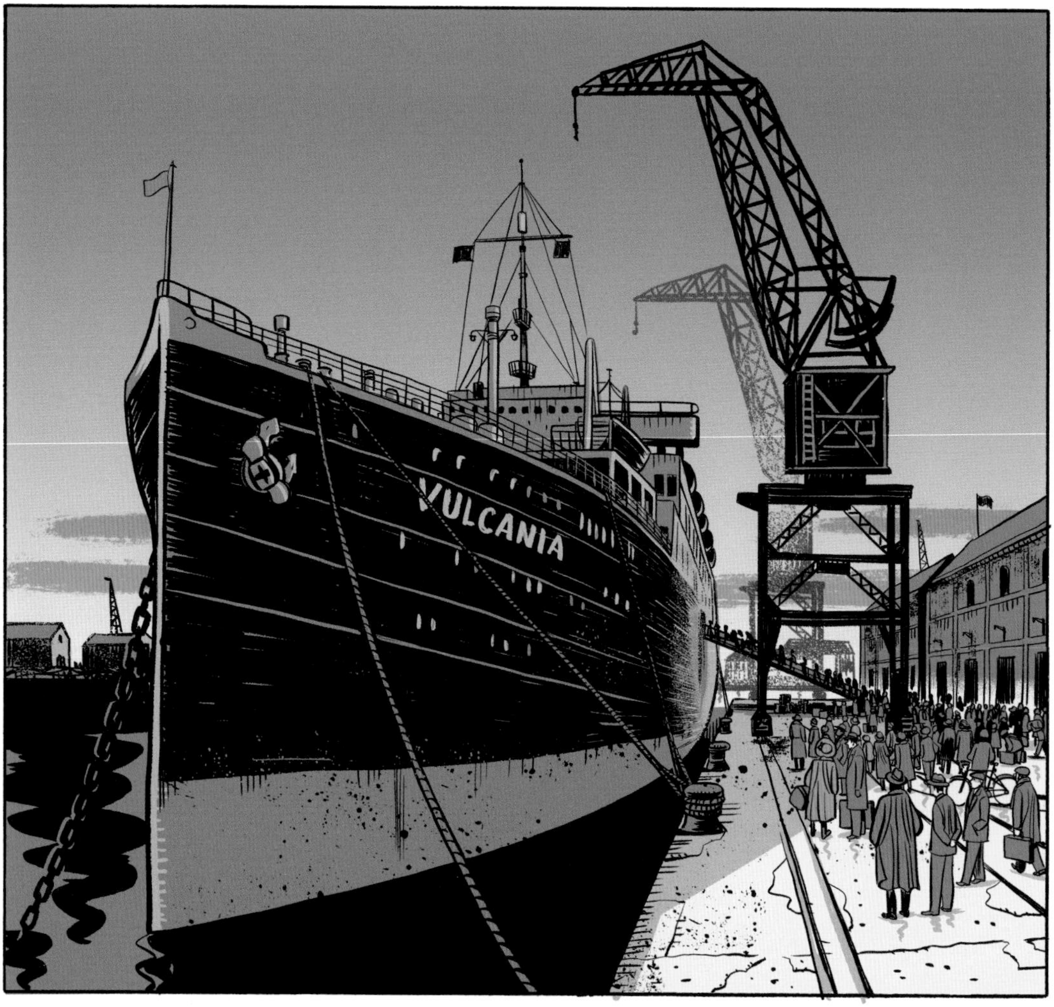
VULCANIA

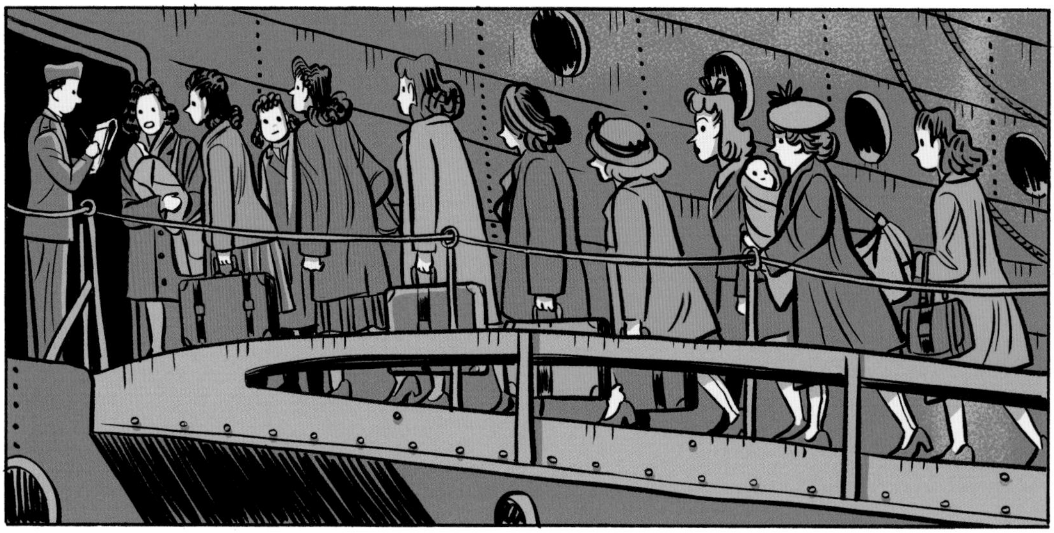

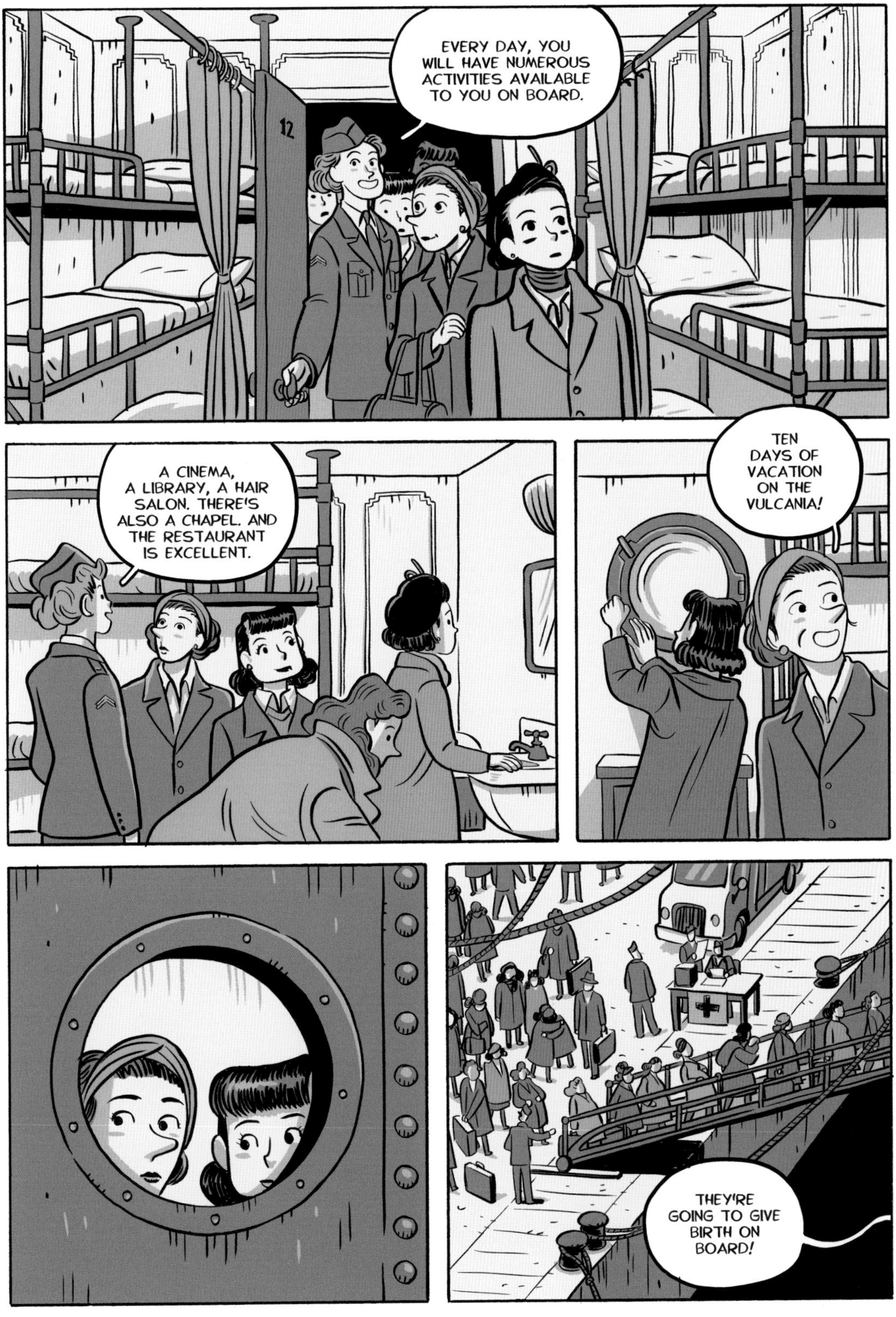

EVERY DAY, YOU WILL HAVE NUMEROUS ACTIVITIES AVAILABLE TO YOU ON BOARD.
12
A CINEMA, A LIBRARY, A HAIR SALON. THERE'S ALSO A CHAPEL. AND THE RESTAURANT IS EXCELLENT.
TEN DAYS OF VACATION ON THE VULCANIA!
THEY'RE GOING TO GIVE BIRTH ON BOARD!

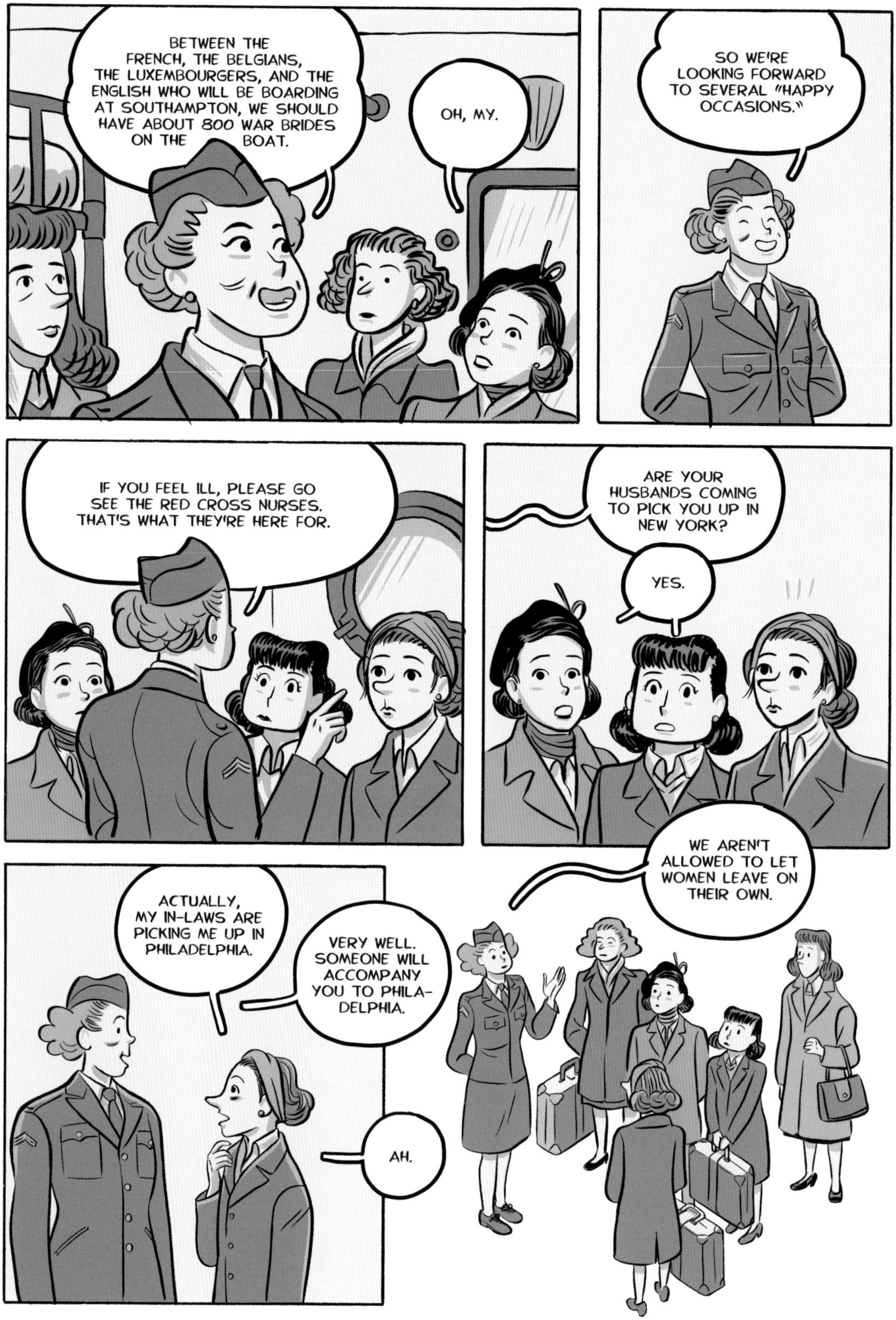
BETWEEN THE FRENCH, THE BELGIANS, THE LUXEMBOURGERS, AND THE ENGLISH WHO WILL BE BOARDING AT SOUTHAMPTON, WE SHOULD HAVE ABOUT 800 WAR BRIDES ON THE BOAT.
OH, MY.
SO WE'RE LOOKING FORWARD TO SEVERAL "HAPPY OCCASIONS."
IF YOU FEEL ILL, PLEASE GO SEE THE RED CROSS NURSES. THAT'S WHAT THEY'RE HERE FOR.
ARE YOUR HUSBANDS COMING TO PICK YOU UP IN NEW YORK?
YES.
ACTUALLY, MY IN-LAWS ARE PICKING ME UP IN PHILADELPHIA.
VERY WELL. SOMEONE WILL ACCOMPANY YOU TO PHILA-DELPHIA.
AH.
WE AREN'T ALLOWED TO LET WOMEN LEAVE ON THEIR OWN.

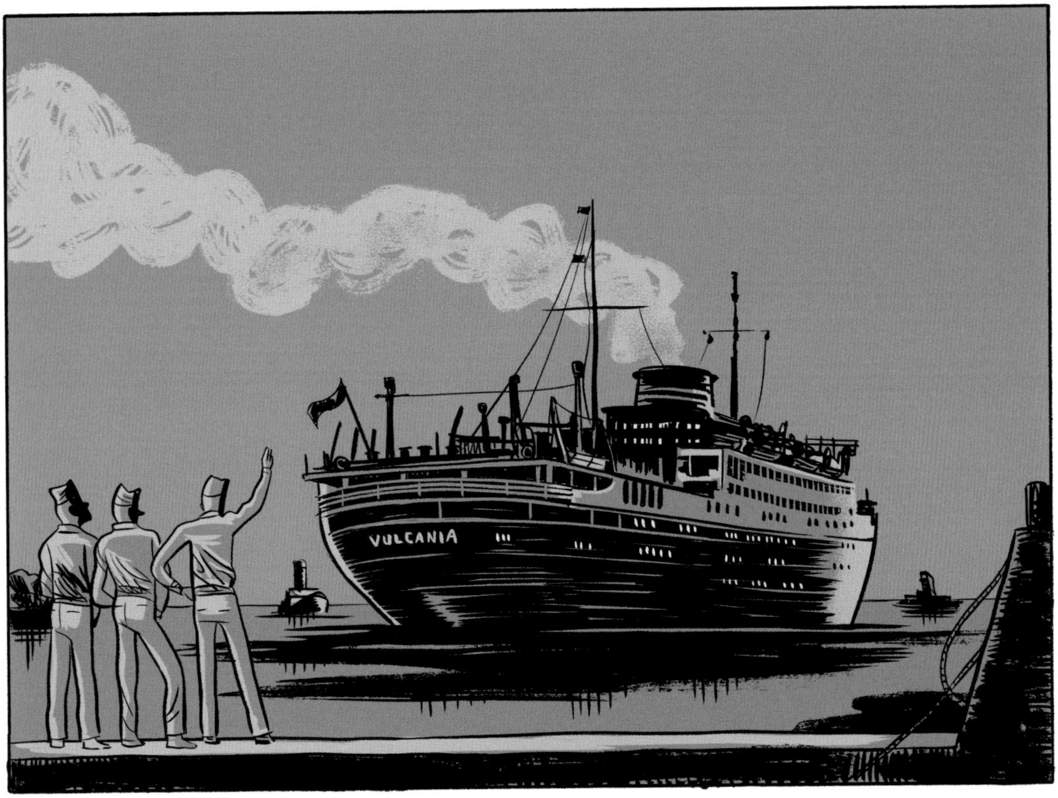
VULCANIA

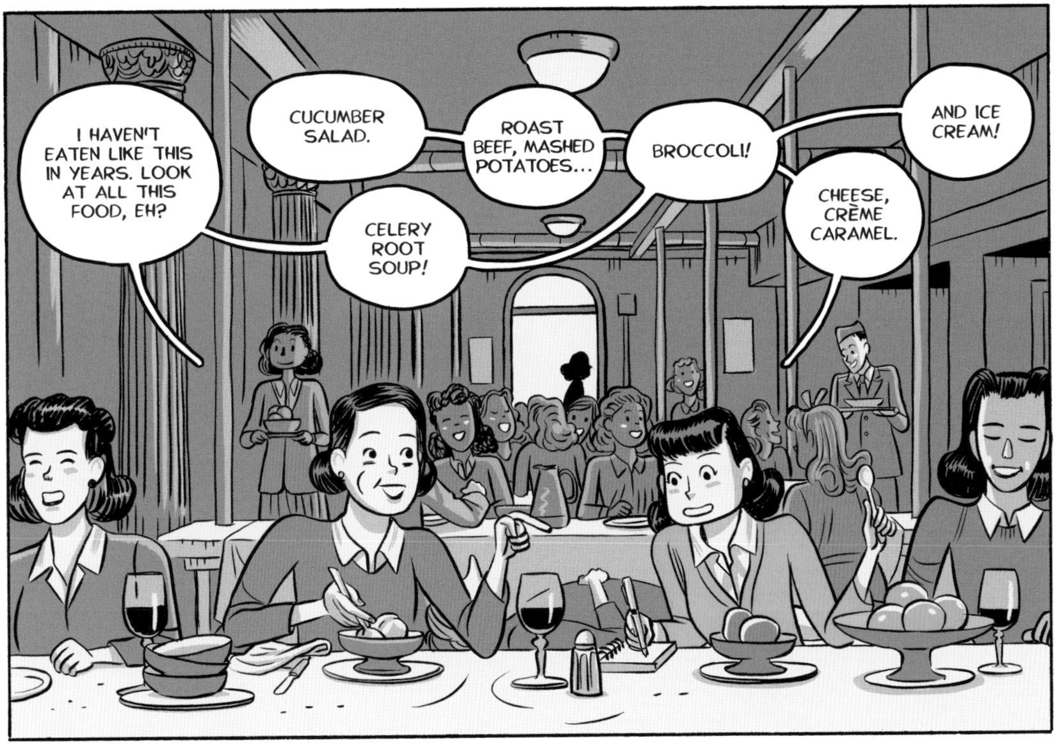
I HAVEN'T EATEN LIKE THIS IN YEARS. LOOK AT ALL THIS FOOD, EH?
CUCUMBER SALAD.
CELERY ROOT SOUP!
ROAST BEEF, MASHED POTATOES...
BROCCOLI!
AND ICE CREAM!
CHEESE, CRÈME CARAMEL.

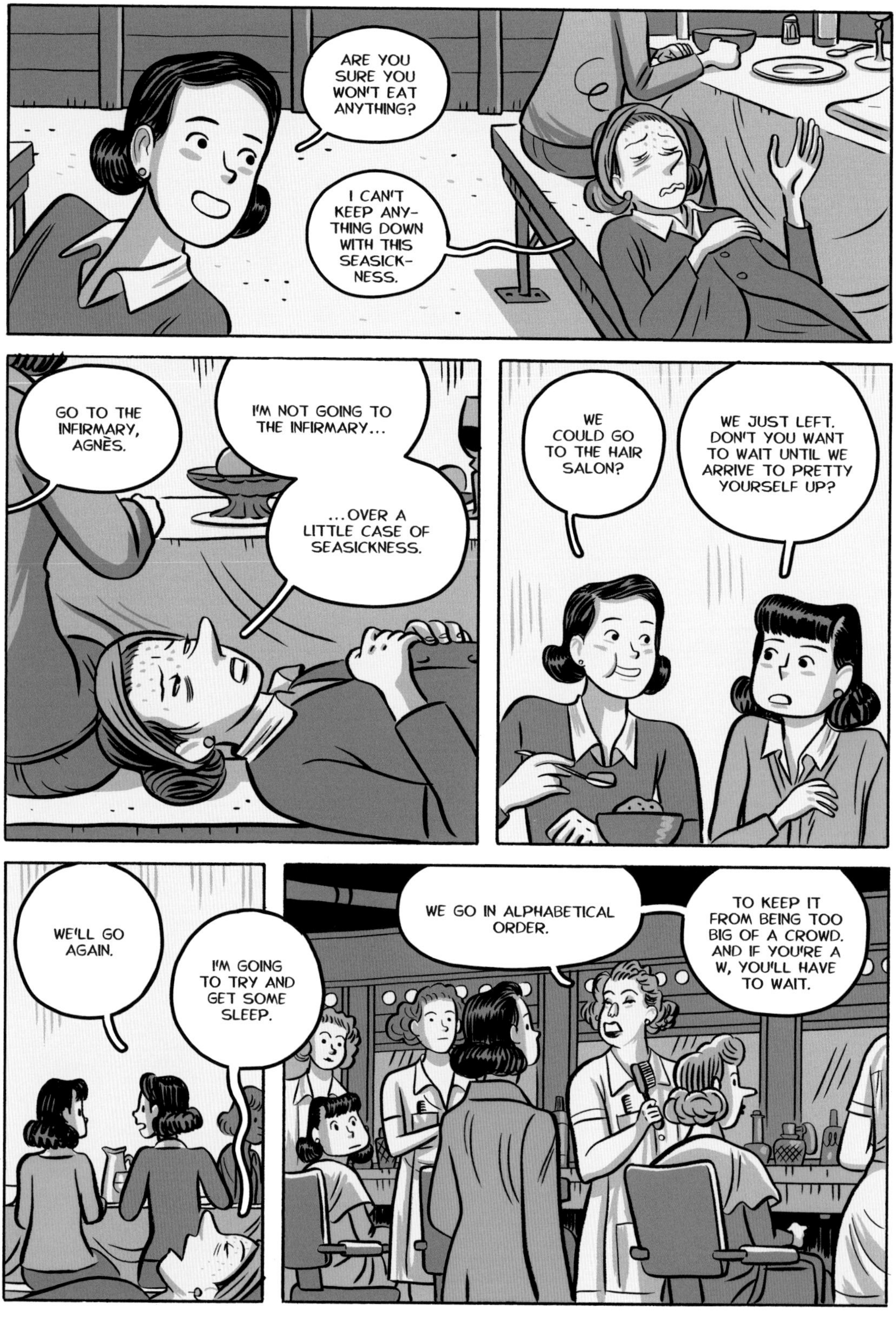
ARE YOU SURE YOU WON'T EAT ANYTHING?
I CAN'T KEEP ANY-THING DOWN WITH THIS SEASICK-NESS.
GO TO THE INFIRMARY, AGNÈS.
I'M NOT GOING TO THE INFIRMARY...
...OVER A LITTLE CASE OF SEASICKNESS.
WE COULD GO TO THE HAIR SALON?
WE JUST LEFT. DON'T YOU WANT TO WAIT UNTIL WE ARRIVE TO PRETTY YOURSELF UP?
WE'LL GO AGAIN.
I'M GOING TO TRY AND GET SOME SLEEP.
WE GO IN ALPHABETICAL ORDER.
TO KEEP IT FROM BEING TOO BIG OF A CROWD. AND IF YOU'RE A W, YOU'LL HAVE TO WAIT.

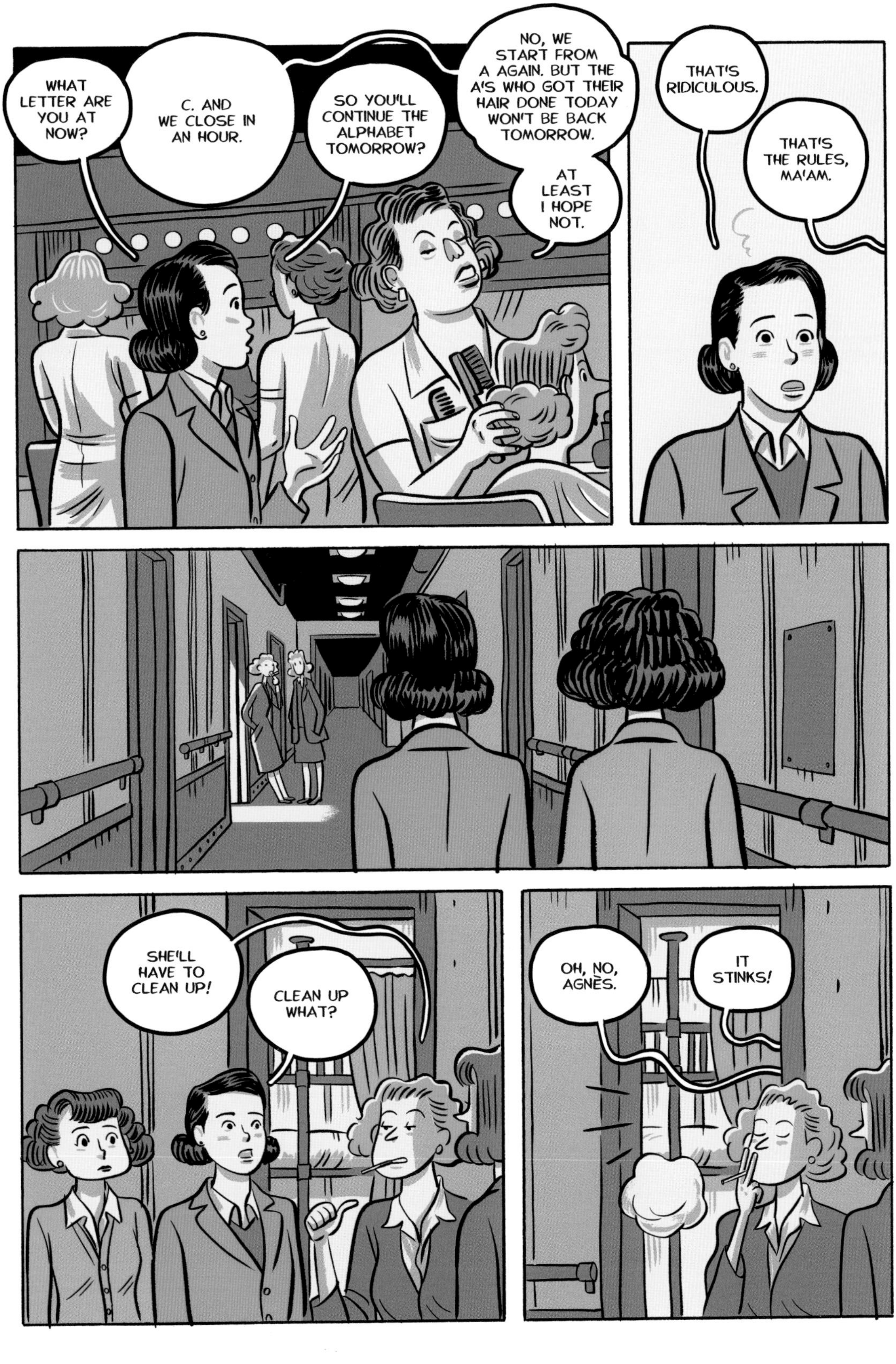
WHAT LETTER ARE YOU AT NOW?
C. AND WE CLOSE IN AN HOUR.
SO YOU'LL CONTINUE THE ALPHABET TOMORROW?
NO, WE START FROM A AGAIN. BUT THE A'S WHO GOT THEIR HAIR DONE TODAY WON'T BE BACK TOMORROW.
AT LEAST I HOPE NOT.
THAT'S RIDICULOUS.
THAT'S THE RULES, MA'AM.
SHE'LL HAVE TO CLEAN UP!
CLEAN UP WHAT?
OH, NO, AGNÈS.
IT STINKS!

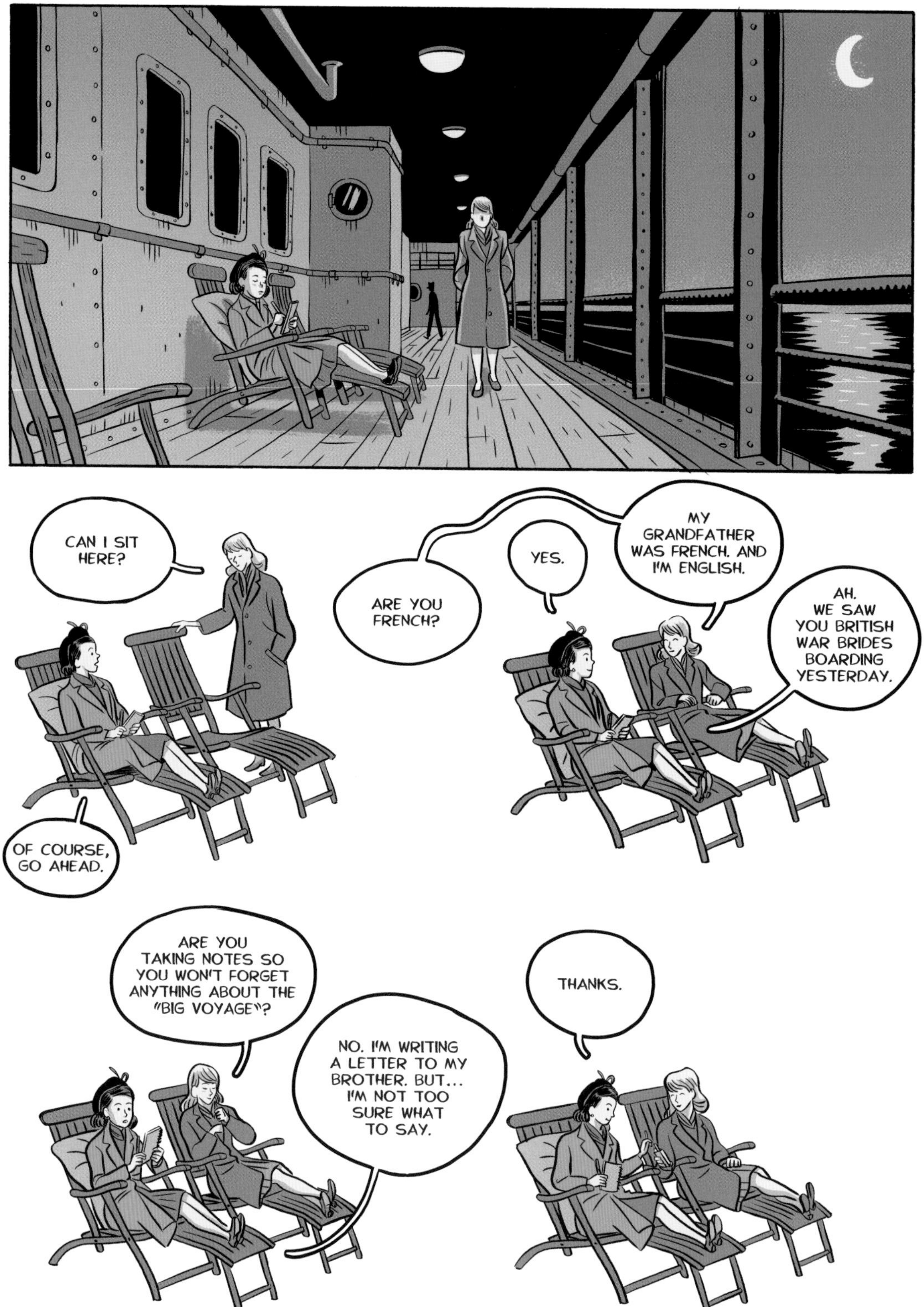
CAN I SIT HERE?
OF COURSE, GO AHEAD.
ARE YOU FRENCH?
YES.
MY GRANDFATHER WAS FRENCH. AND I'M ENGLISH.
AH. WE SAW YOU BRITISH WAR BRIDES BOARDING YESTERDAY.
ARE YOU TAKING NOTES SO YOU WON'T FORGET ANYTHING ABOUT THE "BIG VOYAGE"?
NO. I'M WRITING A LETTER TO MY BROTHER. BUT... I'M NOT TOO SURE WHAT TO SAY.
THANKS.

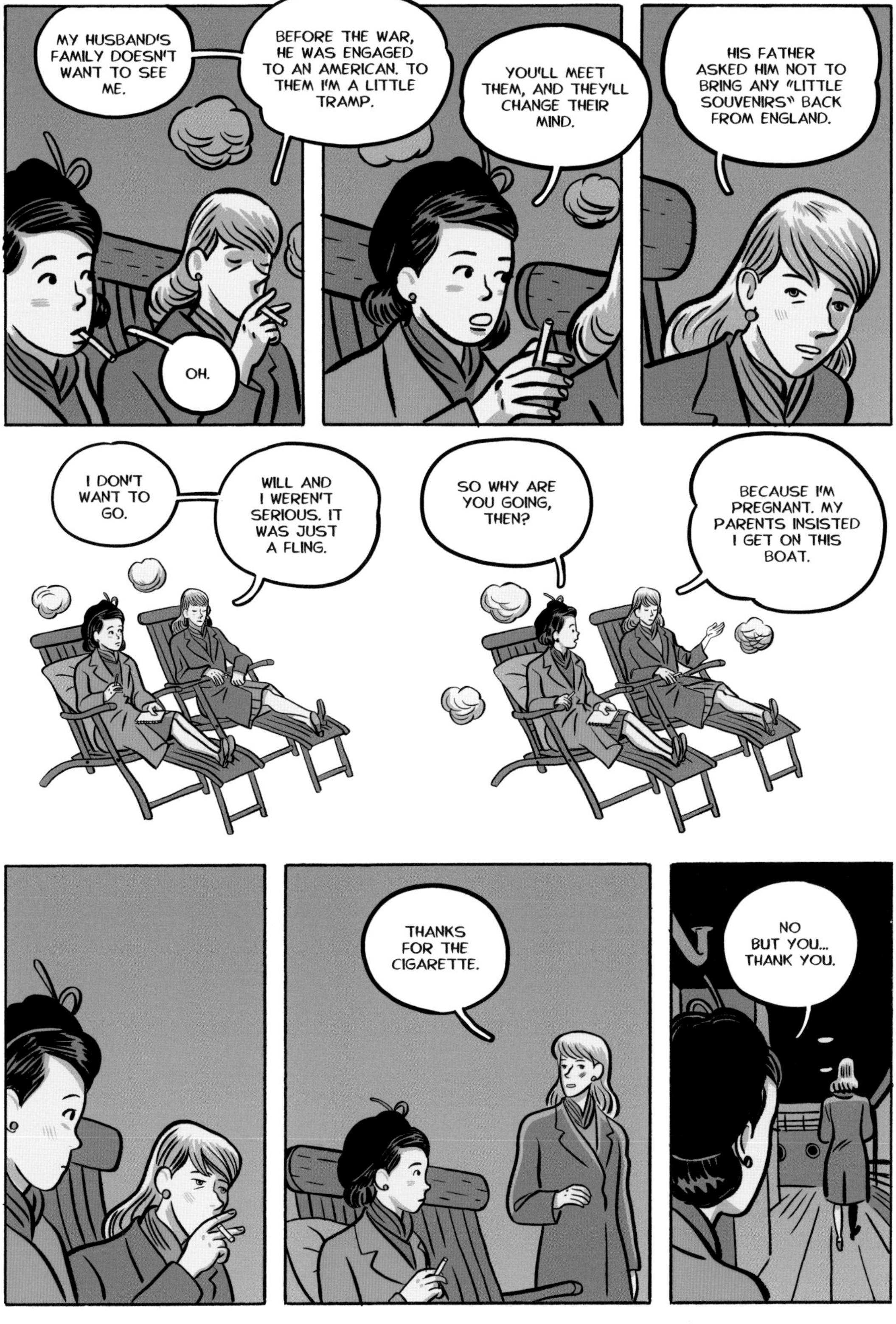
MY HUSBAND'S FAMILY DOESN'T WANT TO SEE ME.
BEFORE THE WAR, HE WAS ENGAGED TO AN AMERICAN. TO THEM I'M A LITTLE TRAMP.
OH.
YOU'LL MEET THEM, AND THEY'LL CHANGE THEIR MIND.
HIS FATHER ASKED HIM NOT TO BRING ANY "LITTLE SOUVENIRS" BACK FROM ENGLAND.
I DON'T WANT TO GO.
WILL AND I WEREN'T SERIOUS. IT WAS JUST A FLING.
SO WHY ARE YOU GOING, THEN?
BECAUSE I'M PREGNANT. MY PARENTS INSISTED I GET ON THIS BOAT.
THANKS FOR THE CIGARETTE.
NO BUT YOU... THANK YOU.

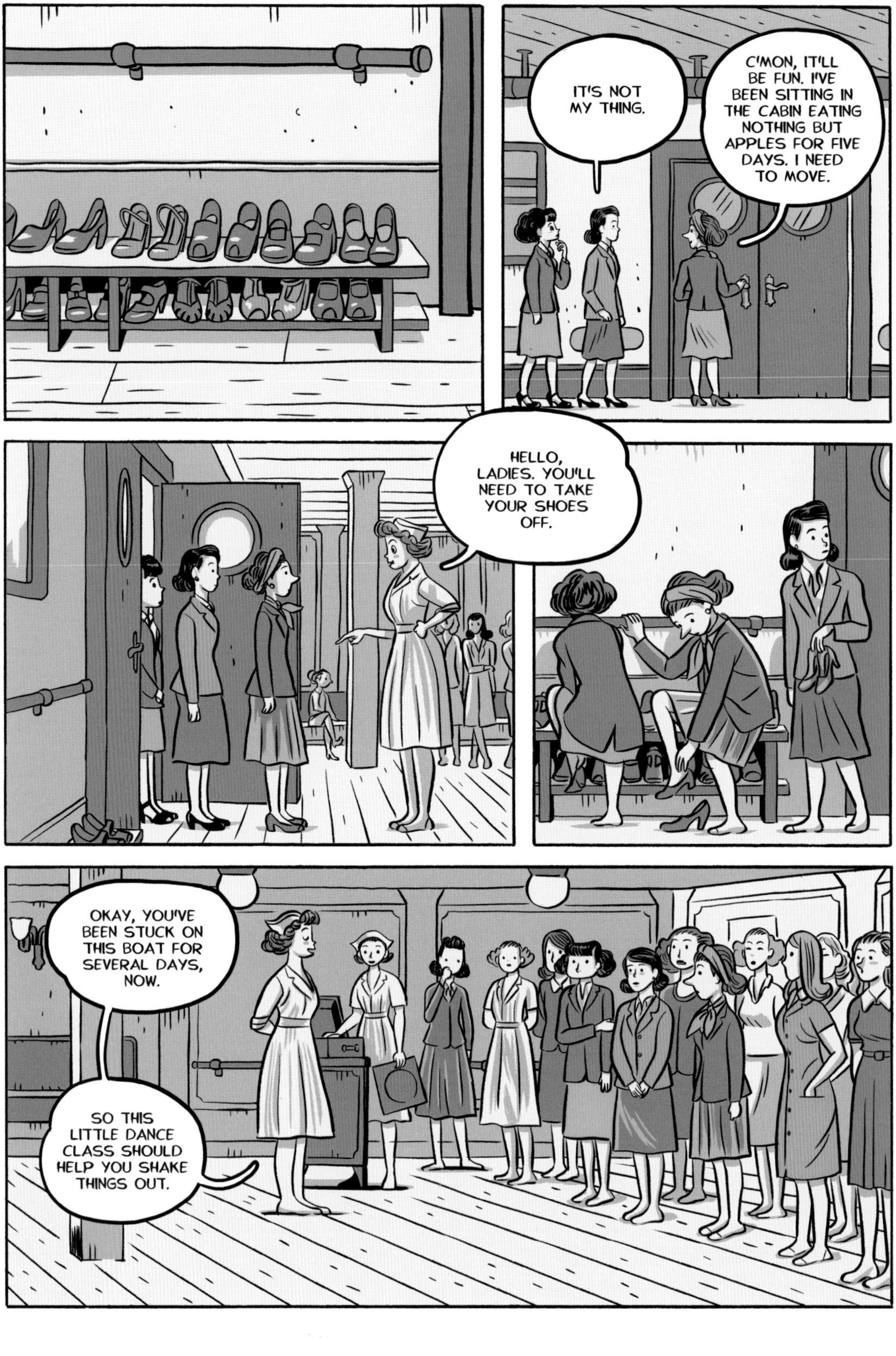
IT'S NOT MY THING.
C'MON, IT'LL BE FUN. I'VE BEEN SITTING IN THE CABIN EATING NOTHING BUT APPLES FOR FIVE DAYS. I NEED TO MOVE.
HELLO, LADIES. YOU'LL NEED TO TAKE YOUR SHOES OFF.
OKAY, YOU'VE BEEN STUCK ON THIS BOAT FOR SEVERAL DAYS, NOW.
SO THIS LITTLE DANCE CLASS SHOULD HELP YOU SHAKE THINGS OUT.

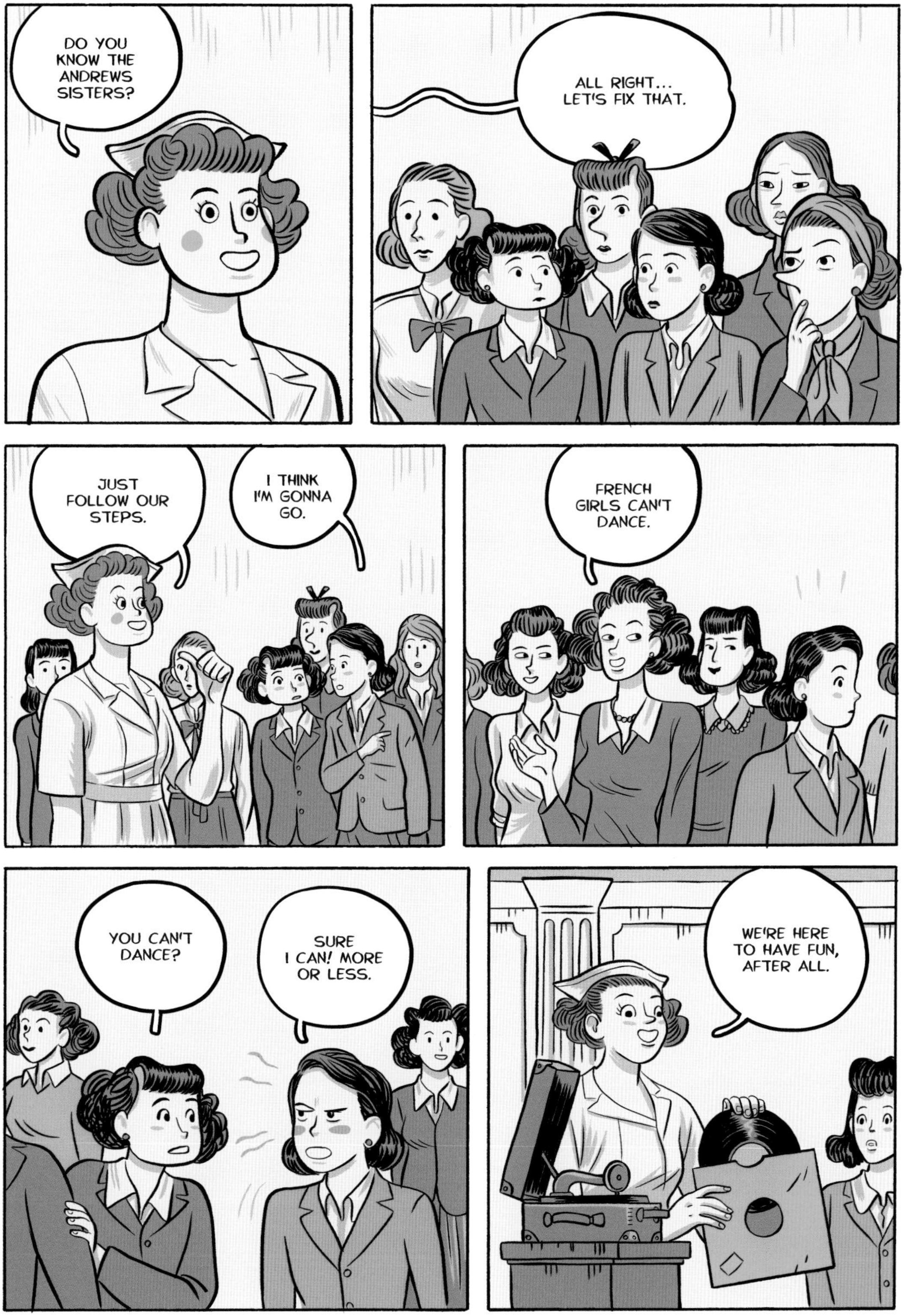
DO YOU KNOW THE ANDREWS SISTERS?
ALL RIGHT... LET'S FIX THAT.
JUST FOLLOW OUR STEPS.
I THINK I'M GONNA GO.
FRENCH GIRLS CAN'T DANCE.
YOU CAN'T DANCE?
SURE I CAN! MORE OR LESS.
WE'RE HERE TO HAVE FUN, AFTER ALL.

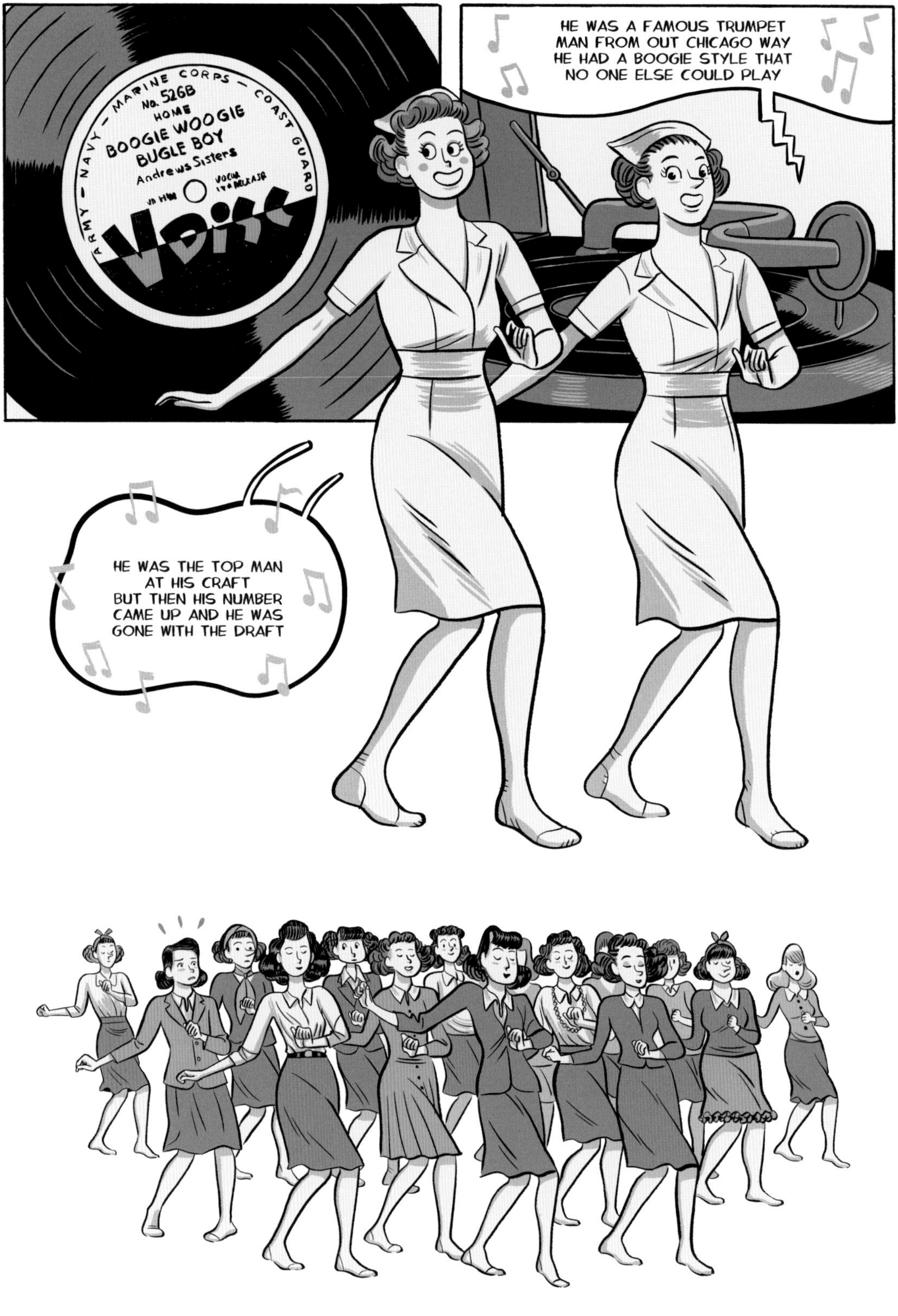

ARMY — NAVY — MARINE CORPS — COAST GUARD
No. 526B
HOME
BOOGIE WOOGIE BUGLE BOY
Andrews Sisters
V DISC
HE WAS A FAMOUS TRUMPET MAN FROM OUT CHICAGO WAY HE HAD A BOOGIE STYLE THAT NO ONE ELSE COULD PLAY
HE WAS THE TOP MAN AT HIS CRAFT BUT THEN HIS NUMBER CAME UP AND HE WAS GONE WITH THE DRAFT

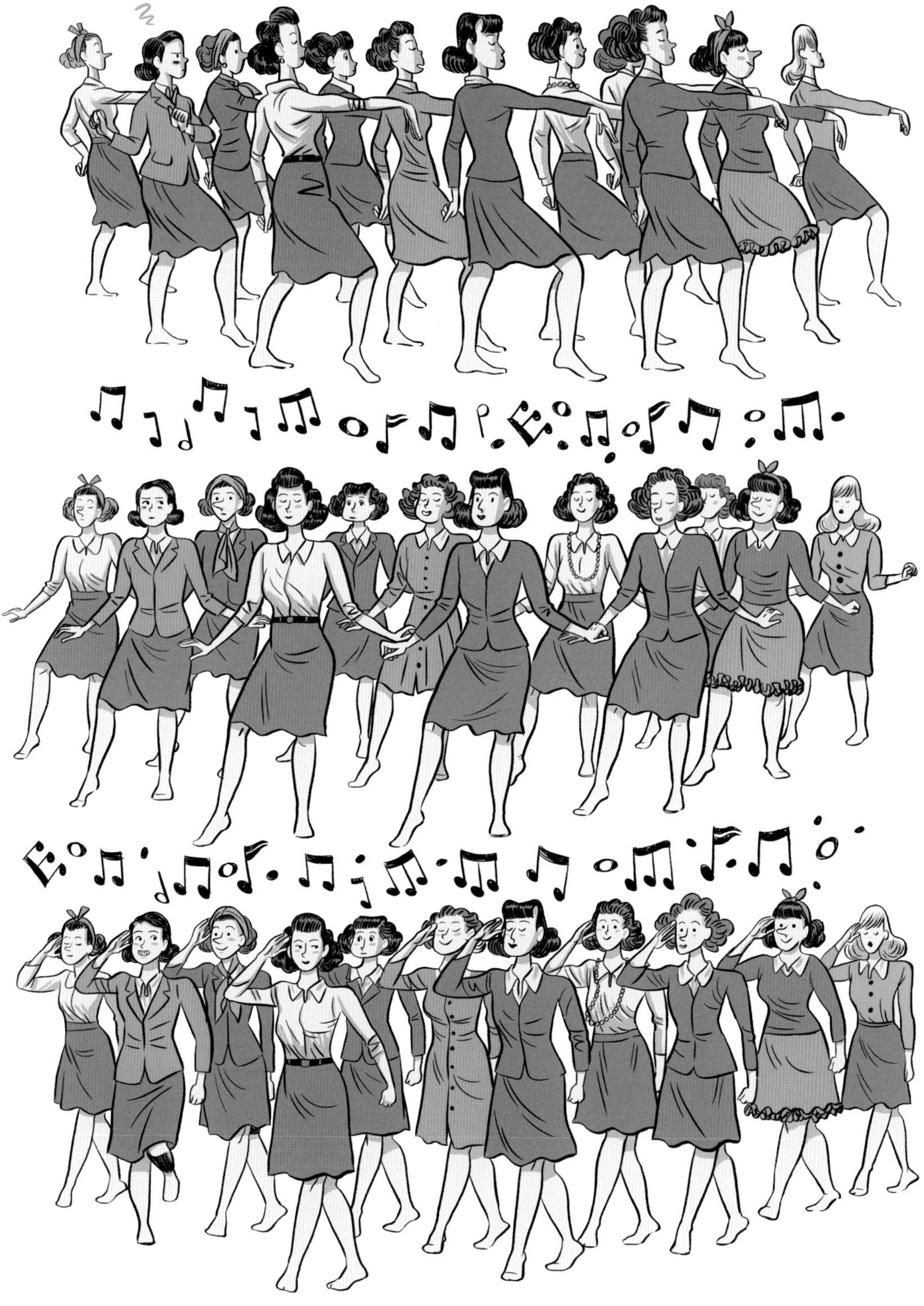

THEY CLAP ♪♪ THEIR HANDS AND STAMP THEIR FEET ♪♪ BECAUSE THEY KNOW HOW HE PLA

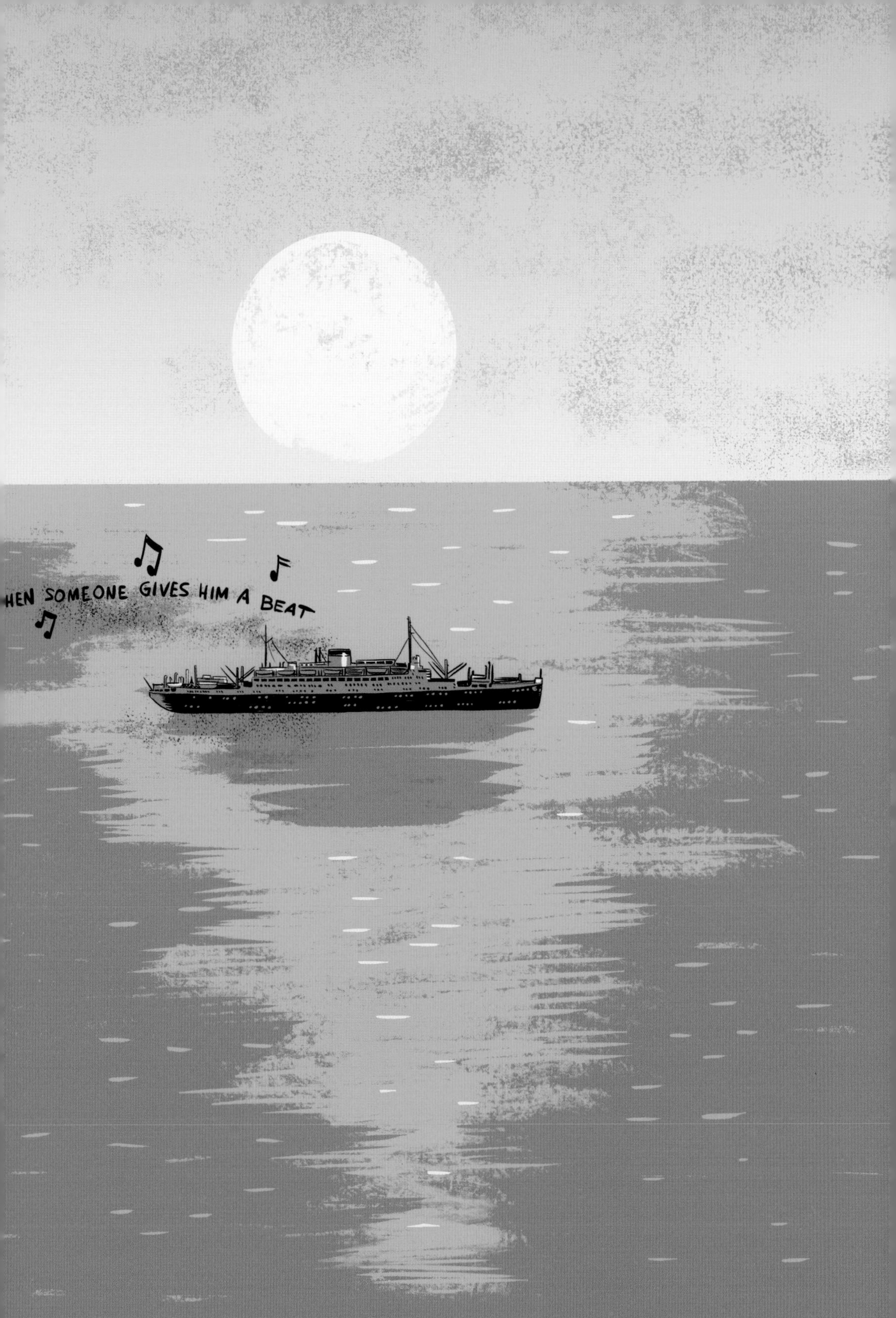
HEN SOMEONE GIVES HIM A BEAT

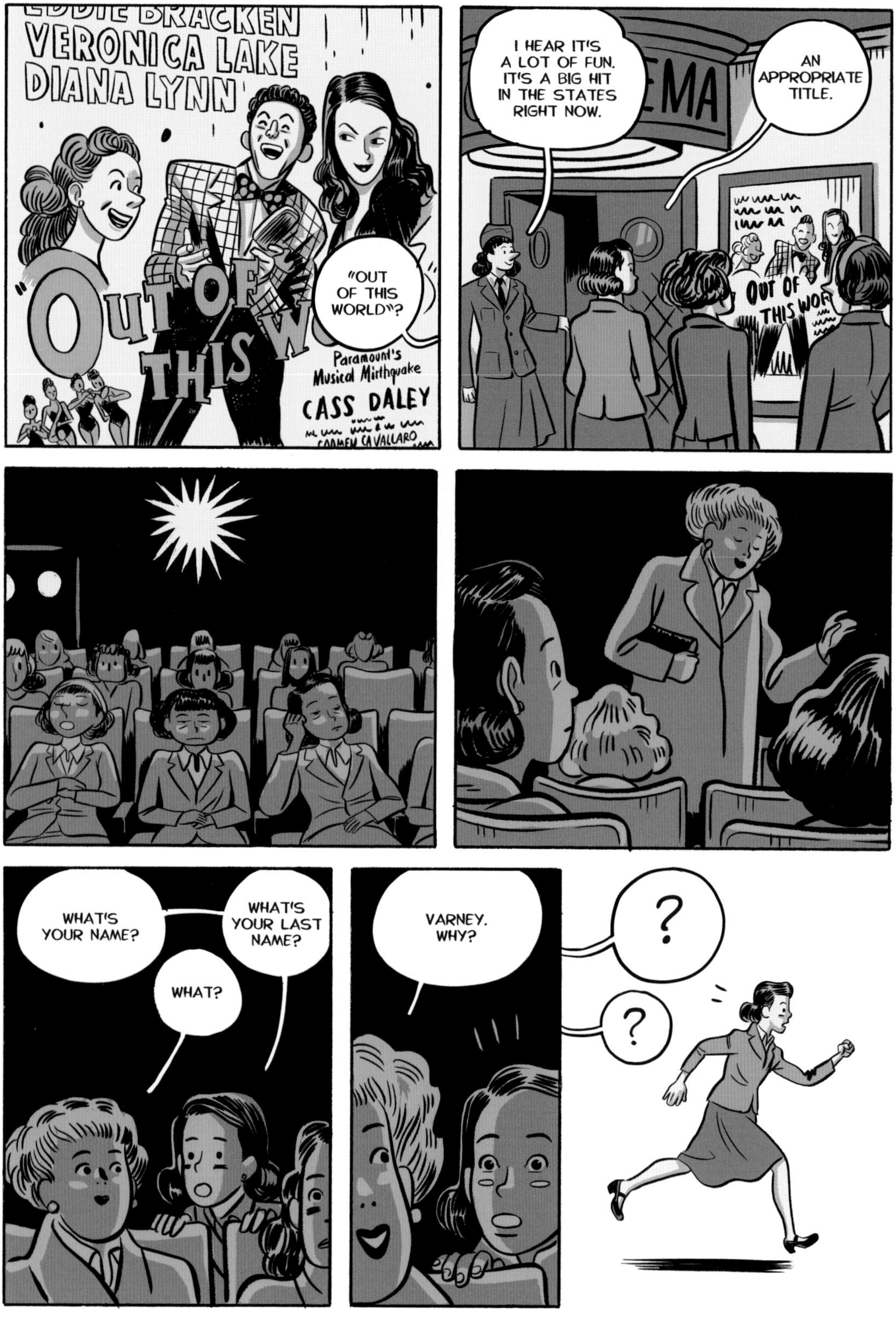
EDDIE BRACKEN
VERONICA LAKE
DIANA LYNN
"OUT OF THIS W
"OUT OF THIS WORLD"?
Paramount's Musical Mirthquake
CASS DALEY
CARMEN CAVALLARO
I HEAR IT'S A LOT OF FUN. IT'S A BIG HIT IN THE STATES RIGHT NOW.
AN APPROPRIATE TITLE.
EMA
OUT OF THIS WOR
WHAT'S YOUR NAME?
WHAT'S YOUR LAST NAME?
WHAT?
VARNEY. WHY?
?
?

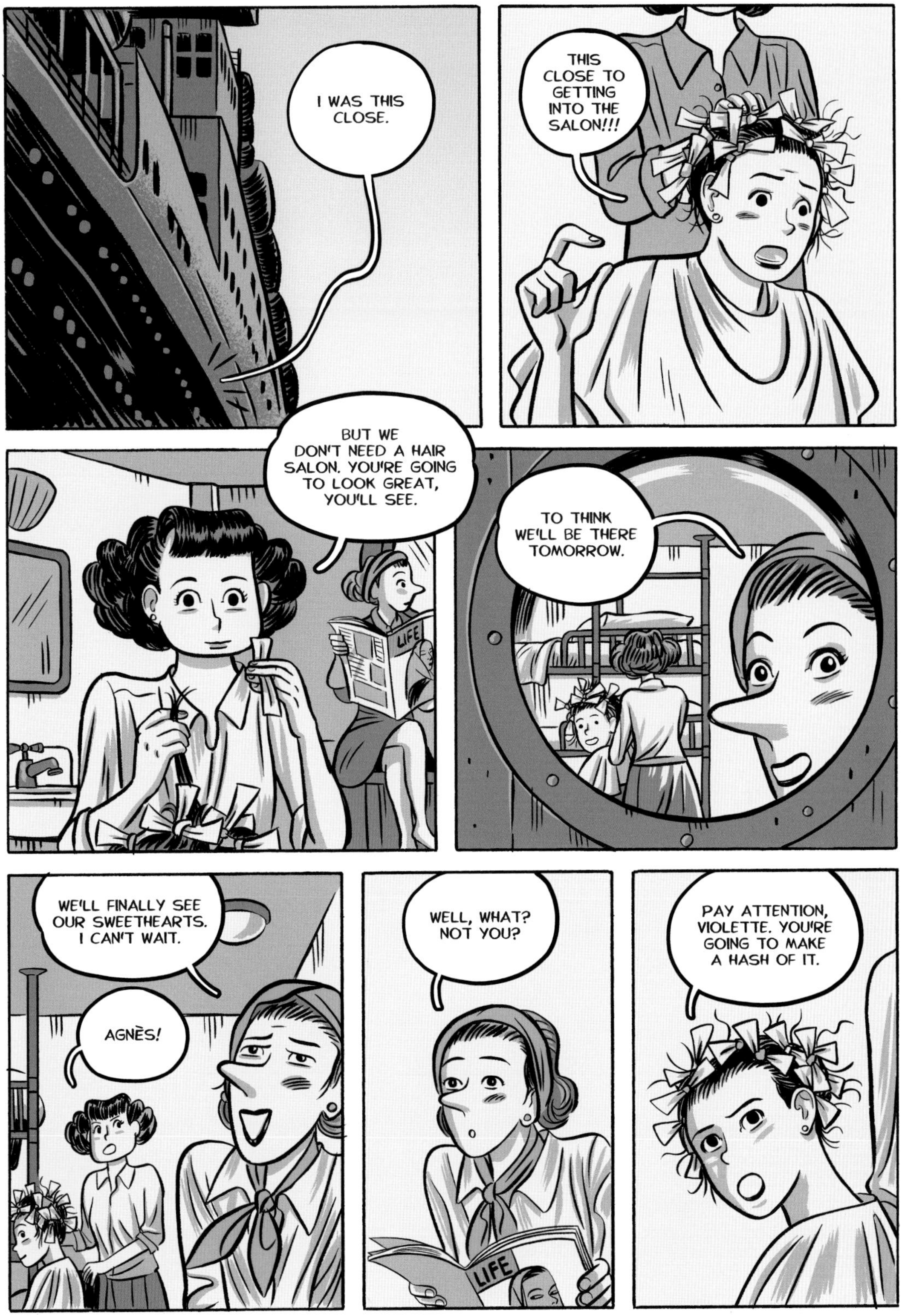
I WAS THIS CLOSE.
THIS CLOSE TO GETTING INTO THE SALON!!!
BUT WE DON'T NEED A HAIR SALON. YOU'RE GOING TO LOOK GREAT, YOU'LL SEE.
LIFE
TO THINK WE'LL BE THERE TOMORROW.
WE'LL FINALLY SEE OUR SWEETHEARTS. I CAN'T WAIT.
AGNÈS!
WELL, WHAT? NOT YOU?
LIFE
PAY ATTENTION, VIOLETTE. YOU'RE GOING TO MAKE A HASH OF IT.

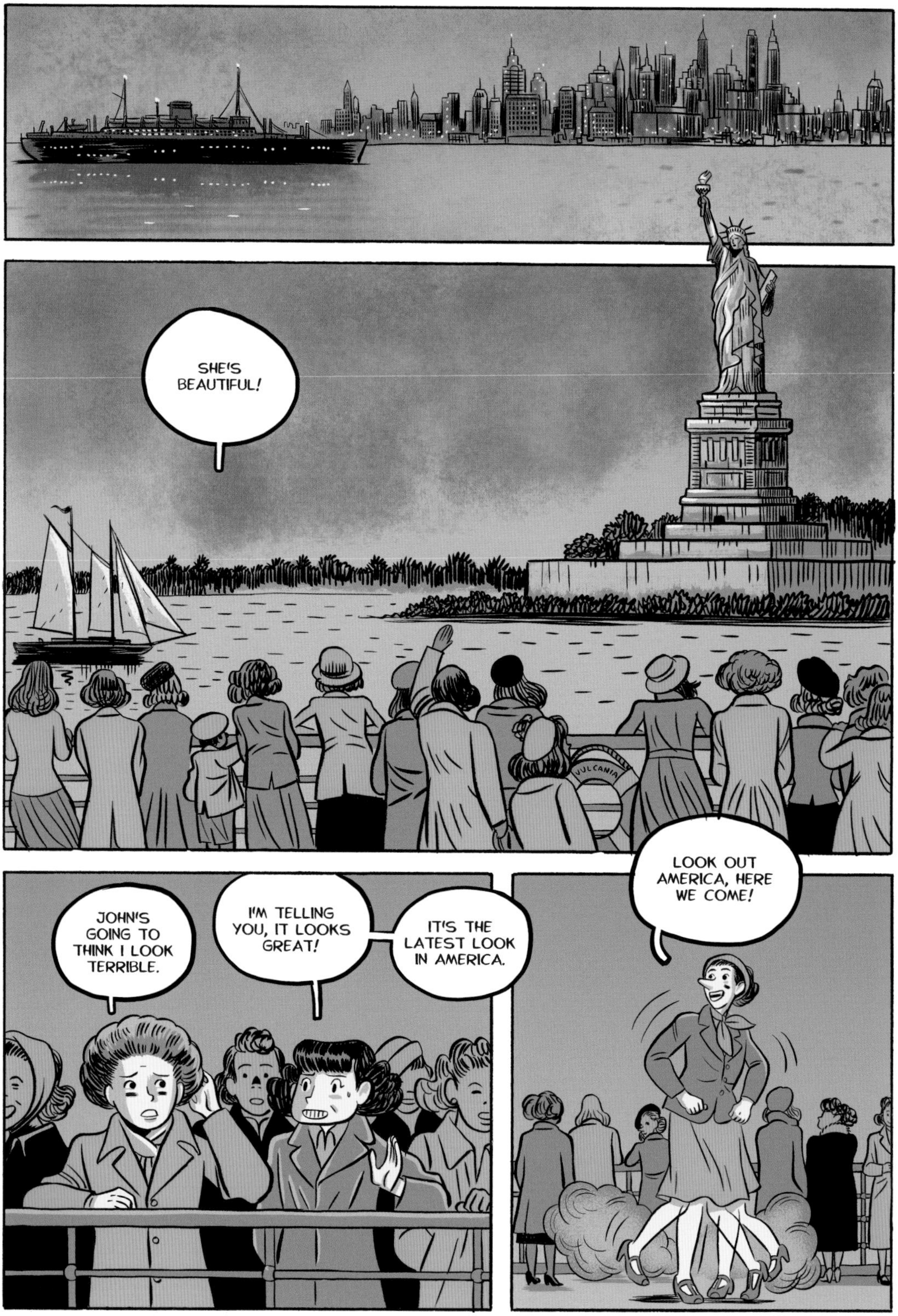
SHE'S BEAUTIFUL!
VULCANIA
JOHN'S GOING TO THINK I LOOK TERRIBLE.
I'M TELLING YOU, IT LOOKS GREAT!
IT'S THE LATEST LOOK IN AMERICA.
LOOK OUT AMERICA, HERE WE COME!

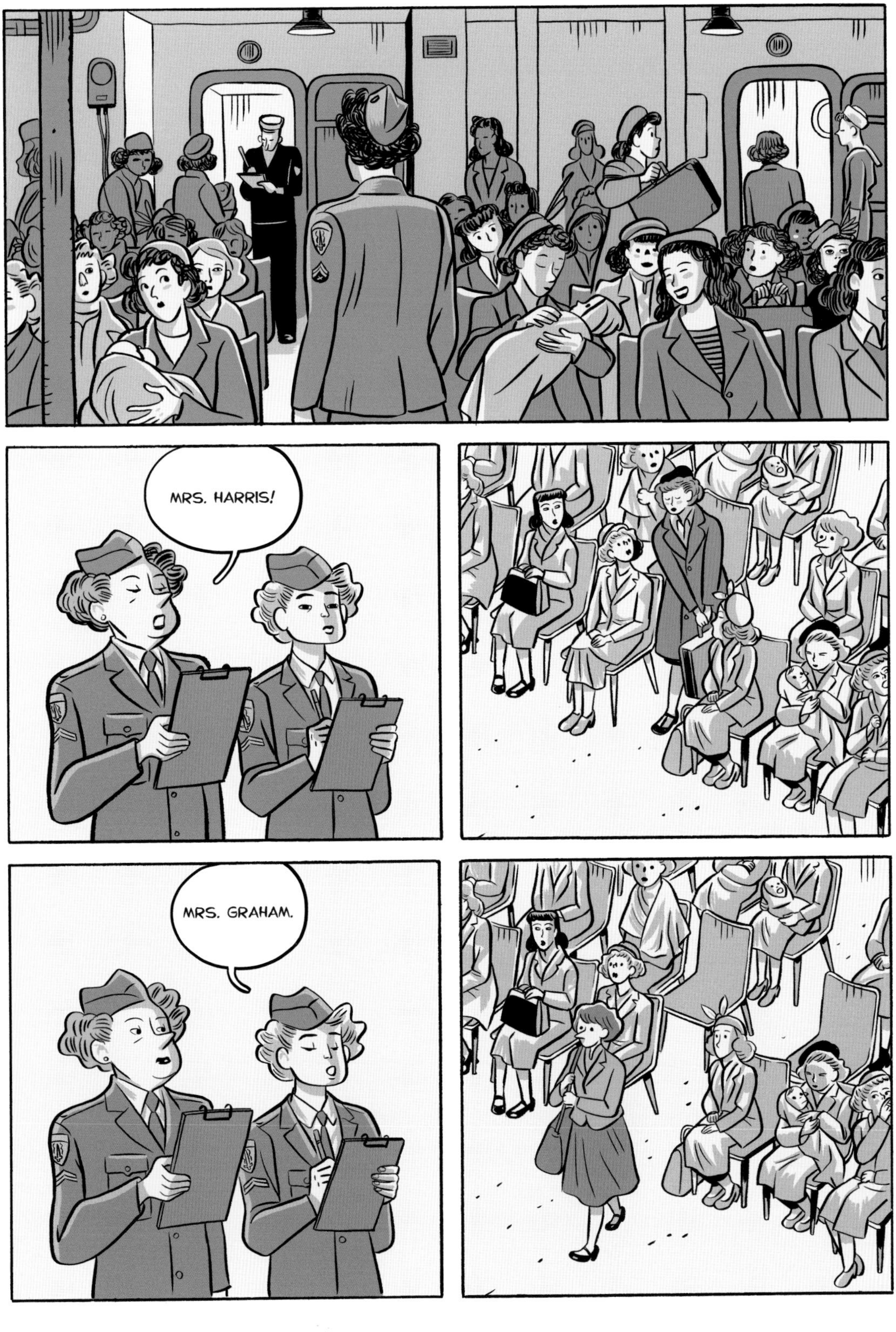
MRS. HARRIS!
MRS. GRAHAM.

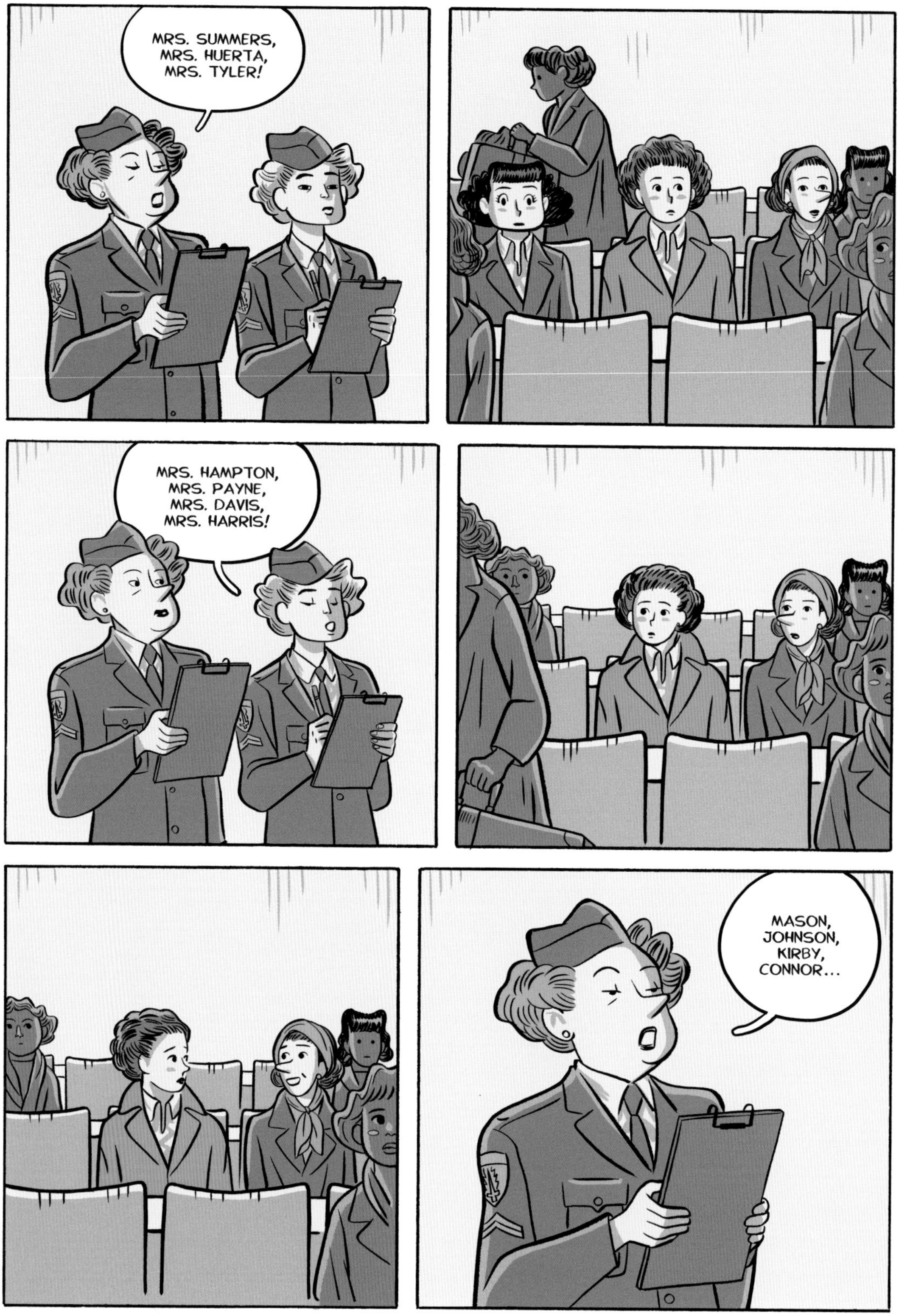
MRS. SUMMERS,
MRS. HUERTA,
MRS. TYLER!
MRS. HAMPTON,
MRS. PAYNE,
MRS. DAVIS,
MRS. HARRIS!
MASON,
JOHNSON,
KIRBY,
CONNOR...

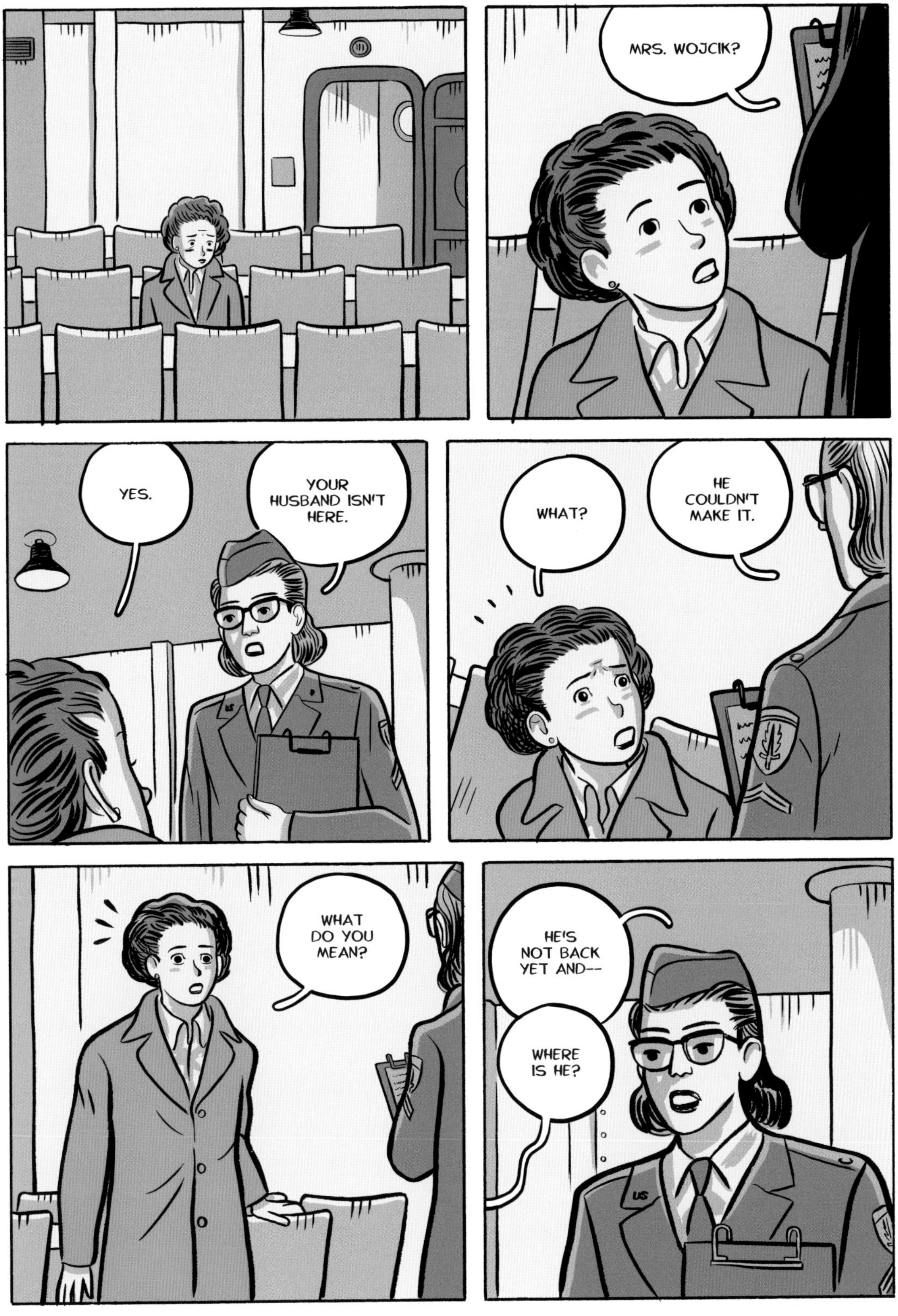
MRS. WOJCIK?
YES.
YOUR HUSBAND ISN'T HERE.
WHAT?
HE COULDN'T MAKE IT.
WHAT DO YOU MEAN?
HE'S NOT BACK YET AND--
WHERE IS HE?

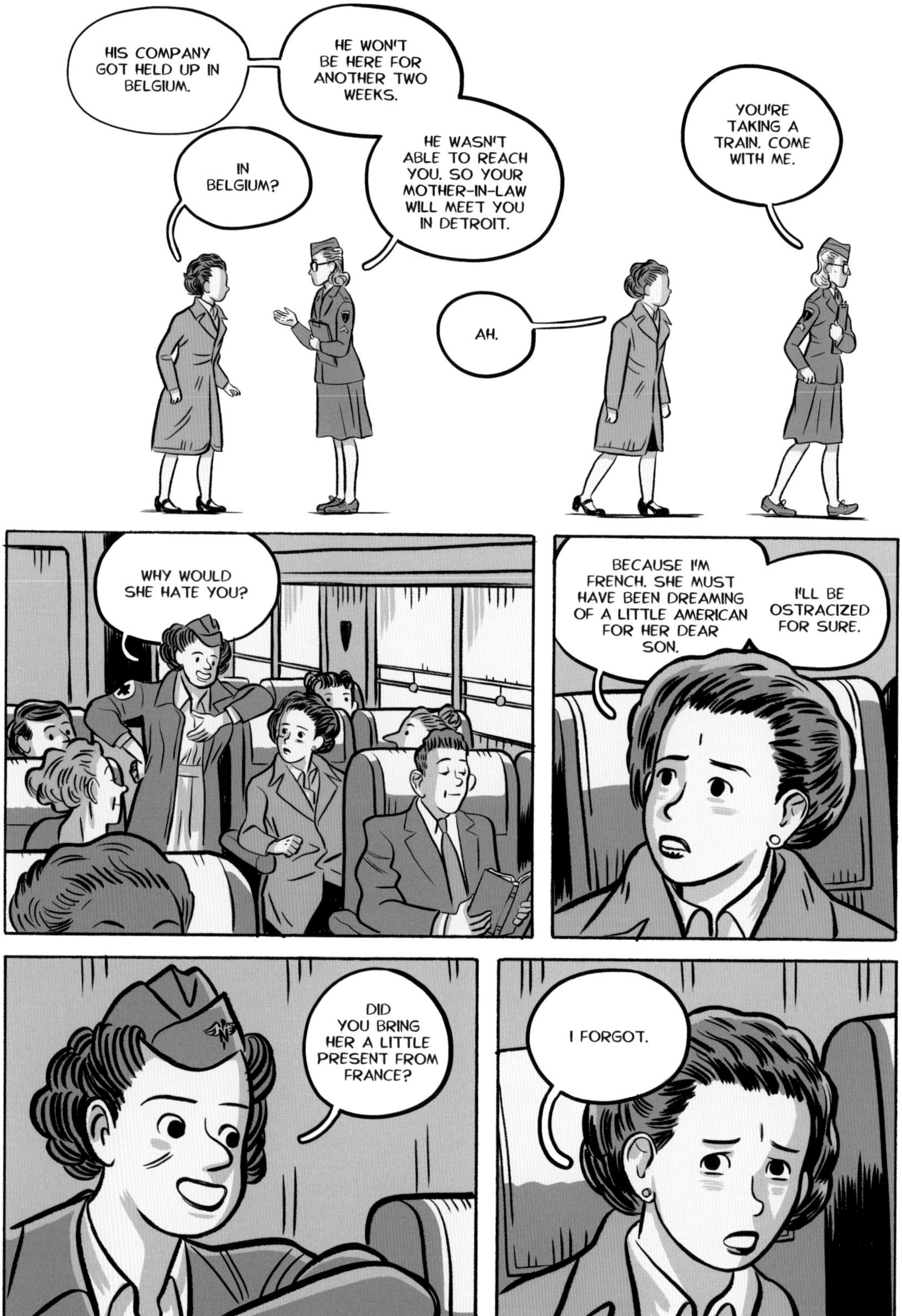
HIS COMPANY GOT HELD UP IN BELGIUM.
HE WON'T BE HERE FOR ANOTHER TWO WEEKS.
IN BELGIUM?
HE WASN'T ABLE TO REACH YOU. SO YOUR MOTHER-IN-LAW WILL MEET YOU IN DETROIT.
AH.
YOU'RE TAKING A TRAIN. COME WITH ME.
WHY WOULD SHE HATE YOU?
BECAUSE I'M FRENCH. SHE MUST HAVE BEEN DREAMING OF A LITTLE AMERICAN FOR HER DEAR SON.
I'LL BE OSTRACIZED FOR SURE.
DID YOU BRING HER A LITTLE PRESENT FROM FRANCE?
I FORGOT.

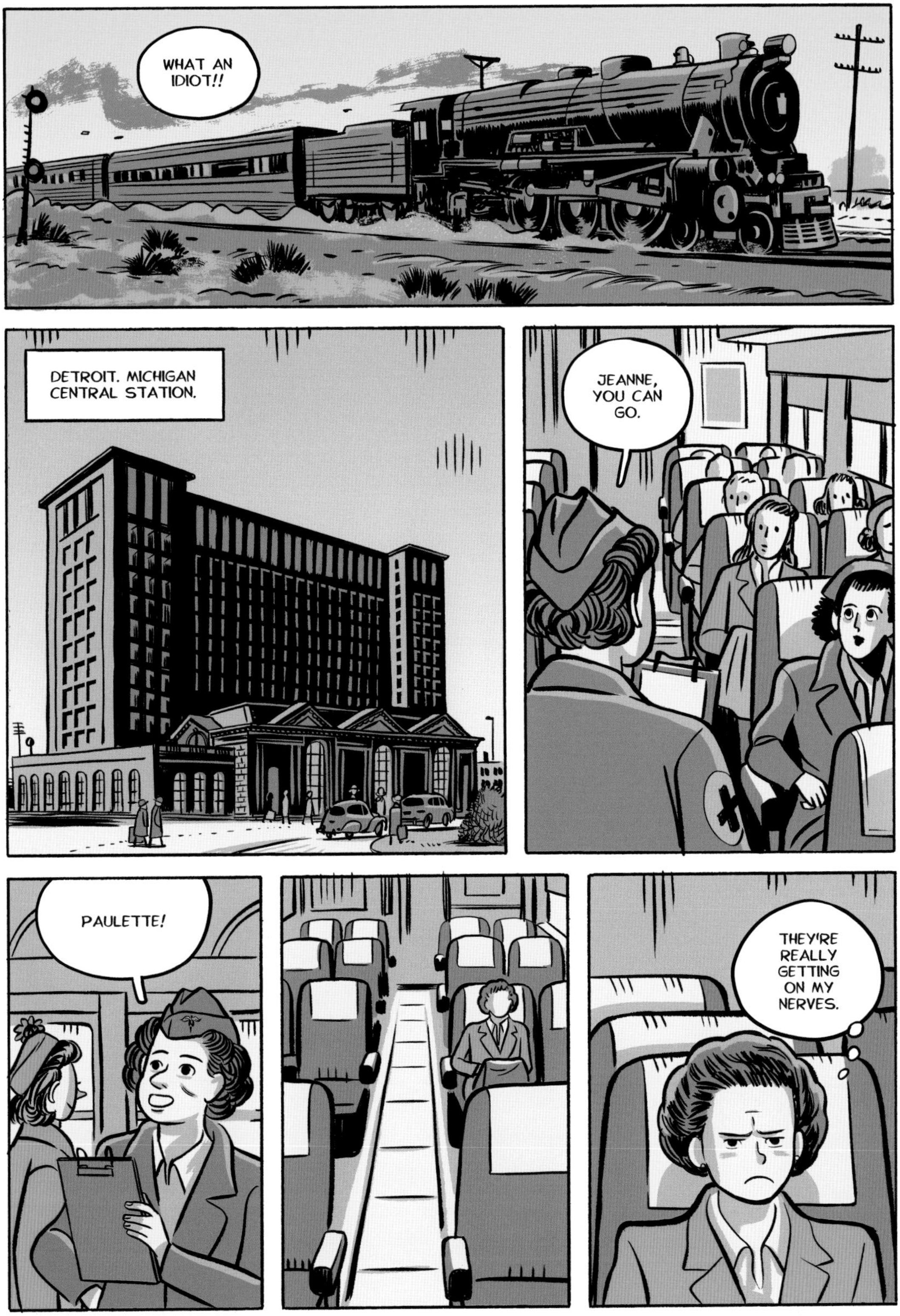
WHAT AN IDIOT!!
DETROIT. MICHIGAN CENTRAL STATION.
JEANNE, YOU CAN GO.
PAULETTE!
THEY'RE REALLY GETTING ON MY NERVES.

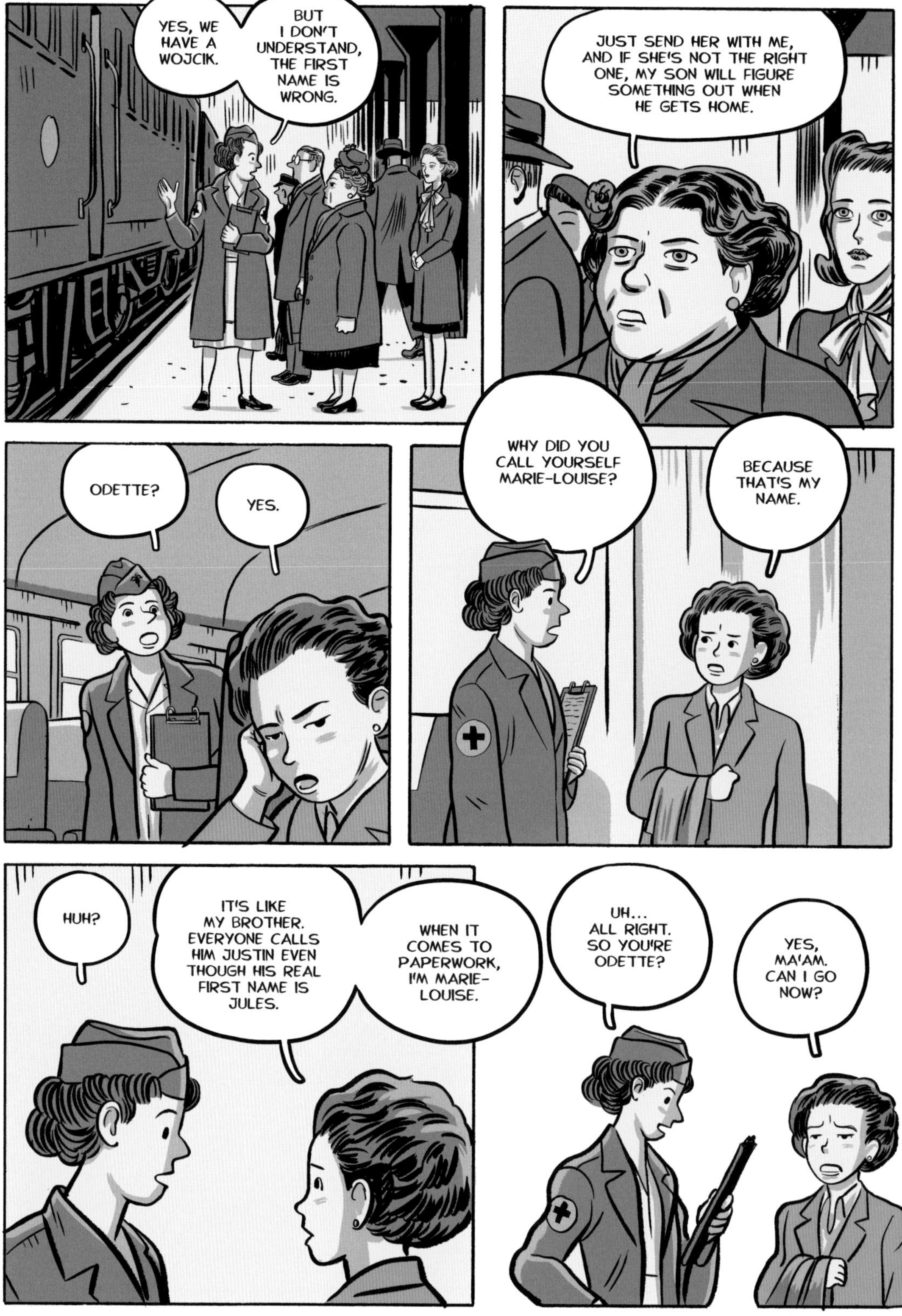
YES, WE HAVE A WOJCIK.
BUT I DON'T UNDERSTAND, THE FIRST NAME IS WRONG.
JUST SEND HER WITH ME, AND IF SHE'S NOT THE RIGHT ONE, MY SON WILL FIGURE SOMETHING OUT WHEN HE GETS HOME.
ODETTE?
YES.
WHY DID YOU CALL YOURSELF MARIE-LOUISE?
BECAUSE THAT'S MY NAME.
HUH?
IT'S LIKE MY BROTHER. EVERYONE CALLS HIM JUSTIN EVEN THOUGH HIS REAL FIRST NAME IS JULES.
WHEN IT COMES TO PAPERWORK, I'M MARIE-LOUISE.
UH... ALL RIGHT. SO YOU'RE ODETTE?
YES, MA'AM. CAN I GO NOW?

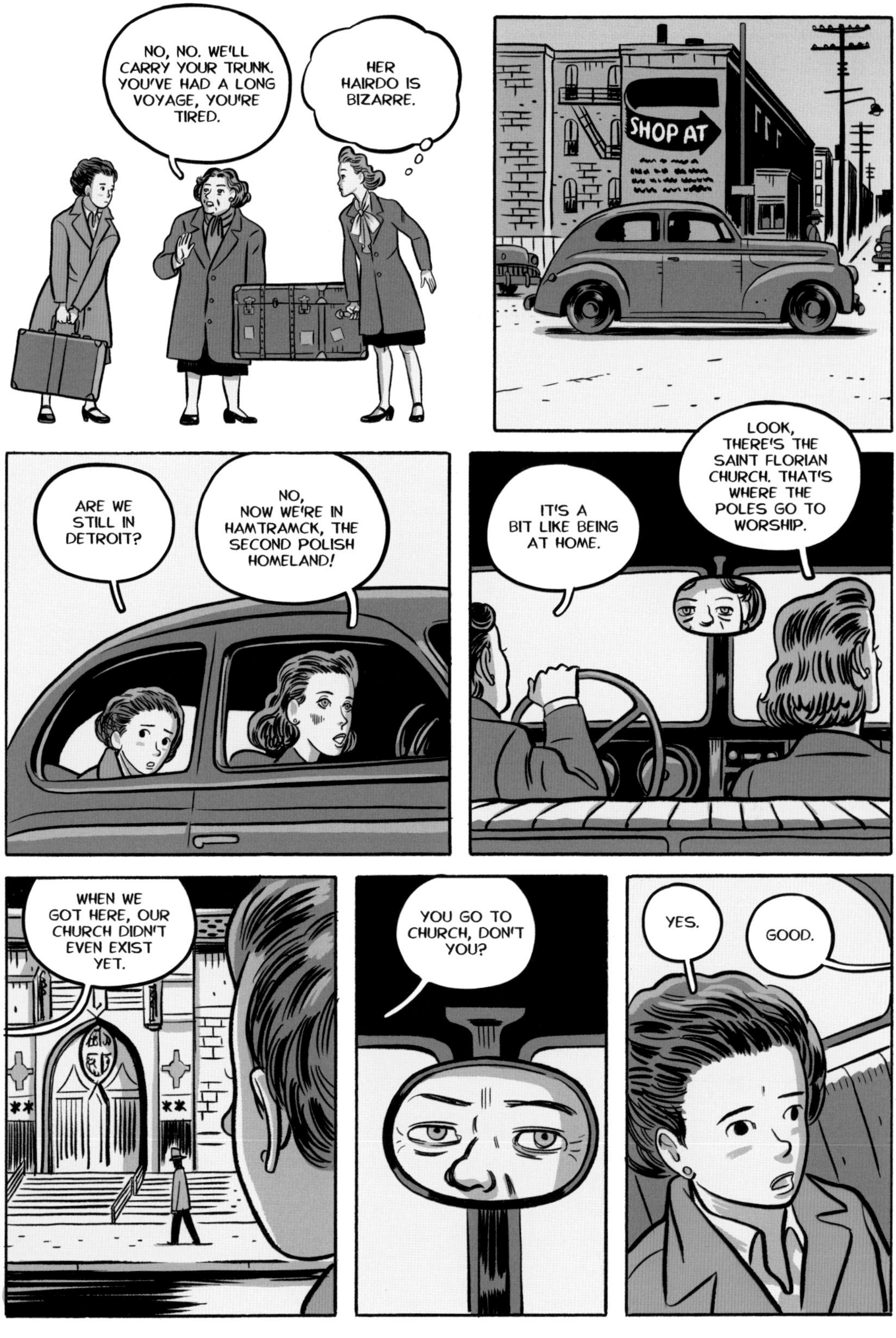
NO, NO. WE'LL CARRY YOUR TRUNK. YOU'VE HAD A LONG VOYAGE, YOU'RE TIRED.
HER HAIRDO IS BIZARRE.
SHOP AT
ARE WE STILL IN DETROIT?
NO, NOW WE'RE IN HAMTRAMCK, THE SECOND POLISH HOMELAND!
IT'S A BIT LIKE BEING AT HOME.
LOOK, THERE'S THE SAINT FLORIAN CHURCH. THAT'S WHERE THE POLES GO TO WORSHIP.
WHEN WE GOT HERE, OUR CHURCH DIDN'T EVEN EXIST YET.
YOU GO TO CHURCH, DON'T YOU?
YES.
GOOD.

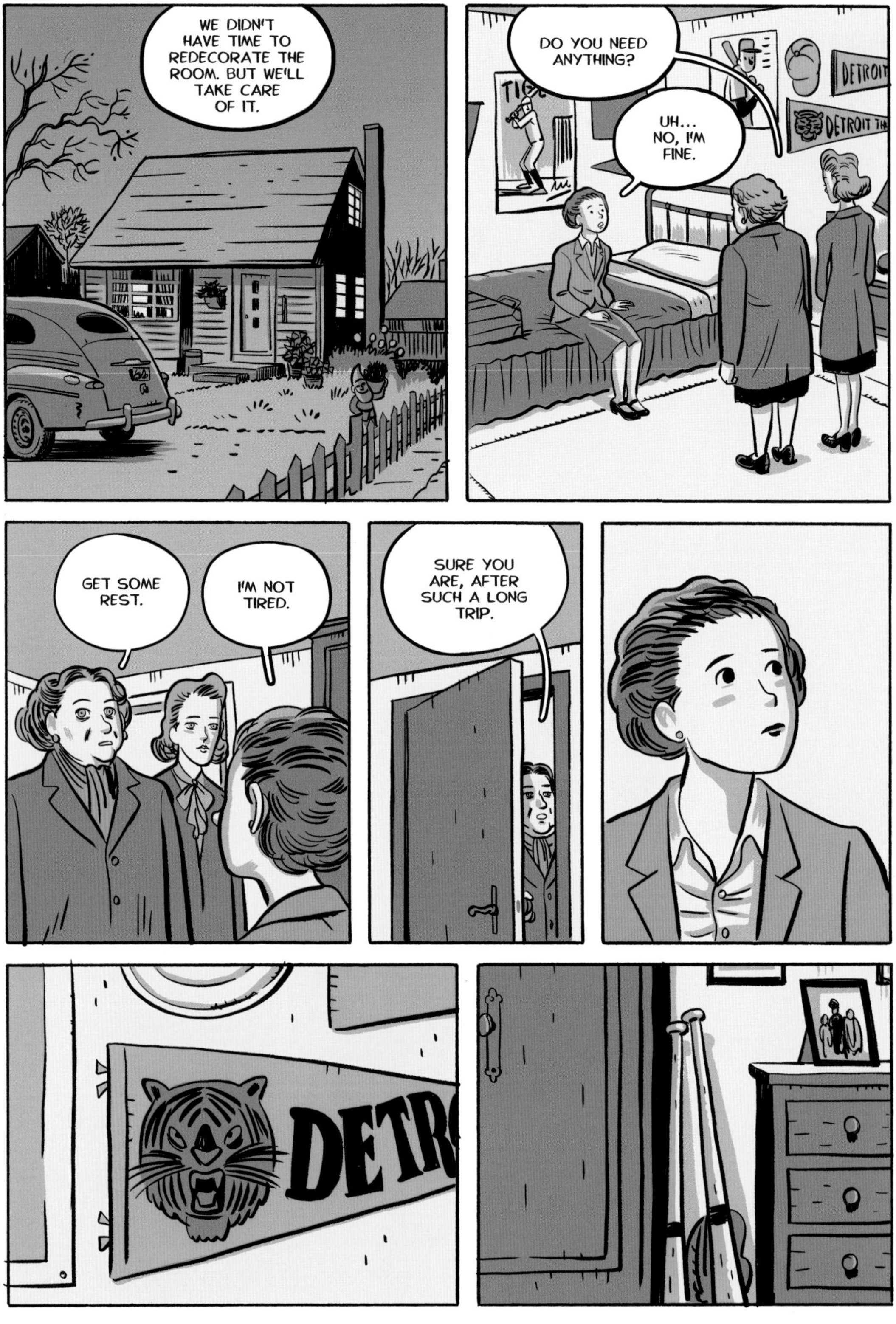
WE DIDN'T HAVE TIME TO REDECORATE THE ROOM. BUT WE'LL TAKE CARE OF IT.
DO YOU NEED ANYTHING?
UH... NO, I'M FINE.
GET SOME REST.
I'M NOT TIRED.
SURE YOU ARE, AFTER SUCH A LONG TRIP.
DETROIT
DETROIT TI
DETR

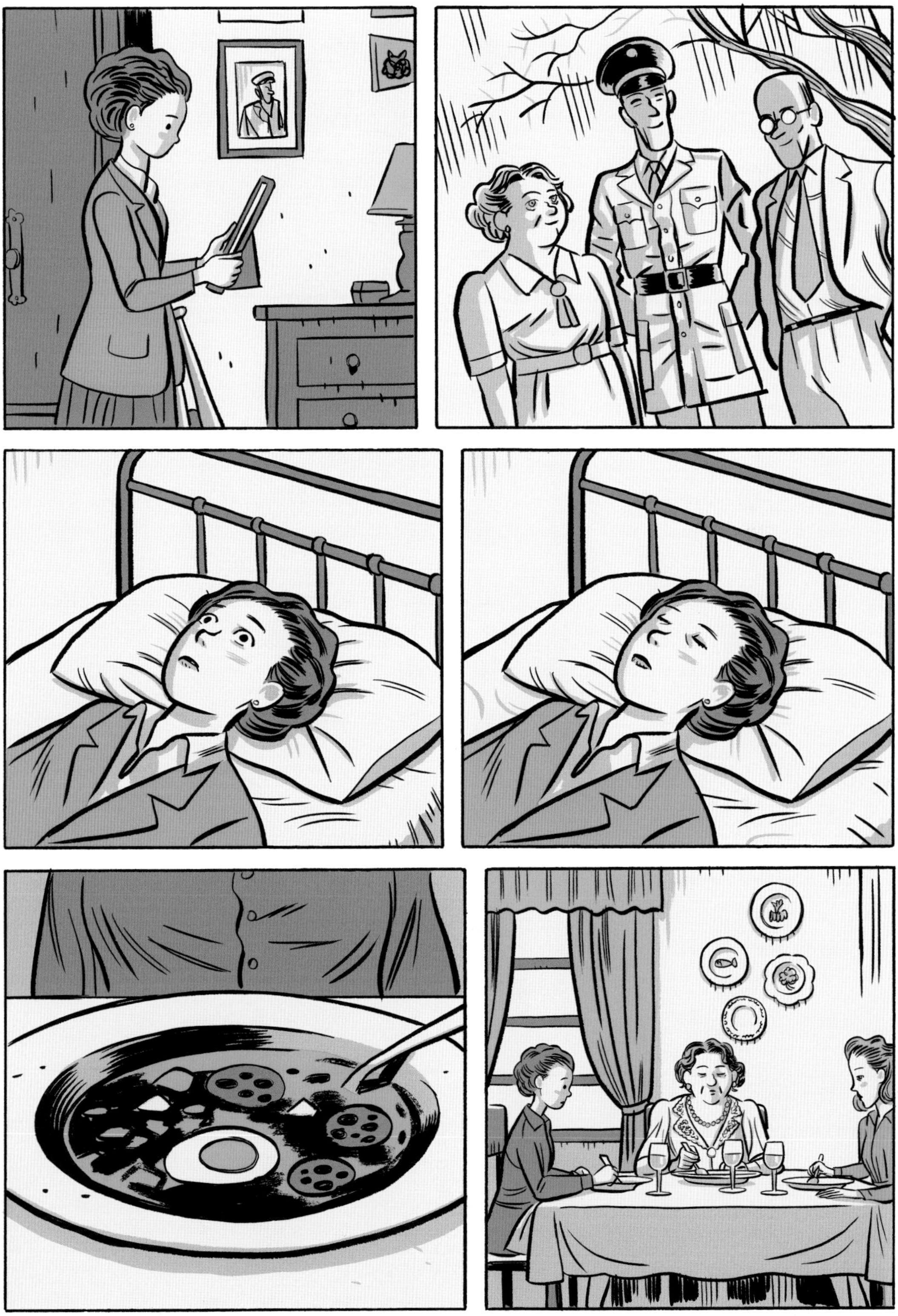

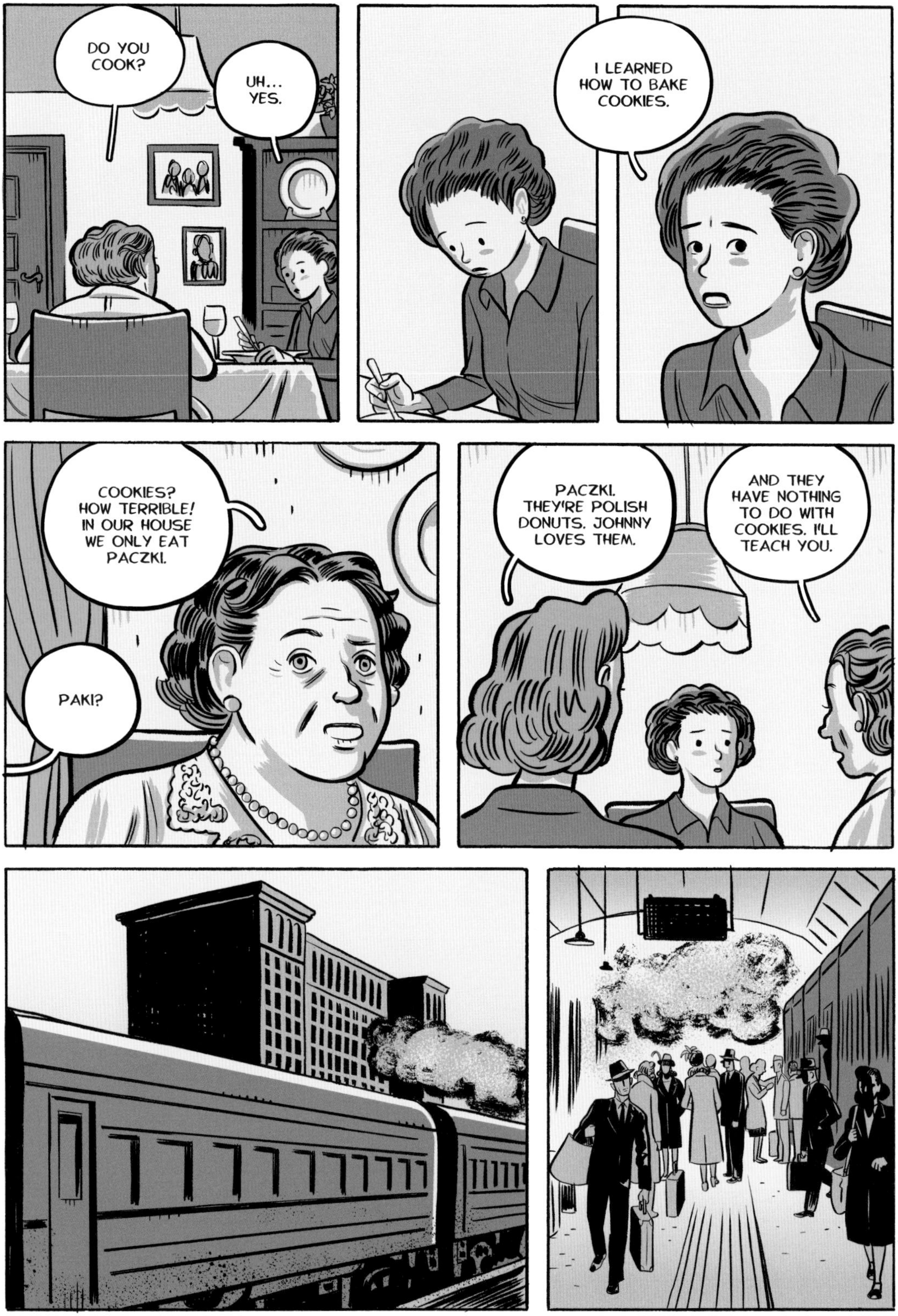
DO YOU COOK?
UH... YES.
I LEARNED HOW TO BAKE COOKIES.
COOKIES? HOW TERRIBLE! IN OUR HOUSE WE ONLY EAT PACZKI.
PAKI?
PACZKI. THEY'RE POLISH DONUTS. JOHNNY LOVES THEM.
AND THEY HAVE NOTHING TO DO WITH COOKIES. I'LL TEACH YOU.

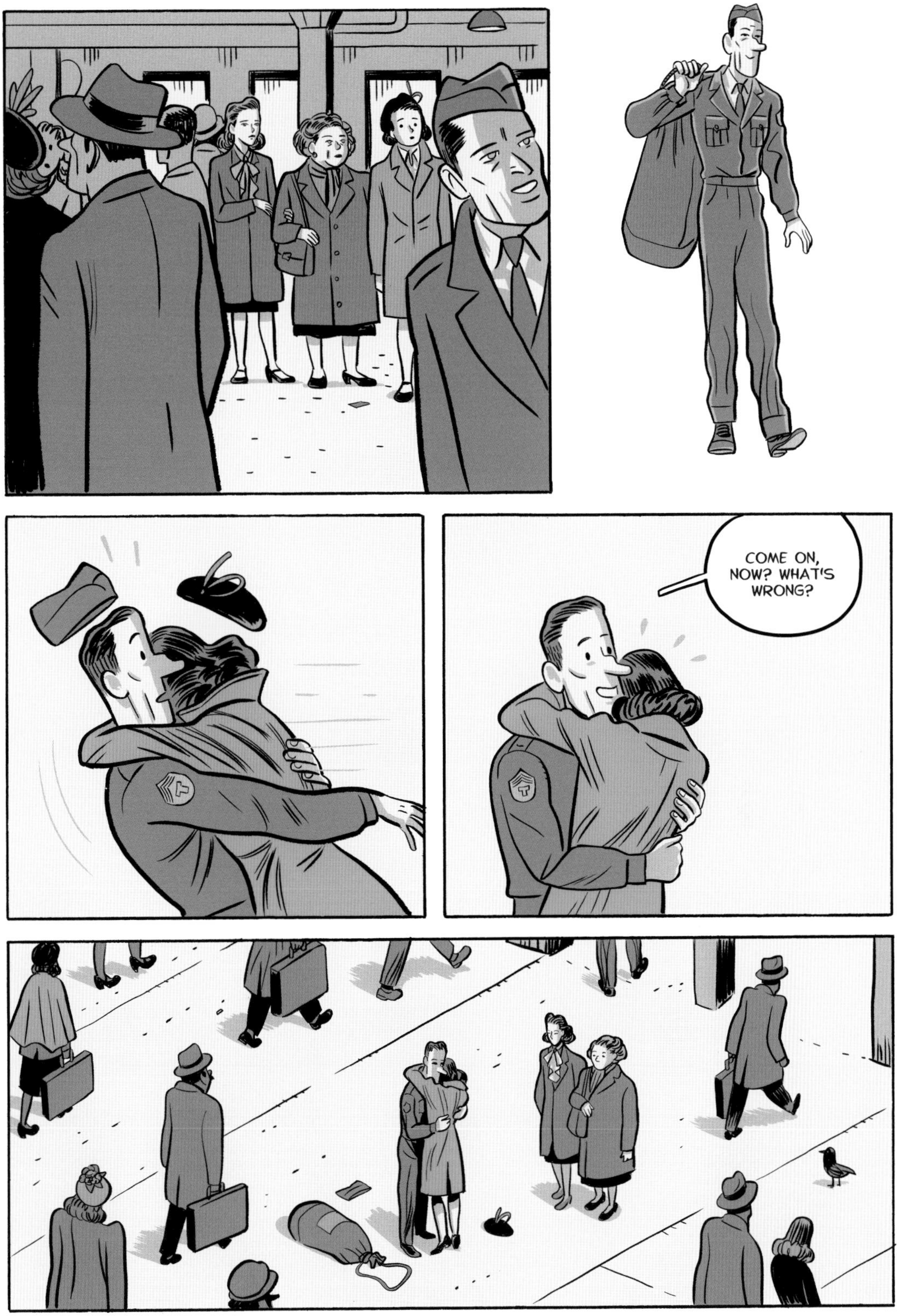
COME ON, NOW? WHAT'S WRONG?

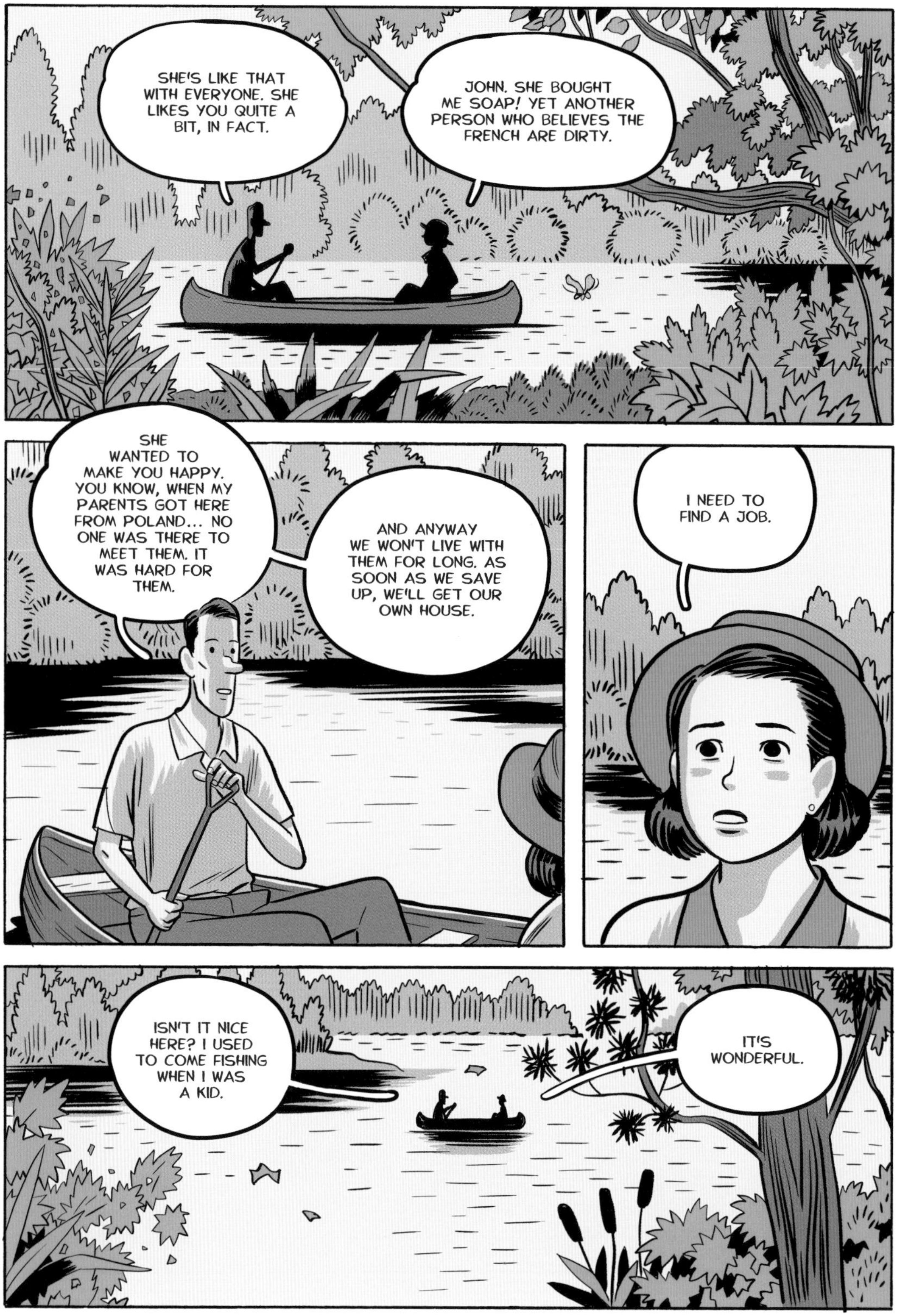
SHE'S LIKE THAT WITH EVERYONE. SHE LIKES YOU QUITE A BIT, IN FACT.
JOHN. SHE BOUGHT ME SOAP! YET ANOTHER PERSON WHO BELIEVES THE FRENCH ARE DIRTY.
SHE WANTED TO MAKE YOU HAPPY. YOU KNOW, WHEN MY PARENTS GOT HERE FROM POLAND... NO ONE WAS THERE TO MEET THEM. IT WAS HARD FOR THEM.
AND ANYWAY WE WON'T LIVE WITH THEM FOR LONG. AS SOON AS WE SAVE UP, WE'LL GET OUR OWN HOUSE.
I NEED TO FIND A JOB.
ISN'T IT NICE HERE? I USED TO COME FISHING WHEN I WAS A KID.
IT'S WONDERFUL.

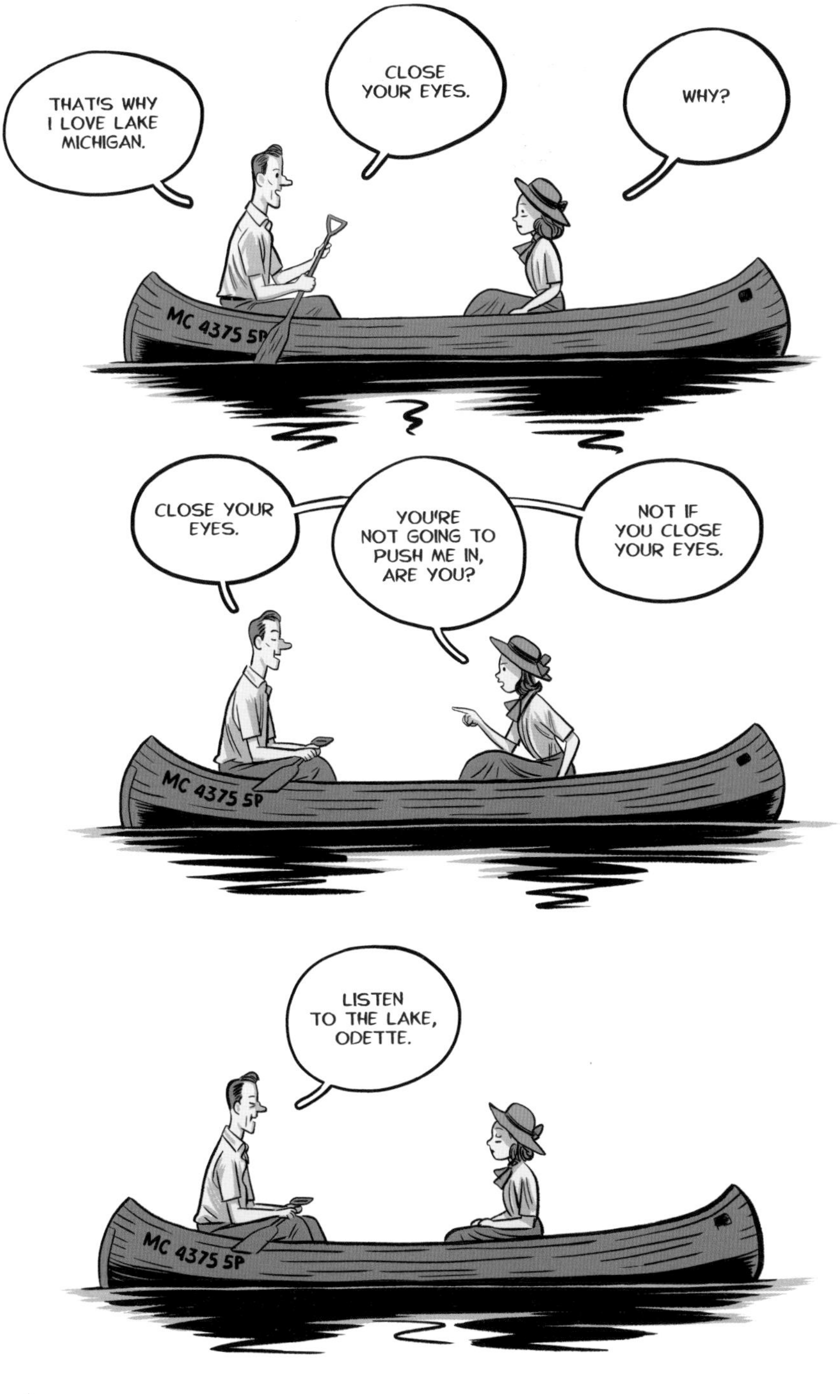
THAT'S WHY I LOVE LAKE MICHIGAN.
CLOSE YOUR EYES.
WHY?
MC 4375 5P
CLOSE YOUR EYES.
YOU'RE NOT GOING TO PUSH ME IN, ARE YOU?
NOT IF YOU CLOSE YOUR EYES.
MC 4375 5P
LISTEN TO THE LAKE, ODETTE.
MC 4375 5P

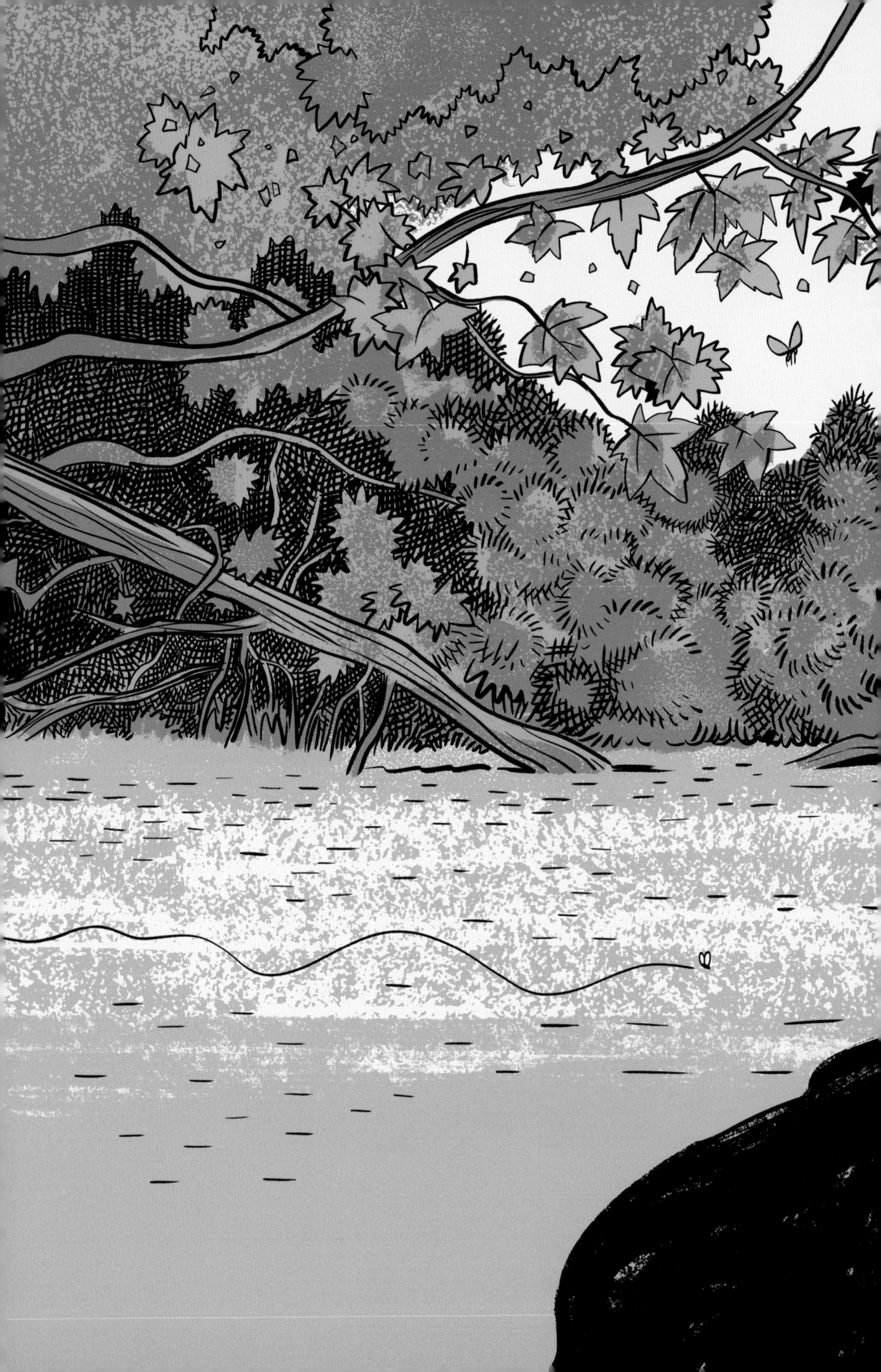

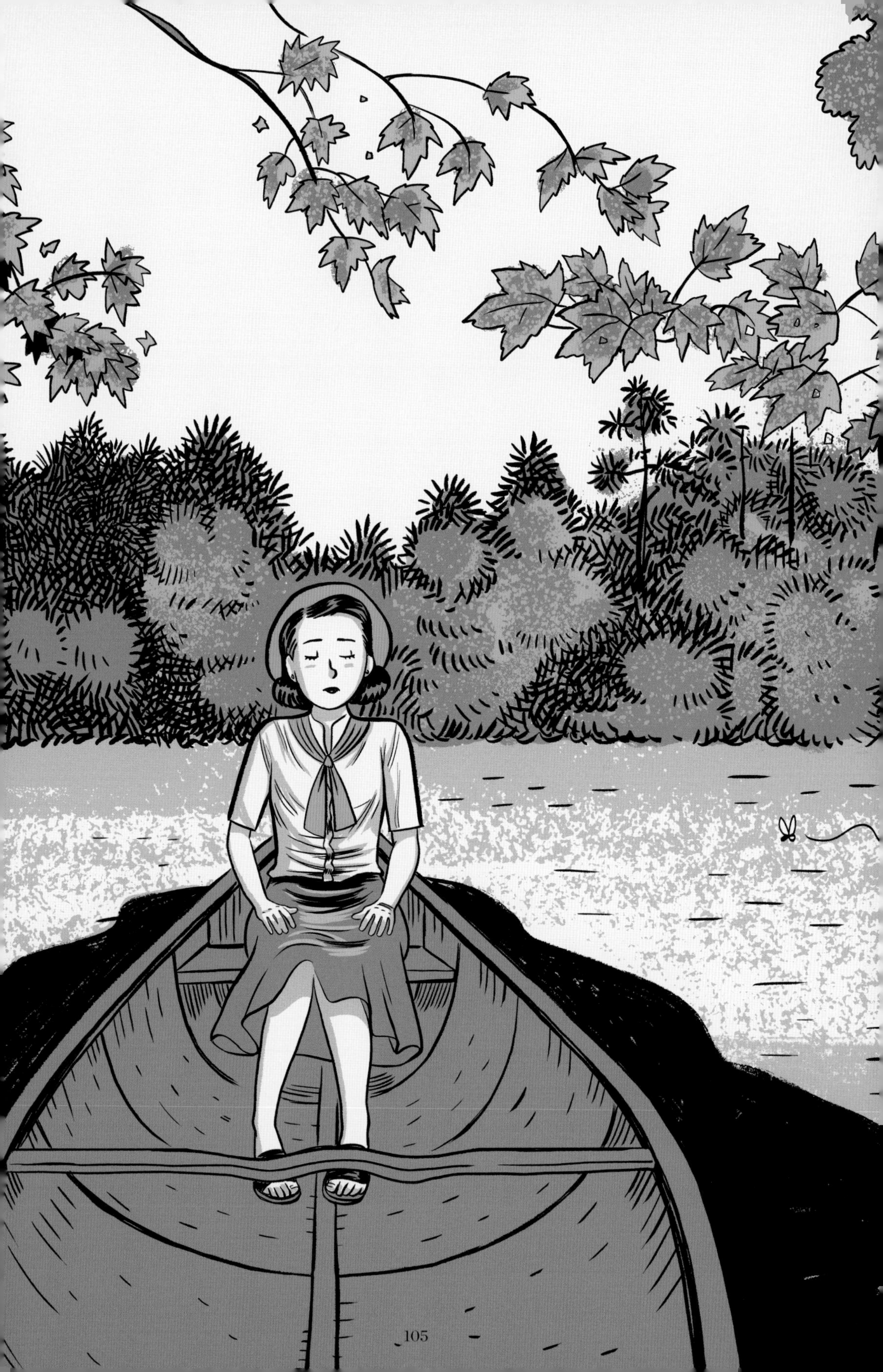

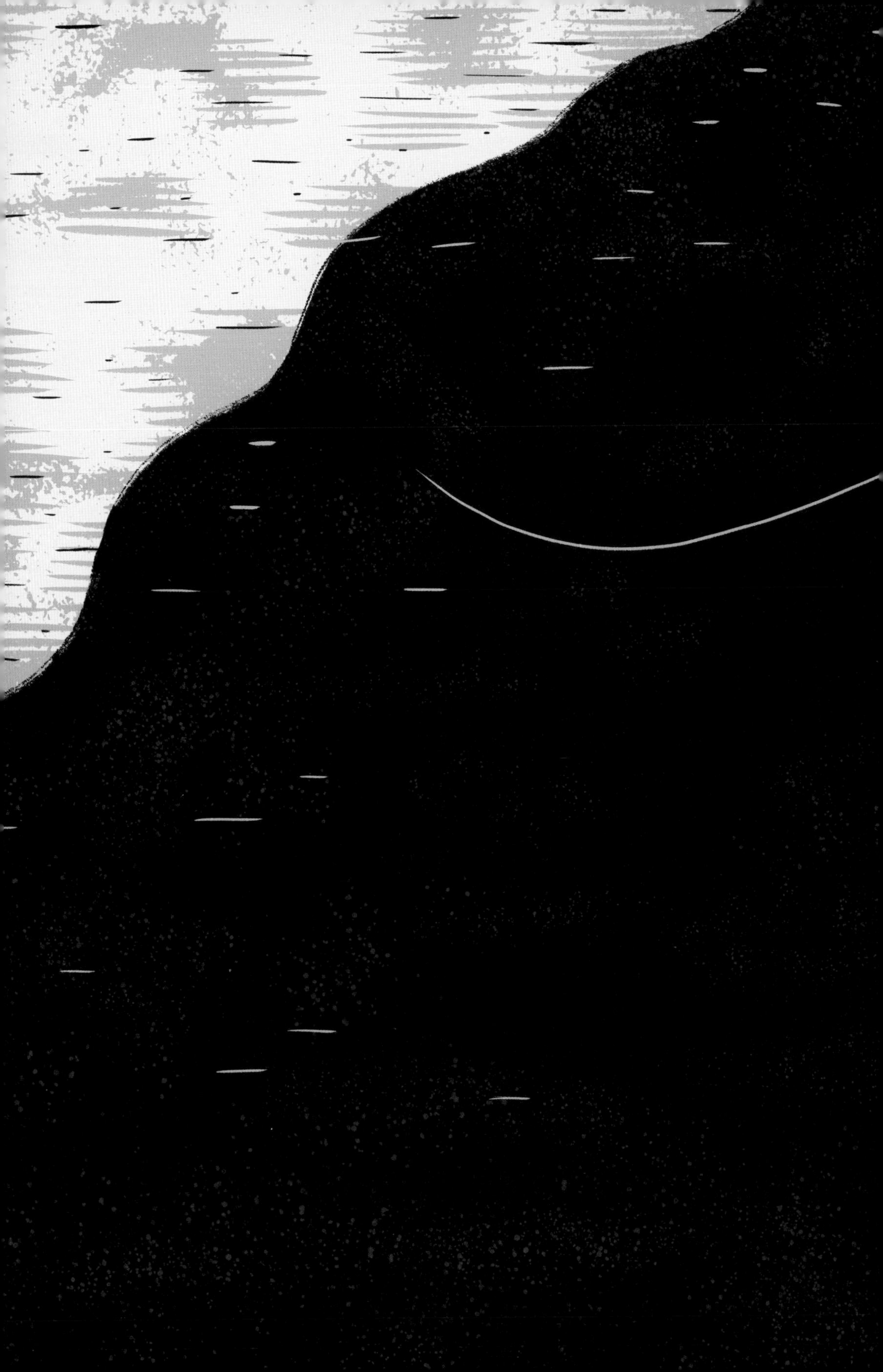

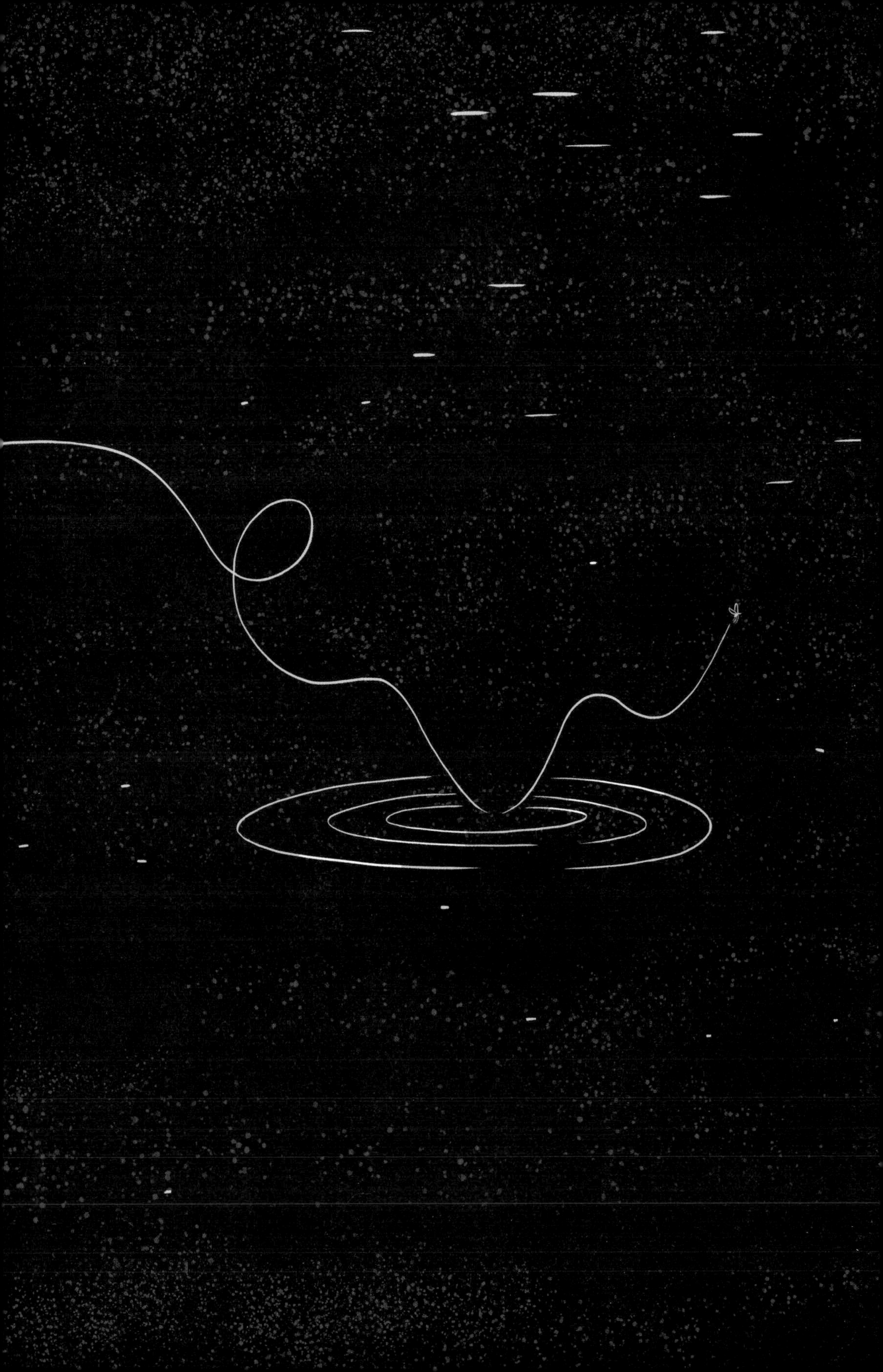

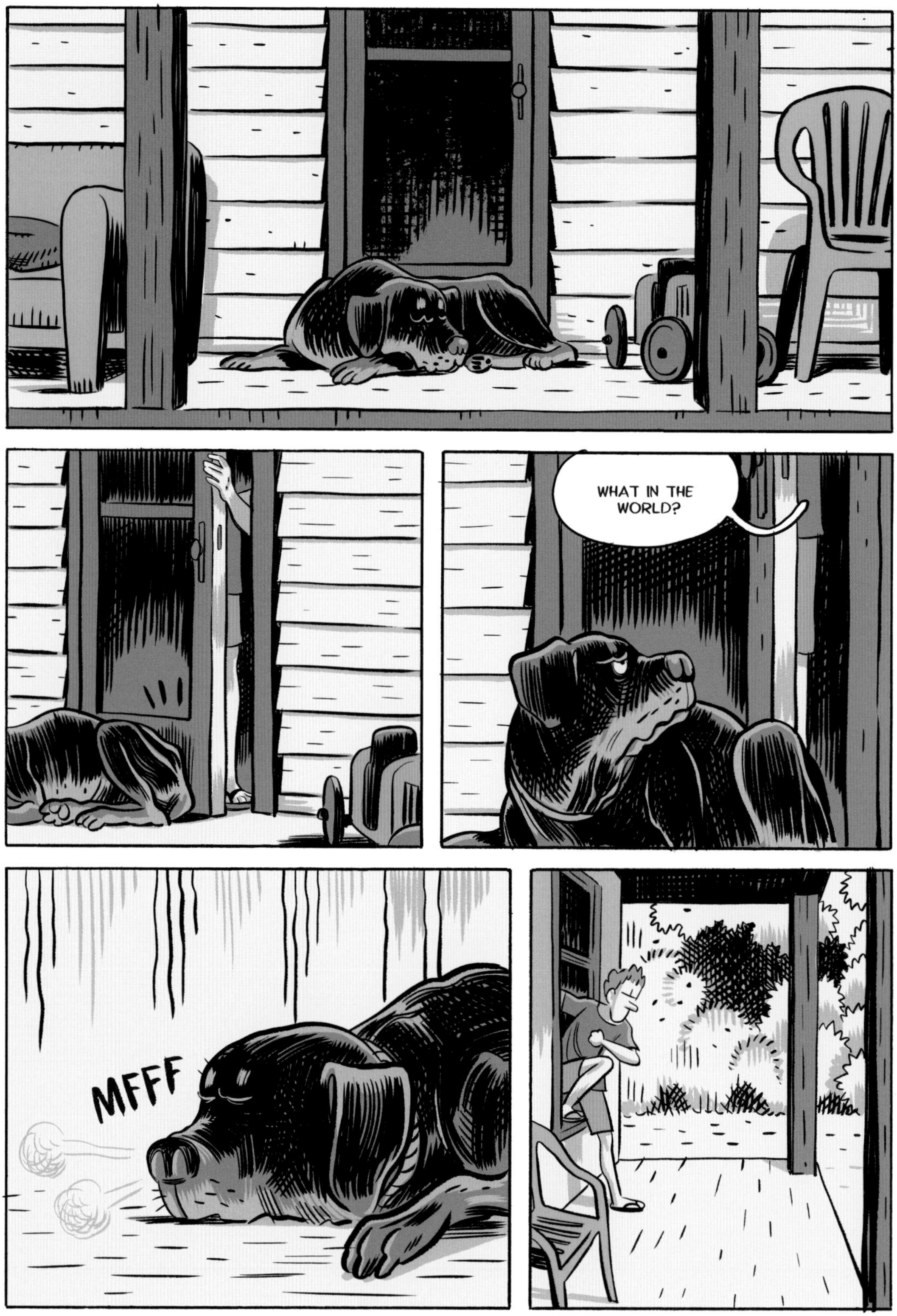
WHAT IN THE WORLD?
MFFF

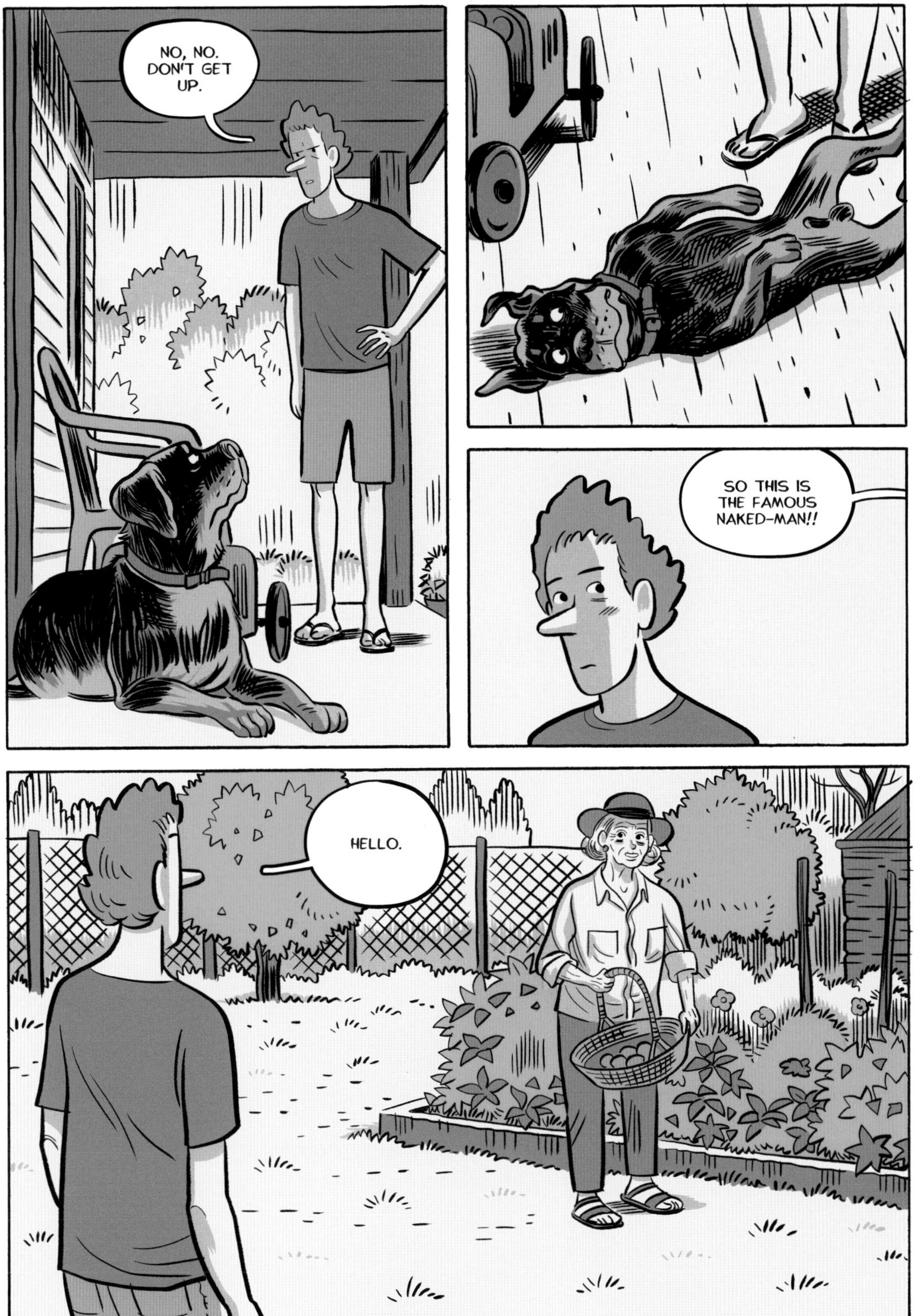
NO, NO. DON'T GET UP.
SO THIS IS THE FAMOUS NAKED-MAN!!
HELLO.

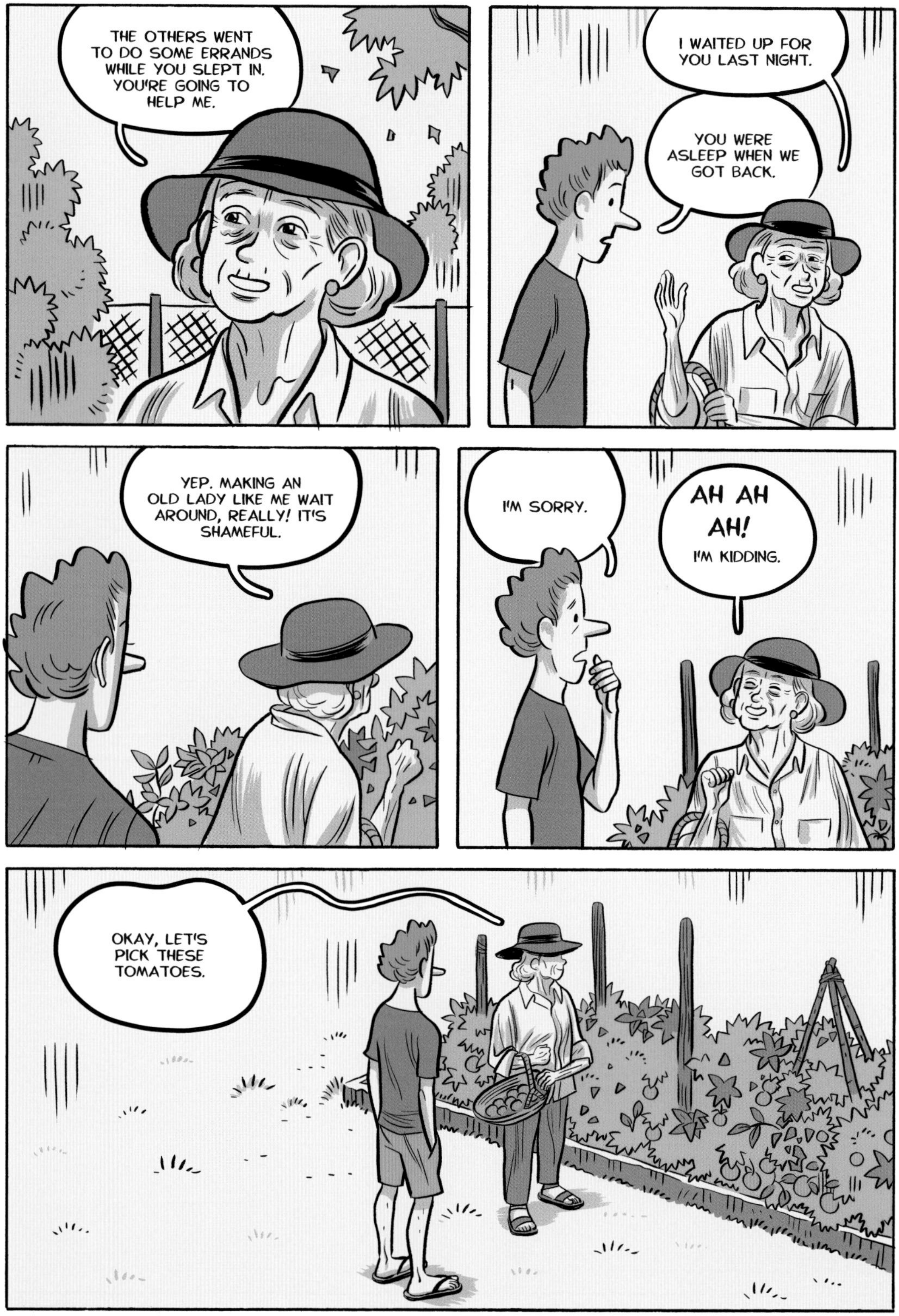
THE OTHERS WENT TO DO SOME ERRANDS WHILE YOU SLEPT IN. YOU'RE GOING TO HELP ME.
I WAITED UP FOR YOU LAST NIGHT.
YOU WERE ASLEEP WHEN WE GOT BACK.
YEP. MAKING AN OLD LADY LIKE ME WAIT AROUND, REALLY! IT'S SHAMEFUL.
I'M SORRY.
AH AH AH!
I'M KIDDING.
OKAY, LET'S PICK THESE TOMATOES.

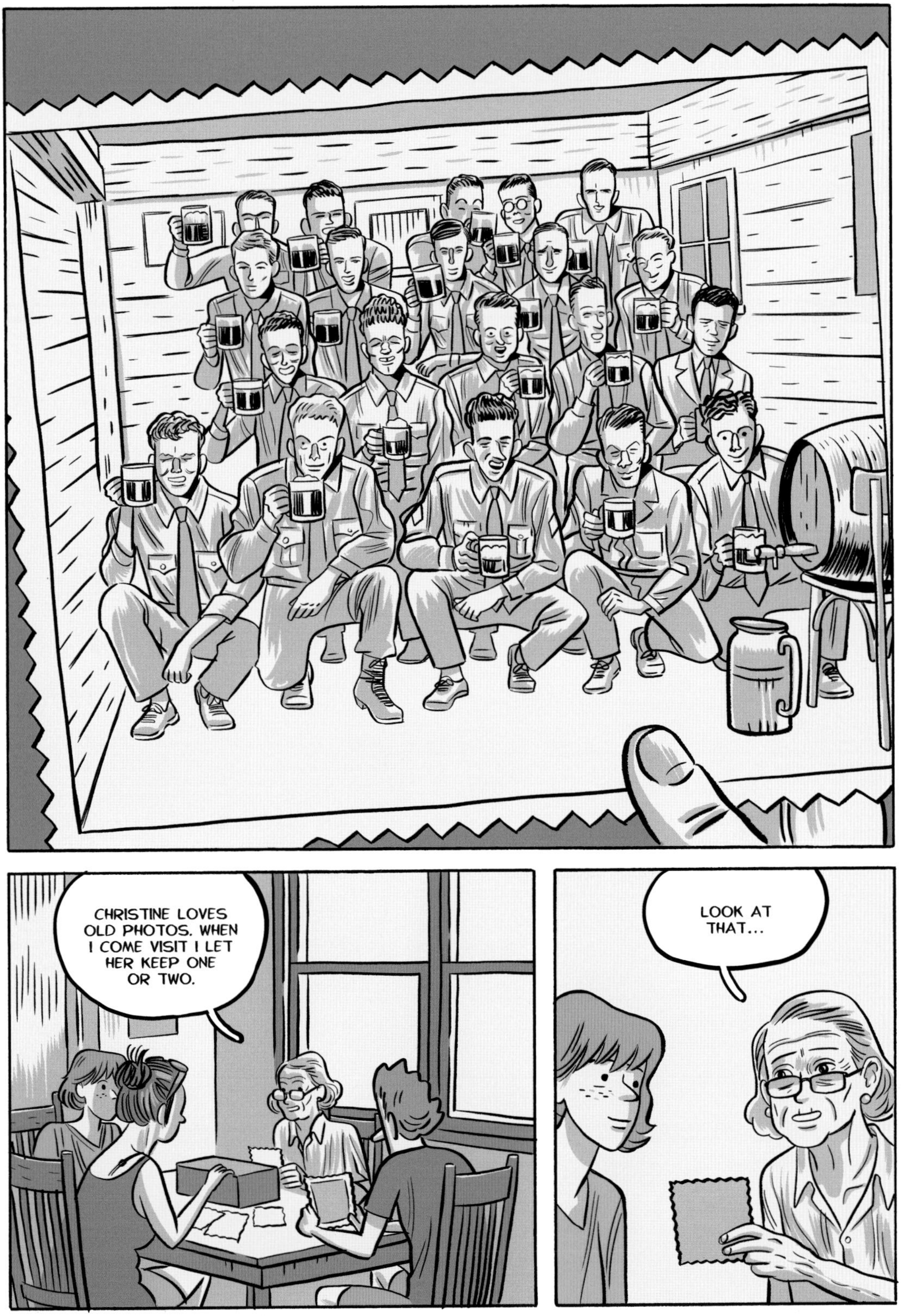
CHRISTINE LOVES OLD PHOTOS. WHEN I COME VISIT I LET HER KEEP ONE OR TWO.
LOOK AT THAT...

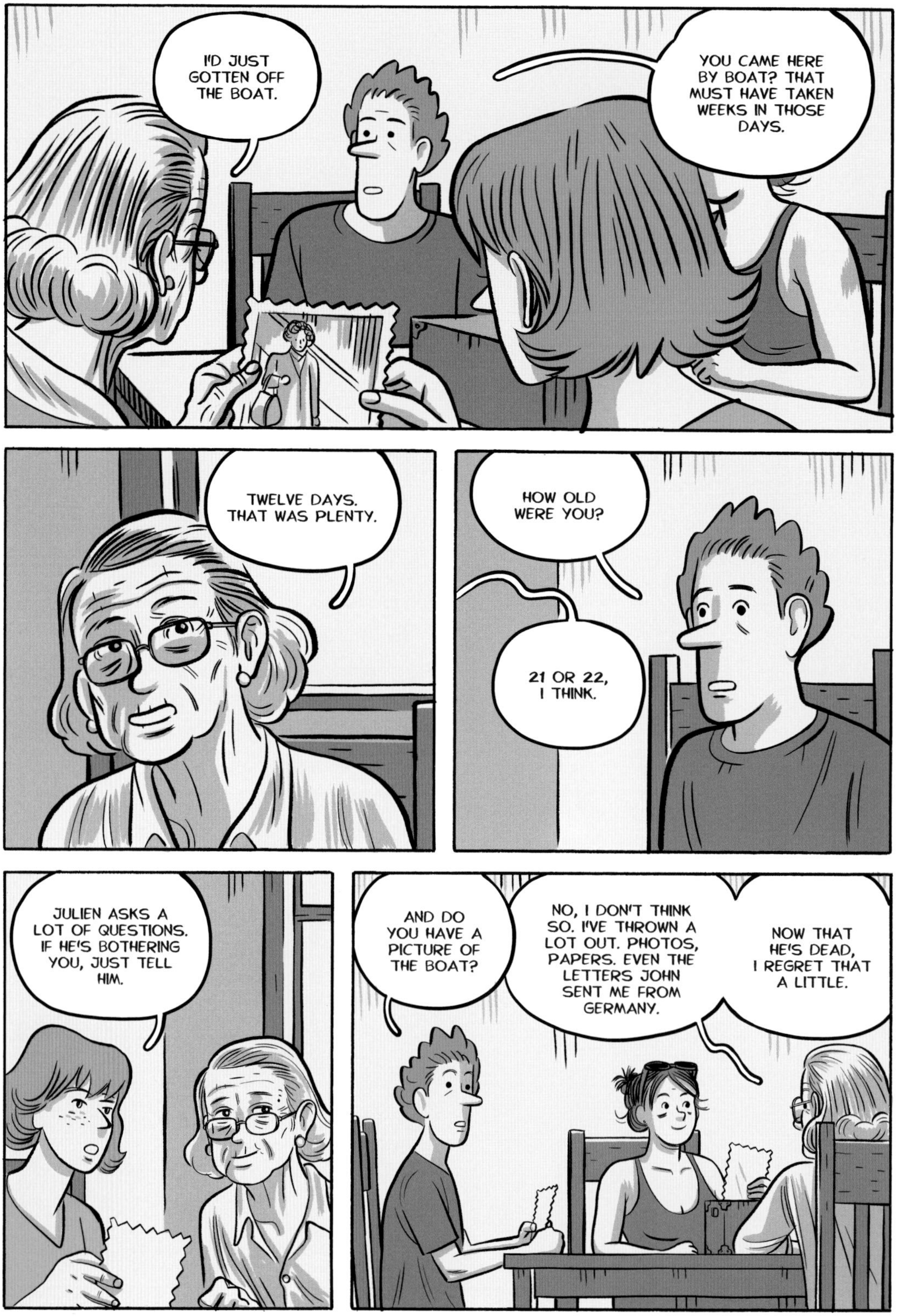
I'D JUST GOTTEN OFF THE BOAT.
YOU CAME HERE BY BOAT? THAT MUST HAVE TAKEN WEEKS IN THOSE DAYS.
TWELVE DAYS. THAT WAS PLENTY.
HOW OLD WERE YOU?
21 OR 22, I THINK.
JULIEN ASKS A LOT OF QUESTIONS. IF HE'S BOTHERING YOU, JUST TELL HIM.
AND DO YOU HAVE A PICTURE OF THE BOAT?
NO, I DON'T THINK SO. I'VE THROWN A LOT OUT. PHOTOS, PAPERS. EVEN THE LETTERS JOHN SENT ME FROM GERMANY.
NOW THAT HE'S DEAD, I REGRET THAT A LITTLE.

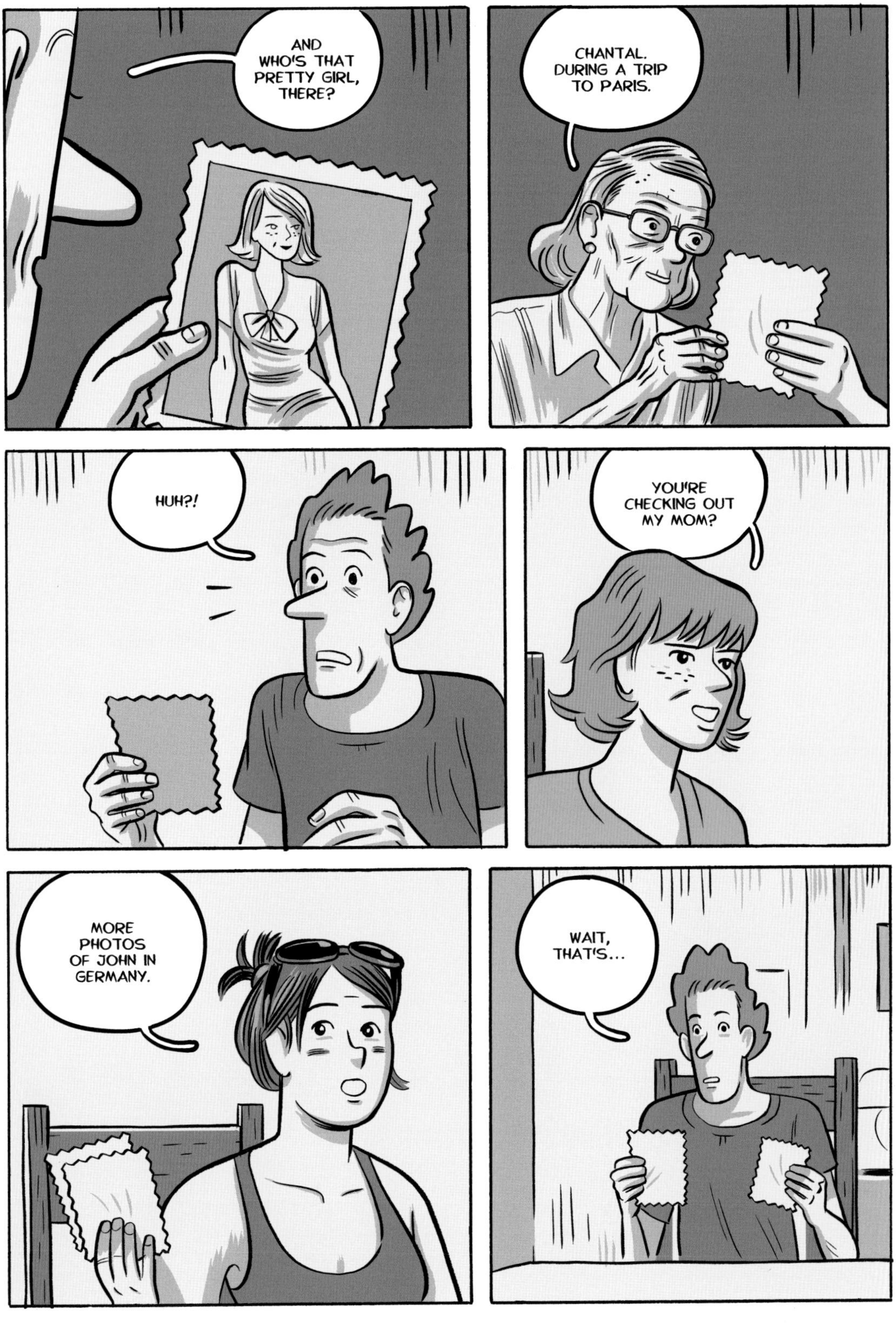
AND WHO'S THAT PRETTY GIRL, THERE?
CHANTAL. DURING A TRIP TO PARIS.
HUH?!
YOU'RE CHECKING OUT MY MOM?
MORE PHOTOS OF JOHN IN GERMANY.
WAIT, THAT'S...

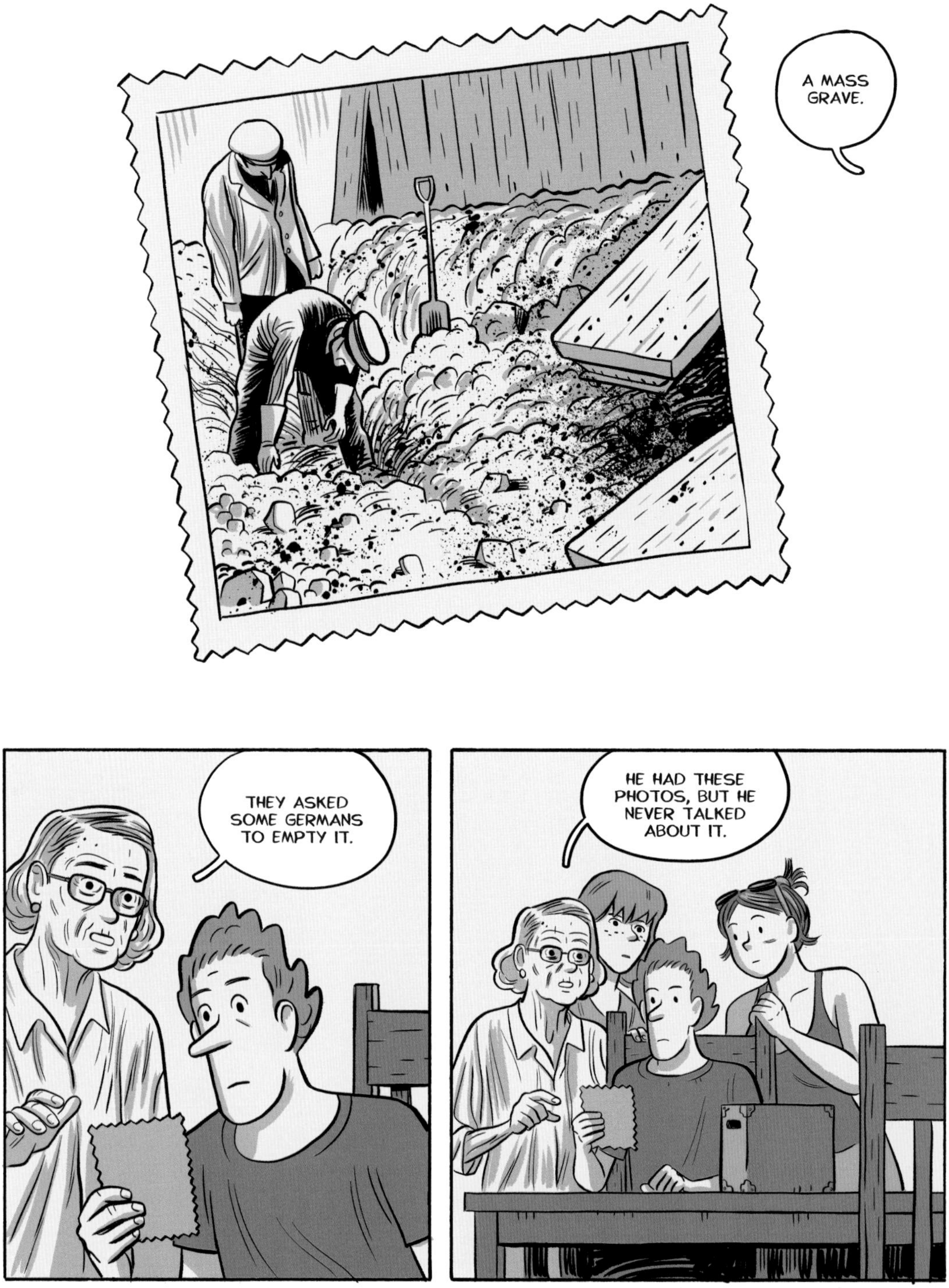
A MASS GRAVE.
THEY ASKED SOME GERMANS TO EMPTY IT.
HE HAD THESE PHOTOS, BUT HE NEVER TALKED ABOUT IT.

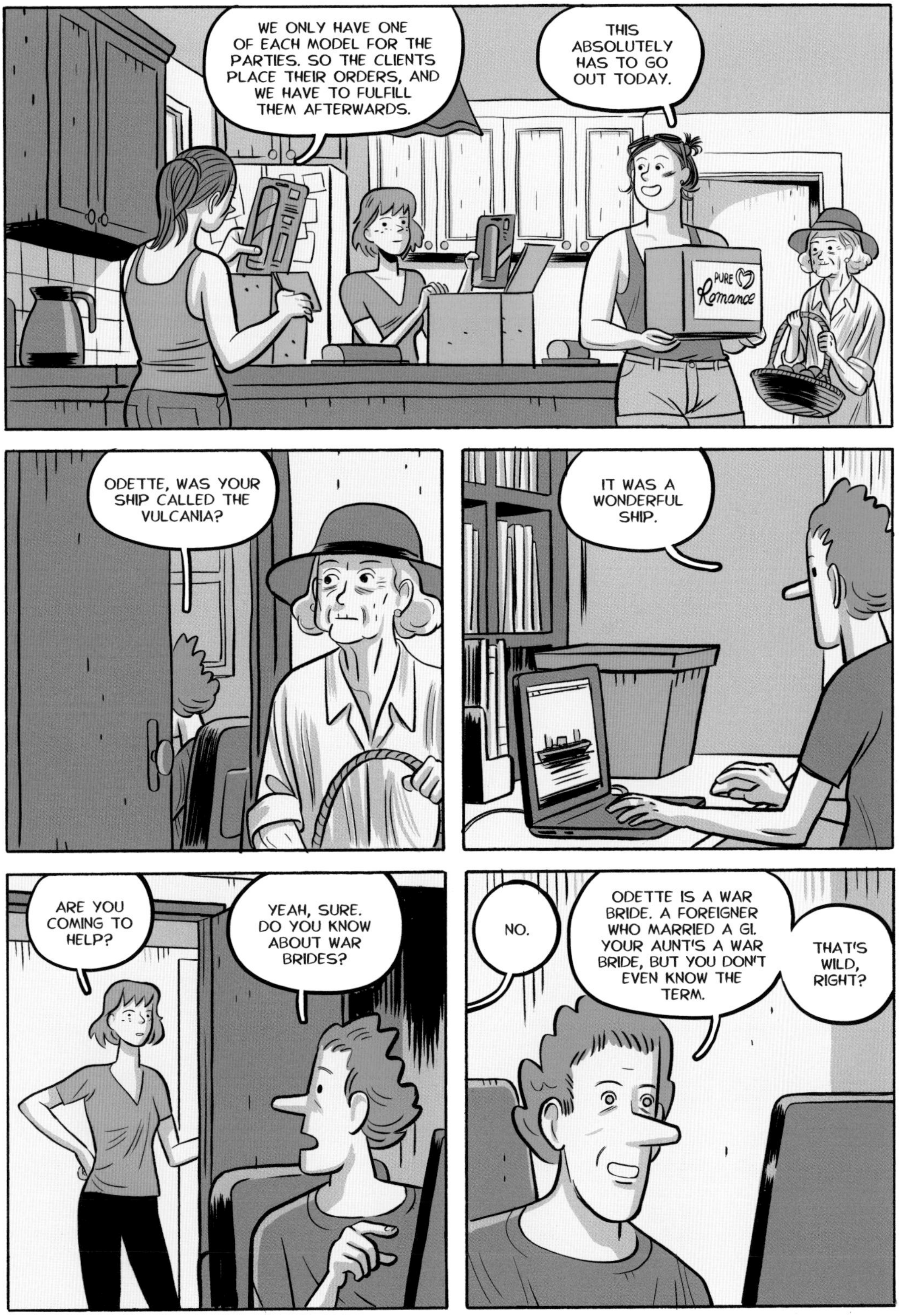
WE ONLY HAVE ONE OF EACH MODEL FOR THE PARTIES. SO THE CLIENTS PLACE THEIR ORDERS, AND WE HAVE TO FULFILL THEM AFTERWARDS.
THIS ABSOLUTELY HAS TO GO OUT TODAY.
PURE Romance
ODETTE, WAS YOUR SHIP CALLED THE VULCANIA?
IT WAS A WONDERFUL SHIP.
ARE YOU COMING TO HELP?
YEAH, SURE. DO YOU KNOW ABOUT WAR BRIDES?
NO.
ODETTE IS A WAR BRIDE. A FOREIGNER WHO MARRIED A GI. YOUR AUNT'S A WAR BRIDE, BUT YOU DON'T EVEN KNOW THE TERM.
THAT'S WILD, RIGHT?

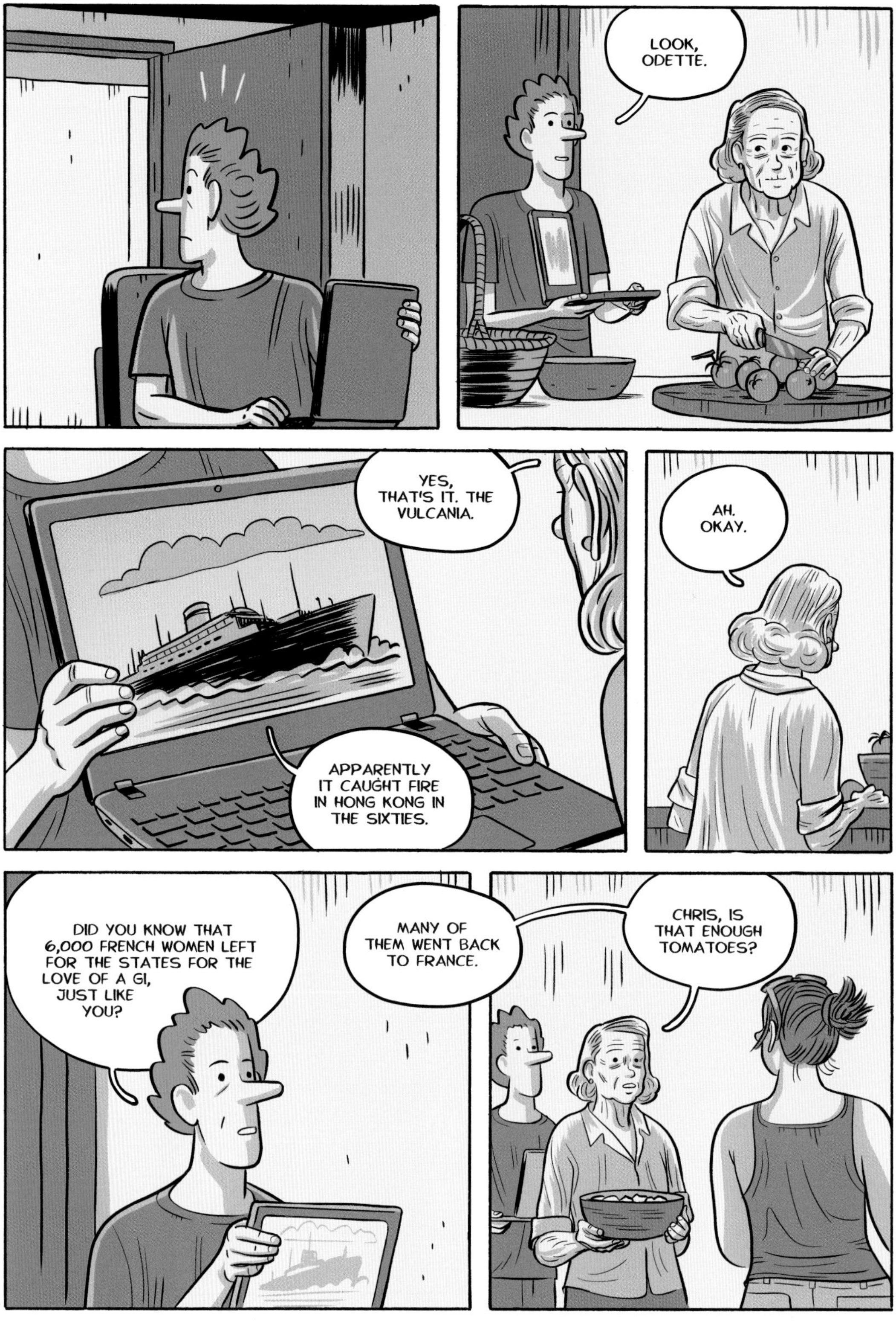
LOOK, ODETTE.
YES, THAT'S IT. THE VULCANIA.
APPARENTLY IT CAUGHT FIRE IN HONG KONG IN THE SIXTIES.
AH. OKAY.
DID YOU KNOW THAT 6,000 FRENCH WOMEN LEFT FOR THE STATES FOR THE LOVE OF A GI, JUST LIKE YOU?
MANY OF THEM WENT BACK TO FRANCE.
CHRIS, IS THAT ENOUGH TOMATOES?

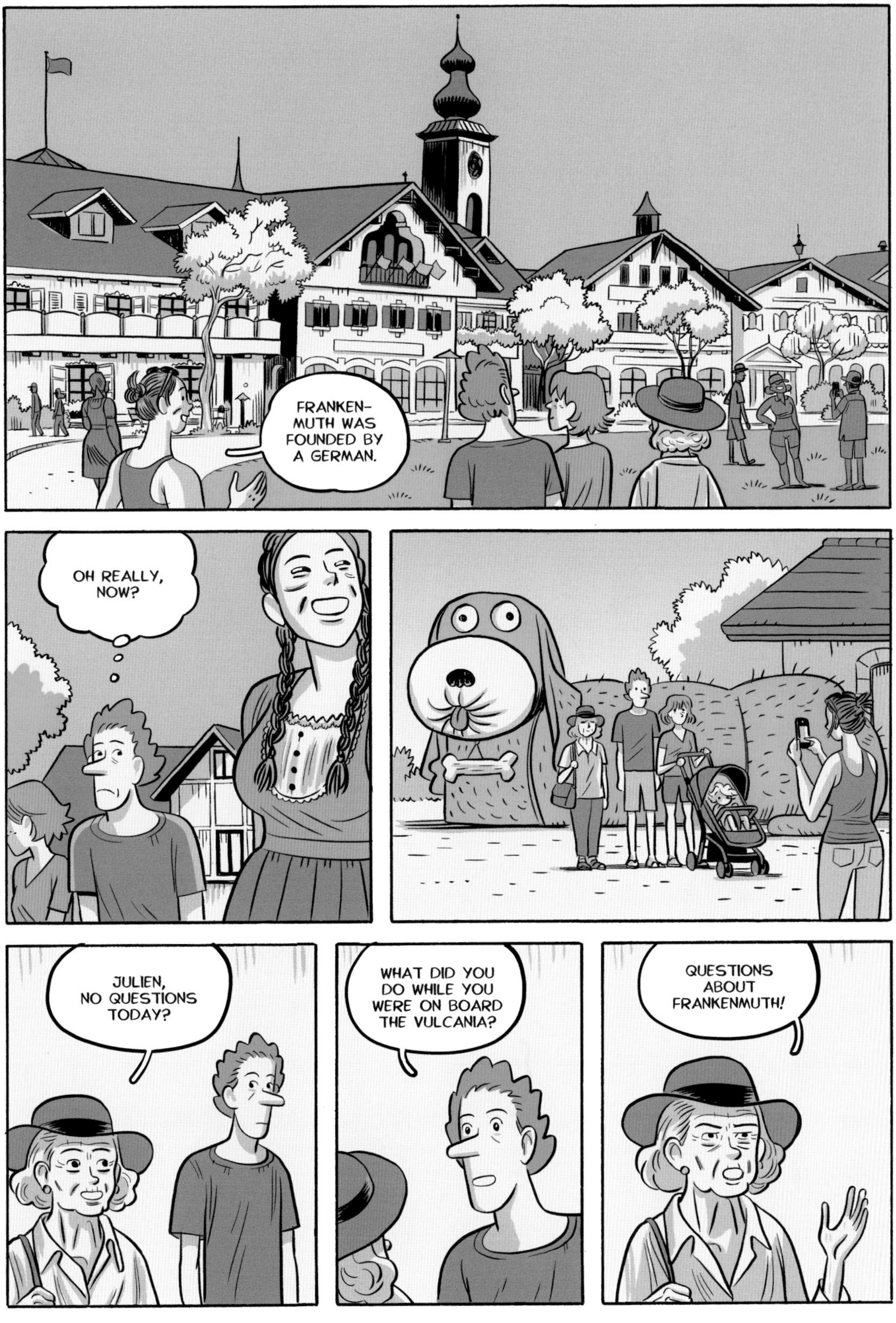
FRANKEN-MUTH WAS FOUNDED BY A GERMAN.
OH REALLY, NOW?
JULIEN, NO QUESTIONS TODAY?
WHAT DID YOU DO WHILE YOU WERE ON BOARD THE VULCANIA?
QUESTIONS ABOUT FRANKENMUTH!

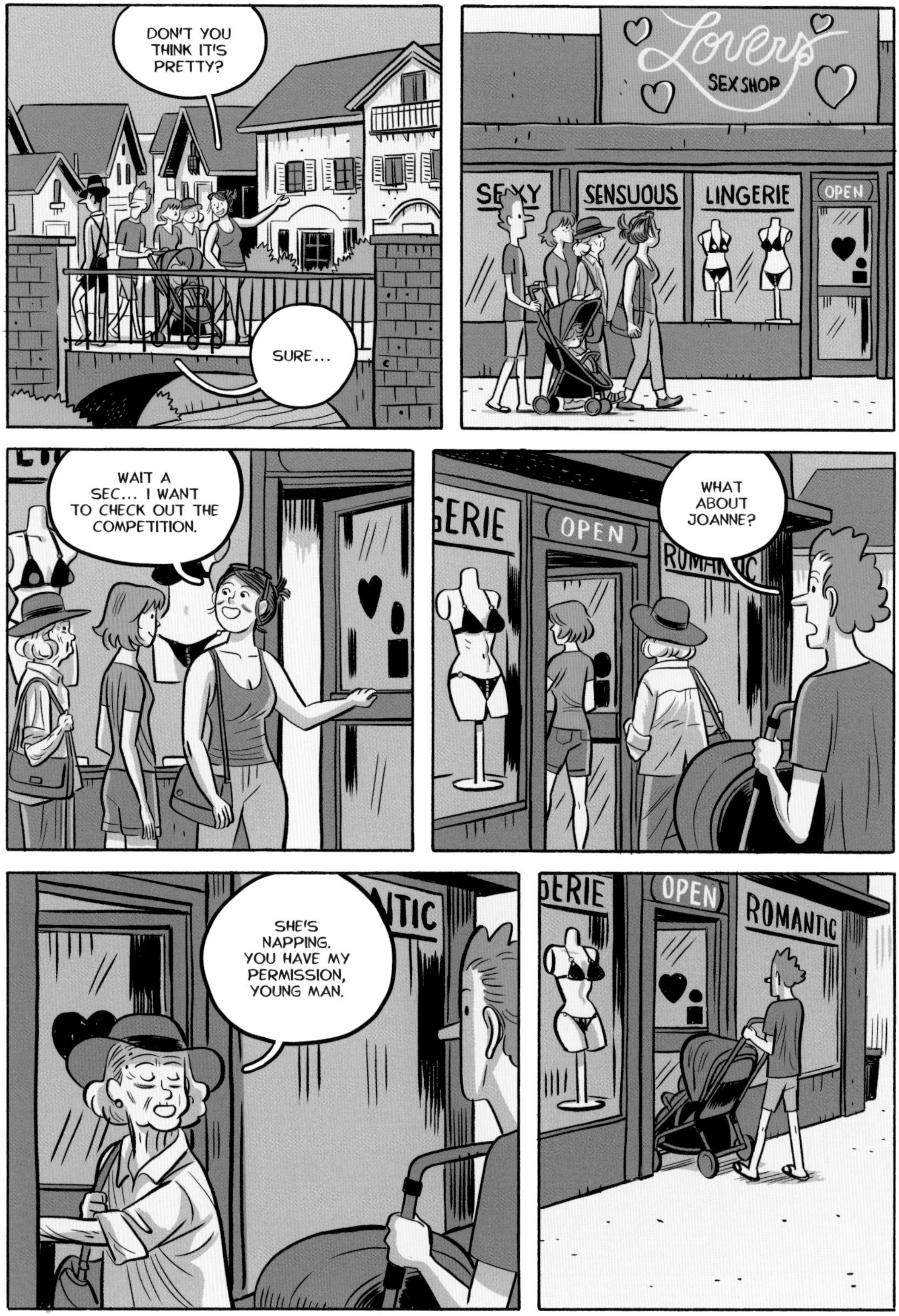

DON'T YOU THINK IT'S PRETTY?
SURE...
Lovers
SEX SHOP
SEXY
SENSUOUS
LINGERIE
OPEN
WAIT A SEC... I WANT TO CHECK OUT THE COMPETITION.
GERIE
OPEN
WHAT ABOUT JOANNE?
SHE'S NAPPING. YOU HAVE MY PERMISSION, YOUNG MAN.
OPEN
ROMANTIC

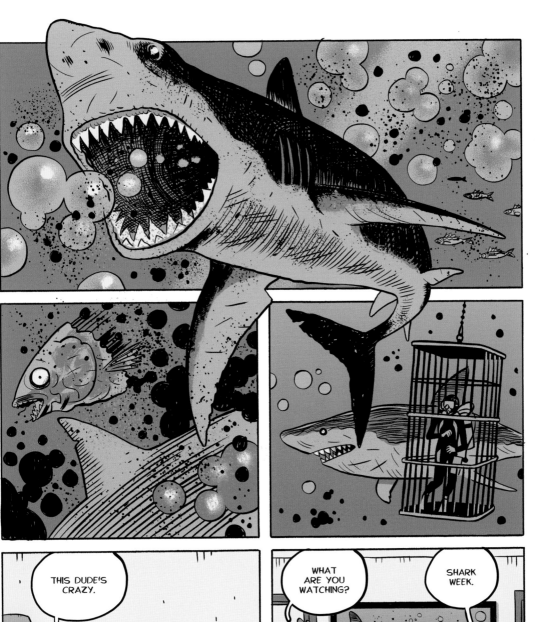

THIS DUDE'S CRAZY.

WHAT ARE YOU WATCHING?

SHARK WEEK.

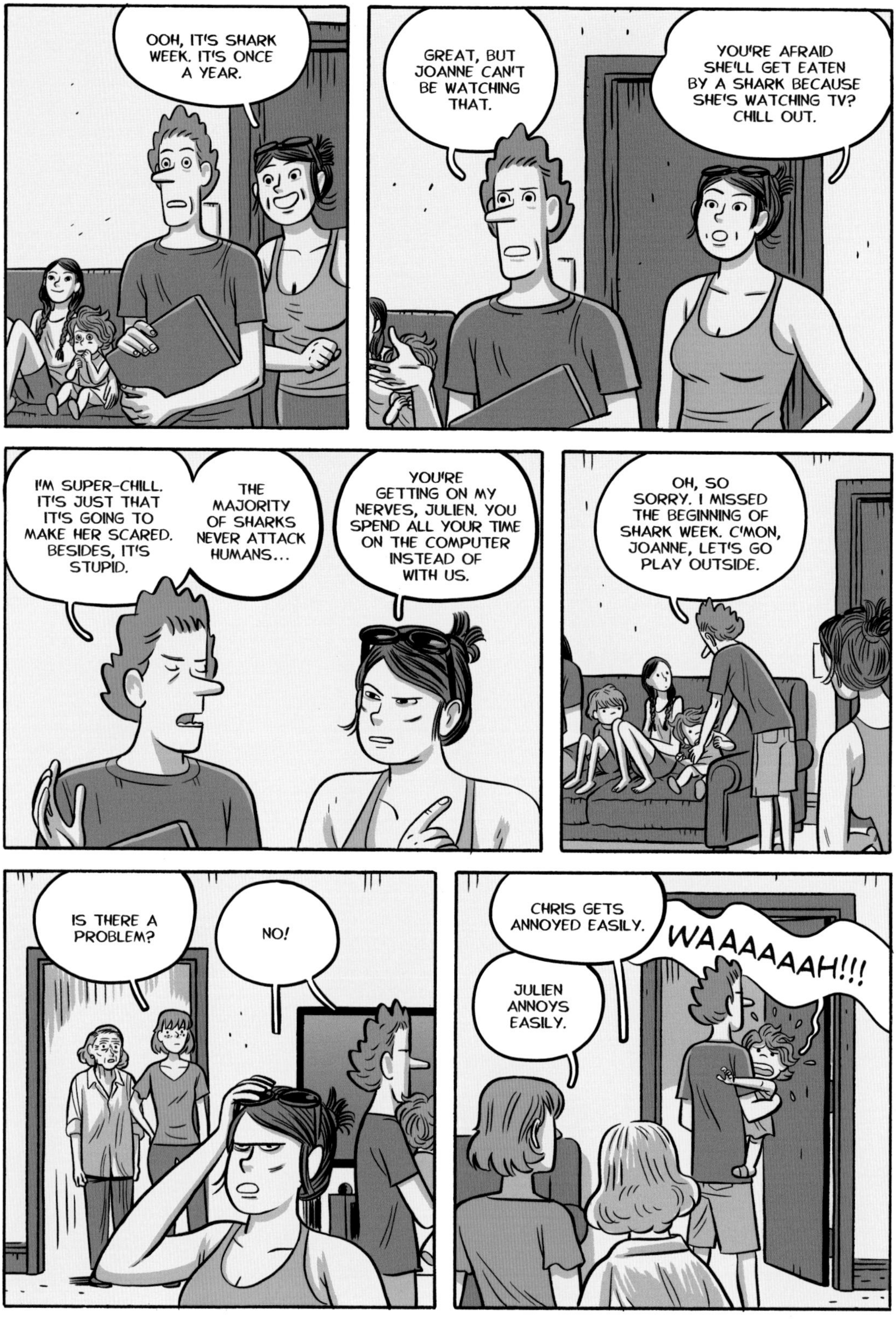
OOH, IT'S SHARK WEEK. IT'S ONCE A YEAR.
GREAT, BUT JOANNE CAN'T BE WATCHING THAT.
YOU'RE AFRAID SHE'LL GET EATEN BY A SHARK BECAUSE SHE'S WATCHING TV? CHILL OUT.
I'M SUPER-CHILL. IT'S JUST THAT IT'S GOING TO MAKE HER SCARED. BESIDES, IT'S STUPID.
THE MAJORITY OF SHARKS NEVER ATTACK HUMANS...
YOU'RE GETTING ON MY NERVES, JULIEN. YOU SPEND ALL YOUR TIME ON THE COMPUTER INSTEAD OF WITH US.
OH, SO SORRY. I MISSED THE BEGINNING OF SHARK WEEK. C'MON, JOANNE, LET'S GO PLAY OUTSIDE.
IS THERE A PROBLEM?
NO!
CHRIS GETS ANNOYED EASILY.
JULIEN ANNOYS EASILY.
WAAAAAAH!!!

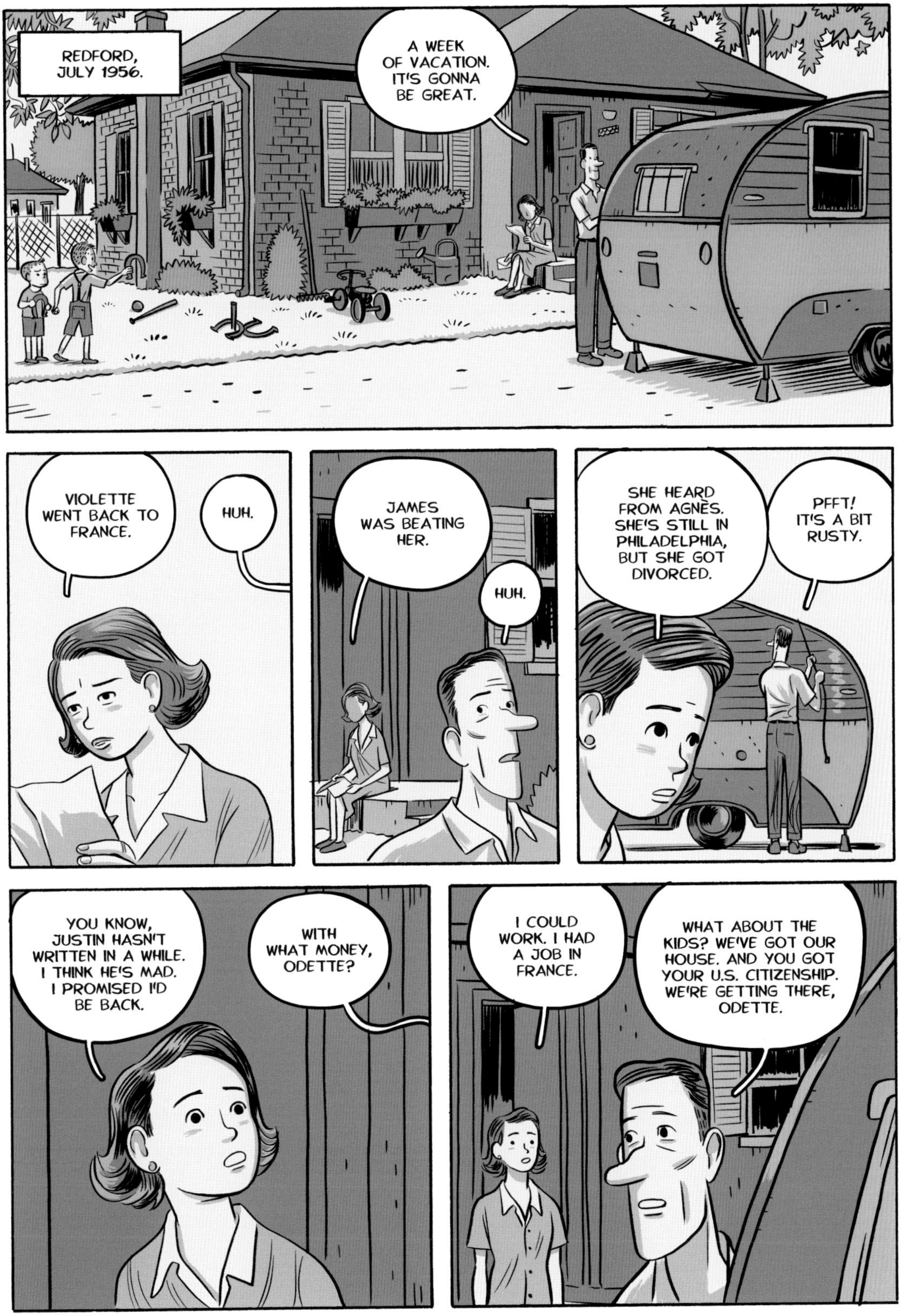
REDFORD, JULY 1956.
A WEEK OF VACATION. IT'S GONNA BE GREAT.
VIOLETTE WENT BACK TO FRANCE.
HUH.
JAMES WAS BEATING HER.
HUH.
SHE HEARD FROM AGNÈS. SHE'S STILL IN PHILADELPHIA, BUT SHE GOT DIVORCED.
PFFT! IT'S A BIT RUSTY.
YOU KNOW, JUSTIN HASN'T WRITTEN IN A WHILE. I THINK HE'S MAD. I PROMISED I'D BE BACK.
WITH WHAT MONEY, ODETTE?
I COULD WORK. I HAD A JOB IN FRANCE.
WHAT ABOUT THE KIDS? WE'VE GOT OUR HOUSE. AND YOU GOT YOUR U.S. CITIZENSHIP. WE'RE GETTING THERE, ODETTE.

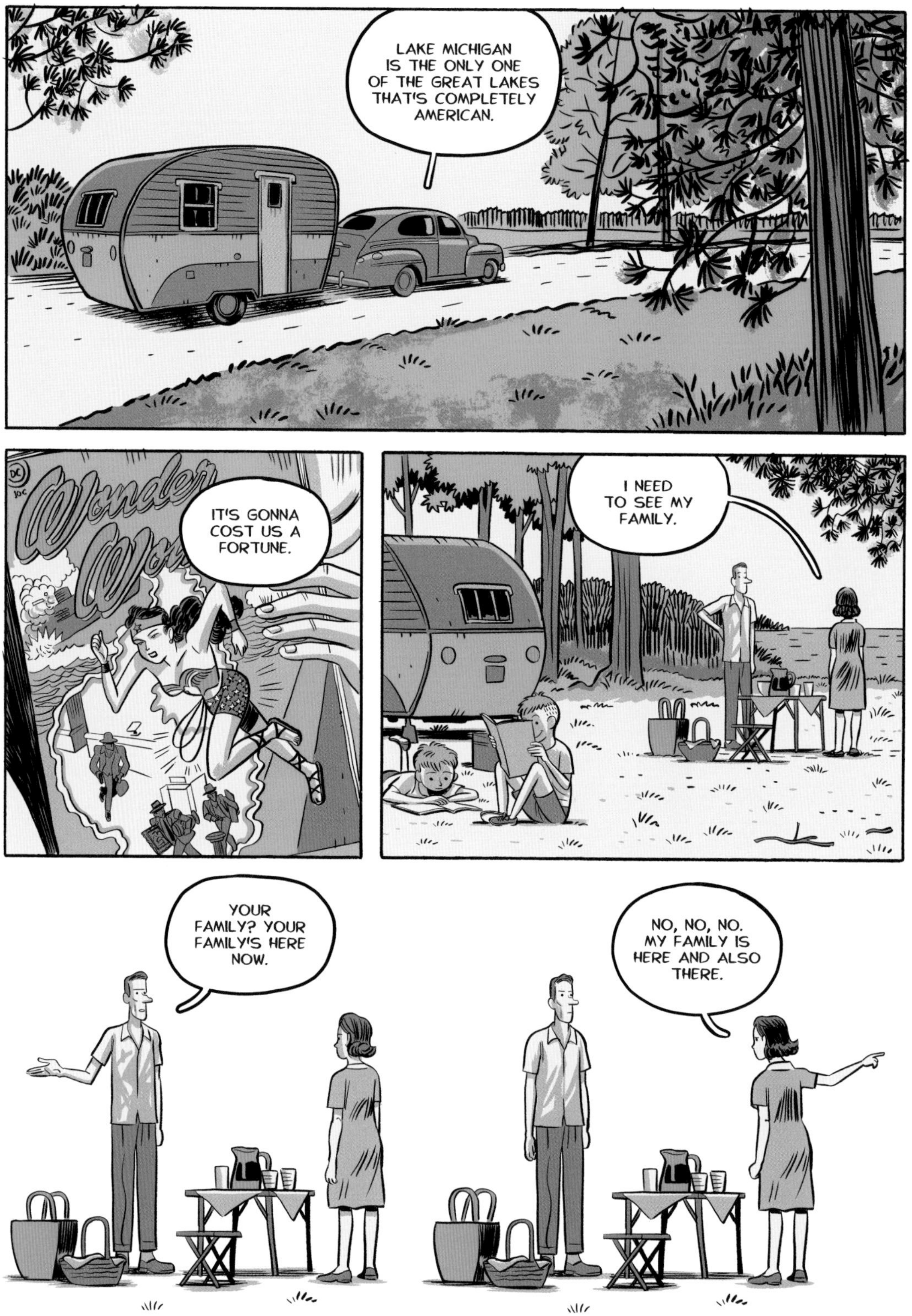
LAKE MICHIGAN IS THE ONLY ONE OF THE GREAT LAKES THAT'S COMPLETELY AMERICAN.
IT'S GONNA COST US A FORTUNE.
I NEED TO SEE MY FAMILY.
YOUR FAMILY? YOUR FAMILY'S HERE NOW.
NO, NO, NO. MY FAMILY IS HERE AND ALSO THERE.

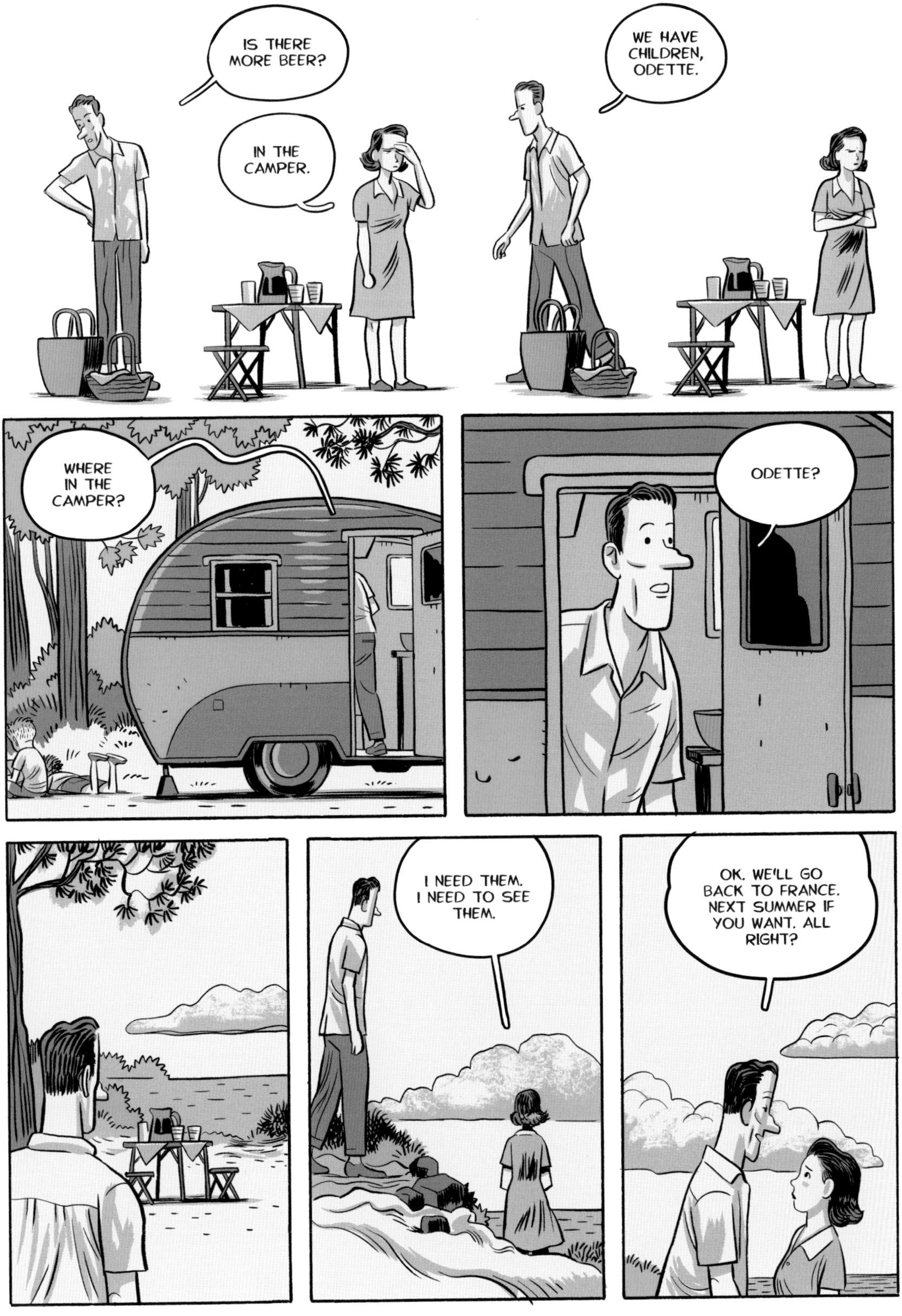
IS THERE MORE BEER?
IN THE CAMPER.
WE HAVE CHILDREN, ODETTE.
WHERE IN THE CAMPER?
ODETTE?
I NEED THEM. I NEED TO SEE THEM.
OK. WE'LL GO BACK TO FRANCE. NEXT SUMMER IF YOU WANT. ALL RIGHT?

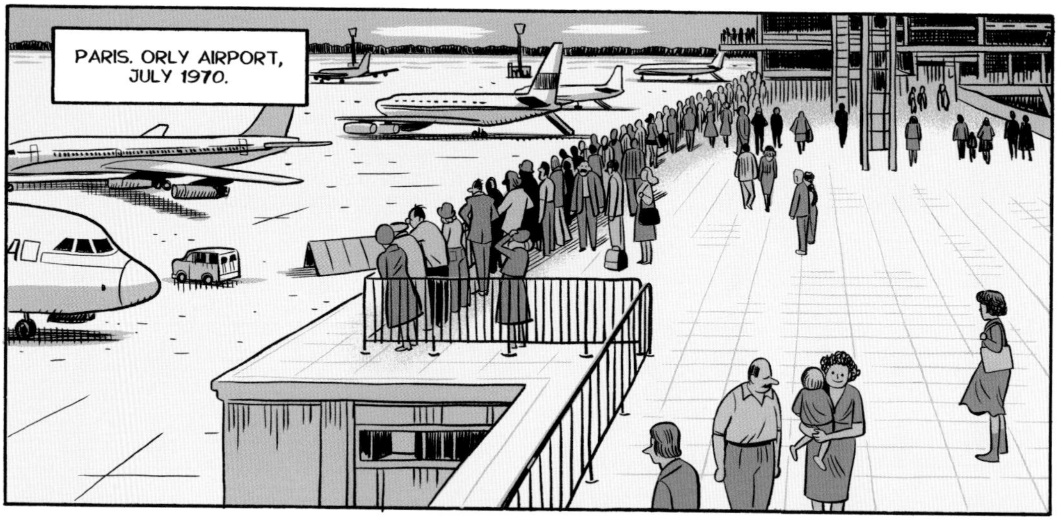
PARIS. ORLY AIRPORT, JULY 1970.

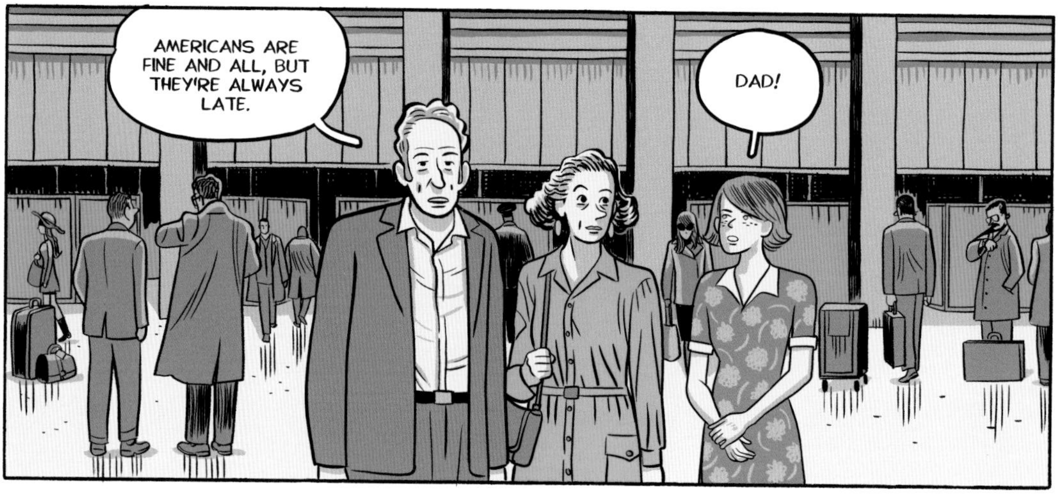
AMERICANS ARE FINE AND ALL, BUT THEY'RE ALWAYS LATE.
DAD!

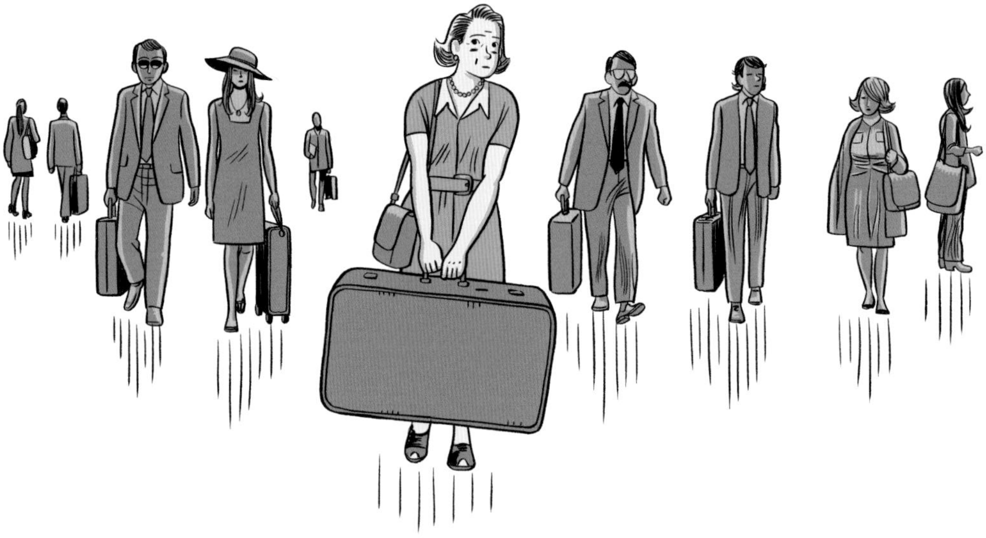

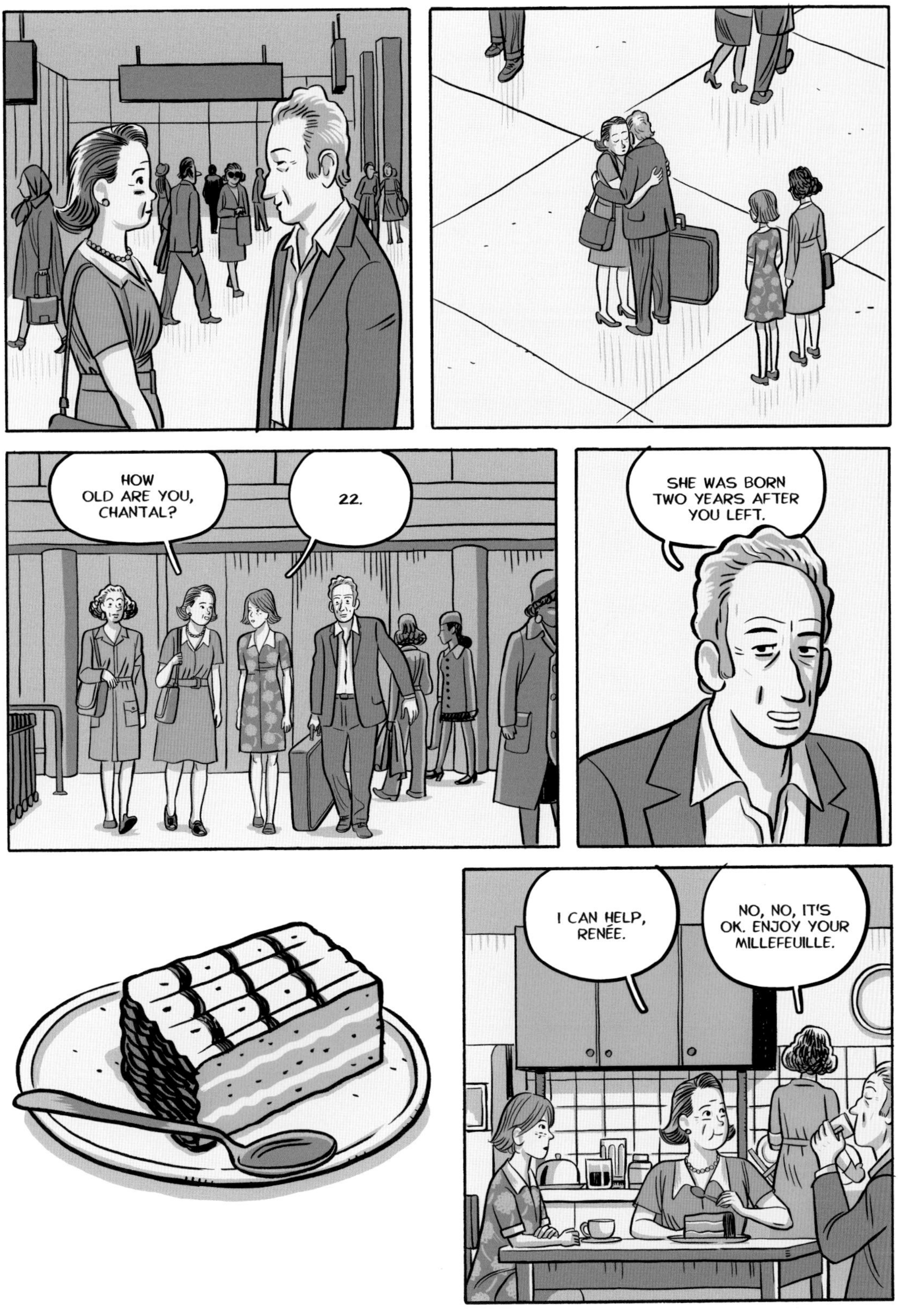
HOW OLD ARE YOU, CHANTAL?
22.
SHE WAS BORN TWO YEARS AFTER YOU LEFT.
I CAN HELP, RENÉE.
NO, NO, IT'S OK. ENJOY YOUR MILLEFEUILLE.

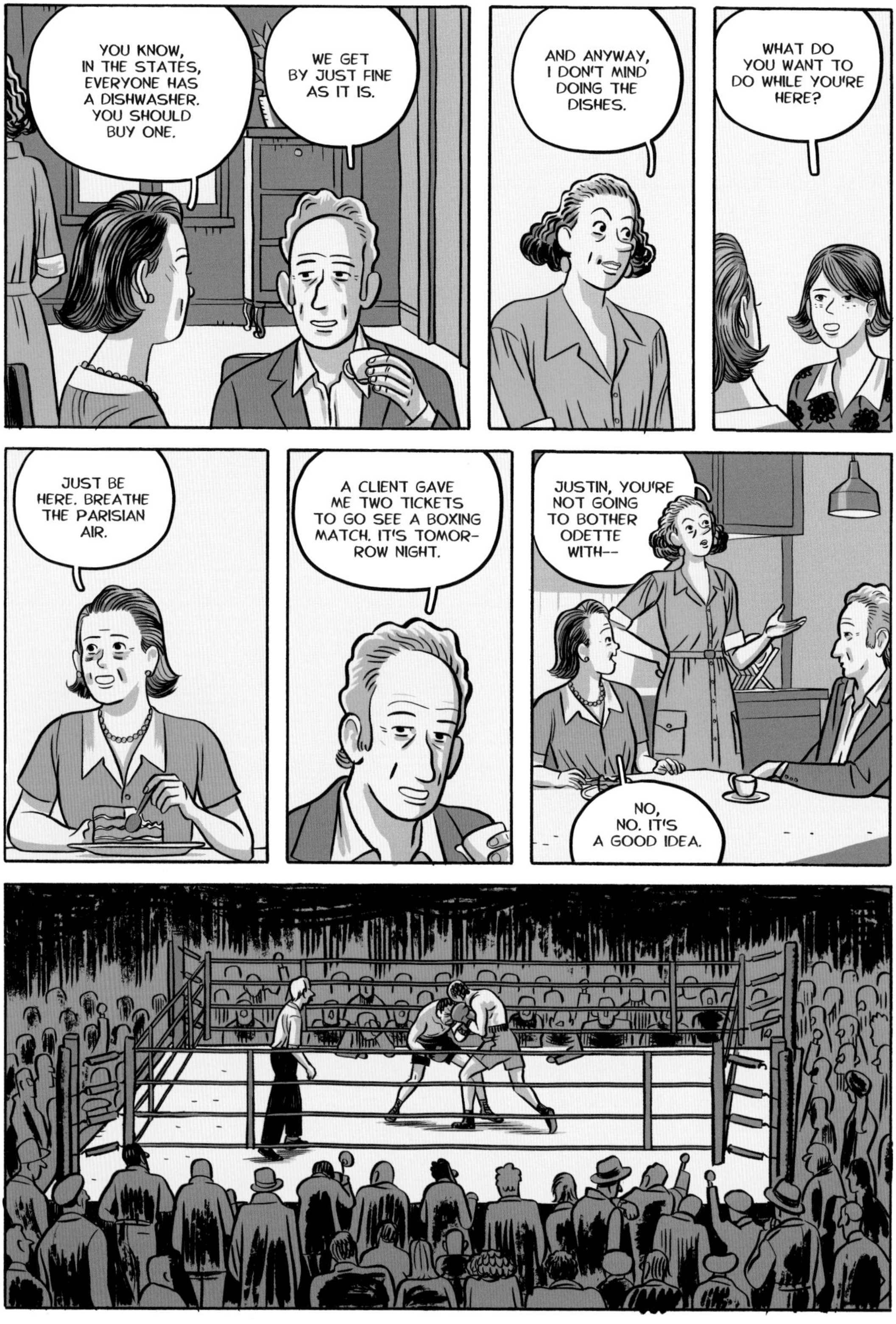
YOU KNOW, IN THE STATES, EVERYONE HAS A DISHWASHER. YOU SHOULD BUY ONE.
WE GET BY JUST FINE AS IT IS.
AND ANYWAY, I DON'T MIND DOING THE DISHES.
WHAT DO YOU WANT TO DO WHILE YOU'RE HERE?
JUST BE HERE. BREATHE THE PARISIAN AIR.
A CLIENT GAVE ME TWO TICKETS TO GO SEE A BOXING MATCH. IT'S TOMORROW NIGHT.
JUSTIN, YOU'RE NOT GOING TO BOTHER ODETTE WITH--
NO, NO. IT'S A GOOD IDEA.

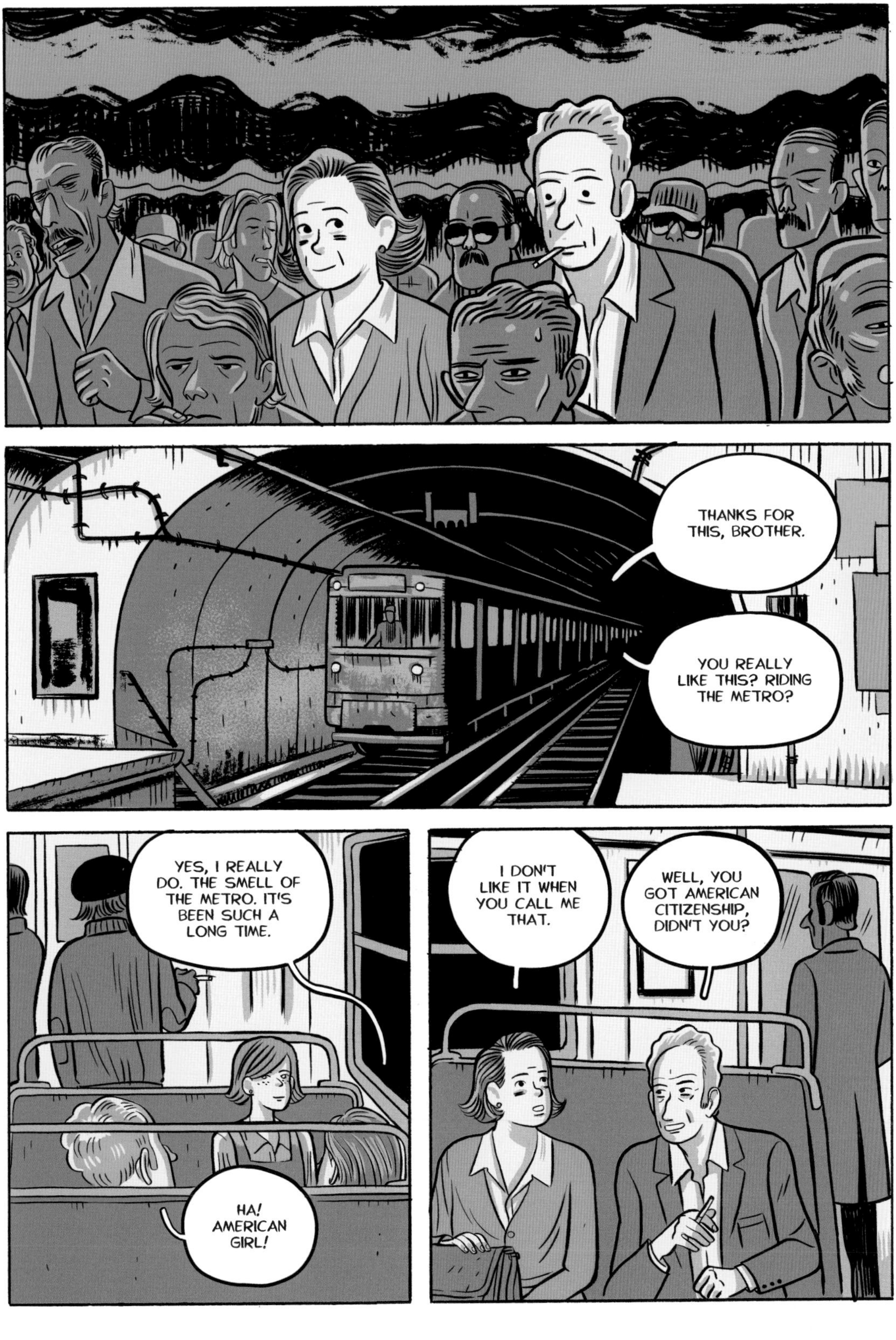
THANKS FOR THIS, BROTHER.
YOU REALLY LIKE THIS? RIDING THE METRO?
YES, I REALLY DO. THE SMELL OF THE METRO. IT'S BEEN SUCH A LONG TIME.
HA! AMERICAN GIRL!
I DON'T LIKE IT WHEN YOU CALL ME THAT.
WELL, YOU GOT AMERICAN CITIZENSHIP, DIDN'T YOU?

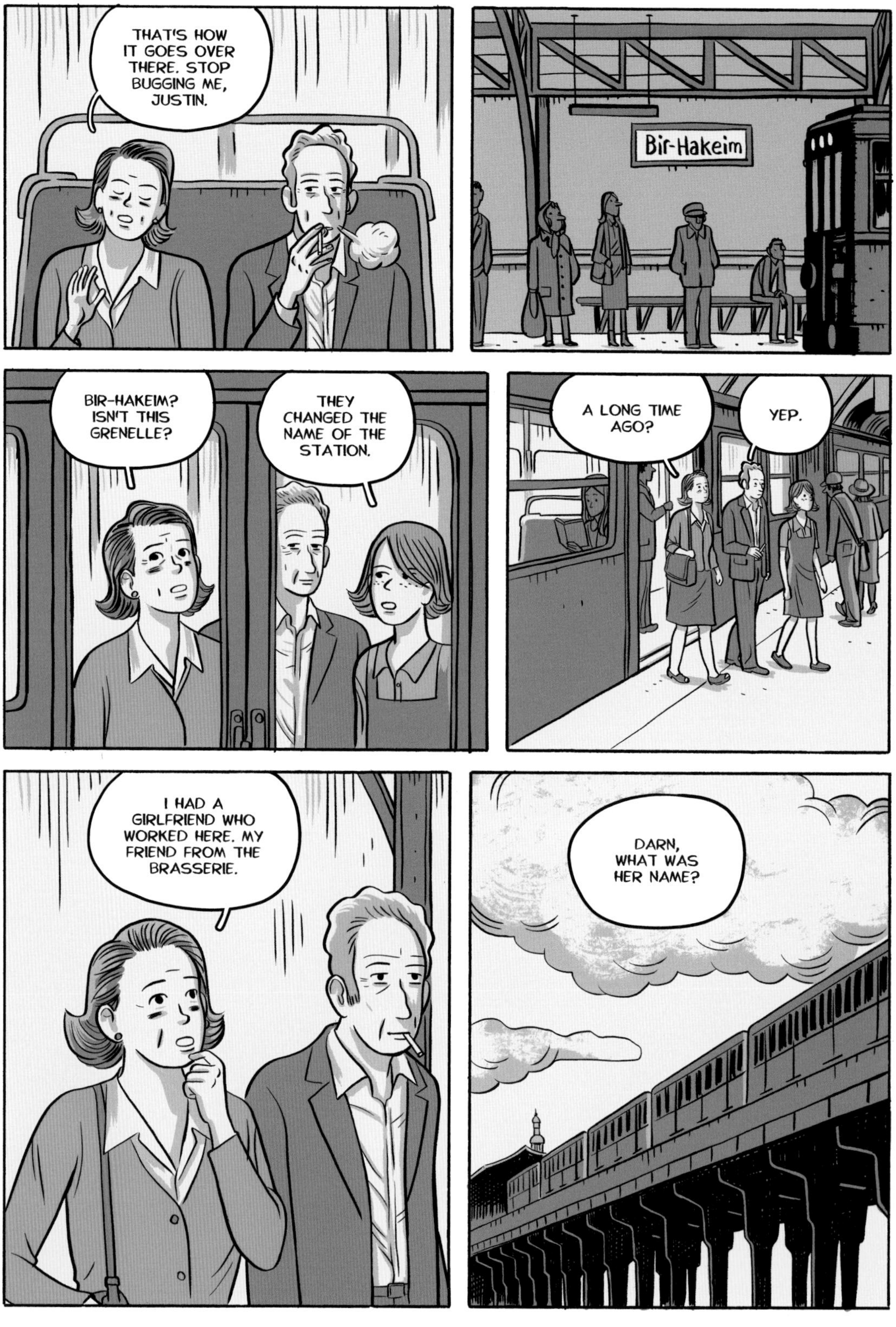
THAT'S HOW IT GOES OVER THERE. STOP BUGGING ME, JUSTIN.
Bir-Hakeim
BIR-HAKEIM? ISN'T THIS GRENELLE?
THEY CHANGED THE NAME OF THE STATION.
A LONG TIME AGO?
YEP.
I HAD A GIRLFRIEND WHO WORKED HERE. MY FRIEND FROM THE BRASSERIE.
DARN, WHAT WAS HER NAME?

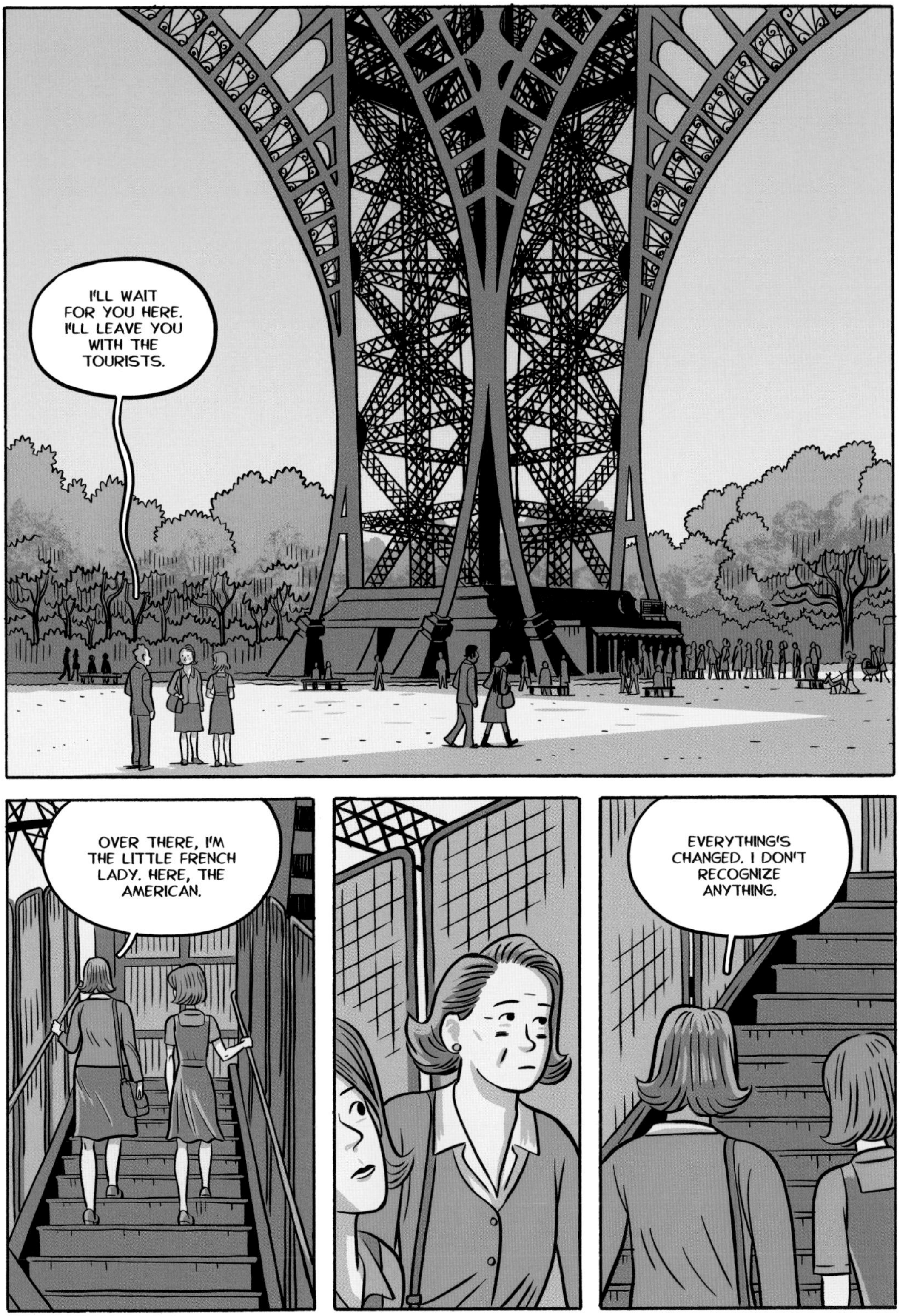
I'LL WAIT FOR YOU HERE. I'LL LEAVE YOU WITH THE TOURISTS.
OVER THERE, I'M THE LITTLE FRENCH LADY. HERE, THE AMERICAN.
EVERYTHING'S CHANGED. I DON'T RECOGNIZE ANYTHING.

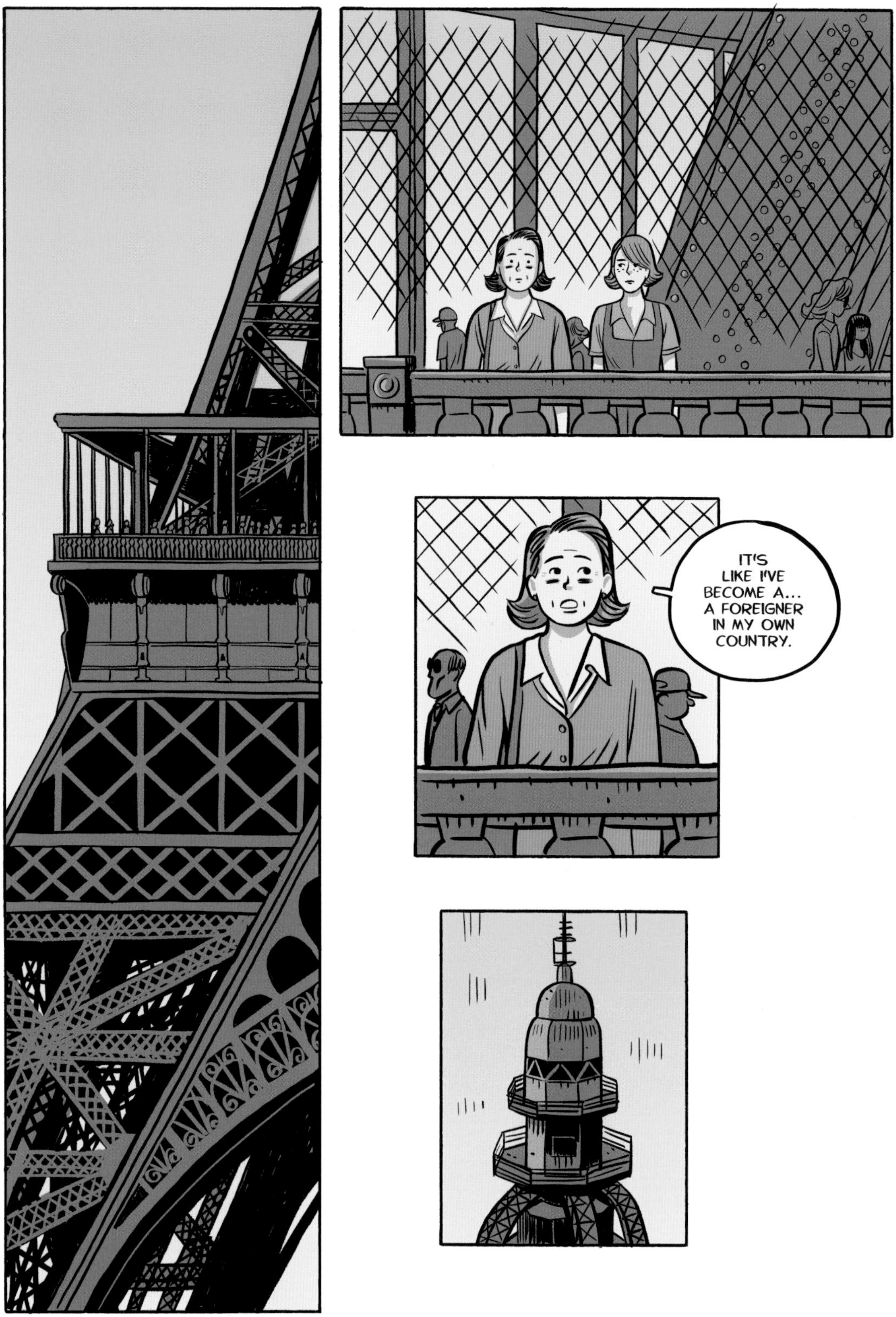
IT'S LIKE I'VE BECOME A... A FOREIGNER IN MY OWN COUNTRY.

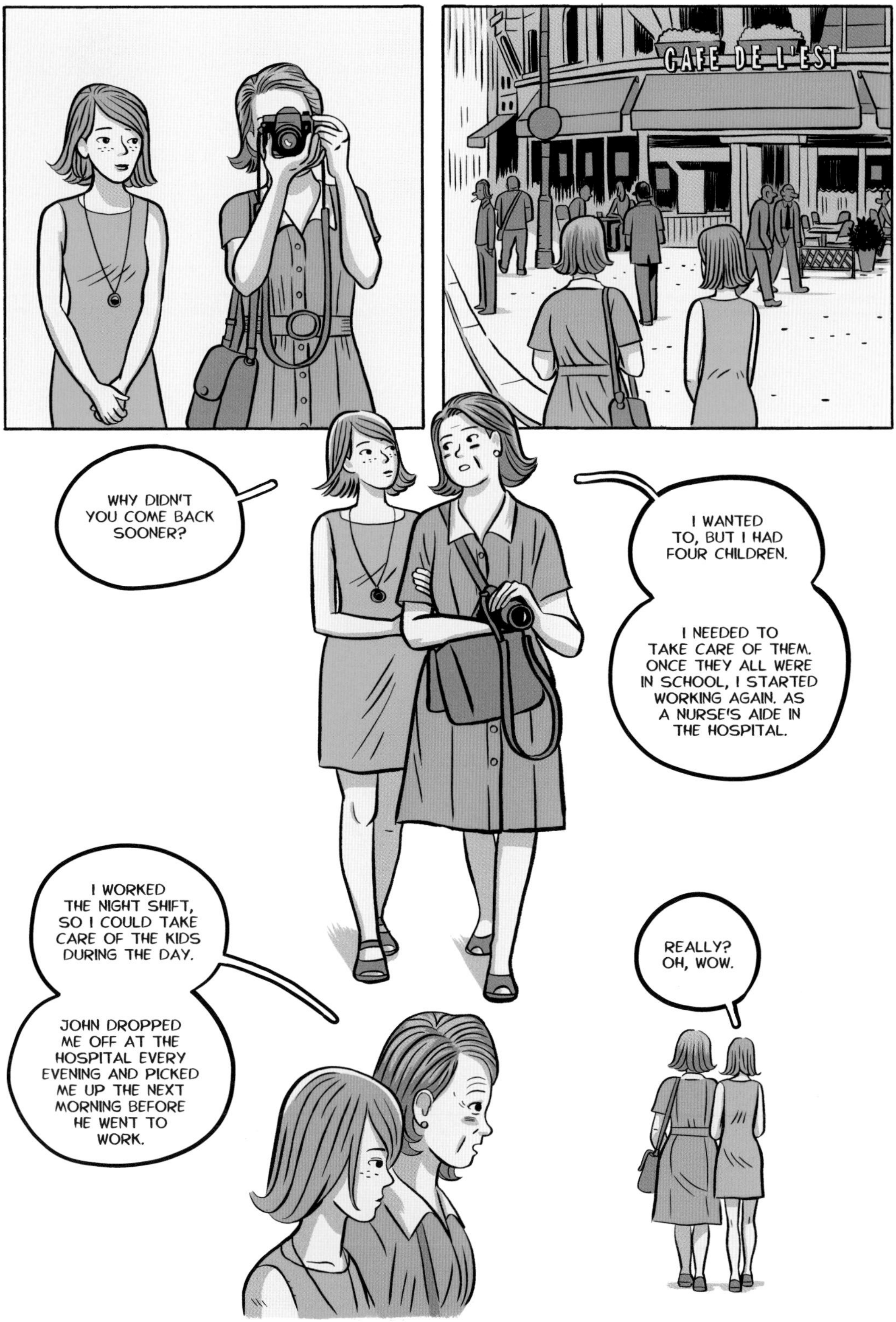
CAFE DE L'EST
WHY DIDN'T YOU COME BACK SOONER?
I WANTED TO, BUT I HAD FOUR CHILDREN.
I NEEDED TO TAKE CARE OF THEM. ONCE THEY ALL WERE IN SCHOOL, I STARTED WORKING AGAIN. AS A NURSE'S AIDE IN THE HOSPITAL.
I WORKED THE NIGHT SHIFT, SO I COULD TAKE CARE OF THE KIDS DURING THE DAY.
JOHN DROPPED ME OFF AT THE HOSPITAL EVERY EVENING AND PICKED ME UP THE NEXT MORNING BEFORE HE WENT TO WORK.
REALLY? OH, WOW.

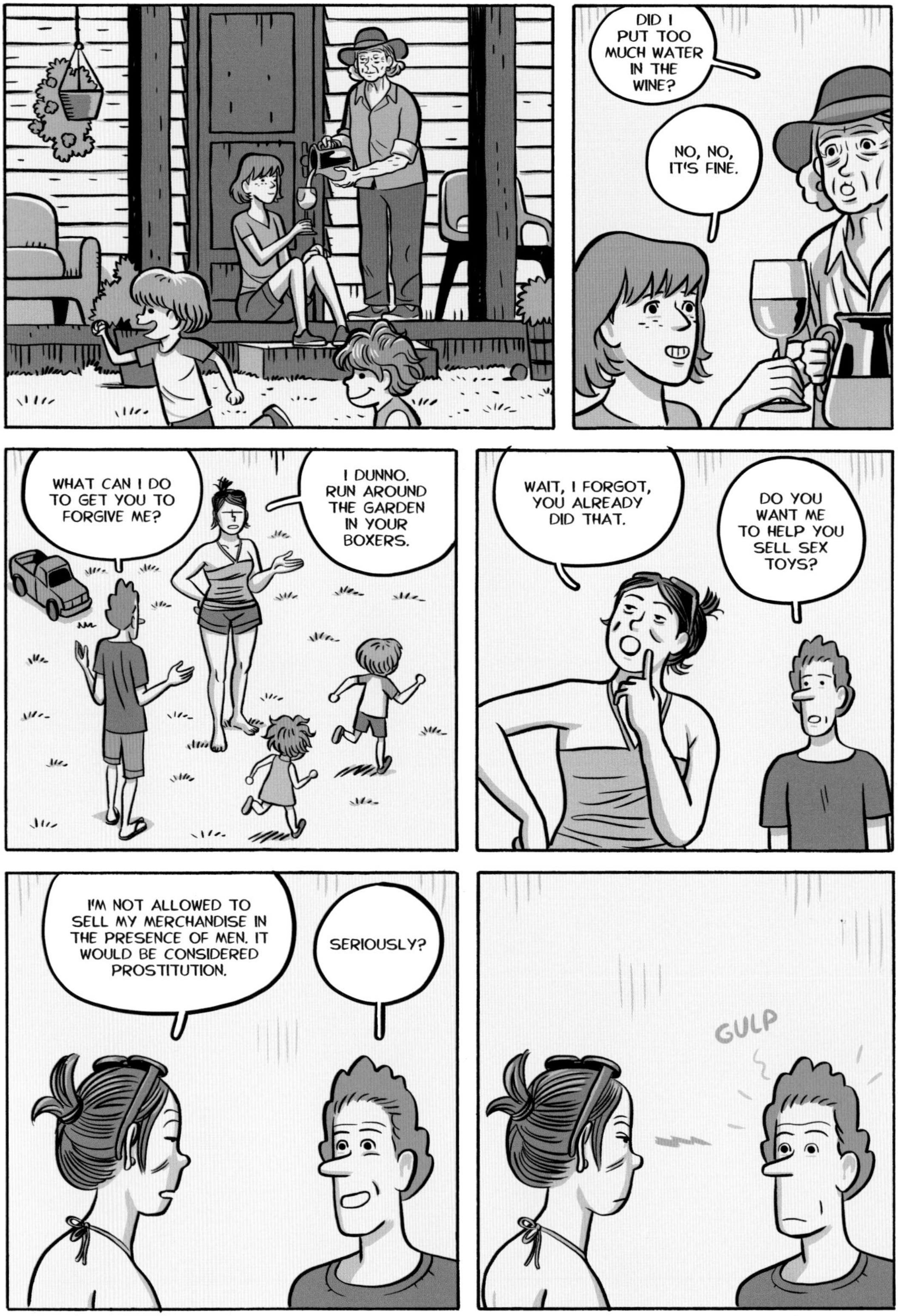
DID I PUT TOO MUCH WATER IN THE WINE?
NO, NO, IT'S FINE.
WHAT CAN I DO TO GET YOU TO FORGIVE ME?
I DUNNO. RUN AROUND THE GARDEN IN YOUR BOXERS.
WAIT, I FORGOT, YOU ALREADY DID THAT.
DO YOU WANT ME TO HELP YOU SELL SEX TOYS?
I'M NOT ALLOWED TO SELL MY MERCHANDISE IN THE PRESENCE OF MEN. IT WOULD BE CONSIDERED PROSTITUTION.
SERIOUSLY?
GULP

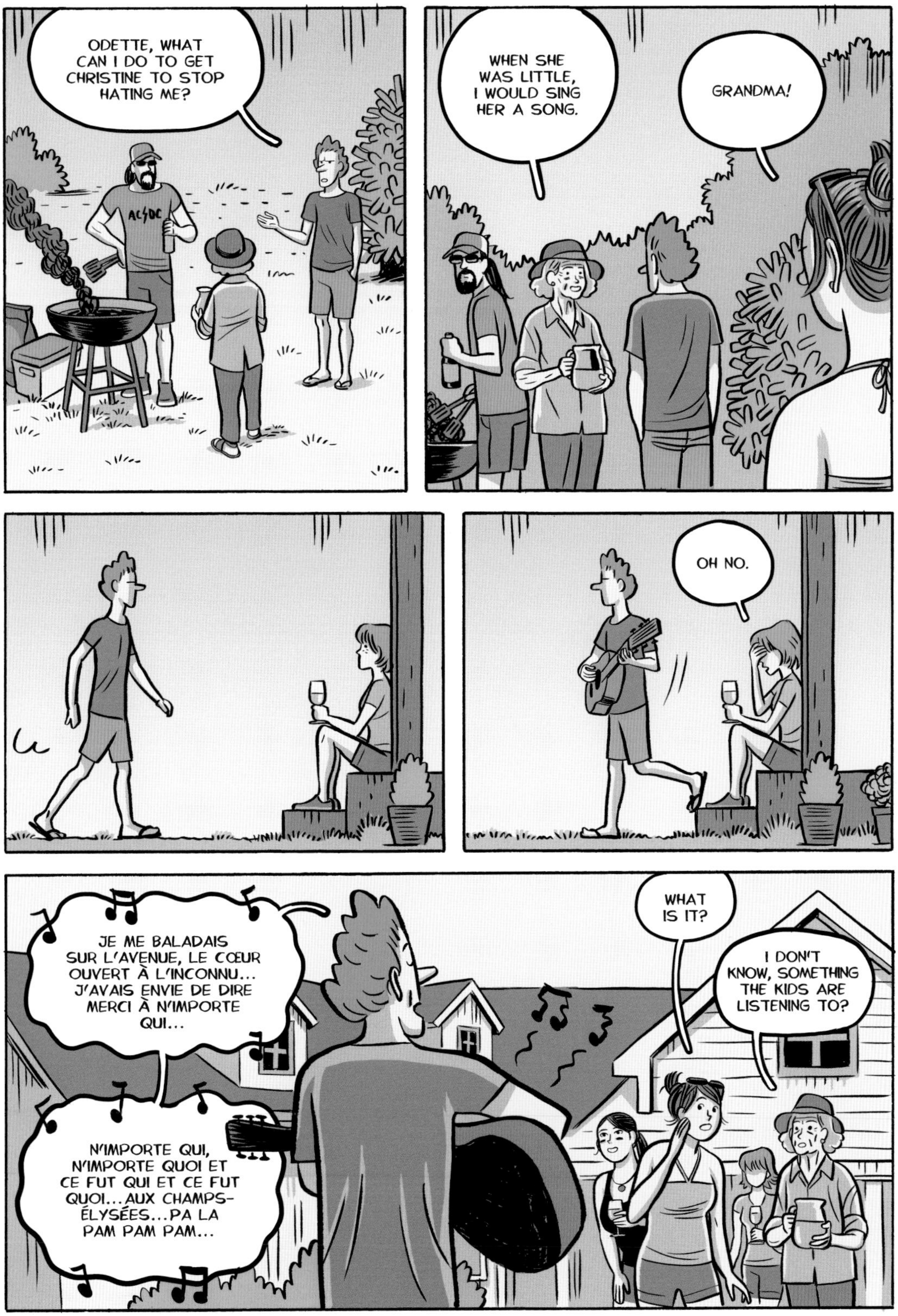
ODETTE, WHAT CAN I DO TO GET CHRISTINE TO STOP HATING ME?
AC/DC
WHEN SHE WAS LITTLE, I WOULD SING HER A SONG.
GRANDMA!
OH NO.
JE ME BALADAIS SUR L'AVENUE, LE CŒUR OUVERT À L'INCONNU... J'AVAIS ENVIE DE DIRE MERCI À N'IMPORTE QUI...
N'IMPORTE QUI, N'IMPORTE QUOI ET CE FUT QUI ET CE FUT QUOI...AUX CHAMPS-ÉLYSÉES...PA LA PAM PAM PAM...
WHAT IS IT?
I DON'T KNOW, SOMETHING THE KIDS ARE LISTENING TO?

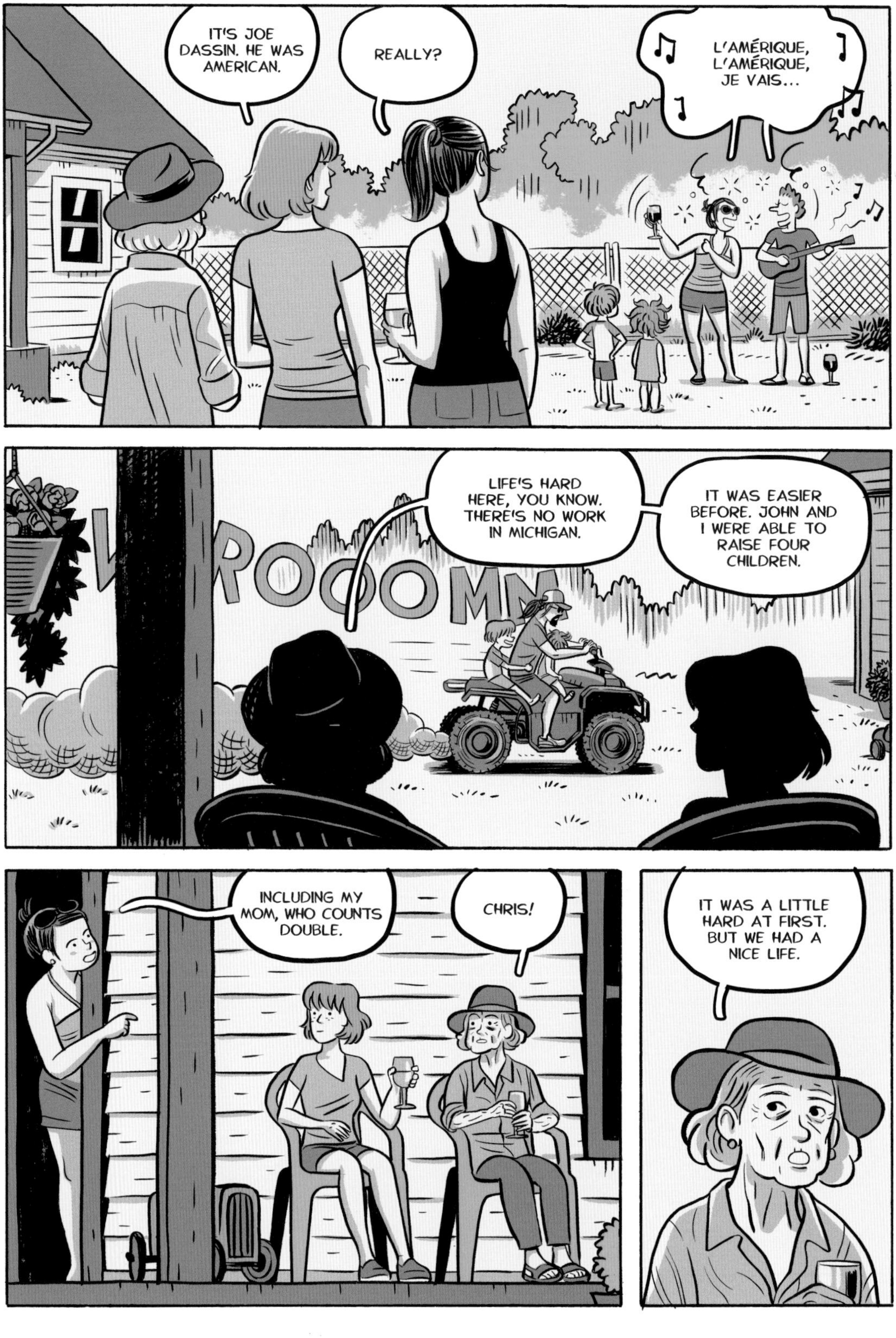
IT'S JOE DASSIN. HE WAS AMERICAN.
REALLY?
L'AMÉRIQUE, L'AMÉRIQUE, JE VAIS...
VROOOMM
LIFE'S HARD HERE, YOU KNOW. THERE'S NO WORK IN MICHIGAN.
IT WAS EASIER BEFORE. JOHN AND I WERE ABLE TO RAISE FOUR CHILDREN.
INCLUDING MY MOM, WHO COUNTS DOUBLE.
CHRIS!
IT WAS A LITTLE HARD AT FIRST. BUT WE HAD A NICE LIFE.

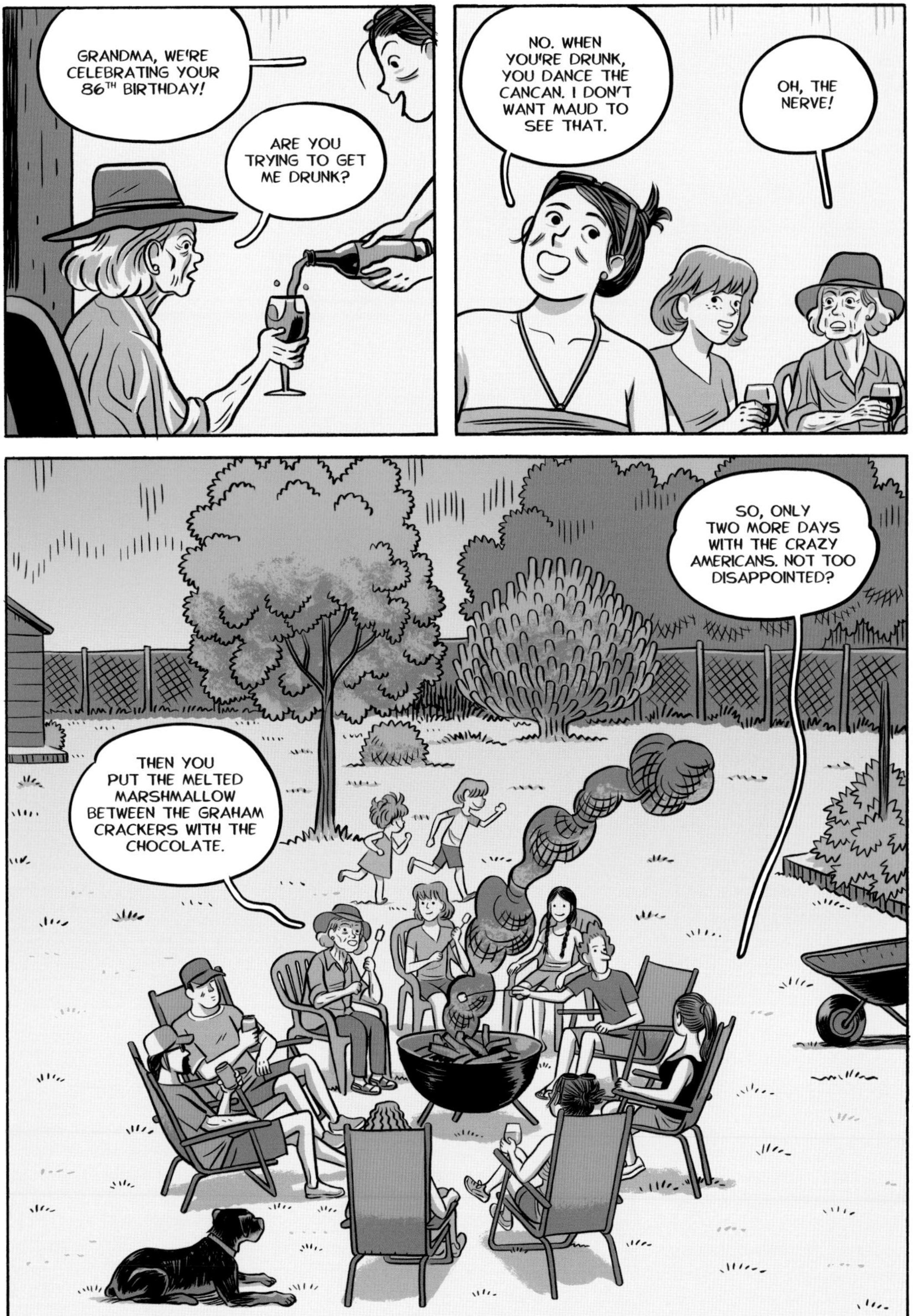
GRANDMA, WE'RE CELEBRATING YOUR 86TH BIRTHDAY!
ARE YOU TRYING TO GET ME DRUNK?
NO. WHEN YOU'RE DRUNK, YOU DANCE THE CANCAN. I DON'T WANT MAUD TO SEE THAT.
OH, THE NERVE!
SO, ONLY TWO MORE DAYS WITH THE CRAZY AMERICANS. NOT TOO DISAPPOINTED?
THEN YOU PUT THE MELTED MARSHMALLOW BETWEEN THE GRAHAM CRACKERS WITH THE CHOCOLATE.

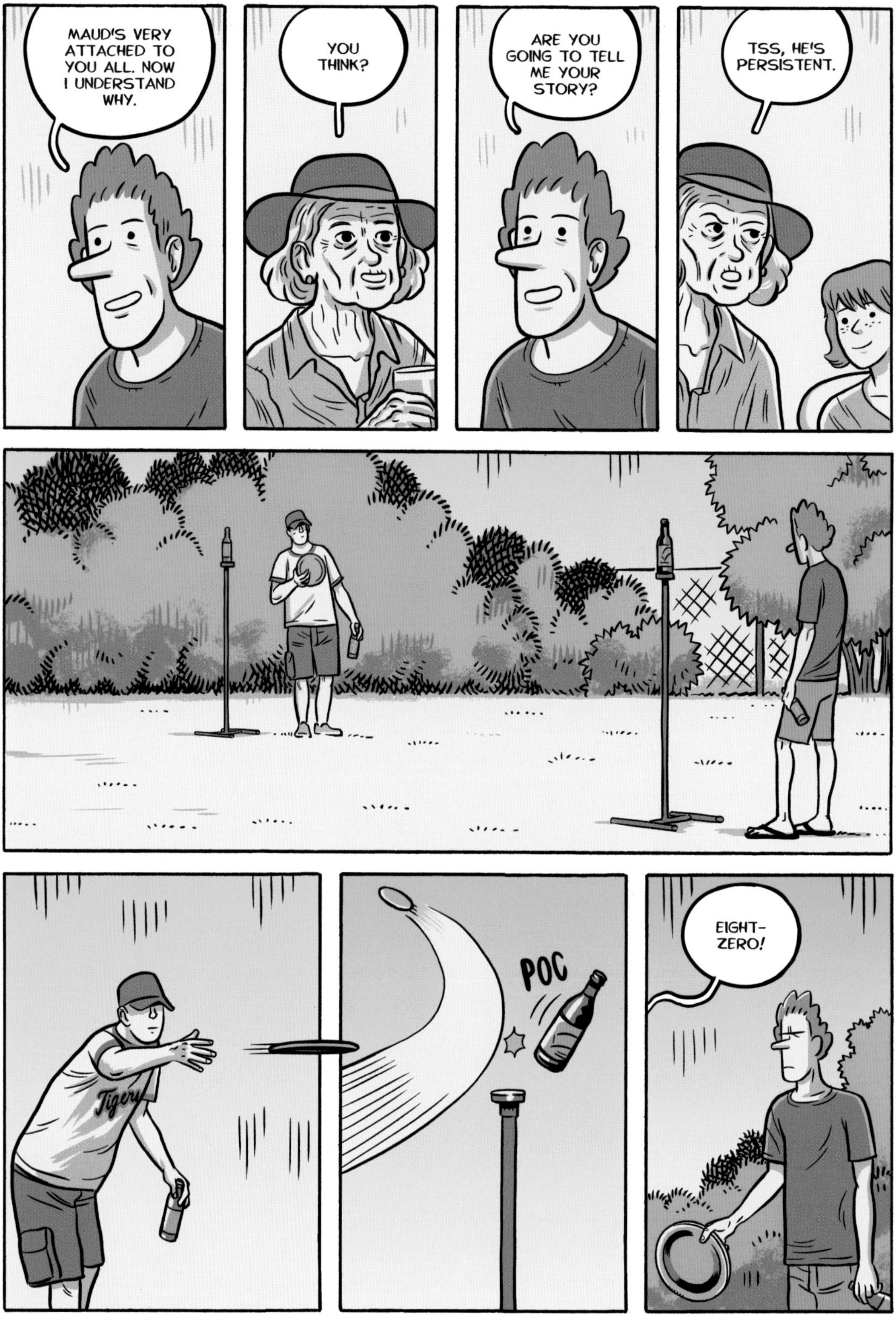
MAUD'S VERY ATTACHED TO YOU ALL. NOW I UNDERSTAND WHY.
YOU THINK?
ARE YOU GOING TO TELL ME YOUR STORY?
TSS, HE'S PERSISTENT.
Tigers
POC
EIGHT-ZERO!

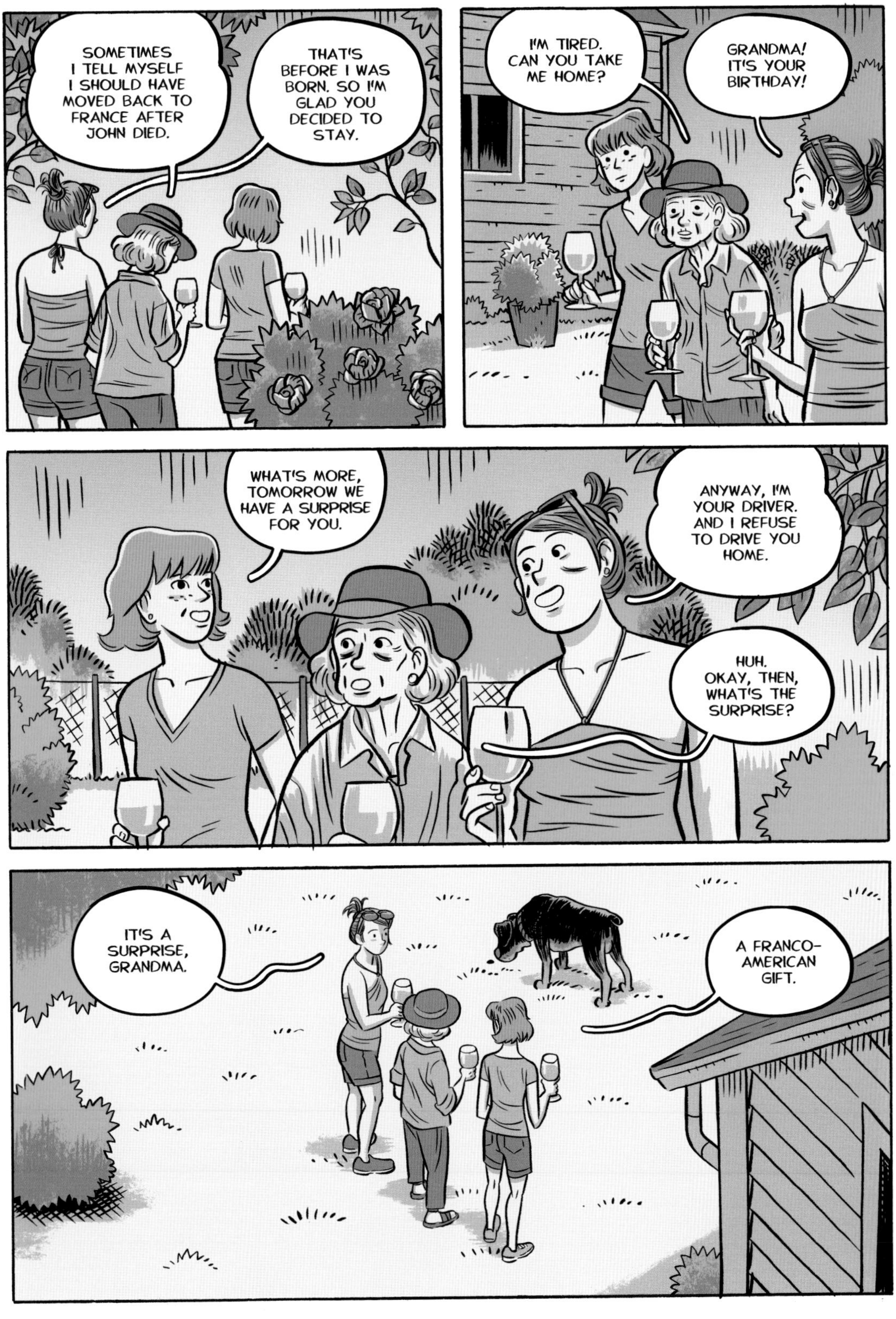
SOMETIMES I TELL MYSELF I SHOULD HAVE MOVED BACK TO FRANCE AFTER JOHN DIED.
THAT'S BEFORE I WAS BORN. SO I'M GLAD YOU DECIDED TO STAY.
I'M TIRED. CAN YOU TAKE ME HOME?
GRANDMA! IT'S YOUR BIRTHDAY!
WHAT'S MORE, TOMORROW WE HAVE A SURPRISE FOR YOU.
ANYWAY, I'M YOUR DRIVER. AND I REFUSE TO DRIVE YOU HOME.
HUH. OKAY, THEN, WHAT'S THE SURPRISE?
IT'S A SURPRISE, GRANDMA.
A FRANCO-AMERICAN GIFT.

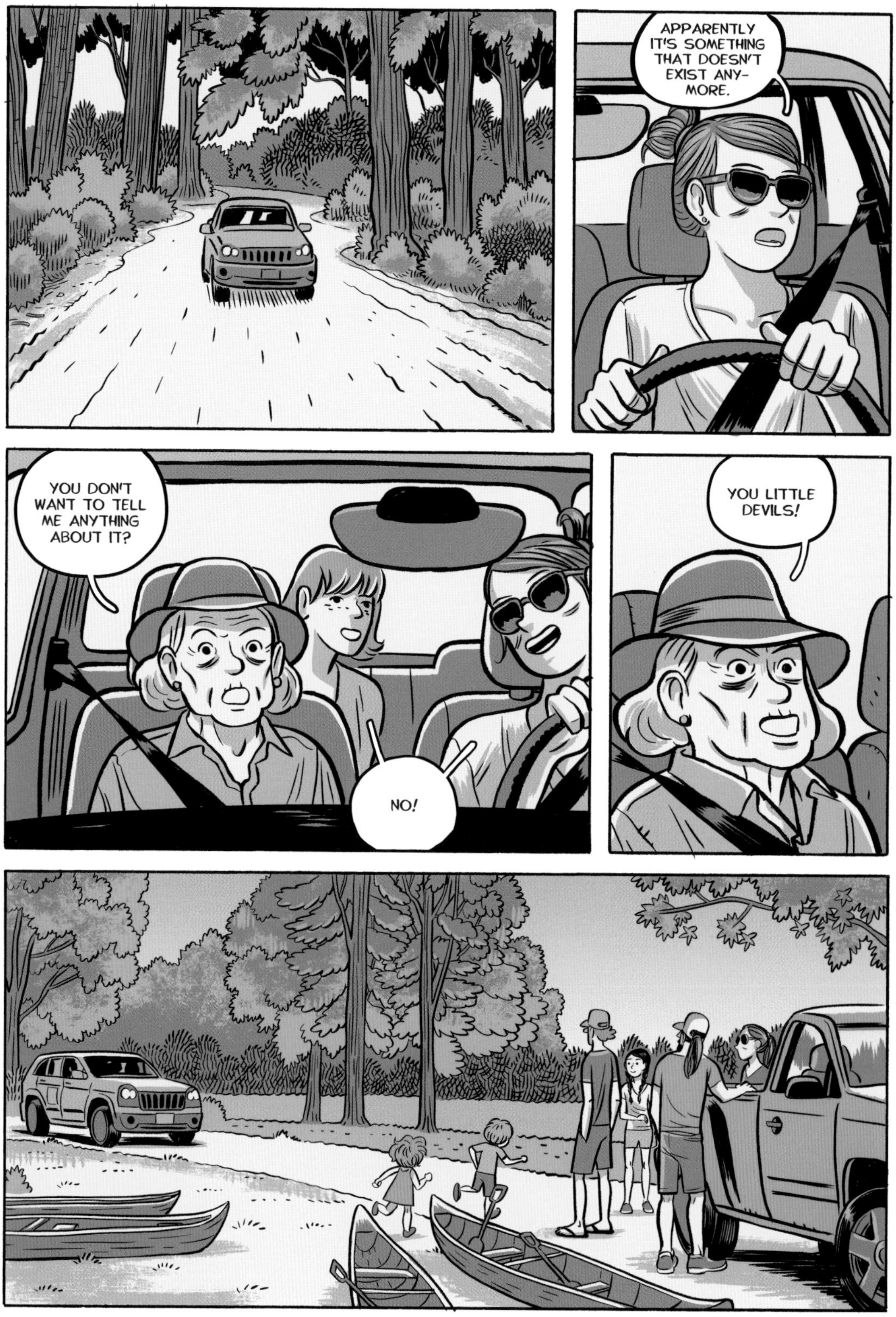

APPARENTLY IT'S SOMETHING THAT DOESN'T EXIST ANY-MORE.
YOU DON'T WANT TO TELL ME ANYTHING ABOUT IT?
NO!
YOU LITTLE DEVILS!

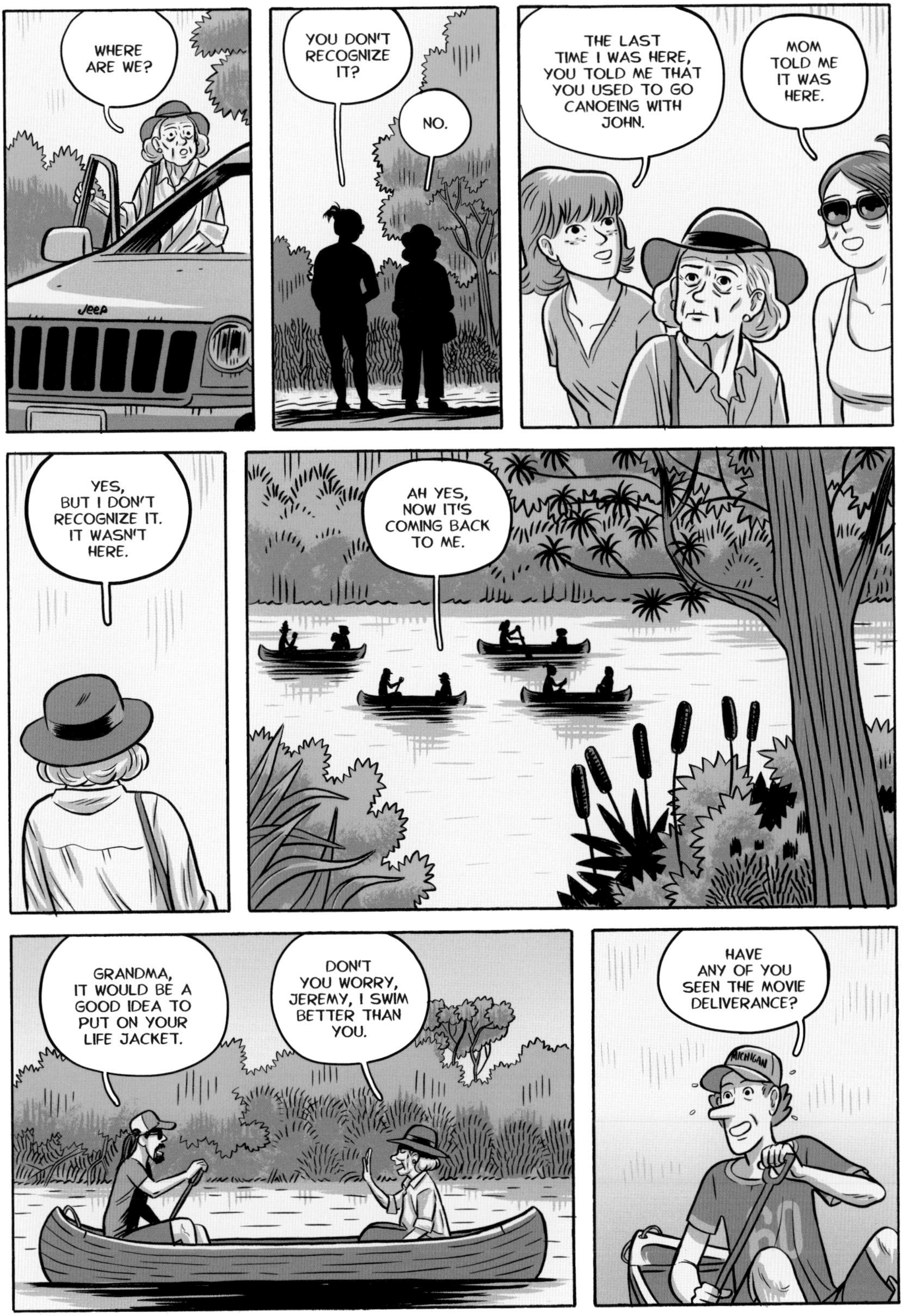
WHERE ARE WE?
JEEP
YOU DON'T RECOGNIZE IT?
NO.
THE LAST TIME I WAS HERE, YOU TOLD ME THAT YOU USED TO GO CANOEING WITH JOHN.
MOM TOLD ME IT WAS HERE.
YES, BUT I DON'T RECOGNIZE IT. IT WASN'T HERE.
AH YES, NOW IT'S COMING BACK TO ME.
GRANDMA, IT WOULD BE A GOOD IDEA TO PUT ON YOUR LIFE JACKET.
DON'T YOU WORRY, JEREMY, I SWIM BETTER THAN YOU.
HAVE ANY OF YOU SEEN THE MOVIE DELIVERANCE?
MICHIGAN

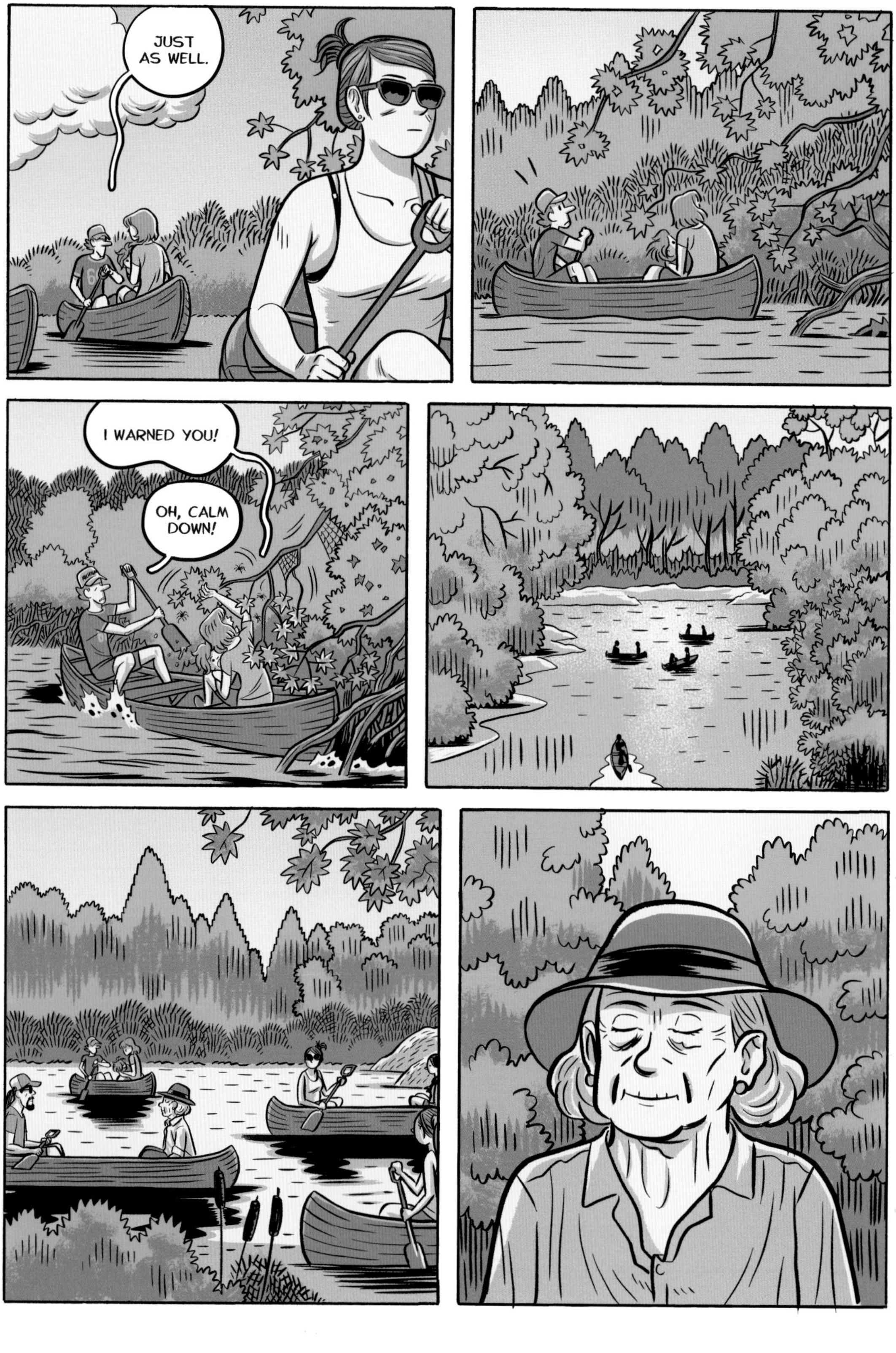
JUST AS WELL.
I WARNED YOU!
OH, CALM DOWN!

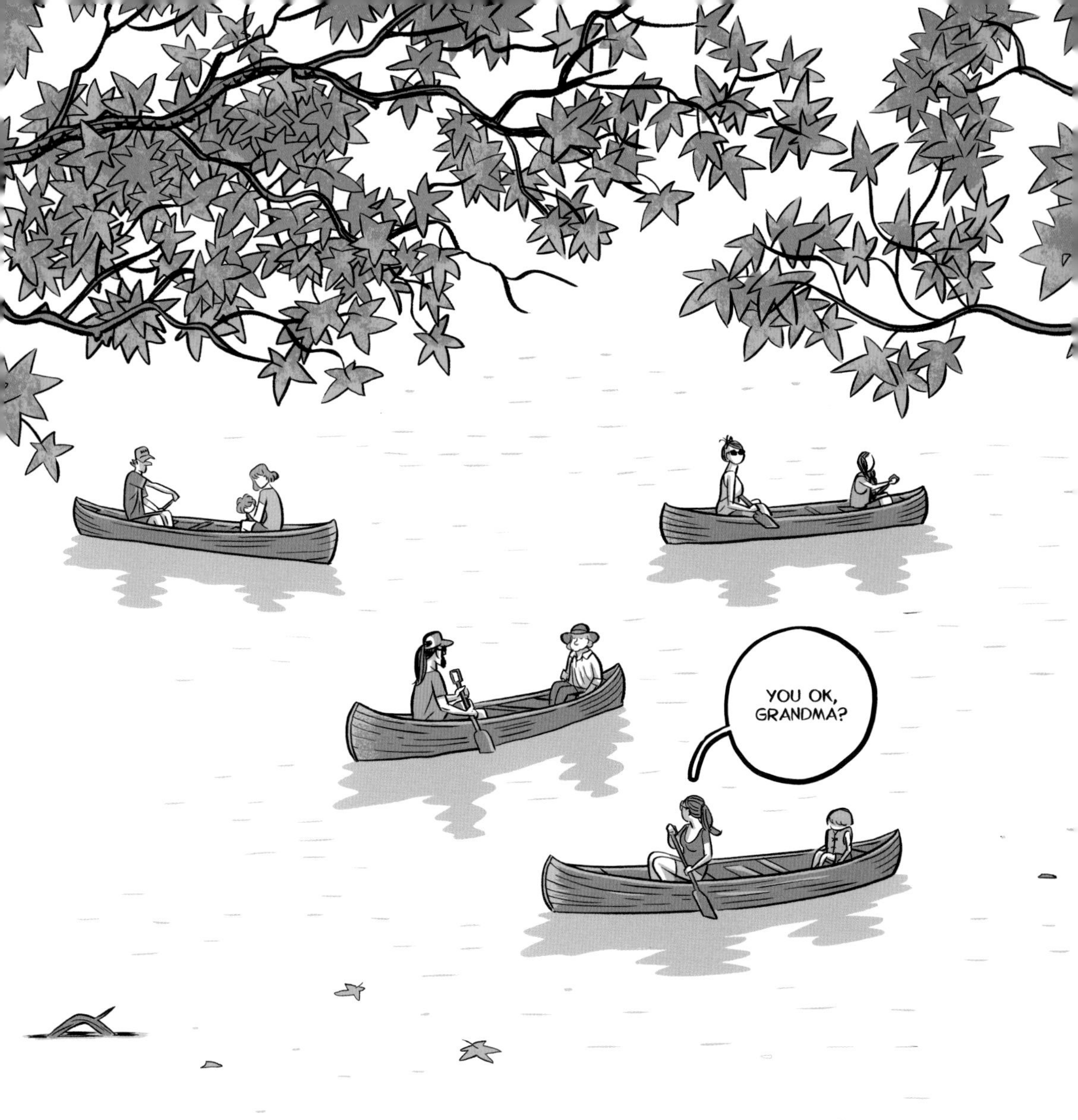
YOU OK,
GRANDMA?

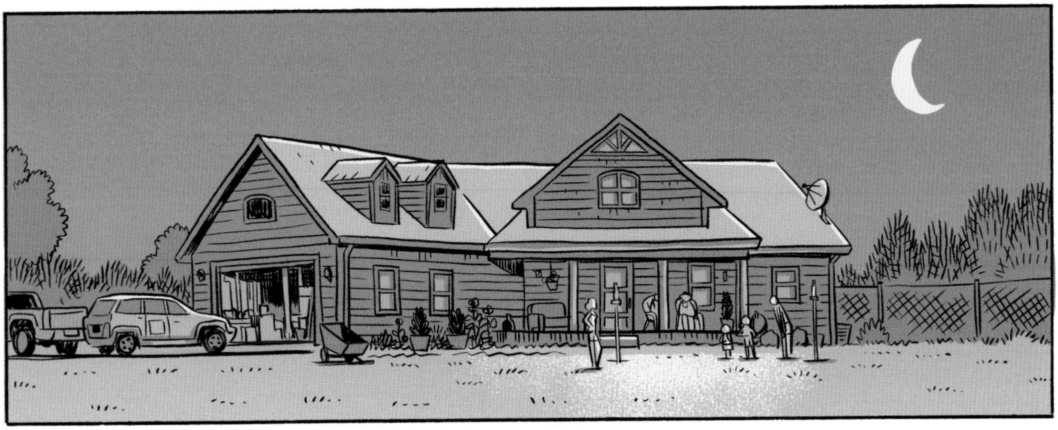

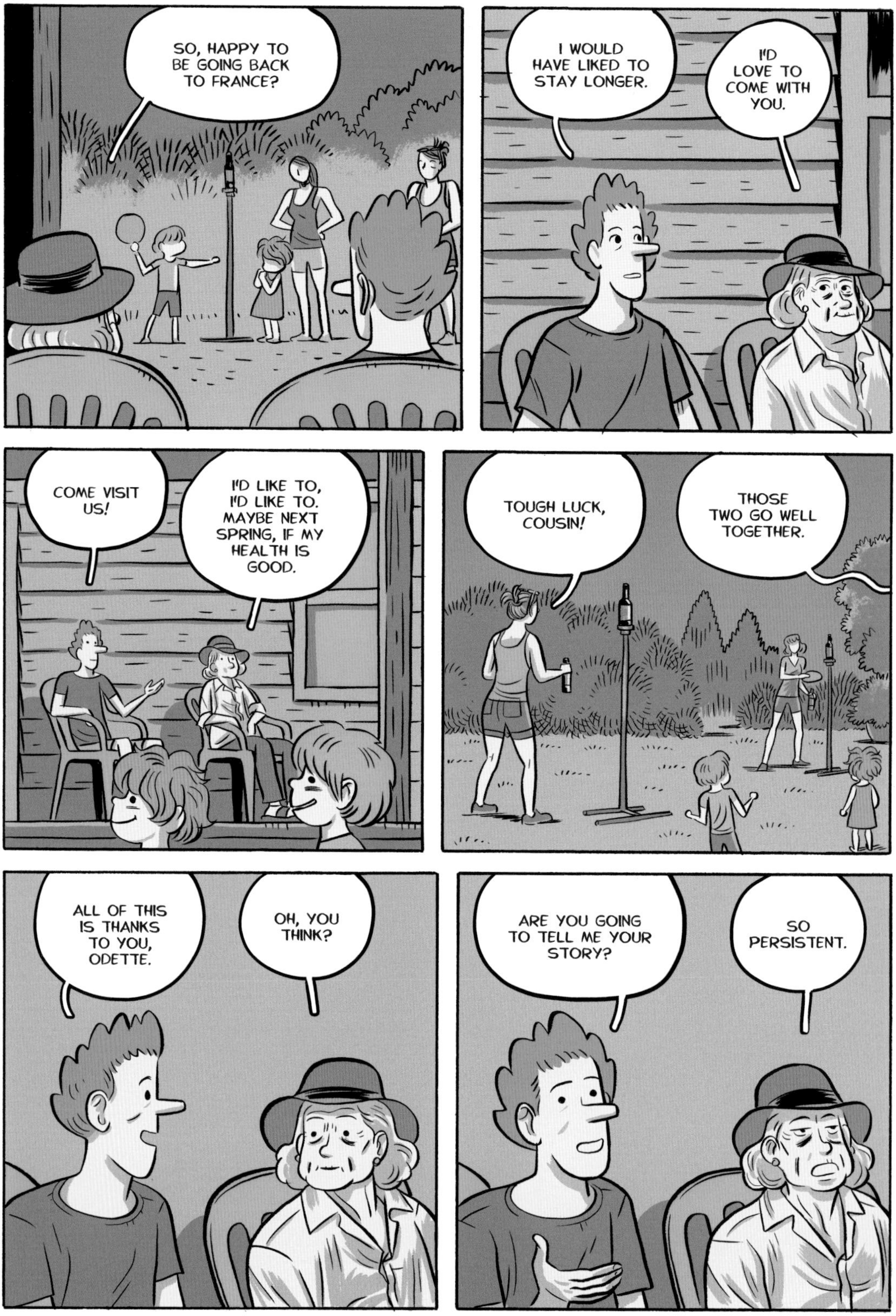
SO, HAPPY TO BE GOING BACK TO FRANCE?
I WOULD HAVE LIKED TO STAY LONGER.
I'D LOVE TO COME WITH YOU.
COME VISIT US!
I'D LIKE TO, I'D LIKE TO. MAYBE NEXT SPRING, IF MY HEALTH IS GOOD.
TOUGH LUCK, COUSIN!
THOSE TWO GO WELL TOGETHER.
ALL OF THIS IS THANKS TO YOU, ODETTE.
OH, YOU THINK?
ARE YOU GOING TO TELL ME YOUR STORY?
SO PERSISTENT.

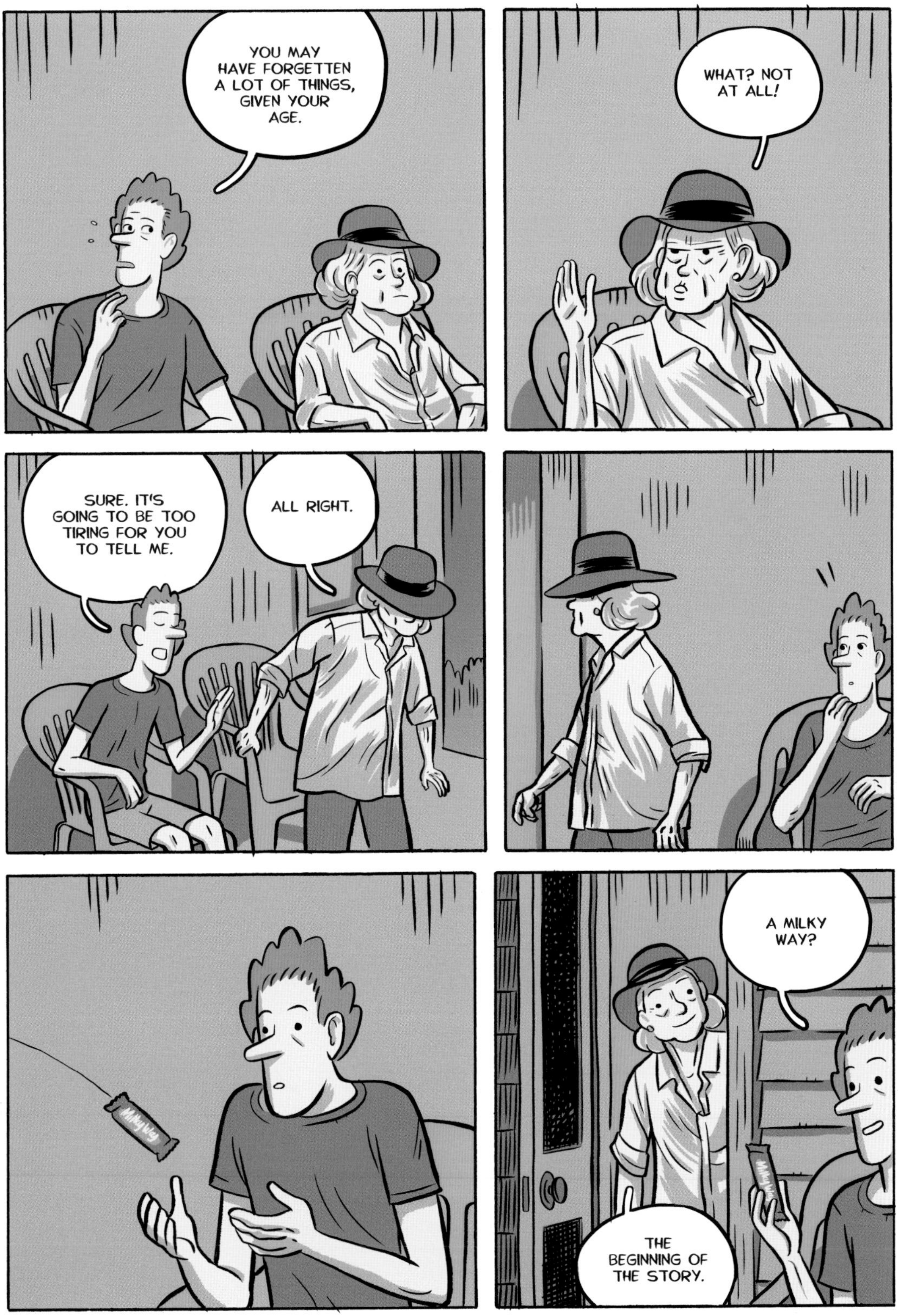
YOU MAY HAVE FORGETTEN A LOT OF THINGS, GIVEN YOUR AGE.
WHAT? NOT AT ALL!
SURE. IT'S GOING TO BE TOO TIRING FOR YOU TO TELL ME.
ALL RIGHT.
A MILKY WAY?
THE BEGINNING OF THE STORY.

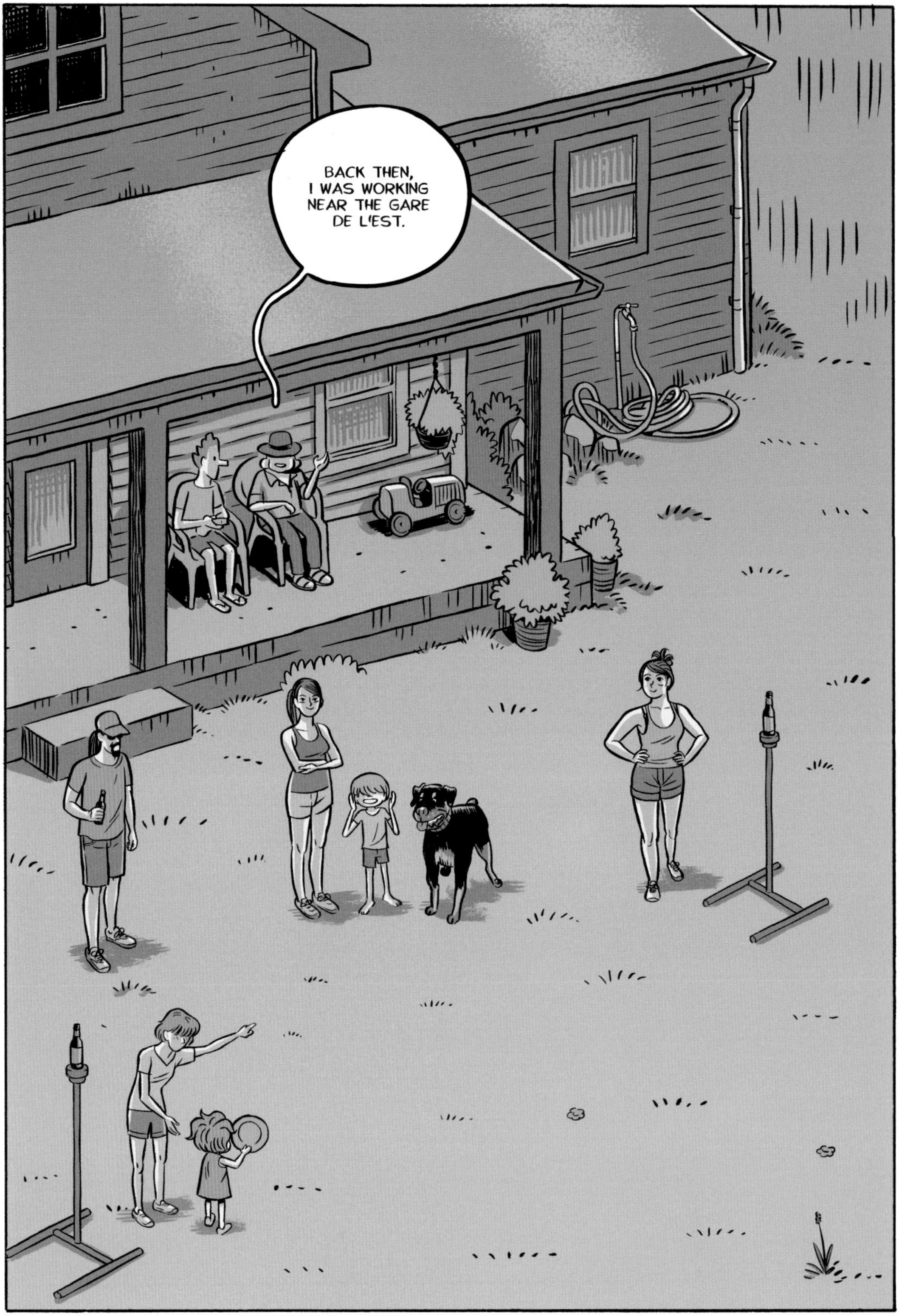
BACK THEN, I WAS WORKING NEAR THE GARE DE L'EST.